D1097944

CASTLES
AND
CAVERNS
Zeld and the Invaders

CASTLES
AND
CAVERNS

Zeld and the Invaders

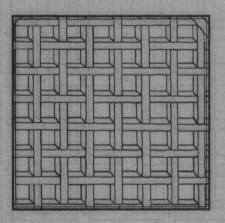

By
J. D. Raisor

First Edition of 1000 copies # *758*

ISBN 978-0-938717-75-1
Summary: Zeld's first year at Castles and Caverns School of Knighthood is plagued with enemies and secret plots which he must overcome to reclaim his lands and title.
[1 Medieval – Fiction. 2 Christian – Fiction. 3 Family Saga – Fiction. 4 Schools – Fiction. 5 Magic – Fiction. 6 Historical – Fiction.]

Printed in USA

Book Design
Gary B. Shumway

Published by Shumway Publishing Co.
shumwaypublishing@squarespace.com

They say that dedicating a book is one of the most exquisite acts of love one can perform. I would argue that it is even more beautiful to dedicate this one to you without saying your name.

But that won't quite do.

Thirty years ago I married a tomboy with scraped up knees and a love for animals.

We have eight children, fourteen grandchildren and have raised more cats, dogs, chickens, ferrets, pigs, gerbils, mice, fish, small birds and rabbits than I care to mention. We have yet to find an elephant for sale, but as soon as we do I will know it's time to enlarge the dog pen.

Anyway this book is dedicated to her: my Heather of pink and blue.

J. D. Raisor

To Caryl my fellow writer—

Happy Reading

J. Dmi Raiser

CONTENTS

Glossary

Ballista: War machine that shoots giant arrows.

Catapult: War machine that flings heavy loads.

Derrick: Medieval lifting machine. Crane.

Ditty: Song or poem.

Dukedom: Much like a king has a kingdom, a duke has a

dukedom and an earl has an earldom.

Fencing: Sword fighting.

Fortnight: Two weeks.

Garderobe: Toilets or bathroom.

Gong Farmer: Bottom level farmer that works with human
and animal waste.

Manky: Old, rotten or worthless.

Mongonel: War machine that can fire arrows or small rocks.

Mum: Mother.

Onager: Large catapult.

Portcullis: Grid style gate lowered to keep invaders out.

Posh: Extravagant.

Queue: Line of people or items.

Rakish: Evil.

Romp: Outing.

Sinister: Evil. Coats of arms that face left are sinister.

Wagon Park: A place to park wagons.

Welch: Older spelling of Welsh. Welch is also a surname.

Zwiehander: Two handed German sword.

axehead until it flung free of the handle and spun away into the darkness.

Peter looked panicked but used the opportunity to bash Godfrey headlong with his shield, one quick blow after another drove Godfrey backward. After the third hit Godfrey dropped his sword. On the seventh blow Godfrey's feet left the ground and he landed hard on his back. Peter placed the blunt tip of the axe handle securely against Godfrey's throat.

"Do you yield?" Peter asked triumphantly while staring down into Godfrey's face.

Godfrey didn't answer.

Peter asked again, "Do you yield?"

Then in the stillness of the night a mechanical sound rang out and echoed off the castle walls. It was the sound of a mongonel. Five arrows sprang out of the ancient rapid-fire war machine striking Peter in the back, penetrating through his armour and deeply into his body. The recoiling wind blew the elfin cloak off the face of Peter's assailant. An assassin named Grunfeld stood on the battlefield exposed.

Peter sank to his knees, spoke only one word, "Zeldain." Then fell forward landing next to Godfrey.

"Treachery!" shouted out a de Saxon soldier at the walls.

Several men ran to close the main gate but none of them made it. Twenty of Hesse's men dressed in elfin cloaks for invisibility and carrying mongonels had slipped into the castle during the duel. They doffed their cloaks and opened fire. Poisoned arrows flew freely and the de Saxon soldiers dropped like apples in a gale.

With tears streaming down his face, Zeldain, Peter's oldest son, rushed his little brother back into the safety of their room in the tower.

Lord Barrack de Saxon, Peter's brother, sounded the retreat on his horn. The few remaining soldiers ran for the secret exits. Catherine ran into the boy's room atop the tower and collected Zeldain while Penny, her handmaiden, lifted Wolfgang. They escaped through a secret passage in the wall which led them to the stables where they exited the castle in the back of a wagon driven by a faithful soldier.

Once they had journeyed down the road a half mile they ran into Lord Barrack who was preparing the local villagers for a coun-

Prologue

Peter de Saxon's new suit of armour, made that very year in1220 AD, squeaked as he turned around and looked up to find the window in the high tower. He spied the person he was looking for; namely, his wife Catherine. Then he spied above her something he had not expected, the heads of his two little boys watching him from atop the battlements on the tower. He smiled as they had obviously sneaked out of bed to watch him.

As the portcullis lifted, Peter emerged alone through the open gate of the castle prepared for battle. He drew his axe and approached his opponent. Godfrey of Hesse had agreed to end the conflict through trial by battle. Peter's men stood on the ramparts, weapons held in readiness. Hesse's army waited anxiously in the darkness. Torches stood upright forming a circle. Peter took his place between two torches opposite of Hesse. This final duel would determine the outcome of the long war which stretched back in time for generations.

Hesse made the first move, lifting his shield with his left arm and swinging his sword from right to left and then quickly back again attempting to catch Peter off guard.

Peter had seen far better swordsmanship than this in his many battles. He waited for the sword to return to its original position then using his shield he swept the sword further to the right. Without a moments hesitation he followed by striking down hard with his axe on Godfrey's shield. The crashing sound rang out loudly and Godfrey nearly dropped to his knees. The shield was mangled; sliced in half and rendered useless by the extraordinarily harsh blow.

Godfrey looked surprised but lunged forward swinging his sword with great speed and accuracy driving Peter backward. After the first four swings Peter used the underside of his axehead to catch the blade of the sword. The axehead wobbled unsteadily. Peter took a quick look; his axe had been sabotaged. The pins that held the head into place were missing. Small scratches revealed that someone had used a tool to remove them.

Peter looked Godfrey in the eyes.

Godfrey returned a sinister smirk. Peter realized someone in the castle had betrayed him. Godfrey pushed firmly against the terattack. He dismounted his horse, turned sharply to Catherine and said, "Peter was assassinated on the battlefield."

"I saw everything," Catherine sighed.

"Take the boys to safety. When Zeldain is of age send him to the Castles and Caverns School where I teach. That is where Peter wanted him to attend and I'll await him there. This is not the end of the de Saxon family. However long it takes, whatever the cost, we will recover our lands and castle and free the people Godfrey of Hesse has taken from us. Zeldain is the lawful heir. God has passed the mantle to the boy and he will lead us to reclaim our small kingdom. Take my horn. If you're captured use it to signal us as to your whereabouts," ordered Lord Barrack while handing his horn to Wolfgang.

"Where is your son?" Catherine asked.

"Danny is safe – now go!"

Penny climbed down from the wagon to join the villagers. Catherine grabbed hold of Zeldain who was attempting to follow Penny. "I can fight!" he shouted struggling to break free of his mother's grasp.

"Not until you're a squire!" she told him.

Zeldain frowned as this was one of the rules of chivalry; he stopped struggling and simply watched his uncle fade in the darkness as the wagon raced quickly away into the night.

Section One

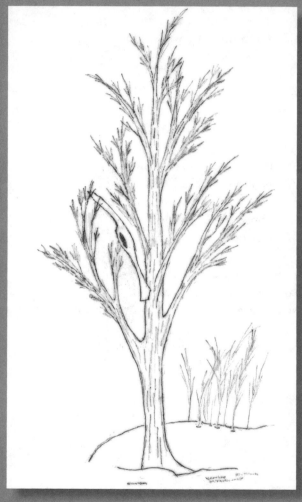

As a "tool" it should be used
on stone, not wood.
A "dwarf" must have lost me in
Zelds neighborhood.

CHAPTER ONE
Going Home

Zeldain heard Wolfgang's signal horn ringing through the late morning air. Anxiously he jabbed his pitchfork into the straw, and then quickly stepped out of the barn. Looking up he saw his brother standing atop a large rock near the mountain road. Wolfgang pointed to Zeldain's right. Zeldain scanned the horizon and spied a cloud of dust rising. Wolfgang draped the horn's leather strap around his neck; then, cupped his hands to his mouth and shouted out, "They're coming!"

The farm consisted of two buildings, a farmhouse and a shabby barn. A curved wooden fence stretched around a small plot of rock-filled pastureland and each end of the fence reached one of the small buildings. A wooden gate met the narrow winding road that wandered around the mountain.

Zeldain dashed toward the sparsely furnished farmhouse. Catherine, his mum, joined him. Together they pulled the bed away from the wall and then Zeldain lifted the cool smooth capstone in the floor revealing the family's secret hiding place. Zeldain's twelve-year-old heart pounded while he helped count out the gold coins in sets of ten. Catherine dropped the coins into a soft leather purse until she reached a thousand. They raced to the nearby road where Wolfgang waited in the warm midday sun. Catherine hadn't caught her breath yet when a party of riders drew near.

"Me Lord," Catherine said loudly trying to compensate for her breathlessness. She spoke using the peasants' vernacular.

The Earl stopped; then, turned his head toward her cautiously. Catherine, a blonde haired woman around thirty years of age, looked thin with long arms, legs and neck. Zeldain understood his mum wanted to appear as a hard working peasant woman living in a farmhouse beyond the bounds of Christendom. He also knew such a position meant she shouldn't speak to the gentry even if she were the only English speaking peasant for hundreds of miles.

"Pardon, me Lord, but me master asked that I stop you and offer payment in exchange for your riderless horse," Catherine said while bowing.

"Who is your master?" asked the Earl.

"Peter de Saxon," she answered as truthfully as she could. Both her boys twinged nervously when they heard their father's name.

"He is offering this money," said Zeldain with a bow, showing proper English etiquette, as he held up the purse.

"Ten thousand silver coins is my price and not a farthing less," said the Earl definitively.

A hard lump formed in Zeldain's throat as he reluctantly handed away the purse with the thousand gold pieces in it and said, "Me Lord gave me this bag of coins and says he'll pay precisely this amount." He knew it was a considerable risk handing this much money over to a total stranger but without the horse, Zeldain couldn't attend school.

The Earl took several moments to count the coins, his stewards nervously awaiting his answer.

"Your master knows the price well. The horse is sold, but not the saddle. I will take this money and saddle to the widow Rachel, she'll need them. Many thanks."

Zeldain felt both pleased and relieved their charade had worked. Catherine's story sounded real to him. After all, no peasant would have a purse full of coins, nor would they need such an excellent warhorse. Zeldain smiled at his mum with a glint of happiness in his eyes. Only an hour ago a stranger had stopped and told them about the horse and now he owned it.

The steward walked the large light grey horse over to Zeldain handing him the reins. "His name is Lightning," said the steward respectfully as the Earl's entourage filed past.

What a grand name, Zeldain thought, as he stepped closely and cautiously toward the Paladorian. He pulled from his pocket a small round sour apple and offered it to the horse. Lightning looked Zeldain in the eyes. Then slowly stretching out his neck, the horse bit the apple. Zeldain nervously checked to make sure he still had all his fingers. He moved to Lightning's left, holding out the remaining portion of the apple. After the horse's second and

CHAPTER TWO

Visitors

A dwarf holding a map marched ahead of the handcarts, which were pulled by dwarves stretching out in a queue up the mountain road. As they drew near, the leader approached Catherine.

"I'm Damart. Please allow me to introduce my wife Gutrace," the leader said graciously in English with a bow. Zeldain noticed something new. The dwarves brought their wives and children along.

Damart asked Catherine, "Are you the English woman we're searching for?"

"Are you looking for an English woman?" she asked innocently in English.

"Our assorted lot of miners started as three small groups. We found each other on the way here. I have a map my cousin made for me, so they elected me their leader. My cousin claimed you are an esteemed friend of the dwarves," Damart concluded.

"May I see the map?" Catherine asked politely.

Tiptoeing to look over his mum's shoulder Zeldain saw the map started in England and took the travellers directly to their farm. Zeldain's panicked eyes met his mother's. He knew this map meant death to their family if it landed into the wrong hands. He could see the same concern in his mother's eyes.

"What would you trade for this map?" Catherine asked while attempting to hide the desperation in her voice.

"Oh, the map is no longer of any value, now we're here. Perhaps we can stay the night and burn it in a bonfire of friendship. We dwarves don't want others to know where our mines can be found. But first, let us make certain the roads to the mines we are looking for are clear, then we'll celebrate," Damart suggested.

The dwarves belonged to a short, stocky race of humanoids known for their powerful arms, broad chests and short legs. Generally, the men grew long hair and beards, which they braided to keep out of their work.

Catherine, after examining the map, gave the directions to the two closer mines and told them the third would take two hours to walk to.

"Take Lightning and one of the dwarves up the road and find this mine for them," Catherine told Zeldain. He understood his mother wanted the map destroyed and so did he. His panic ebbed once he saw his mother put her plan into motion.

A dwarf prepared to go with Zeldain at Damart's request. The dwarf took out a quarterstaff for protection.

Seeing the staff, Catherine frowned. The dwarf said in dwarfish, "In case we find a snake on the road," and waved his hand in a snakelike manner. The motion of the snake seemed to satisfy her that the quarterstaff wasn't meant for her son's head.

Zeldain whistled for Lightning and his grand horse came running through the trees. The dwarves looked impressed. When the dwarf holding the quarterstaff tried to mount, Lightning wouldn't allow it. He turned his hindquarters toward the dwarf and kicked with both rear legs. The dwarf dove hastily out of the way.

Only after Zeldain calmed the horse and motioned for the dwarf to come did the horse let the dwarf near. Zeldain distracted Lightning with a carrot; then, he mounted and helped the dwarf up.

Zeldain enjoyed the ride up the mountain with the dwarf. The air felt cool and crisp on Zeldain's face and the scenery was magnificent. The horse's hooves hit the road in a rhythm of clip-clop, clip-clop. After travelling for a few moments the dwarf introduced himself, "Bushby, I Bushby."

"Zeldain, Zell - dain," the boy repeated slowly.

"Zell-dame," the dwarf said, trying to say it correctly.

"Bushby," replied Zeldain politely.

As they listened to the horse's hooves, the dwarf began singing. To Zeldain's surprise Lightning showed his approval by prancing as if in a parade. The dwarf sang louder. Zeldain slowly translated the words in his mind, like seben for seven, dwarfolk for dwarves, but the words Snow White revealed the song's true message. The

10

dwarf's song echoed all over the mountains. After a while, Zeldain learned the ditty and joined in the singing.

Time passed quickly and the pair arrived at the location of the mine entrance. The ground consisted mostly of mountain stone with a stream running on the right side of the road. An alcove opened up on the left with mature pines and black soil. The dwarf compared the mountainside with the map for a moment; then, wedged his quarterstaff in a small crack, prying open a rather large entrance. Zeldain's mouth fell wide open, as he had never seen a secret passage before.

"Amazing!" he exclaimed.

Bushby and Zeldain explored the mine for a moment; then, Bushby went outside and tied a blue rag to a tree. With the location marked and the mine open the companions headed back before darkness fell.

When they arrived, Zeldain found the tents and handcarts arranged to form a large circle in the pasture, and in the centre they had stacked wood for a bonfire. The women cooked while the men inspected the farm. The dwarves appeared most impressed with the stone wall on one side of the house. They looked at the other walls and scratched their heads as if to ask why did you build only one wall with stone? Zeldain showed them the pile of rocks at the side of the house. Their faces lit up as if they understood the house wasn't finished. Then they used their mining axes to reshape the waiting stones into blocks. Before long, the dwarves had made enough blocks to finish a side wall.

Zeldain greedily began placing the stones into their proper position. He secretly hoped the blocks would keep coming and Wolfgang joined him, but Catherine stopped the process. "We'll work on that tomorrow," she said. "Tonight we'll have a celebration with our new mates."

After darkness fell, the dwarves lit the bonfire, and sang songs about the Goddess on the Moon, what to do when your dog won't stop barking, and other silly songs. Each family sat in front of their own tent. The dwarves showed their dancing. Long shadows from the firelight peaked across the dwarven tents each time the performers leapt to indicate the next phase of the dance. To bring the grand evening to a spectacular close, Damart burned the map in a dwarven ceremony of friendship.

The dwarves hurriedly packed their belongings the next morning to make up for lost time as the caravan awoke late. Before the dwarves left they gave Wolf his first masonry lesson. The handcarts headed up the road to their destinations while Zeldain checked the fishing traps and Wolf worked on the house.

The dwarven women and their children trudged down from the mines every couple of days. One of the dwarven men came with them for protection. Zeldain hurriedly refilled their water barrels at a nearby stream with a bucket. Catherine took lessons in dwarfish so she could communicate with the new neighbours. Catherine also learned how to make cages to catch rabbits and birds. Her long fingers served her well and she made several cages to use around the farm.

While Catherine had her lessons Zeldain and Wolf received masonry lessons from whichever dwarven man had made the journey down the mountain. They learned everything from how to hold the axe, to where to strike the stones for best results.

By mid-August the house was completely rebuilt in stone with a much better roof, a nice kitchen with a stone fireplace and a new bedroom had been added. The pastureland laid rock free with the fence pushed back, framing a larger space. Crops grew on little plots of land close to the stream.

One afternoon the dwarves from the farthest mine came staggering to the farm. Large bats had ferreted their way into the mine and attacked them. Bushby had been bitten so many times that they carried him the last mile. Catherine directed the injured into the house and laid them on the beds. She dressed and bound their wounds with long rags she tore from an old dress.

"We all here?" asked Dort weakly.

They weren't. One of the children named Tula had gone missing. The boys went out to the barn and removed their swords from their hiding place.

Zeldain whistled loudly and Lightning ran toward him. He leapt onto Lightning's back. Wolf ran to join him. Zeldain and Wolf locked arms and Wolf spun up onto the horse's back. The boys charged up the mountain, Zeldain's sword in his right hand and Wolf's in his left.

"To the rescue!" they yelled with their swords outstretched as they rode through the gate.

Catherine ran after her boys calling them back but they had already ridden out of range and Zeldain couldn't hear her. As they rode away, she called out absentmindedly, "And where did you chance upon those swords?"

In route to the mine, the boys counted six dead bats. Each had an eighteen-inch wing span and the size of the bats frightened Zeldain. Wolf looked scared too.

When Zeldain and Wolf reached the camp, they couldn't find Tula. They called for her and searched in odd places. Finally they found her curled up, hiding in a small chest. She lifted the lid but weakened by the bat bites couldn't run far. The boys scooped her up and ran for Lightning.

Wolf screamed painfully and dropped to his knees as one of the bats sunk its teeth into Wolf's exposed back.

Zeldain moved into position holding his sword above his head. "Hold perfectly still," he said and then swung his sword. Wolf froze and Zeldain sliced the bat in two. The impact forced the bat's fangs to tear out of Wolf's back. Again Wolf screamed in pain and blood flowed down his back.

Zeldain lifted Tula and Wolf onto Lightning. Three bats attacked Zeldain while mounting his horse. The bats unsuccessfully tried to bite through Lightning's thick hide and he knocked them sprawling with his head. One dropped to Lightning's right side and he stomped it with his hoof. Once the children were mounted, Lightning galloped quickly away and wouldn't stop until they were safe.

The rough ride bounced the boys and Tula around harshly. Occasionally, a bat would attack and the boys would defend themselves with a sword. Tula sat between them and it proved to be the safest place.

The three children didn't reach the farm until after dark. Catherine ran out and smothered her boys with kisses; then, seeing their injuries, she ushered them into the house for treatment. Tula had been saved, but despite Catherine's best efforts, Bushby died.

The women and children cried and the men appeared worried. The de Saxon family grieved even more than the dwarves. Zeldain's family hadn't had a chance to grieve for their father, Peter. They had no time as they were forced to flee England and establish a new life in exile. They grieved not only for Bushby, but for their father as well.

The dwarves built a fire and gathered around it, sitting on stones. They waited to see how the injured would fare.

Zeldain felt overwhelming sadness and wandered off into the trees so no one would see him cry. The full impact of his father's death came crashing down upon him and he found it hard to breathe as his throat choked with emotion. His chest ached and so did the bones in his face. Then the tears flowed. He sank to a kneeling position hidden in the trees. He swiped at the tears on his face, but more instantly took their place. Memories of his father flashed through his mind, his father teaching him how to shoot a bow and how it felt to ride on his father's shoulders. Zeldain fancied himself a king back then, but that existence died long ago.

Zeldain felt his mother's arms gathering around him. He sobbed for a while as his mum held him tight. Moments later Zeldain and his mum made their way back to the bonfire and they sat next to Wolf. The three of them gazed into the fire with Catherine in the centre, Wolf on her left, and Zeldain on her right. Both boys snuggled into their mother's arms and rested their heads on her shoulders.

They awoke in the morning still outside by the fire pit. Catherine checked on the injured inside the house. All the remaining dwarves had miraculously survived the dark and terrible night.

The dwarves from the two remaining camps came the next evening and carried Bushby away on a four-man stretcher they lifted onto their shoulders. Bushby lay covered with leaves and the remaining dwarves marched behind the stretcher in two queues forming a funeral procession. They left singing a mournful song.

The dwarves buried Bushby in a hidden location on the mountain. Zeldain didn't understand why the dwarves handled the funeral arrangements the way they did, but he respected their ways.

After the funeral a group of dwarves loaded a handcart and headed for the town of Blackdane to buy healing ointments for the injured. Catherine gave them a few gold coins to help with the cost.

It took the dwarves a week and a day before they returned to the farm. They brought back, among other things, some scar removal cream. Catherine rubbed the cream on her boys and they laughed, as the cream tickled something fierce. Zeldain noticed the dwarves had no reaction at all. To Zeldain's surprise, he discovered

14

dwarves aren't ticklish.

The dwarves also brought back twine and three fruit trees for the family. This confused Zeldain because his mother hadn't asked for such things.

Damart explained, "We had enough money for what we needed and spent a little extra to improve the farm. Because you've been such generous friends, we brought you these trees and a special gift to go with them. I daresay, it is a strange gift but we think you'll enjoy it."

The dwarves planted the three saplings near the stream where they'd receive plenty of water and sunshine. Then Damart brought out the gift. It was a brown bottle full of liquid with two markings on the side. Damart poured the contents into three dwarven water barrels he had placed at the side of each tree. The dwarves mixed the contents into the water thoroughly by using long sticks. Then they poured the concoction from the barrels around each tree.

A strange stretching sound came from the trees and in a matter of seconds they grew triple in size and produced fruit. Everyone clapped. The boys watched the entire proceedings with interest. "Outstanding," said Zeldain.

Zeldain watched as Wolf slowly approached one of the trees. Zeldain thought he saw something small and furry on a branch, but a moment later it had vanished. It kept disappearing and reappearing. Wolf slowly moved toward it and then hastily jumped up snatching it. He'd caught a young mountain sprite.

Wolf calmed it by petting it and humming to it gently. As he continued to hum, the mountain sprite nestled on Wolf's shoulder and purred. The tan coloured sprite had a long black tail. Obviously, a bit of the concoction had accidentally splashed on him causing him to grow to this unusual size. Being so young, he still had the appearance of a rodent, as his human features hadn't developed yet. Zeldain smiled. Somehow, the sprite looked like a proper pet for Wolf.

"May ve pick de golden vim?" a Viking woman asked Catherine with a look of great anticipation on her face. She and several companions arrived one afternoon at the farm. She stood pointing to the yellow flowers blooming nearby.

Catherine waved her arm toward the flowers and the women excitedly ran for them, carrying baskets and bags. They filled them as full as they could and then paid Catherine. Zeldain felt pleased to see them pay his mother in gold coins. He didn't understand why they'd do it, but he felt better about leaving, knowing his mother had an income, even if by mistake.

For the last few days before Zeldain's upcoming journey he and Wolf spent every minute together. The two of them did all they could for their mum as Zeldain would leave for school soon. Wolf's sprite, which he named Hammer, became quite tame and went everywhere with the boys, usually riding on Wolf's shoulder.

All too soon the morning came for Zeldain to leave. The boys stood side by side as Catherine gave Zeldain her farewell and handed him his travelling provisions.

"This is your food, tuition money and your passage money to England. Under no circumstances are you to reveal the location of your family to anyone. When you reach Blackdane, go to the dockyard straightaway and ask if any dwarven ships are sailing for England. Don't go on a Viking ship if you can help it." She held out the two purses. "I've stuffed both purses with straw, so they won't jingle as you ride. You'll need to hold the food basket on your lap. Come home, if you can, in the summer and always mind this thought, 'you are a child of destiny'. God be with you, son." She hugged him, kissed his face several times and then stood in the doorway of the house to wave goodbye.

Zeldain turned to Wolf. "Do your best," he said, placing one hand on Wolf's shoulder.

Zeldain and Wolf unhitched the horse from the drag cart and led it to the front of the barn where they kept the swords. Zeldain removed his sword and mounted Lightning. Wolf lifted up the food basket. Zeldain held up his sword and yelled as he saw his father do many times when he rode out on adventures, "VICTORY IS OURS!"

As Zeldain rode away, he looked over his shoulder several times and spied his mother still waving. He would miss his family but he couldn't worry about them, nor did he allow himself to worry about other things, like how he would find his way to England before the Vikings discovered he was a prince of noble birth. Zeldain, full of youthful bliss, felt as if he could take on the entire world, even if it meant riding cheerfully into the jaws of death.

Chapter Three

The Jaws of Death

Zeldain travelled along the mountain road looking for every lost item that had ever been dropped since the beginning of time. He found pottery shards that appeared to have mysterious writings on them. Zeldain hoped they'd lead to a lost treasure someday. He kept the shards and a long stick he could use as a quarterstaff.

When he rode into the Viking village, he saw the straw houses, the town hall and port. He wondered how such a little place could make the English feel so horrorstruck. One grandiose fire would wipe them out. He wandered through the streets toward the port. He addressed no one in Blackdane and no one addressed him.

When Zeldain reached the dockyard, he saw a dwarf sitting next to a ship coiling a rope. "Hello," said Zeldain once he reached the docks in his best but unpolished Danish. The dwarf remained silent, because he didn't know Danish.

"D'you know English?" the boy asked hopefully.

The dwarf looked up and answered with a wink. But Zeldain didn't see it, as only just then one of the Viking boatmen within earshot yelled, "DIS BOAT GOES TO ENGLAND AND SUUN."

"How much?" the boy asked, having already forgotten his mother's warning.

"For vat?"

"Safe passage."

"Tu England?"

"YES, TO ENGLAND!" Zeldain yelled back.

Several men laughed.

"De usual rate vill du. Ve are a cargo ship and yuu vill have tu sleep on de deck," the captain explained.

"The price includes me horse as well."

"Yah, dat goes vith out vords."

"When do we leave?" asked Zeldain.

"As suun as de ship is fuuled, yuu arc lucky tu find us, yust before leaving time." The sailor added, "Come on board vile yuu still can."

Zeldain examined the Viking ship. At the bow of the ship towered a large carved figure of a sea monster's head. The decoration had been painted in dark tones but it also showed a fair amount of bright red. A single red and white sail waited for hoisting up the only mast. Atop the mast sat a small crow's-nest, where a sailor would be assigned to keep watch. Rowing oars waited to be lowered into the water on both the port and starboard sides of the ship. The stern of the ship held two small rooms, the kitchen and the captain's quarters.

Zeldain felt exhausted from his long ride. He found a place at the bow of the ship where the crates formed what resembled a stall. Both he and Lightning slept.

After two hours he awoke, then went to the stern of the ship to pay for his passage. He handed the captain the purse his mum had given to him. The sinister captain, Koren the Cunning, counted the money and said, "Yah, dis is de proper amount."

All the men smiled as they cast off. As the ship pulled away from the waterfront, Zeldain saw the dwarf giving him some sort of salutation by holding up two crosses. The boy waved.

"I'M A CHRISTIAN TOO," he yelled in English. "GOD BE WITH YOU!" The Vikings smiled and waved in mocking gestures to the dwarf. Some blew him kisses and sang a Viking song:

"How sweet is life upon the sea? It's easy money for you and me."

The dwarf had attempted to warn the boy but to no avail. Zeldain had no idea the captain of the ship, who had already taken Zeldain's money to use on the campaign against the English, further planned to kill him and to confiscate his horse. Tears streamed down the dwarf's face and he waved goodbye to the boy who surely sailed away to a watery grave.

Unaware of the danger Zeldain returned to his stall. He slept until nearly dark when a bell tolled. He walked down to the galley and found venison stew with rolls. He ate well. When he returned to his horse, he found a couple of sailors admiring it.

18

"His name is Lightning," he said as if introducing a guest.

"He is beautivul," one of the sailors said.

"A real prize, Vere did yuu steal him?" asked another.

"Me mum traded for him."

"Traded vat? Vere does yuur mutter live boy?" a sailor questioned.

Zeldain didn't fall for that simple trick as he minded his mother's warning. "On the moon," he replied cleverly. "Her name is Olga; she is the Goddess of the Moon. She only comes out when the moon is full and takes the 10 best horses she can find," Zeldain teased.

The Viking sailors smiled and laughed.

"Maybe I vill kill yuur futter, marry yuur mutter and den all de yorses vill be mine," said a sailor teasing back.

"Me father is the Man on the Moon. You can kill him if you want, but first you'll have to reach the moon and then find your way through a sea of horse droppings. I recommend a Viking ship with plenty of hands for rowing. Oh, and it would help if they had terrible colds, so they couldn't smell the ocean," Zeldain said.

The Vikings laughed; then, shuffled off to bed with a delightful story to tell their fellow sailors. The reprieve was only temporary. After all, the horse was a magnificent prize and the puny boy couldn't defend it, but another night would do as well.

In the morning Zeldain wandered to the galley and asked the cook if he could help with breakfast. The galley consisted of a smallish room at the stern of the ship with a large bowl shaped metal table. Hot coals burned in the bowl. The cook roasted sausages on long thin rods that reached across the table.

"Ven one side is cuuked yuu turn dem over," said the cook pointing to sausages in both cooking stages. Zeldain had never seen shish kabob cooking before.

"Does it work with apples?" Zeldain asked, tipping his head to one side in a questioning manner.

"Yah, all kinds of tree fruits and ground fuuds tuu," Guulmate answered. Then he added in a quiet tone, looking furtively from side to side, "Yuu are a fine lad, as suun as yuu can yuu get avay from dis ship. Guulmate vill say notting."

"Why should I leave? The crew fancies me."

"Yah, but day fancy yuur yorse better dan yuu, lad. Some vant yuu dead. So, yuu get avay vile yuu still can."

Zeldain didn't know what to think about Guulmate's warning. He pulled his last two apples from his pocket. He speared them on a rod and hung them over the hot coals.

While the rest of the crew ate sausages, Guulmate and Zeldain had sausages with roasted apples. The hot juice ran in streaks between Zeldain's fingers. The cook laughed and pointed to Zeldain's messy face. Still laughing he handed Zeldain a galley rag to wipe his hands and face. The cook added more wood to the hot coals which restarted the small fire. He handed Zeldain two pails, which showed signs of heavy use.

Pointing to them he said, "Sea vater and de other guud vater."

Zeldain carried the first one and walked to the edge of the boat, tied a rope around the handle and lowered it toward the sea when a sailor grabbed hold of the pail and scolded him. Zeldain couldn't understand a word he said because he spoke too hastily. The sailor untied the knot and slowly tied a new knot, so Zeldain could learn it. The sailor then untied the knot and handed the pail and rope back to Zeldain. The boy tied the knot the sailor showed him. The sailor watched as the pail filled with sea water. The sailor also showed Zeldain how to recoil the rope and where to place it when he finished.

When Zeldain returned to the galley, he found the cook waiting for him with the other pail. He pointed to a barrel not far away. Zeldain exchanged the full pail for the empty one. He found a ladle hanging from the barrel and ladled water into the pail. Another sailor gently lifted the pail out of his hands and with one motion plunged the pail into the barrel and pulled it out full. He held the pail above the large barrel for a moment to let the drippings run back inside. Zeldain carried the pail back to the galley.

"Vash and rinse," the cook said placing the second pail on the coals to heat. The cooking rods and serving platters didn't take long to wash. The crew had used their own knives to spear the sausages.

Zeldain got along well with the crew. In fact, he got along so well the captain had a hard time finding anyone to murder him.

The next day Bjorren the Bold and Koren stood on the starboard side of the ship. Bjorren said. "It is terrible luck tu kill de son of a Goddess. Besides he learned de sheet bend knot in tirty seconds. It is a shame tu murder such a talented boy – only because he owns a fabulous yorse."

"He is English. Ve vill kill him sooner or later - it is only a matter of time," barked Koren.

"So, is dis de enemy of our mighty captain?" Bjorren asked mockingly, "Young English boys who have not yet learned tu tie deir knots?"

"Yuu see him as a boy, and yuu are blind. In fifteen years he vill become a poverful enemy vit allies. Someday he vill send boats tu Denmark tu raid our shores," Koren scolded.

"In fifteen years we vill all be deat and the vorld vill belong tu pigs dat fly," countered Bjorren.

"If you von't kill him den who?"

"No man on dis ship. De crew vould mutiny before day vould kill him."

"Dan ve'll let nature du it. Inform de crew dat ve are letting him off at de virlpool and no man vill varn him," Koren proclaimed.

Bjorren understood from Koren's tone the punishment for warning Zeldain was death.

"Vat if he lives?" Bjorren demanded.

"No vone has ever survived de virlpool. Large ships half sunk dere," Koren reminded him.

"Yah and what if de young half-god lives?"

"Dan he goes free."

"Vat about de yorse?" questioned Bjorren.

"If de boy lives, de yorse is his," Koren said bitterly, staring out to sea with the look and sound of a rakish scoundrel.

Bjorren slipped past Koren to tell the crew. Within minutes he warned every sailor.

Zeldain noticed the crew seemed out of sorts for the rest of the day. A quiet mood prevailed at dinner time. The men sat sour-faced on the rowing benches nearest the kitchen awaiting their meal.

Zeldain spent the day watering, feeding and grooming his horse. He also helped in the galley. Guulmate taught him how to make scones. Zeldain smothered them with honey and butter. The invigorating smell of the hot bread brought the crew to the galley. Guulmate told the crew of the boy's diligence in cooking the meal. They stopped eating and looked disheartened at the food. A Viking superstition stated that anyone sharing a condemned man's last meal would ultimately share his fate. They looked at each other for a solution.

Then Guulmate asked, "Vould yuu deny de fuud given tu yuu by de son of de Goddess of de Muun?" The Vikings also held the belief that they'd be sorely cursed if they defied the will of a God or Goddess.

Zeldain didn't understand what they said but when everyone stopped eating and stared at him he thought he should say something, so he held up his scone and yelled, "VICTORY IS MINE!"

The crew couldn't understand Zeldain's words, so Koren intervened during the awkward silence and explained the boy had taken the ritual challenge of death. This cheered up the crew and they feasted as the ritual required. Koren gave permission to open a cask of ale and turned the occasion into a celebration.

Koren sat back, enjoying the party. The boy's death couldn't be blamed on him and Koren had never heard of any boy Zeldain's age surviving a Viking death ritual. The boy had cooked the customary meal. He had invited his mates to watch, or so it appeared. Everything fell properly into place, according to the Viking custom.

Koren smiled a broad yet devilish grin. "Vonce de yorse loses de boy in de virlpool it vill swim back for de ship and tu his new master - me!" Koren whispered to himself.

That night Zeldain went to bed with a full belly for the second night in a row. He'd worked much harder on the farm for a far worse meal. He fancied the seafaring life which seemed an incredible adventure and the Vikings treated him well. Then he minded what Guulmate told him, that some admired his horse more than him and they wanted him dead. Perhaps the time had come for him to abandon ship. He took a squint, searching the horizon but saw nothing but birds far away. With no land in sight, he'd have to trust his luck until morning.

CHAPTER FOUR

How Do I Get Off?

Zeldain kept waking up imagining an assassin slowly creeping toward him in the moonlight with a knife. He checked often but found no one on the deck of the ship. When the sun rose, he finally relaxed and slept for three hours. He awoke with a yawn and rubbed his eyes. He stretched for a moment, sat up, and then stood on his feet. He walked from his stall to the galley and found the cook saved him some boiled eggs with hardtack from morning's breakfast.

The cook used a hammer to open a well-supplied crate, full of new pots and pans. Zeldain saw hardtack, clean plates, candles, torches, and, tucked into the corners, knives and spoons.

"This looks like a whole kitchen. Why not use this new stuff instead of the old?" Zeldain asked loudly.

Guulmate slammed the lid onto the top of the crate barely missing Zeldain's head and scolded him. "Yuu should keep yuur lips tight locked or de captain vill know dat yuu know tu much," Guulmate said angrily, "Many men half gone tu a vatery grave because day know tu much."

"I'm sorry Guulmate. I'll try to do better," Zeldain apologized, although he had no idea what he had done wrong.

"Yuu help me vith de fish, Yah?" asked Guulmate more cheerfully.

"Yes," answered Zeldain.

He knew how to clean fish but felt surprised to see the large multicoloured scales reflecting the late morning sun. He watched as Guulmate put different parts from the fish into certain pails which sat on the port side of the deck. The heads went in one pail, most of the innards went into another, followed by a third pail for special innards only some fish had. The crew busily hung a rather large fish net to dry. Zeldain had many questions but dared not ask them.

Suddenly, a terrified voice from the crow's-nest yelled, "Dragon!"

The crewman climbed down as hastily as he could. The crew ran to the middle of the boat and formed a long queue from stern to bow, each holding a heavy crate. Perspiration dripped from the crew's horrorstruck faces. Zeldain found it hard to breathe and his heart pounded ferociously in his chest.

As the large headed, bright red dragon flew past the ship it chanced upon its future victims. Zeldain felt the dragon's gaze, and then a gigantic wave of panic overwhelmed him. It felt one hundred times worse than any fear he had previously endured. This fear didn't merely twinge his heart; instead, it completely surrounded it in an icy grip. His breathing nearly stopped and he couldn't move for several seconds. The dragon circled round and blasted a ball of flames which hit the starboard edge of the sail. Guulmate quickly threw a bucket of water on the flames. The four-legged monster circled again, and this time dove past the ship. Its wings produced the strongest gale Zeldain ever felt.

Two crew members lost their balance and fell overboard and the port side of the boat lifted out of the water seven feet. The remaining crewmen threw their crates toward the rising port side to add weight. The boat rocked heavily from port to starboard but didn't capsize. Lightning jumped and kicked furiously.

The dragon came around for a third pass, flying low, this time with a greater force of wind. The crewmen's faces froze with fear. Zeldain cleared the deck by tossing the fish buckets into the galley, even though his muscles didn't want to move.

He missed with one bucket and hit the doorframe which sent fish heads flying backwards through the air. When the dragon descended it saw the fish heads, and swerved to avoid what looked like arrowheads flying its way. As it did, it slammed into the fishing net. This left the dragon momentarily stunned by the collision. One of the crates cracked open and battleaxes scattered across the port side of the ship.

The crew was in shock. Then, Bjorren collected a battleaxe and let out a war cry. The whole crew took up the axes and attacked in unison. Zeldain drew his sword from his belt and attacked the dragon's left side on the starboard side of the ship.

The dragon still had plenty of fight left in it. Another fiery blast erupted, turning two crew members into flaming balls. They hastily jumped into the ocean to douse the flames.

Zeldain couldn't inflict any damage against the hard dragon scales. He slipped the tip of his sword under a scale and thrust it in with all his might. The dragon whipped its tail tossing Zeldain to the deck of the ship. His sword protruded from the dragon like a silver cross.

He yelled, "Me sword," as he thought of it being lost forever when the dragon flew away. Guulmate heard him and with the hammer he had used to open the crate he pounded the pommel, driving the sword deep into the dragon's body. A wild blast of flames shot through the air. Another burning man jumped overboard. A second swing from Guulmate, and the dragon leaped, flapping its wings to escape, which caused the boat to rock heavily.

"De beast vill capsize de ship," yelled Bjorren.

The crew threw ropes over the top of the dragon preparing to tie it down. Meanwhile, the dragon knocked Guulmate half way across the boat with his tail. Zeldain rose to his feet and grabbed the hilt of the sword. Using all his might, he pulled. The sword sprang from the wound like a cork from a bottle and blood gushed everywhere. In a final attempt to free itself, the dragon twisted its head around and bolted back the direction it came from. This exposed its vulnerable underside and with a powerful blow Bjorren swung his battleaxe into the dragon's neck and punctured its windpipe. After a few death throes the dragon lay motionless.

The crew immediately ran to rescue their injured mates who'd gone overboard and checked on the damage to the ship. Koren unfortunately became one of the fireballs that had jumped into the water. The crew placed him in his cabin next to the galley along with the other injured crew members. Zeldain found Lightning on the other side of the dragon. Lightning had kicked the dragon repeatedly causing what appeared to be massive injuries.

The crew acted swiftly and butchered the dragon, keeping the useable parts of course. Zeldain had heard some medicines came from dragon parts and watched intently. Bjorren removed the dragon's fire gullet which resembled a leather purse, only with a three foot long neck at the top.

Guulmate's work kept him the busiest of them all. He removed an eye and rubbed liquid from the eye on the wounded men's burns. He kept the remaining fluid in a brown bottle. Next he peeled away the skin from the skull. He used a battleaxe to crack the skull open and placed the brain into a bucket of fresh water. He carried the bucket to the sea monster head, then cut the wings off and dragged them to the bow as well. With the wings gone, loads more space became available on the deck.

Guulmate asked Zeldain to hold a wing that hung over the edge of the boat. While Zeldain held the wing in place, Guulmate sliced the brain in half; then, used one half of the brain as a type of glue to stick the wing to the ship. Guulmate and Zeldain repeated the process on the other side. The wings made a magnificent decoration. The ship truly resembled a sea monster.

The crew removed the teeth and filled the galley with dragon meat. The larger bones were set out to dry. The second eye floated in a bucket of fresh water, while the scales of the dragon sat on the deck sorted according to their size. Lightning had two enormous horns stashed in with him. The dragon's lungs hung in the fishnet. The tongue swayed back and forth while hanging like a sausage on the galley door next to the liver and the heart.

The thick blood covering the deck slowly dried. The crew finished searching the innards for treasure and cutting out the claws. The ship reeked with the foul stench of the dragon.

Bjorren at first appeared pleased with the progress, and then shouted, "VERE IS DE BRAIN?"

Guulmate shouted back, "I USED IT!"

"For vat?" demanded Bjorren angrily.

Guulmate showed him the wings on the ship.

"Du yuu tink day vill vork?"

"Vy not?"

Bjorren laughed and then shouted loudly, so everyone could hear him, "DIS VAS A GREAT BATTLE MEN! ONE DAT YUU VILL BE PROUD TU TELL YUUR GRANDKIN ABOUT!"

The crew nodded approvingly. Bjorren walked around the ship to Zeldain and said, "More den half belongs to yuu, I vould say."

"I don't understand," replied Zeldain.

"Dis dragon vas huge and yuu and yuur yorse tuuk avay more den half de strength. Yuu half done svell."

Zeldain explained that Guulmate drove the sword in, but Bjorren had already left to go praise the other crew members.

Soon the wounded men could stand on their feet. As their burns quickly healed, they stood looking out the door of the cabin watching the dragon shrink into pieces. After a while the dragon's blood finished drying on the bottom of the ship. To Zeldain's jaw dropping surprise, the crew rolled it up like a rug. He joined in and found it felt like leather. Zeldain had never heard of dragon's blood leather before.

He asked Guulmate warily, "What is this used for?"

Guulmate replied secretively, "Poisoned pruuf leadder armour."

Zeldain asked tactfully, "If there's anything else you can tell me - I'd like to learn all about dragons."

Guulmate explained things as he pointed to the different parts of the dragon.

"Big byones are lightning byolts

Lungs, sea vater in and guut vater out

Dragon cryings heal vounds

Dragon scales no byurns

Gullet is dragon fire on English

Teeth tu make lightning arrows

Claws are sharp spears

Meat for fuud

Yorns tu sell

Dese meats tu make yuu strong," Guulmate said as he pointed to the tongue, liver and heart hanging on the galley door.

"Thank you," said Zeldain when he finished.

He didn't understand everything Guulmate said. However, he wanted to avoid 'dragon fire on the English' and Zeldain felt certain Guulmate had tried to warn him, once again, to leave the ship. After all he could only find one Englishman on board. Zeldain searched in vain for the shoreline.

The boat turned sharply on a new course as if the wind had made a sudden change. Zeldain looked up, only to find the sail taken down for repair. He wondered how the boat could possibly move so quickly. Bjorren called everyone to the bow to see the new addition. What the crew saw was simply beyond belief: the dragon wings flapped and the boat moved at triple the usual speed.

"Don't forget tu add dis part of de story for yuur grandkin," Bjorren teased. "Credit for dis goes tu Guulmate."

"De idea vas inspired by de lad," Guulmate explained. "How else can his mutter come down from de moon?"

The good fortune impressed the crew as well as the leadership of Bjorren, Guulmate and Zeldain. They sang an Old Norse song about Thor's war hammer. With the song, the last of Zeldain's panicky feeling subsided.

Although Zeldain couldn't tell what they sang about, he could tell a jolly crew from a miserable one. The crew had an enormous amount of work to do before dark. The entire crew, including Zeldain, received new leather armour. The crew finished Zeldain's vest and leggings first. The oversized leather armour felt soft on the inside but tough on the outside. Guulmate told him, "It is tuu big on purpose, because yuu are still growink." Zeldain thanked the whole crew and meant it.

Darkness fell as only the stars shone that night. A few clouds would have blocked out all the light. The boat came to a stop. Then, Koren the Cunning called the crew together. He spoke quickly in Danish and Zeldain couldn't understand him.

"As you know men, de lad has taken the challenge of de virl-pool. Vell, ve're here on the coast of England and it torments me tu tell you, it's time for his test. It's times like dese when I ask myself, who are ve to interfere with de vill of the Gods? I know dat ve vould like to cheer de lad to victory but ve must remain silent. Only in our hearts and minds can ve cheer. Silent on de outside but cheering for our lad on de inside. This is our duty and our honour. Let no man abandon his duty tonight. May his mutter de Goddess of de Moon protect him," Koren said in mocking reverence.

Bjorren led Lightning to the starboard edge of the boat. Guulmate spoke to Zeldain pointing to a small white stripe that appeared in the darkness he said, "Dat is de shore of England. Ve can not go dere. Yuu and yuur yorse vill have tu svim tu de shore."

Zeldain gathered his things and handed them to Guulmate. Zeldain jumped into the water and whistled for Lightning who jumped without hesitation. Zeldain climbed on Lightning's back, and then reached up for his belongings. He wedged his sword into his rope belt. His money bag holding the tuition and pottery shards had never left his side. Using a rope, Guulmate lowered

28

his food basket. Guulmate had placed in it a brown bottle along with some dragon meat and hardtack and last of all came the quarterstaff.

"Guud luck," said Guulmate.

Bjorren spoke as loudly as he dared, "Vikings of dis ship I give yuu Zeldain Halfgod."

Zeldain kicked his heels into Lightning's side.

"God be with you," he called back quietly.

Lightning swam straight for the shore. Suddenly the current of the whirlpool tossed them to the left. Zeldain wondered what Lightning had in mind. He grabbed the horse's mane with one hand, while the other held onto his basket and quarterstaff. Then, things really went awry.

He couldn't tow Lightning back in the right direction. Lightning continued to go left. The harsh ocean current felt strong, like the mountain wind pulling on Zeldain's legs. In the fight to stay on Lightning he dropped the food basket and quarterstaff and grabbed hold of Lightning's mane with both hands. The horse continued to go left even though the beach grew farther and farther away. Zeldain could see his quarterstaff going around in circles. His basket with the dragon meat sank like a rock. Lightning snorted to clear the sea water that had splashed into his nose.

The ship sat silently as Zeldain struggled. He wanted to cry out for help but it might alert someone to the presence of the Vikings and if that happened, Guulmate could be killed. Lightning took them out to sea and the crew couldn't see them in the darkness. They kept looked straight ahead, while Lightning swam on the port side of the ship attempting to break free of the whirlpool's current. The crew could see something going around in the whirlpool but couldn't quite make it out. They waited. Koren told them, if necessary we'll wait until dawn, which really meant, we're not leaving without my new horse.

CHAPTER FIVE

Where is Me Son?

On this same particular night someone scaled the walls of the McMarr Manor and tried to steal the horses. The horses in the barn neighed loudly. They had been trained to stay put, so the intruder moved on. It could have been anyone fumbling around in the darkness, pirates, thieves, Vikings, Christians who challenged Jens McMarr Sr.'s unorthodox beliefs, non-Christians who hated him for his beliefs or a prank by some local farm boys.

It only took a few seconds for Jens Sr. to arrive at the scene in his nightshirt, he merely followed the noise. Jens Sr. stood more than six-feet tall, heavy set, with a full sized stomach and powerful arms. His dark bushy beard and blonde hair were peppered with grey. His hair coupled with his watery blue eyes, gave him the appearance of an old timer. His trey born sons, Oles, Oars and Odin had blonde hair, blue eyes and pale skin with freckles. They trailed behind their father along with his eldest son Jens Jr., who had uncharacteristically dark hair, eyes and skin.

What resembled a six-legged milk cow wandered across the manor yard in the moonlight. Upon closer examination, someone was escorting the cow toward the front gate. Jens Sr. calmly told his boys to surround the cow. He slipped over to a woodpile and pulled out a hidden axe. No tools or weapons were permitted in the open at the manor, as raiders could easily use them. Jens Sr. had taught his sons to give their enemies no advantage.

The family surrounded the six-legged cow. To their amazement the other two legs belonged to a girl. She had long brown hair curled at the ends with a touch of red highlights. She had big blue beautiful eyes and a nice smile.

"What'll we do with her Dad?" Oles asked, excitedly.

"We'll turn her over to the sheriff," he said.

"Oh please, sir, not the sheriff," the girl cried. "If he catches me again, I'll go to prison."

"It's your doing, Lass, not mine," replied Jens Sr.

She ran over to Jens Jr. and put her arms around him.

"Please don't let them take me away," she sobbed. Then she lifted her head straight up and yelled, "NOW!"

Suddenly, both the girl and Jens Jr. lifted magically through the air and over the wall. It took several minutes for Jens Sr. and his sons to saddle their horses, light torches and open the gate. This gave the kidnappers a sizeable lead. In the darkness, Jens Sr. and the three boys had a difficult time following the trail. The night shadows of the woods played tricks on their eyes and they were compelled to suspend the search. They did much better in the early morning light, but by then they were too late. The McMarrs followed the trail to the ocean and there it ended. They stared into the distance looking for something, anything.

Then Odin shouted, "THERE HE IS!"

A dark figure of a boy riding a horse floundering in the ocean came into view. The search party rode out into the sea with their hearts beating wildly to retrieve him. They led the fatigued horse to shore. The horse's mane ensnared the boy's hands tightly and he leaned forward with his wet hair covering his face. The boy, exhausted from his ordeal, could not speak. Before the sun had cleared the horizon, everyone stood on dry ground. Once on shore, Jens Sr. pulled his son's hair back for a better look at his face. Only then, did they discover they hadn't saved Jens Jr., but someone else.

Jens Sr. eyed the boy up and down, this time in the light. The boy wore an unusual and oddly oversized suit of leather armour. The horse came from Denmark's Paladorian stock. Both the boy and the horse lay exhausted on the rocks. Oles spied a Viking ship with wings. The men on board stood at the starboard side of the ship, intently searching the shoreline.

The McMarrs hid themselves and their horses in the rocks.

Zeldain, though exhausted, spied the ship and with his remaining strength he stood holding his sword straight up and yelled, "VICTORY IS MINE!"

The sword glistened in the morning sunlight and the crew cheered, but Koren went into a fit of rage. He accused the crew of cheating him out of the horse and he threw things around the deck. Bjorren commented, "He's de son of de Goddess of de Moon. She sent him here tu test us before ve go tu battle. Be tankful she didn't find us unvorthy."

Koren remained bitterly silent as the Viking ship reversed course. Zeldain collapsed onto the beach and the McMarrs hurried to carry him home. Once revived, he ate six eggs and a half pound of bacon for breakfast. Afterward, he climbed into the bed at the manorhouse's guestroom. Lightning, on the other hand, lay moaning in one of the stalls with a belly full of seawater.

Jens Sr. went into the guestroom and checked on the boy at noon. "What's your name lad?" he asked.

33

"I'm Zeldain de Saxon."

Jens Sr. appeared surprised, "Are you from the de Saxon family living in exile?"

"Yes."

"I know your family. We felt deeply saddened when we heard about the dreadful attack on your castle, and the death of your father. Why have you come to Scotland, lad?"

"Scotland?" the boy croaked, "I'm supposed to be in England. I'm attending the Castles and Caverns School of Knighthood. It starts sometime soon."

"Aye, lad, the school does start soon. Me boys are planning to attend as well. Last night me son Jens Jr. fell victim to a kidnapping plot. We searched for him all night and when we found you in the water, we thought you were he. Tell me about the Viking ship - did they steal away me son?" Jens Sr. asked.

"No, they coveted me horse. I paid them for safe passage to England and when we reached the shore, they put us overboard and told us to swim to the beach. Me horse couldn't go the direction they pointed, so we swam all night in the darkness," Zeldain said.

"There is a whirlpool, not far from where we found you, that's strong enough to sink a ship. I believe they sent you to die and planned to rescue the horse. That's the way with Vikings. If they think you're protected by a god, they'll let nature kill you, so they can remain blameless," Jens Sr. explained.

"Let me explain a few other things you clearly need to know, lad. The second part of your name is 'dain', you came here by Viking boat and your horse is Paladorian. By these clues I know your mother is living in the Paladorian Mountains of Denmark," said Jens Sr. He stopped speaking and watched Zeldain closely. Zeldain's mouth fell wide open in shock.

"That's right, lad, you're teeming with clues. I know your family is in terrible danger, so we must secret away these clues from your enemies before you report to the school. Let's start with your name."

"What's wrong with Zeldain?"

"It is a clue to find your family. If your enemies hear your name, it may start them thinking about Danes, and then Denmark. What if we called you Zello instead?"

"No, I don't much fancy that. What about Zeld?"

"Zeld will do nicely," said Jens Sr., nodding his head in approval. "You must never tell anyone you came with the Vikings, no matter what lad, no matter what. You may say you saw the Vikings and they tried to kill you, but never say you came on a Viking voyage. About the horse, let one of me sons ride your horse to the school and claim it as his own. Meanwhile, you'll ride one of our horses."

"Agreed," said Zeld shaking hands with Jens Sr. "What must I do to keep you from telling anyone where me mum is hiding?"

"We all keep one another's secrets, lad, and I would deem it an honour to count you as me dear mate. I believe the kidnappers took me son, mistaking him as a servant they could recruit into their band of thieves. Other servants have gone missing from time to time. If I'm right, this gives me son a chance to escape on his own and live," said Jens Sr.

"If the kidnappers ever ferret out they've stolen me son, they'll hold him for ransom. Once they receive the money, they'll kill him and make it appear as an accident. Much akin to the Vikings letting nature kill you, they'd let him accidentally drown or take a fall from an insurmountable height. They would never release me son unharmed. For they surely know, I'd destroy the lot if he could tell me where to find them. So, if you will remain silent about Jens Jr., I'll remain silent about your mother. What say you to that?" Jens Sr. asked.

"Silence it is," Zeld answered.

Jens Sr. led Zeld out of the guest bedroom and went into the kitchen where the triplets and another younger boy sat eating their midday meal at a table.

"This is Zeld. He has come to attend the Castles and Caverns School of Knighthood. The Vikings sank his boat and he swam to the shore with his horse. He's quite a lad. You heard his cry 'victory is mine' and you saw how angry the captain became. This lad got the better of him. He's agreed not to tell anyone about Jens Jr.'s kidnapping. Please sit down, over there, and eat," Jens Sr. directed Zeld.

The triplets sat up with a smile when they heard they'd have a new companion going to school with them.

"I'm Oars."

"I'm Odin."

"I'm Oles."

"I'm Dando."

"Is this your first year at the school?" asked Oles.

"Yes," he said looking up and seeing three identical faces. Zeld shook his head to clear his vision.

"What didja say your name was again?" Odin asked.

"Zeld," he responded slowly, "Me name is Zeld."

"Didja see anything of our brother last night?" Oars asked.

"No, I only remember the Viking ship," he answered.

"D'you remember us rescuing you from the water?" asked Oars.

"You rescued me outta the water?" Zeld asked.

"Yes, and your skin was the most wrinkled I've ever seen. Somehow your leather armour stayed dry. What type of leather is that? Where can I buy some? How many Vikings were there? What is the name of your horse? Can I ride him? Where d'you come from? D'you like cheese? Where'd you find that sword? What is the capital of Ireland?" Then laughter erupted as the triplets reached their limit of pestering questions. They loved this mettlesome game and began laughing at the questions they asked.

"'D'you like cheese?' Where'd that come from?" Odin asked Oles.

"I dunno but it was funny," Oles responded. All three faces laughed.

"What is the capital of Ireland?" one of them repeated and they laughed again.

The triplets and Dando went outside, mounted their horses and rode out the gate. Zeld watched them leave. A woman walked into the kitchen.

"Hello, me name's Marta McMarr." Marta had blonde hair with a womanly figure, blue eyes reminiscent of her sons' and pale skin

"Me name is Zeld," he responded turning his head to see her. Then he asked, "Are you their mother?"

"Yes, they're trey born," Marta told Zeld.

"At first I thought they were a three-headed monster," said Zeld.

"They are," Marta answered smiling.

36

"I'm the boy from the sea," Zeld stated in a matter of fact tone.

"Oh, how did you enjoy playing merman for a night?" she teased.

Zeld understood perfectly where the boys picked up their sense of humour.

"I didn't much like it at all," he muttered, glancing down.

When he looked up, he found Marta had left. A large clump of bread and a bowl of beef stew sat next to him. Zeld ate the food and went out to find his horse.

Lightning appeared pleased to see him, but the look disappeared once he stood in his rough cut timber stall. Zeld hugged his horse and thanked him for saving their lives. A raspy sound in Lightning's breathing caught Zeld's attention. Zeld looked around for someone to tell, but he couldn't see anyone in the yard. He entered the manorhouse but found no one in the kitchen or the guestroom. Finally, he overheard voices, so he followed the sounds until he came to a posh den where Jens Sr. and Marta explained to someone the details of the search.

Zeld poked his head into Jens Sr.'s posh den but said nothing. His shadow gave him away and Jens Sr. motioned him in. He said, "This is Zeld. He's the lad we fished out of the ocean earlier this morning. He also saw the Viking ship, isn't that right, lad?"

"Yes, that's right, I did see the Viking ship," said Zeld as he sidestepped a knee high table and sat on a padded stool next to Marta.

"Are you English?" asked a distinguished, dark haired man with a Norman style goatee, who sat at the nearside of the desk.

"Yes, I'm English."

"Does this boy work for you, Jens Sr.?" the man asked.

"No. He's a school lad starting at Castles and Caverns this year," Jens Sr. answered.

"That's correct," stated Zeld.

Zeld turned to Jens Sr., "Me horse is ill. Methinks he has seawater in his lungs."

The man looked up from his parchment.

"Did the Vikings chase you into the water?" the distinguished man asked.

"Yes, if it weren't for me horse's ability to swim, I would've drowned," Zeld stated firmly.

"Thank you, Zeld, I'll put out a warning. Oh, I imagine the town healer might have something for seawater in the lungs. It would be a shame to lose such a talented horse," the man said as he retrieved his parchment and rose to his feet.

"I'll catch you McMarrs up later," he said buttoning his top button as he stood in the doorway and turned sharply to walk away. Zeld heard him take two footsteps, and then he heard no sound at all. Zeld leaned over to see the man but he had vanished without trace.

CHAPTER SIX

Healers

"You and me should go straightaway into town and find the healer," Jens Sr. suggested to Zeld as he stepped around his desk in his posh den.

"Certainly," replied Zeld.

The two of them walked to town because all of the manor's horses were used on the search. Thick vegetation surrounded them on both sides and even in the space between the ruts foliage tried to reclaim the coach way. As they walked, side by side, they talked.

"Who was that well-dressed man at the manor?" Zeld asked politely.

"King Henry's clerk. It's his job to report problems, so the king can decide what to do about them," explained Jens Sr.

"Did the king know when me family's castle fell under attack?"

"Oh, yes."

"Why didn't he help us?"

"King Henry tried, but his men fell into an ambush. You see, Godfrey of Hesse planned for years to take your father's castle. He set up ambushes for all of your father's allies."

"Doesn't King Henry have a grand army?" asked Zeld, with a sinking feeling in his stomach. He also felt a bit confused as to why the king would not have used them.

"Yes, but most of it is stationed in the Holy Land," explained Jens Sr. "There was one other sizeable concern: King Henry had no experience leading a rescue army."

"Did me father lack experience as well?" Zeld asked, hoping to hear his father was a military genius.

"No, your father had built an army and placed his brother, Lord Barrack, over it. After Godfrey of Hesse's troops captured the castle, Barrack rallied the villagers and the few men who escaped the slaughter for a counterattack. One of the survivors told me

Barrack was struck down by a traitor who stabbed him in the back with a poisoned sword but Barrack managed to kill the traitor before the poison went into full effect. Despite Barrack's loss, the counterattack took place giving your mother enough time to get away to safety with you lads in tow."

Zeld felt sad hearing the news about his uncle. He looked crestfallen as the realization sank into his mind that Lord Barrack wouldn't be waiting for him once he reached Castles and Caverns.

"Later, your mother wrote letters to King Henry explaining she and her two sons survived and would live in exile for a time. King Henry used the letters to block Godfrey of Hesse's claim to the land, but Hesse took possession of the castle and lands all the same, which includes the people and animals, as if he held the deed. Hesse profited greatly by this venture. However, he'll lose everything if an heir returns, which means he must murder your entire family in order to truly win," Jens Sr. told Zeld.

"Someday I'll recover me family's lands, castle and people. If he hopes to kill me, he'll be woefully disappointed - I don't plan to die."

Jens Sr. chuckled at Zeld's odd sense of determination.

"King Henry and I would both celebrate at seeing you reclaim your castle. There would be considerably less trouble in our area if Hesse retreated to Germany," Jens Sr. added.

By the time they reached the village a notice hung on the village board. It stated that a Viking ship had been seen by a young English boy. The villagers didn't act alarmed.

Jens Sr. explained, "They can't read."

Jens Sr. called to the villagers, "This notice says Vikings were already seen this year." The villagers looked unimpressed.

Zeld called out defending his honour, "It's true, I saw them."

The town healer, dressed as a shopkeeper, stood by a wagon. He told the driver to hang on for a moment. The healer was shorter than Zeld, bald on top, with a thin build. But what he lacked in height he made up for in energy.

"Boy, are you English?" he asked abruptly.

"Absolutely," Zeld answered.

The healer then turned to the driver and issued a new set of directions for the delivery which sent the wagon a safer direction, further from the coast.

"Bolt, we've an ailing horse at the manor," Jens Sr. told the shopkeeper.

"What's the problem?" asked the shopkeeper impatiently while looking up into Jens Sr.'s face.

"Seawater in the lungs," Jens Sr. declared.

"I have what you need, let me collect me bag."

"I'm glad you came by. This shipment of star daisies would've been easy pickings for the Vikings."

The healer walked toward the McMarr Manor with his bag in hand. Jens Sr. and Zeld walked quickly to keep up.

"You think he's trudging swiftly now, you should've seen him the other day when a plague broke out in Jeweldurn. He took one of his own potions and outran the horses. He rushed in and out so hastily the Jeweldurnians still haven't figured out who rescued them," Jens Sr. said.

Zeld couldn't keep walking at the healer's quick pace. He and Jens Sr. let the healer go on ahead while they puttered along behind.

"Let me tell you the story of us McMarr's," Jens Sr. volunteered. "My name was originally Jens Marrsen, my father's name was Marrs Olsen. It is the Viking custom to take your father's first name and add 'son' or 'sen' on the end to create your surname."

"When my wife and I converted to Christianity our village went into an uproar. My father pulled me aside and said, 'Scandinavia is no place for a Christian, and your brother Lars must avenge this outrage. Take your wife to Scotland and I will do all in my power to keep you safe from your brother's wrath. Someday, however, I will pass on and your brother and his cohorts will make plans to destroy you. Prepare for that day as it will surely come.' I never laid eyes on my father again."

"Once Marta and I reached Scotland I took the Scottish version of my name, Jens McMarr Sr. It took us fifteen years to build the manor and it contains many of the luxuries of a large scale castle." Jens Sr. pointed out the features of the manor as they approached it. "We have the chapel, Great Hall, which is in the centre of the east and west wings, barracks and stables. The outer wall surrounds everything and is strongly fortified."

By the time Jens Sr. and Zeld reached the stables, the healer had mixed a concoction based on an estimate of the amount of seawater in Lightning's lungs. The healer stood in the horse's stall vigorously shaking the bottle with the elixir.

"Jens Sr., would you keep a bucket of fresh water in readiness? I imagine the horse will be slightly dehydrated when we finish. Boy, come 'round and persuade your horse to drink this."

Nervously, Zeld leaned over and held Lightning's mouth open while the healer poured the concoction down the horse's throat. When the horse finished drinking the healer bellowed, "GIVE HIM ROOM!"

Zeld quickly slipped through the rails of the stall and backed away. His nervousness grew as the horse rose hastily to his feet, neighing in distress. Then steam spewed from Lightning's nose. Puff, puff, puff, followed by a small steady gush of steam and then a larger gush with a low whistle, followed by an even larger gush with a high whistle. Finally the steam poured from the horse's mouth, nose, and ears. Then with a small popping sound it stopped. The horse looked at the men and nodded his head in approval. Lightning strolled to the bucket of fresh water and drank.

Zeld let out a sigh of relief. The healer turned his attention toward him and made a quick examination. He had already noticed Zeld's drooping shoulders and repeated yawning. Zeld's exhaustion was obvious. He reached into his bag and removed three bottles. Opening the lids he placed one pill from each bottle in Zeld's hand.

He pointed to the pills and said in a knowledgeable tone, "Take the blue ones now and the yellow one in the morning."

Zeld swallowed the two blue pills and kept the yellow one in his hand.

"No dear boy, take the yellow pill in to the manorhouse and place it somewhere. If one holds medicine in ones hand it will lose its potency," explained the healer.

"I didn't know," Zeld muttered a wee bit embarrassed.

"Place it in the drawer of the guestroom," Jens Sr. instructed.

Zeld went into the manorhouse and placed the yellow pill into the drawer. Then he lay down on the bed for a short rest and fell sound asleep.

"You'd better check on the boy. One of those pills was a powerful sleeping agent. He'll sleep for at least three hours. Oh, and no charge today," Bolt added. "King Henry will pay this bill."

"I sincerely thank you for King Henry's hospitality," Jens Sr. teased with a twinkle in his eye.

"Certainly - where is everyone?" Bolt asked.

"We had a raid last night. One of the servant boys is missing and we're still searching," Jens Sr. explained as honestly as he could without revealing the kidnapped person was his son.

"Good luck with your search. If you need me, I'll be at me shop all night concocting potions, as it appears we'll need them. A Viking ship spied on the coast this early isn't the luckiest of signs!" Bolt shouted over his shoulder as he whizzed out the gate at his usual quick pace.

Jens Sr. went inside as soon as Bolt left and checked on Zeld. Finding Zeld asleep he knelt down on his left knee and offered an emotional prayer asking God why he had sent him another de Saxon boy while leaving his son in danger?

When Zeld finally awoke, he stumbled into the kitchen and spied Marta returning wearily from the chapel.

"Have you heard from the rescue party yet?" Zeld asked hopefully.

"No, they'll return soon, tired and hungry. I don't know what to cook for supper." She groaned while taking a seat.

"How about scones?"

"That would be wonderful," she cried, rising to her feet and giving him a smile.

Marta found the flour, yeast, honey, and other ingredients for scones. It had been ages since she'd cooked a meal. Her role changed from a farm girl, to wife and mother, and then to that of a Duchess when Jens Sr. built his army to one hundred men. Together she and Zeld prepared seven huge platters of scones for the rescue party.

Jens Sr. entered the kitchen carrying two buckets of milk and had animal feed stuck to his clothing. Obviously he had worked in the stables. As the horses arrived the riders found the serving table waiting for them out in the courtyard with the platters of scones. The riders dismounted and Jens Sr. led the horses to their stalls.

Once he finished cleaning in the kitchen, Zeld went outside with the others. He took two scones for himself and covered them with his favourite, blackberry jam. His mouth watered as he took his first bite.

One of the servants studied Zeld for a moment, and then asked suspiciously, "Are you English?"

"Yes," he replied. "Why does everyone keep asking me that question?"

"It's the fastest way to know your mates from your enemies," the servant told Zeld.

"I only have one enemy," Zeld remarked with certainty.

"Then you haven't been in Scotland long," concluded the servant.

44 Zeld was taken aback by this comment. He truly hadn't been there long but still couldn't understand what that had to do with how many enemies he had.

As dinner drew to an end Jens Sr. called the milling crowd to attention. The search leaders gave their reports and Jens Sr. gave the assignments for the next day. Only half as many people would search for Jens Jr. as they had covered most of the area already.

With business for the evening completed Zeld went to the guestroom, undressed, said his prayers and climbed into bed. He had nightmares that night. Firstly, the Vikings attempted to kill him. Secondly, he nearly drowned in the ocean with Lightning. Thirdly, he heard the triplets teasing him, "What's your horse's name? Can I ride him? What's the capital of Ireland?" Then several new voices asked, "Are you English? Are you English? Are you English?" Words and phrases followed, "I give you Zeldain Halfgod - I only have one enemy - then you haven't been in Scotland long."

BANG! The door flew open and hit the guestroom wall. The triplets, who were Zeld's age and size, landed on the bed one at a time, causing Zeld to flop up and down. He sat up wide awake. They started in with the questions again, "Would you care to ride with us today? Does your horse like honey in his oats? Can you say Worcestershire sauce? Can you spell Worcestershire sauce? Why is your nose on upside down?"

When they laughed, Zeld seized the opportunity to start on them, "Are dwarves ticklish? What's the name of the Goddess of the Moon? Do dragons lay eggs or give live birth? What's the name of the three-headed monster that lives at the McMarr Manor? Oops, I'd bet me last copper piece you know plenty well the answer to the last one."

Odin sighed, "I imagine we are the answer to that last one."

Oars said, "Correct and for that answer, Zeld's won a fabulous prize selected by our lovely lady especially for him - breakfast in the kitchen."

Oles clapped his hands and cheered as if Zeld had won something valuable.

Zeld hadn't finished yet, "To think me horse and I swam all the way across the sea to go to school. So, what happens when we arrive, me horse and I are landed with YOU three. The capital of Ireland is Dublin. Yes, I like cheese. I, would even eat oats with honey in it, and no, I can't spell Worcestershire sauce."

45

The triplets had been out teased for the moment and they did the only thing they could do. They moved over to one side of the bed and together they lifted the mattress until Zeld fell out the other side.

Then they dropped the mattress on top of him and ran out the door yelling, "Mum, Zeld's awake."

Jens Sr. called up, "Remind him to take the yellow pill."

All three boys ran back to the guestroom, "You're supposed to take a yellow pill. Can we watch? Are you gonna turn into a pink toad?"

Here we go again, Zeld thought. So he yelled, "YES!" The triplets laughed.

"You're gonna turn into a pink toad?" Oles asked, repeating the question.

Zeld held the yellow pill above his mouth and announced, "Good gentlefolk, you're about to see me, the amazing Zeld, attempt to turn meself into a pink toad by swallowing this yellow pill. Those of you with unsteady hearts, please turn away." Zeld then swallowed the pill.

Oars turned away, Odin pointed at Zeld, while Oles squealed in a high pitched surprised voice, "Iiiit'ssss woooorrrkiiinnng." To which Zeld replied, "Ribbit."

The triplets ran out, calling to their Dad, "Zeld didn't want to take his pill, but we made him."

Jens Sr. called all the boys together after breakfast, in the yard, and did something unusual. He held out his hand with his pinky finger and thumb extending out at each end, the other fingers tucked away underneath. The triplets and the younger boy from the day before did the same thing leaving a space for Zeld in a circle. He swiftly followed suit.

"This is our family sign," Jens Sr. explained. "We use this to identify our allies and it might become important by the end of the day - but no one knows for certain."

They followed in a pledge, "Be true to your family, true to your God, and true to your king." Zeld felt a true friendship forming between him and the McMarrs.

Zeld and Lightning spent the day assigned to a search crew. The triplets, along with the other boy from the day before, had the same job, namely, riding back and forth informing the other crews about their crew's progress on the search.

Zeld's crew captain methodically posted lookouts at excellent vantage points; then, his crew searched small woodland areas. If anyone tried to steal away, they would've been seen.

After repeating the process at a few more patches of woods the search changed and the crew investigated possible hiding places. They searched an abandoned cottage in the woods, but found nothing. Zeld pointed out some recent repairs, including new roof beams, however, as far as anyone knew, it meant nothing.

After this search they headed north to see if anyone in that direction had anything to report. The crew rapped on the doors of the little houses in the villages along the way and checked out small caves the right size for hideouts. This search turned up nothing. The farther north they went, the closer to dragon territory they came. The search crew breathed a sigh of relief when they turned around for home.

The end of the day brought no solid clues. When they reached the McMarr Manor, the mood grew bleak.

"We can go out again tomorrow," Zeld told Jens Sr. Zeld wasn't ready to give up the search, not after only two days.

"No," Jens Sr. said thoughtfully, "Tomorrow school starts. You and the triplets must be on your way."

Zeld hadn't known school started so soon. Perhaps they would excuse him for a few days, he thought.

Jens Sr. called the triplets, Zeld and the younger boy, who Zeld had seen several times but couldn't remember his name, "Tomorrow is the first day of school for the four of you. You are going. We've enough men to search without you. Oars, you'll ride Lightning and Zeld, you'll ride Tiger," he said, pointing at the boys. "Tell the school you own the horses you're riding. They must never learn Lightning belongs to Zeld. This is a matter of life and death."

In the morning the boys rode for school.

"How far is it?" Zeld asked, while attempting to look down the road.

"Three hours on horseback," said Oles truthfully.

"- or forever in a wagon," added Oars sarcastically.

"Last year we travelled by wagon several times to visit Jens Jr.," explained Odin.

The triplets attempted to play horse tag along the way but the heavy suits of armour ended the game quickly.

Odin asked Zeld in an overly courteous tone, "Why d'you wear leather armour instead of mail?"

"I don't own any other armour," he informed his mates.

"Tell them you couldn't swim across the sea in your heavy armour. They'll have to believe that, won't they?" suggested Oars.

When Oars turned around his brothers and Zeld had vanished. He'd missed a turn.

"MATES, HEY MATES, WHERE ARE YOU?" he shouted out.

CHAPTER SEVEN

Let the Fun Begin

When Zeld and the triplets arrived at the castle in the early afternoon Zeld could hardly believe his eyes. He found the castle far from complete, in fact only half the outer walls were in place. This didn't surprise the McMarrs but Zeld, a new student, felt shocked. He wondered if the triplets jested with him. He expected a grand castle with trumpeters announcing everyone's arrival. Only the sign out front reading, "Castles and Caverns School of Knighthood" convinced Zeld he'd actually arrived at the right place.

The boys rode through the gate and followed a multicoloured flagged rope that led them to a queue at the stables. Oles walked his horse up to the hostler first. "Name?" the hostler bellowed over the noise of the bustling crowd.

"Oles McMarr."

"Not your name, the name of your horse!" said the hostler unhappily.

"Meadow."

"Mare or Stallion?"

"Mare."

"Age?"

"Seven years."

"Shod or unshod?"

"Shod."

"Breed or markings?"

"Belgian."

"Stall number 18," said the hostler, pointing in the he direction he should lead the horse.

Oars stepped up.

"Name?"

"Lightning."

"Mare or Stallion?"

"Mare?" Oars answered in a questioning tone.

"Stallion," corrected the hostler after leaning back for a look. "Shod or unshod?"

Oars looked to Zeld for help.

Zeld nodded his head and Oars said, "Shod."

"Age?"

Zeld shrugged his shoulders.

"I dunno," said Oars sounding a wee bit flustered.

50 "Breed or markings?"

"Pala, pala, something or other," said Oars uncertainly.

"Paladorian, 10 years of age," replied the hostler knowingly. Then pointing in a different direction, he called, "Stall 42."

Zeld stepped up for his turn and said, "Please Mr. Hostler, I just acquired this horse and I dunno anything about her."

"Him," the hostler corrected. "You have a twelve-year-old Clydesdale stallion. He's shod. Do you know the name?"

"Tiger," answered Zeld.

"Stall 41."

Zeld felt idiotic. He really didn't know much about horses. He walked Tiger back to stall 41 and found a good sized stall with plenty of room and feed. It took a while to remove the saddle as he'd never done it before. The triplets waited for him, queuing to pay their tuition.

The triplets told Zeld the names of the buildings while they waited. The half-built outer wall stood towering in the shape of a horseshoe around most of the existing buildings. The main gate faced eastward and was positioned in the bottom centre of the horseshoe. The Great Hall with its adjoining kitchen sat inside the main gate and to the north. Its east wall became a portion of the outer wall with a kitchen door also exiting the castle. North of the Great Hall rested an archery range.

Inside the courtyard and to the south was the hostler's house and the stalls for the staff's horses. South of that were the stalls for the student's horses. The chapel, with a towering white cross, resided to the west of the hostler's house. West of that stood the library. Again moving west sat the largest of the four barracks. A golden lion had been painted on the door and directly underneath it the words "Lion Gate" stood out in silver.

"What does Lion Gate stand for?" asked Zeld.

"That's the name of the barracks for the Brotherhood of Earth," answered Oles.

"Yeah, four barracks and four brotherhoods," added Odin, pointing out the other three barracks. Zeld saw two long and narrow barracks located north of Lion Gate which were labelled "Smoky Glen" and "Eagle Loft". The doorway to Smoky Glen framed a picture of a green glen with sleepy smoke rolling from a hovel and Eagle Loft showed an eagle with talons extended to land on its nest. North of them was the fourth barracks called "Galleon Cove". Its picture consisted of a ship anchored in a blue water lagoon. Several storage sheds kept their place near the fourth barracks.

Two outdoor classrooms sat between Smoky Glen and Eagle Loft and the Great Hall. Chicken coops, a hay barn, granary, indoor and outdoor classrooms were all located in the southwest area, built outside the security of the walls. Two bathhouses, one for staff and one for the students, were built over the stream to the north. Living quarters for the staff sat to the northeast, also outside the walls. Rails which clearly indicated the jousting lanes were further east. By the time the boys looked the school over, they found themselves at the front of the queue.

A friar sitting behind a writing table called, "Name?"

"Me name or me horse's name?" Odin answered with a question of his own.

"Your name this time," chuckled the friar. "And we'll ask for your name one more time today. Only, you'll sign it in a book."

"Odin McMarr," he stated proudly.

The friar wrote down the name. When he looked up, the triplets stood in such a way they appeared to have one body with three heads.

"Our parents are brother and sister," they called out in unison, to the friar's eye bulging surprise. Then the triplets stepped apart.

"Three of you?" he asked looking a bit lightheaded.

"Yes, why not?" answered Odin.

"Why not indeed. I need the names of the other two boys," he requested, still a little shocked.

"Oles McMarr and Oars McMarr," answered Odin.

51

"That is a total of 60,000 silver or 6,000 gold pieces," stated the friar after writing the names down.

"That's an outrage!" said Oles in a pretendedly angry voice. "We demand a volume discount."

The friar laughed so hard his belly nearly tipped over his table.

"You boys have earned yourselves a role in this year's school play," he said without hesitation.

The McMarr's handed over the six thousand gold pieces. The friar wrote out the receipts, and then turned his attention to Zeld.

"Your name?"

"Zeld."

"Of what place?"

"Me family lives in exile."

The friar wrote Zeld de Exile.

"I know the McMarr boy's parents but I don't know yours."

"Peter and Catherine de Saxon."

"Blimey, I am pleased to make your acquaintance and to know you're still alive," said the friar while shaking his hand. "Do you have a suit of chainmail armour?" asked the friar.

"No."

"Do you have a shield with your family's coat of arms?"

"No, but I remember it well enough."

"Excellent. Did you bring the money for tuition?"

"Yes," answered Zeld taking out the purse his mother had given him.

The friar opened the purse and counted out two thousand gold pieces, several bits of wet straw and five pottery shards.

"You may keep the straw and pottery shards," the friar said jovially.

"It's a treasure map," said Zeld as he hastily collected the shards.

Zeld found it rather odd that the friar didn't ask him if he were related to Lord Barrack de Saxon; after all, his mother said he had been a teacher at the school. Zeld wondered if he should ask about his dearly departed uncle, but then realized by doing so he might place himself into jeopardy.

Zeld joined the triplets. They helped a new student put on his chainmail armour. He introduced himself as James O'Day. Zeld saw other families assisting their sons put on their armour. Zeld couldn't help much because he didn't know where the pieces went or how they held together.

The school swarmed with people. Some worked in the Great Hall setting up tables and benches while the cooks remained busy dashing in and out of the kitchen.

A group of stonemasons continued construction on one wall of the castle. The stonemasons had rows of the biggest stones Zeld had ever seen. One crew lifted the stones, with a derrick, while another crew manhandled them into position. Zeld could see numbers written on each stone. He wished Wolf could see it. He hadn't missed his family too much, but this sight filled him with a longing for home.

A loud metallic ringing sound caught Zeld's attention. All the fifth-year students were called to the Great Hall. The staff welcomed them back by shaking their hands, issuing new Castles and Caverns long, sleeveless, dark blue tunics with a fancy silver C&C pattern centred on the chest. Then the fourth-year students paraded in, followed by the third-year students. The herald called for everyone in the Great Hall to be seated.

From talking to the McMarrs, Zeld understood by the third year he'd be a squire. He watched the older students and tried to imagine himself as a brave and noble, battle-ready, squire.

The second-year students came next. They were given a smaller light blue tunic of a page, with flap sleeves and the same C&C pattern on the chest. Finally the first-year students were called to the door.

The herald cried, "The announcing ceremony will begin." He called the first name on his list.

"Edward of Peele, son of Ross and Bridget of Peele."

Edward nervously stepped forward into the room. At a table sat three friars and two knights, waiting to judge the coat of arms for each new student, and place each boy into their proper brotherhood. Edward signed the school's registry book at the table. A friar gave him the tunic of the older boys, because he was of age to be a squire. A picture of a tree adorned his shield. The men at the table discussed the picture and agreed on the Brotherhood of Fire.

The Brotherhood of Fire, the smallest brotherhood, cheered to have a new member. They held up their shields and pounded loudly on the front of them with the flat side of their swords three times. CRASH, CRASH, CRASH!

The herald called, "Gilbert Stuart, son of Cajun and Bernice Stuart."

The assignment seemed simple for most coats of arms. The school organized itself into four brotherhoods. Firstly, the Brotherhood of Earth, which included all the boys who had land animals on their coats of arms. Secondly, the Brotherhood of Water accepted the boys with coats of arms depicting ships, fish, water monsters and such. Thirdly, the Brotherhood of Air encompassed coats of arms with birds, dragons and other flying things. Fourthly, the Brotherhood of Fire included those coats of arms that didn't fit any of the other categories.

"Sullivan de Bruce, son of Garden and Elizabeth de Bruce," announced the herald.

Sullivan coat of arms showed a spider swinging on a silver thread.

Following a short discussion that consisted of attempting to decide if the spider stood on the earth or flew on the thread, a friar announced, "He belongs in the Brotherhood of Air."

Hoops and hollers greeted the announcement from the Brotherhood of Air as they pounded their shields with their swords three times.

"Zeld de Exile, son of Peter and Catherine de Saxon," the herald announced.

All of the effort to disguise Zeld's identity had come to naught. Zeld had no idea they'd announce his parents' names when they asked for them. Zeld unhappily walked into the Great Hall and bent over to sign the book. He recorded his name as Zeld de Exile. At least his family's location remained a secret. When he stood up, he found a swarming beehive of activity. He saw smiling faces, angry faces, shocked faces, and a few that appeared totally lost. Zeld felt crestfallen as so many of the boys pointed at him and spoke to each other in whispers. Zeld looked out of place wearing Dragon's blood armour instead of chainmail. He didn't carry a shield with his coat of arms and he knew it would be a problem as well.

One of the friars suggested placing him in the Brotherhood of Fire. The friar that served as head of the committee said, "No, we'll ask him a few questions."

Turning to Zeld he asked, "Does your family possess a coat of arms?"

"Yes, it's a picture of a two-headed eagle on a golden-brown background," Zeld answered.

The head friar at the table asked Friar Martin to open the Heraldry Book of England. They promptly turned to the section on winged animals and studiously searched through each picture. Sadly, the book did not contain the picture Zeld described.

"How do we know he's of noble birth?" asked Friar Martin.

The friar in charge looked very old with thin silver hair and brown aging spots, yet he had a boyish charm about him. He asked thoughtfully, "Has any member of your family attended a school of knighthood?"

"Yes, me father attended this school. He told me he slept in an underground room and had classes all over the valley," Zeld stated, hoping the new clue would help.

"That would've been in the early years," commented a friar at the table.

"Friar Martin, will you retrieve the school's registry book from that period," asked the friar in charge. Friar Martin left with a puzzled look on his face as if he weren't exactly sure where the book was stored.

Meanwhile, Zeld took a moment to examine the Great Hall. On his right towered high windows that rose to peaks, in the Norman style. The wide kitchen doorway sat positioned on the south side of the east wall with a huge open roasting pit on the north side on the same wall. Long tables were set end to end filling the hall from north to south, while the head table ran east to west. The number of boys in each brotherhood varied so the amount of empty spaces varied for each section as well.

Zeld spied Friar Martin entering the library by using a key, and then returning while carrying the book in question. Thick dust billowed from the book as Friar Martin set it down with a thud.

"Repeat your father's name again, would you?" asked the friar as he waved his hand to clear the dust in the air.

"Peter de Saxon," responded Zeld.

"Here it is in year three," said Friar Martin after looking through several pages in the book, "Peter de Saxony was assigned to the Brotherhood of Air. He's the son of Kildain and Blair de

Saxony."

The friar sharply turned his head toward the lot of boys from the Brotherhood of Air and said, "Be prepared." Then he stood to address the room.

"I want to call your attention to a lad that went to school here a few years ago. When he came, he'd been raised as a peasant and he'd just learned of his noble birth. His name was Robin of the Hood. Robin first arrived, poorly outfitted, much more so than Zeld. Today, a school exists in his name, which we compete with regularly. Zeld will attend Robin's former brotherhood, THE BROTHERHOOD OF AIR!" he shouted.

Members of the Brotherhood of Air banged their shields wildly three times and cheered, as they were traditionally the second smallest group. Zeld received the tunic of a page; then, was escorted to the Brotherhood of Air's tables. A boy whose shield had the picture of the sun on it greeted him. He introduced himself as Robert O'Day.

The McMarr triplets were introduced one at a time, and each assigned to the Brotherhood of Air as well. Their coat of arms consisted of a white cross with wings standing out against a black background. This depicted Jens McMarr Sr.'s conversion to Christianity and departure from Norway.

"Brothers always go to the same brotherhood," they told Zeld as they sat by him.

The herald announced, "James O'Day son of Thomas O'Day and a daughter of a king's knight."

James' shield looked the same as Robert O'Day's, both having pictures of a yellow sun except James' shield had a blue strip behind the sun.

Robert looked furious to see James attending the school. In an angry voice, he called James' mother terrible things and they drew their swords. The staff restrained them and reminded them of the rule of safe haven. The turmoil started all over again when the friar announced James O'Day would join the Brotherhood of Air.

"HE'LL NOT BE IN THE SAME BROTHERHOOD AS I!" Robert shouted out.

The friar stated the rule, "Brothers always go to the same brotherhood." The word 'brothers' made both of them fume. Zeld thought, the dwarves never acted that way nor the McMarrs. Even the Viking crew never acted this way.

Zeld felt glad his brother Wolf and he got along. Zeld had never seen such a display of rage. The anger seemed to linger in the air, making those in the Great Hall feel extremely uncomfortable.

Forgetting his English roots for a moment, Zeld thought, the English are weird. I wonder if they're always fighting against themselves. Brother against brother and Lord against Lord would turn everything into chaos.

After the announcing, a total of six new pages joined the Brotherhood of Air. The boys removed their armour and the entire school sat to a feast.

Several large roasted pigs were brought in on huge silver platters with boiled potatoes and carrots. It had been ages since Zeld attended a true feast. The triplets actually behaved like gentlemen for a change. The only ones that didn't seem to enjoy themselves were the brothers O'Day, who shot angry looks at each other the entire time.

When the feast ended, a friar came to each table and dropped off a wooden bucket. The boys from each brotherhood emptied their scraps in it. The Brotherhood of Earth needed two buckets as they had the greatest number of boys. Zeld and Oars carried their scraps to the wagon waiting on the other side of the kitchen. Kitchen scraps already filled the wagon by the time Zeld and Oars found it.

As they placed the bucket atop the smelly heap, Zeld heard a clanging sound and looked to see if they'd damaged anything. He found a large treasure chest that resembled the one the friar used to collect the tuition money, buried under the scraps. The treasure chest looked unharmed.

When they returned to their table, another friar called for all the first-year pages to come with him. Oars nudged Zeld, "That means us."

Once at the benches of the outdoor classrooms the friar said, "I'm Friar Timothy and I'll give you the royal tour."

Friar Timothy stood tall and strong, his appearance resembled a knight rather than that of a friar. His frock looked dull and mostly the brown colour had faded to a tan. He had light brown hair and blue-green eyes with a fair complexion.

Zeld saw things they had missed before; namely, storage pits, a delivery area for the stonemasons and all sorts of battle stations in readiness on the walls. The tour lasted thirty minutes. The sun had nearly gone down and the shadows from the buildings stretched across the castle yard.

As the tour concluded, the friar asked, "Are there any questions?"

Zeld wished to clear up a matter that had puzzled him. His hand went up and the friar called on him.

"How much do peasants pay for kitchen scraps?"

"Peasants don't pay for kitchen scraps."

"Then why do they need such a large treasure chest in the scrap wagon?"

The friar motioned for a small treasure chest and asked, "This size?"

"No, bigger," Zeld held out his hands indicating a larger treasure chest, and then added. "Similar the one used to hold the tuition money." The friar appeared alarmed. He told the boys to draw their weapons and follow him.

Zeld ran cautiously behind the friar to the library, his sword drawn but feeling rather giddy, because he didn't know who or what to attack. The friar went into the library alone. He returned hastily.

"Come with me," he called urgently.

Zeld felt a mounting uneasiness; his sword hand grew sweaty from the tension. Friar Timothy ran over to the hostler's stable where he located a metal ring suspended from an overhanging log. He hit the ring with a nearby hammer. Zeld's ears rang with pain because he was too close to the bell. The entire school came running.

"The tuition money is gone. I believe it was stolen by thieves in the scrap wagon," said the friar.

"Squires, mount up," called a knight with a deep commanding voice, "Two minutes, just two minutes," the knight added with a strong sense of alarm in his voice.

Greg the hostler appeared with four saddled horses. He hurried the horses to the knights who hastily mounted.

"Pages stand guard," said the knight, his voice booming across the courtyard. The pages sheathed their swords and attempted to keep out of the way of the horses.

Squires riding bareback and carrying swords and shields surrounded the knight. The knight ordered, "Pursue and take captive." The horses charged through the gate leaving a heavy trail of dust behind them.

Friar Timothy instinctively took command and gave orders like a knight commander, "Robert O'Day, take two pages and go check on the kitchen staff; then, bring me word. Swen and Swan Christiansen, light the torches on the towers. You boys lock the gate," he yelled in Zeld's general direction. Zeld and the McMarr boys pushed against the heavy wooden gate and it swung closed. "Tyre and Crispyn search the grounds. Send everyone to the Great Hall. You boys there," he called, waving his hand in the direction of several pages. "Go with Friar Stephen to the archery shed and take twenty-five bows and as many arrows as you can carry. Bring them to the front gate – pip pip."

Zeld and the other boys near the gate brought the locking beam down. It slammed with a terrible crash, echoing throughout the castleyard. "Well, I daresay, it's down," muttered Odin, looking around sheepishly.

Pages scampered everywhere obeying the orders, including lighting the towers. The kitchen help, which had been found bound and gagged, were released. A group of boys returned to the front gate with bows and arrows. The stonemasons and their families gathered in the Great Hall with the hostler and the kitchen staff. The friars joined the pages at the front gate. A feeling of extreme tension filled the castle.

Meanwhile, the search party on horseback broke into three groups. One group headed east on a road that went to the nearby village of Baden. A second raced for the mines to the north where the local dwarves worked. The third charged towards the farms, south of the castle.

The first lot, which headed for the village, found a trail of scraps that had spilled from the back of the wagon. Their knight commander blew his horn and the other two groups broke off their pursuit and manoeuvred back towards the sound. The driver of the wagon raced on the road ahead. He ran the horses as hastily as he could. The knight blew his horn three times giving the attack command.

The squires drew their swords and speedily caught the wagon. A thief, who had hidden among the scraps, jumped out with a quarterstaff and struck the lead squire. The solid blow glanced off his shield.

Another squire slipped off his horse into the back of the wagon. A third squire took hold of the quarterstaff but couldn't pull it from the thief's hand. The thief tugged as firmly as he could, attempting to pull the squire off his horse. The squire simply let go of the quarterstaff and the thief fell off the other side of the wagon, hitting the ground with a bone-crushing thud.

The driver drew a dagger and swung it blindly at the squire sneaking up on him, cutting his right arm. The wound did not deter the squire. He grabbed the driver by the hair with his left hand and launched him into the back of the wagon. He used his sword's pommel to break the thief's nose; then, knocked him unconscious with a blow to the forehead. Several other squires stopped the wagon.

The thief that fell off the wagon couldn't escape the charging horses which nearly trampled him to death.

The two thieves were placed in the back of the wagon and taken to the castle. Upon examination, the treasure chest's lock was found missing, but it appeared all the gold remained inside. The missing lock made the robbers appear to have an inside man.

When the squires reached the castle, the knight with the deep voice ordered the grounds searched. "If we find the lock, then we'll find the accomplice," surmised Sir Tavish nobly as he explained his thinking to Father Michael, the schoolmaster. He also ordered all the students and staff to examine the thieves to see if they could identify them.

A couple of the new pages claimed these men helped them put on their armour before the announcing ceremony. At the time they appeared to be members of the staff merely doing their duties. The friars also identified them as family members helping the pages put on their armour. Both the pages and the friars claimed a dark-haired girl helped them as well. Oars told the knight a girl with long brown hair had kidnapped one of their servants at the McMarr Manor. He meant Jens Jr. but Oars had to keep his brother's identity a secret. Zeld felt a flash of inadequacy as he realized the McMarr's were loads better than he at hiding information.

The missing lock finally turned up under the bed of a first-year page. The knight took him privately into an office for questioning. The page told the knight he hadn't yet been assigned a bed. Upon further inquiry the knight confirmed this, which meant the thieves had used the lock to cause confusion.

The knight then released the pages and squires for prayers and bed. After prayers in the chapel, the first-year pages received bed assignments. Most of the staff stayed up late evaluating the performance of the school and attempting to determine how the money went from the library to the wagon. That night the staff sent for the king's clerk and the local sheriff.

61

Zeld, Oars, Odin, Oles, Sullivan and James were assigned the six beds closest to the door of Eagle Loft barracks, the permanent quarters for the Brotherhood of Air. Eagle Loft consisted of a rectangular room with two rows of beds standing as sentries spaced properly down the outside walls, leaving a walkway down the centre. A heavy wooden door rested on one end and on the far end was an empty fireplace with a mantelpiece above and a hearthrug below. Brass torches burned in their brackets which hung on the walls.

While the boys stowed their belongings in bins under their beds, the older ones teased the new ones.

"So, d'you like frigid breezes in the wintertime?" inquired Tyre Stevens. "It's awfully drafty by the door."

Crispyn of Orange obviously had a new tease in mind. "Remember three years ago on this very night when the giant attacked? Poor Ralph of Durham, he never knew what hit him. That giant reached in and whisked Ralph away as he was the page sleeping closest to the door. His mum endeavoured to close the school. 'Castles and Caverns is unsafe,' she wrote to King Henry. I guess having her son devoured by a giant was a wee bit much for her to take." Crispyn bent down and pushed his clothing bin under his bed, and then stood up and continued. "Regretfully King Henry's men never found the giant either. They found a note written in giant informing everyone he'd come back when he felt hungry again. Giants eat only once every three years, don't they, Angus?"

Angus couldn't answer through his silent giggling. On the other hand, the triplets seized the moment and fired questions faster than ever. "Was it really a giant or was it the cold hand of the plagues of Egypt like me brother said? Did the giant grab him with his hand or with his tongue? Did the giant come here on purpose or was he lost? Can you spell tongue? Did the giant like cheese? D'you like cheese? How many eyes did the giant have? What colour were they? What is the capital of Giantopia? Didja know we can keep this blarney up all day?"

"Your brother warned us about you, but he didn't tell us you were trey born. Hey, where is Jens Jr. anyway?" asked Crispyn alertly.

"He is on a purchasing mission in the south somewhere," lied Oars.

"Didn't make it back in time," declared Oles.

"Probably got married," said Odin.

Friar Timothy came back to make sure the beds were properly made. Pointing his finger to the older boys, he scolded, "No short sheeting. Squires, this means you." They laughed.

"Did the Brotherhood of Earth try some tomfoolery on a page again this year?" asked Angus ap Forrest.

"No, they broadened their horizons and hazed several pages this year," replied Friar Timothy in the same scolding tone.

The younger pages looked cautiously at their beds. They examined them but didn't find anything out of the ordinary.

Oars told Friar Timothy his brother didn't make it back from London for the start of school. "He'd better arrive soon, as he'll have to make up his schoolwork," Friar Timothy warned.

The friar smothered the torches hanging in the wall brackets and said, "Goodnight."

The Brotherhood of Air fell asleep before long. Sleeping, that is until James O'Day jumped out of bed with a howl, scratching and throwing down his blankets.

Robert O'Day asked with a sneer, "What's the trouble, did you wet the bed?"

"No, it's itching powder, as if you didn't know," replied James in much the same tone he had used earlier. No one saw or heard Robert walk over to James' bed but James insisted Robert did it somehow. After the blankets received a vigorous shaking out, James climbed back to bed. Quiet again descended over the room. Robert O'Day fell asleep with an impish grin on his face as if he had gotten away with something. Lucky for him no one in the barracks had ever heard of magical shoes of silence!

CHAPTER Eight

School Days

"Chapel in fifteen minutes," called Friar Timothy as he awoke the boys in Eagle Loft early the next morning. Zeld pulled himself sleepily out of bed, dressed quickly, and made it inside the chapel on time. Apparently, his brotherhood was the only one not having a spot of trouble. After chapel the six new boys received their schedule for the semester.

"You can look it over while eating breakfast," Friar Timothy told the six.

The boys hurried over to the Great Hall for breakfast. The cooks served hot porridge with milk and fruit alongside. Most of the boys turned their noses at it, but Zeld and James dived right in without complaint. The first-year pages sat together looking over the schedule.

Awake and arise 6:30 a.m.
Chapel at 6:45
Breakfast at 7:00
1- 8:00 a.m. Friar Martin   Aid for humans and animals
2- 9:00 a.m. Sir Jaydan Razor   Characters and Creatures
3- 10:00 a.m. Sir Roger Fitzwayne Battle Preparations
4- 11:00 a.m. Friar Timothy   History and Geography
Midday meal at 12:00
5- 1:00 p.m. Friar Marcus   Feudalism, Genealogy, Heraldry
6- 2:00 p.m. Sir Drain Bracken   Armour and Armament
7- 3:00 p.m. Friar Jonathan   World Religions
8- 4:00 p.m. Sir Tavish Macdonald Field Exercises
Supper at 5:00
Time for homework and school sports or teams.   Library open.

Friar Martin called for the first-year pages to join him for class. As the six boys walked across the yard, the other first-year pages followed.

"Why weren't you at breakfast?" James asked.

"Fighting," someone called back.

"With the older boys?"

"No, with our half-brothers," a rude voice snapped back.

Friar Martin stopped at the stables where the hostler waited for the boys.

64

"In case you've forgotten, I'm Friar Martin. This is Greg the hostler. We'd an exciting night last night. Our forces, by means of their horses, pursued the money robbing thieves. Our hostler will teach you how to examine your horse following a chase. Pay close attention as this is something you'll use repeatedly throughout your lives."

The hostler stood only four inches taller than Zeld with a stocky build and an energetic personality. He also knew his craft. He had brown eyes and hair and sported a moustache. He gave a demonstration on the horse's hooves, teaching the pages how to properly remove trapped mud and inspect for caltrops. "A horse's worst enemy is the caltrop," the hostler taught. He pulled out a bag containing several sharp jagged spikes. He threw six of them on the ground one at a time."

Zeld stared silently at the caltrops. Somehow they sent an icy-cold shiver through his body.

"No matter how you throw these, they always land with a sharp point standing straight up. One caltrop will cripple a horse or a knight if stepped upon. Last night serves as a prime example of when to use caltrops. The darkness coupled with the horses running at a full gallop made for extraordinarily bad conditions. The thieves could've easily hidden caltrops in the food scraps that spilled out upon the road. We could've lost a dozen horses or more," the hostler informed the pages.

"Fortunately, we didn't lose a single horse, but we did have some minor problems. The wet food scraps caused a couple of our horses to slip. We're lucky none of them fell. I found these two horses with pulled muscles early this morning," the hostler said, bringing the horses forward.

He demonstrated how to examine horses for pulled muscles by massaging the horse's legs with his hands. At one point the horse flinched, revealing the injury. Zeld watched closely as he had never seen this type of work before. It reminded him of magic.

"This mare will need three to four days rest. Then we'll evaluate her progress."

Friar Martin assigned the boys to inspect their horses that night.

"I am Sir Roger Fitzwayne and this is Battle Preparations class. Please sit in a semicircle." The archery targets waited in the distance directly behind Sir Roger. The shooting lanes, which were lined with white stones, stretched between the targets and the class. Zeld took his place as directed and listened intently.

"The outcomes of most battles are determined before the battle begins. The better prepared army almost always wins. Rare exceptions have occurred when someone in the course of the battle acquires a warlord ability. This of course is what happened to Robin Hood and remained his life time secret of success. He always shot bull's-eyes. For today's lesson we'll string the bows and shoot a few arrows."

On Zeld's turn he awkwardly strung his bow. Then he lifted it toward the sky and held his breath as he slowly pulled back the string. He nervously lowered his bow until he thought the arrow would hit the target, and then he smoothly released the string. Zeld's arrow skyrocketed over the top of the target. In fact, all of his arrows did the same thing. Zeld felt disappointed because he had no idea what he did wrong and he worried Sir Roger might throw him out of the class; after all, he couldn't hit the broadside of the Great Hall if his life depended on it. The poor shooting caught Sir Roger's attention but he didn't scold Zeld, as some instructors did in similar situations at other schools, because this would violate his vow of knighthood.

At the end of class, Sir Roger called, "Those pages that need further instruction, namely, those that didn't hit the target, are to meet with me during homework time for personal instruction. Class dismissed." Zeld felt badly because he knew this meant him.

After the midday meal Zeld passed the king's clerk driving a wagon holding the two thieves from the night before. "I'm off to

London," he called to Sir Tavish. Zeld didn't know it, but the clerk also carried an official report for King Henry and other papers requesting rewards for the boys that helped apprehend the robbers.

Sir Tavish Macdonald taught Field Exercises, Zeld's final class of the day. Zeld recognized his voice at once. Sir Tavish had taken charge when the money went stolen. He stood the tallest, heaviest and strongest of the knights and had ample muscles to prove it. On top of his oversized body sat an oversized head. Thick black hair covered most of his body and his eyes resembled small black dots.

The class met at the front gate of the castle. "I want to personally thank you pages for all your help last night when we had our incident." Sir Tavish continued, "In about three weeks time, the English schools of knighthood and the naval academies, along with a couple of other schools, will compete in this year's first tournament. The events include foot and horse racing, wagon racing and horse rescue as well. Cash prizes will go to the winners," he said while folding his arms and tilting his head forward. "Today we'll determine who is fastest in the foot races. Everyone follow me," he called with a wave of his arm.

The class hiked their way south down the road until they came to an area with rails lining one side of the road. Sir Tavish timed the boys at various rail lengths. When Zeld's turn arrived he did his best, but was too slow to win a spot on the team.

"Tomorrow we'll test for the horse racing events. Oh, and mind your homework," called Sir Tavish as an afterthought.

Zeld went straightaway to see Tiger in his stall.

"Hello there, Tiger," he whispered gently.

He brushed Tiger with one hand while checking for problems with his other. Finding nothing, he finished in a hurry. He had one other homework assignment that night, so he ran to the archery range. Sir Roger stood next to Brian Boru showing him how to properly place his arrow across the bow.

"The nock and the notch feather rest on the outside of the bow," Sir Roger taught Brian.

Zeld's shadow crossed in front of the two of them.

Sir Roger looked up and said, "Take up a bow and string it."

Zeld sheepishly walked over to the bows and selected the one he'd used earlier that day. He strung it and waited patiently for his turn. After a couple more tries, Brian could hit the target.

Sir Roger turned his attention to Zeld. Sir Roger stopped on the way and collected a beanbag from the supply shed. Zeld took a right good look at Sir Roger. His average height made him the shortest of the knights. Sir Roger had a stocky build with a muscular chest. He had light brown thinning hair, green eyes, tan coloured skin and a pleasant disposition.

"Zeld, I noticed your arrows went adrift today but I also noticed they landed in a straight line. Have you had lessons before?" asked Sir Roger.

"Me Dad taught me to shoot when I was young."

"I want you to take this beanbag and throw it to me." Zeld hesitantly took the beanbag and waited for Sir Roger to stop backing away. When he did, Zeld tossed the bag underhand through the air in an arching motion.

"Did you see the beanbag rise into the air, and then drop so I could catch it?" asked Sir Roger.

"Yes."

"Is that how you shoot your arrows, I mean, in an arching pattern?"

"Yes," Zeld said.

"As I suspected. And I suppose you learned to shoot with a toy bow and arrow?" asked Sir Roger in a knowledgeable voice.

"Yeah," said Zeld with his jaw dropping in surprise.

"You'll shoot bulls-eyes in 10 minutes or less," Sir Roger predicted. "You see, the toy bow didn't have enough spring to shoot the arrow very far, so you had to compensate by aiming high. I want you to throw the beanbag to me again, but this time I want you to throw it hard and fast. Don't worry about hitting me. I promise, I won't cry," he said standing nobly at his full height, his chest out, with his elbows extended away from his body and his fists resting on his hips. His green cape flowed in the slight breeze behind him.

Zeld took the beanbag and threw it as hard as he could, right at Sir Roger, who caught the beanbag, and then pretended to cry, "You hit me."

Zeld laughed and as he did he felt the pressure to do well melt away.

"This time I want you to throw the beanbag straight at me heart," ordered Sir Roger tossing the beanbag back to Zeld.

Zeld took the beanbag and threw it fast and true at Sir Roger's heart. Sir Roger let the beanbag hit him in the chest.

"Excellent," said Sir Roger. "Take up your bow and let's go shoot a target using this new strategy."

Zeld and Sir Roger went to the range and Zeld nervously took aim. Sir Roger adjusted the bow and told Zeld to pull the string all the way back to his check. Zeld nervously let the first arrow go. It hit the target on the top right.

"This time mind what your father taught you about shooting straight," Sir Roger said.

68

Zeld drew the next arrow more confidently. He placed the arrow directly above the bull's-eye, and then lowered his bow until he aimed straight at the centre. He let the arrow go and it fell only just short of the bull's-eye.

"As the arrow flies through the air, it does fall slightly. Do you see how far the arrow fell from dead centre?" Sir Roger asked showing his excitement.

"Yes."

"Excellent, compensate by aiming exactly that far above centre," Sir Roger instructed.

Zeld's third arrow hit the bull's-eye and so did his fourth and fifth.

While Sir Roger helped a few more students, Zeld shot another ten arrows. Nine of the ten hit the bull's-eye. When practice ended Zeld helped pack away the equipment and walked to dinner with Sir Roger. After witnessing Zeld's dramatic improvement, James O'Day asked Sir Roger if he'd given Zeld a bull's-eye amulet. Zeld didn't understand and Sir Roger simply said, "No, he improved through his own efforts."

Dinner came late, but Zeld thought the delicious chicken pie more than made up for the delay. Father Michael spoke with the cook in the kitchen doorway near the House of Air's tables, to see if a problem had arisen. After all, late dinners were uncommon for the cook.

"Sir, I mean Father, our kitchen isn't big enough to serve this many people. Dinner will be late every night," the cook sobbed. Zeld had once been told, 'never trust a skinny cook'. Well this being the case he knew he could trust Mrs. Palfreeman many times over. Her salt and pepper hair surrounded her plump red face which held her two small dark eyes. Her red face shone even brighter than usual when she wore white, which she did, when serving meals.

Father Michael promised to see what he could do. The number of students had grown steadily each year and the school had grappled with similar problems in the past.

That night at bedtime when Friar Timothy came into Eagle Loft, Zeld asked, "Who is Father Michael?" The other new boys turned to hear the answer as well.

"He is the schoolmaster of Castles and Caverns. He's a relative of King Henry and he nearly ran the country while King Henry finished school here," Friar Timothy explained. "King Henry was only nine when he became king and naturally depended on older, wiser men for a time. The king had full confidence in Father Michael and he became a trusted adviser. In fact, it was Father Michael who came up with the idea to have the English schools run by knights and friars together. This change freed two hundred knights for duty on the crusades. Father Michael is an incredible man and a loyal friend of the king."

Zeld finally understood what Jens Sr. meant when he spoke of King Henry's inexperience. No wonder our castle fell and me father died, thought Zeld. A mere squire led the rescue effort.

That night Zeld had a terrifying nightmare about the attack on his family. His mother ran in and snatched him up in her arms. Another woman carried Wolf. They ran through a hole in the wall he'd never seen before; then, climbed into a wagon. He looked back and saw the family's castle. To his right he could see soldiers gathering in a ditch and peasants running to join them with pitchforks and kitchen knives. Lord Barrack spoke to his mother and they quickly decided to send Zeld to the Castles and Caverns School when he became of age. The woman who held Wolf left them and ran back to help the villagers. Zeld wanted to join them but his mother wouldn't permit him. The driver of the wagon whipped the reins and they fled into the darkness.

Zeld awoke in a panic. He lay in the darkness waiting for his pounding heart to return to normal and wondered what he would've done, had he been the king. Zeld had no clear answers. He didn't know what to do about his current situation either. How would he ever regain his castle?

69

CHAPTER NINE

A Hint of Mystery

We use a measurement system to determine human and animal strength," said Friar Martin, holding up a chart in the Aid for Humans and Animals class. In the background of the Great Hall, Zeld was distracted by the clanging of the breakfast dishes being washed in the kitchen. Friar Martin spoke louder. "For example, a giant is stronger than a knight, trolls have more strength than dwarves or elves and goblins are the weakest of all. You can tell how strong an animal is by its condition, its stance, its ability to manoeuvre and its size. Combat weakens your enemies. The closer an enemy is to unconsciousness, the worse his condition and the less strength he has."

"A man doesn't change in size," blurted out Dewayne of Freemount.

"Yes, he does," assured Friar Martin. "When a man is filled with emotions, I daresay anger or fear, his chest swells and his arms are lifted up and away from himself. When a man is injured or ill, his arms drop and his head hangs to one side. By the end of the year you'll each possess the ability to calculate the exact strength of a person. In time it'll become second nature to you."

"Phenomenal," called Oles.

"Magnificent," suggested Odin.

"Remarkable," commented Oars.

"Most knowledgeable," said Friar Martin.

The boys in class found the comment irresistible and they went throughout the day saying, "most knowledgeable" as many times as possible.

When Zeld saw the horse rescue event in Sir Tavish's class, he felt certain sure he could qualify for the team. All the boys tried out and there were no restrictions, save one; pages paired with pages for the junior division and squires with squires for the senior division. The competition grew fierce. This was a timed event on a measured course which had been laid out west of the school. The competing horse would run over a hill, turn to the right and a rider, standing on the horse's left side, would then vault onto the horse. Next the horse would run and a second rider would vault onto the horse from the right side. After a second turn, the horse sprinted for the finish line.

A ball clock served as the timing device. Five heavy balls hung suspended in a line from an overhanging beam by pieces of string. The clock worked by raising the first ball on a 45 degree angle and allowing it to swing into the other four balls. The inertia from the first ball transferred through the other balls to the fifth ball. It swung away from the others, until gravity pulled that ball down causing a second collision. The first collision made the starting sound and every collision after counted as a second in time.

Oles and Odin attempted it. They finished with a fast time of 23 seconds. Oars and Zeld attempted it with Oars as the first man and Zeld as the second. They finished with a time of 26 seconds.

Zeld realized they could improve their time if they used the same manoeuvre he and Wolf used at the farm. He and Oars traded places as Zeld was used to clasping hands and pulling the second man aboard. They practiced several times until all went smoothly. This cut their time down to 21 seconds. They had the fastest time for the school, beating even the fifth-year students.

Over the next several days, Oars and Zeld practiced regularly. Zeld felt pleased as he could tell they'd gotten a little faster. He watched the squires practicing and found if he used their mounting technique he could spring onto Lightning's back even quicker.

On Saturday morning, Zeld, the triplets, Sullivan de Bruce and James O'Day accompanied five friars to the farms. Each friar drove a wagon in order to carry all the food the school needed for the next week. The farmers waited for the wagons to arrive at what they called the supply station which sat to the south, near the farms. The five wagons were also used to deliver stone fragments from the school's stonemason yard to the farmers.

Loading the wagons with the rocks served as punishment for the squires who hazed the younger boys. As the horses moved along, a familiar clip-clop, clip-clop sound came from their hooves

72

beating on the road.

Zeld thought back to the happy day he and Bushby went up the mountain looking for the mine. Zeld sang the Snow White song. "Seben dwarfolk, seben dwarfolk, dasen ben der names Heir Sleepish, Heir Doctor, Heir Grumpes."

"Where on earth did you learn that song?" Friar Timothy asked.

Zeld opened his mouth to tell him, but then hesitated, "On a road similar to this one."

Friar Timothy looked impressed, "Could you ask the person who taught it to you to come and teach it to the school?"

"No, Bushby died," replied Zeld in a reverent tone.

"I daresay it's certainly a grand song, Zeld. It reminds me of me childhood and the dwarven children I used to play with."

"You used to play with dwarves?"

"Oh, yes," the friar replied happily. "Me best mate growing up was a dwarf named Dort."

"I know him!" Zeld said astonished.

"Not very likely, you see, Dort is a very common name among the dwarfolk," said Friar Timothy.

Zeld sat back listening as Friar Timothy told him about the dwarves.

After awhile, they reached a shady lean-to where a number of farmers waited to load the wagons. The farmers unloaded the stone fragments as soon as the wagons stopped. They seemed pleased to receive it, and Zeld understood how much nicer a stone walled farmhouse was compared to one made from mud and sticks. The pages and friars helped unload. After emptying the first wagon, the pages swept it out and the farmers filled it with food baskets and wooden crates. They filled wagon after wagon with baskets and crates of food. When they finished, the farmers counted the baskets and found one missing.

While searching for the lost basket, Zeld took a moment to view the farms. He saw a couple dozen thatched roof farmhouses. Each house had a barn, fenced fields and various crops in the fields growing in long furrows. He spied pig sties, chicken coops, birdhouses for doves, and pens for geese, rabbits and turkeys. He also saw pastureland and corrals with goats, sheep, horses, cows and oxen. The farmlands included watering ponds for the animals which also served to attract wild water foul.

Smoke rose from the chimneys as the men, women and children went to work in the fields or drove the stout farm wagons to the nearby woods. In the distance Zeld saw a small lumber mill which he supposed supplied the area with lumber.

Finally, someone found the basket in the top of a tall tree. With no ladder nearby, the friars improvised by pulling a wagon close to the tree and James O'Day climbed to the basket. He threw the food down one item at a time to the crowd, and then he tossed the basket. As James climbed down the friars speculated about how the basket found its way there.

"Do you suppose evil spirits haunt this area?" asked one of the friars, showing his superstitious nature.

"No, I imagine one of the farmers played a joke on the pages. You know, to test their manliness," said Friar Timothy.

"You'd think guarding the castle by themselves on the first night of school was test enough!" stated Friar Marcus in a huff.

"Excellent point," Friar Timothy agreed.

The wagons carried the food to the castle's kitchen stoop, where they were unloaded. By the time the wagons were empty the pantry overflowed with food. The head cook, Mrs. Palfreeman, was in a right state and bellowed, "I don't know what we'll do. There is simply not enough room for everything." Zeld could tell the kitchen and pantry were unquestionably too small. The McMarr's kitchen had much more room and shelf space.

After unloading, Zeld wandered off looking for something to do. Some of the boys practiced fencing with wooden swords and he could see a few of them playing horse tag. He had no money but thought he'd go for a romp into town and do some browsing. He saddled Tiger and headed north.

After riding for a while, he found the north road didn't lead to the town. It took him through the greenery and straight to a wooden bridge. Zeld greatly enjoyed his little romp and decided to go on an adventure and see where the road would lead. It continued north past the bridge where he chanced upon a dwarven mine on his right. On his left, across the way, a waterfall splashed into a deep pool of water. Looking around he saw a partially open cave entrance with mining equipment all around but no dwarves.

A small dwarven girl surprised Zeld by opening the cave entrance, so he could enter. He awkwardly opened and closed the door a few times as he had never worked a secret passage before. With the door closed, it appeared to be a natural crack in the rock much like the entrance he saw in Denmark. Zeld found it fascinating.

"HELLO!" he shouted into the darkness. He listened to the echo.

A grumpy voice inside the cavern scolded, "No need to shout. We're right here."

Zeld stepped forward and introduced himself, even though he couldn't see well in the darkness, "I'm Zeld de Exile."

"What do you want?" the same voice asked angrily.

"To make friends," he said politely.

"We already have enough mates, and, besides, you're not a dwarf," the angry voice scolded again.

"Well, where I come from the dwarfolk and me family get along famously."

"Prove it," the angry voice demanded.

Zeld's eyes slowly adjusted and he could see more clearly in the cavern. He showed them the dwarven dance he'd learned and sang the Snow White song.

"So, you spied on a few dwarves once. That's called espionage not friendship," snapped the angry voice that came from a dwarf Zeld thought must do nothing all day but frown.

"You must be Grumpes' grandson," Zeld parried back.

The other dwarves laughed.

"No," another voice interupted, "but you're not far wrong!"

The dwarves laughed again.

"I'm Bushhard," said the cheerful dwarf.

"I'm glad to meet you," said Zeld with a bow.

The dwarves introduced themselves.

"Are you making much money here?" Zeld asked.

"No, our equipment keeps disappearing without trace. We think the stonemasons from the school are taking it, or perhaps the elves," Bushhard concluded.

"I'm a page at the school and I haven't seen any mining equipment there," said Zeld unconvinced.

"We have," Bushhard barked. "The stonemasons are using mining equipment to build the castle."

"How d'you know it's your equipment?"

"We don't but we mark all our items with this unicorn symbol," said Bushhard. He held out a ring with a unicorn design on it. He collected a metal rod and pressed the ring to it. Smoke shot out for a few seconds where the ring touched the rod and when Bushhard removed the ring the image of the unicorn had been burned into it. "If you'll search for this mark, we'll discover the truth one way or the other," said Bushhard.

"We've had trouble with thieves at the castle," explained Zeld, still examining the unicorn mark.

"We heard about that," Bushhard commented.

"We caught the thieves and the money was returned."

"We heard about that too."

"I'll check on the equipment and let you know what I find," promised Zeld.

"Sure you will," said Grumpes sarcastically. "When the moon becomes a triangle."

"I'll bet my new axe against yours he follows through," wagered Bushhard.

"Done," said Grumpes, and the two of them shook hands.

Zeld felt uncomfortable knowing the dwarves bet on his character. He thought it best to go take care of the wager at once. He excused himself and rode for the castle.

When Zeld entered the stonemason's yard they shoed him away. He couldn't enter the yard for safety reasons. The stonemasons had several giant stones to move that day. Zeld would have to bide his time and wait for a better opportunity. Then he thought up a quick plan, perhaps he could sneak into the yard on Sunday.

CHAPTER TEN

Rewards and Spies

Sunday lasts longer than the whole rest of the week put together, Zeld thought. The school considered Sunday a day of rest and no physical activities; namely practicing archery or horse rescue, were allowed. Friar Timothy encouraged reading books from the library, along with prayer.

Zeld, James, Odin, Oles and Oars sat together in the Great Hall and attempted to decide which boy owned the finest horse at the school. Then they visited about their lives before they came to school. Zeld wisely said little. James O'Day, on the other hand, told the lot about his sea voyages with his grandfather and their close calls with pirates.

Zeld spied Robert O'Day listening to the conversation, although he sat with his back toward them, attempting to hide his curiosity.

"My grandfather wanted me to go to the Welch Naval Academy, but my mother insisted on Castles and Caverns. 'That's where your father went and that's where you'll go!'" James said quoting his mum.

Zeld guffawed. "That's what me mum said too."

Oles leaned in with a confession. "Our mum said, 'Jens Mc-Marr Sr., you'll not pay to send our sons to Norway to be corrupted when we've a perfectly good school right here.' Dad agreed, 'You're absolutely right. We can have our sons corrupted right here and save a fortune'." Everybody laughed, even Robert O'Day, who pretended not to listen.

Zeld learned a great amount about the McMarr family, including Jens Sr. and Marta's conversion to Christianity, the land purchase, and his advancing from a farmer to a duke. The brothers McMarr had never met either set of their grandparents.

Zeld told them until he came to Castles and Caverns he'd never even heard the names of his grandparents. He didn't know why their family's surname had changed from de Saxony to de Saxon.

Sir Drain stayed in earshot of the boys in the Great Hall, watching the students. He didn't laugh at the jokes and stories. Sir Drain sat in a chair reading a book, or so it appeared. However, he never turned a single page in the entire time he sat in the Great Hall. Sir Drain's stone-like face and eyes appeared odd to Zeld. He came across as a hard man in looks, deeds and voice with boot black hair except for his brown roots and beard.

78

Later that day everyone attended church and directly afterwards a squire approached Zeld on the way to the Great Hall for dinner. "I saw you practicing the horse rescue event," he said smiling. "You and that McMarr chap hold the record for the best time. I wanted to know where you mastered such a skill. I mean – er – you're amazingly quick and – well – I daresay – much faster than I – and I've worked at it for three years now. Maybe you could show me a few tricks. My name's Matt." Zeld shook his new mate's hand.

Matt stood six feet tall, had blonde hair, blue eyes and a manly square jaw. He wore a squire's tunic with his family's coat of arms on it. The charge of a golden lion with flame-like fur wildly swaying in a strong breeze resembled Matt's blonde hair. All four of the lion's claws were prepared to strike, even as it sat on its hind end, posed as if guarding a sinister secret.

Monday morning the students went back to their classes. Sir Roger's class made arrows instead of shooting them. Sir Drain acted a bit unusual, even hostile, toward Zeld. He taught dodging techniques near the south wall, with Zeld as the guinea pig. Zeld learned to move his body both to the right and the left as quick as a brown hare. Even though he felt happy about learning how to dodge he believed Sir Drain had singled him out for some unknown reason and he felt bad not knowing what he had done wrong.

In Sir Tavish's class the boys continued practicing for their upcoming tournament. Zeld tutored Matt and his time improved by one and a half seconds on the first day. Matt's muscular build kept him from mounting the horse smoothly. Instead he wrapped his arms around the passing horse's neck; then, in a second effort, swung his legs over the horse's back. This lost precious time, but

Matt simply couldn't manage it with the gliding motion Zeld had.

On Wednesday of the third week the king's clerk visited the school. He made a special presentation on behalf of the king after dinner in the Great Hall. The clerk said, "I'm sure you're aware that for a squire to ascertain knighthood he must perform three good deeds of great personal risk and not gain from them in any material way. It is unusual for squires to achieve these deeds while still at school. Mostly they're obtained during the two years of apprenticeship that follow. Tonight we're honoured to grant these certificates of good deeds to Norton Duval and Geoffrey of Hesse."

The entire school gave them a standing ovation. Try as he might Zeld couldn't see the two squires because he sat in the far corner of the room with several crowded tables between him and the front. His line of sight grew worse when everyone stood.

"These good deeds are deserving of a grand presentation," the clerk continued. "Now we have a second presentation." Everyone sat down. "In order to obtain a good deed one must be a squire. It isn't possible to award a good deed to a page. If it were possible, we'd do so tonight. Instead, King Henry has accorded a special gift for the page who discovered the treasure chest in the scrap wagon and alerted the staff. In addition, this same page alerted our King Henry of a Viking ship spying on our coast earlier this year. By changing our usual shipping routes we've avoided the loss of men and material. We present to Zeld de Exile de Saxon this suit of chainmail armour."

The school applauded. Zeld walked sheepishly to the front of the room. He smiled when he saw the rather large treasure chest with a complete suit of chainmail armour inside. The gift both pleased and surprised him. He saw a scroll inside but the clerk refused to let him read it.

"That is a personal letter exclusive to you from the king. Don't open it until you're properly alone," the clerk whispered in a nearly inaudible voice. "Don't share its contents with anyone and read it in the moonlight." The clerk then locked the treasure chest with a key on a red ribbon. He hung the key around Zeld's neck.

Zeld turned cautiously to look at the two squires who had won the good deeds and saw Matt standing behind the clerk. The clerk shook Matt's hand, congratulating him and calling him Geoffrey of Hesse. Zeld swayed on the spot when he heard Matt's real name.

His jolly feeling turned to bitter cold. Painful icicles paralysed his limbs and his stomach dropped several inches. Zeld realized Matt's friendship was nothing more than a scam. He further guessed Geoffrey only wanted to learn his mother's whereabouts.

When the presentation ended, the triplets helped Zeld by carrying his new treasure chest to Eagle Loft. The pages and squires of the Brotherhood of Air stayed awake talking about Zeld's gift long into the night. Zeld waited for hours before he could read King Henry's letter; then, he walked silently to where the moonlight shone through a window.

Dear Zeldain de Saxony,

Nearly three years ago your family suffered its terrible and tragic loss. I rejoiced when I heard you had returned. I wore this suit of chainmail at your age. I hope it fits well enough. I had your coat of arms painted in pride of place. I'm well pleased with the contributions you're making to England. May happiness attend you always.

Your friend,

King Henry Plantagenet III

Then the ink slowly drifted upward, turning into smoke. It hung in the air for a moment, and then returned to the parchment forming new words.

There are two secret compartments in the treasure chest. I have placed in them maps, names and locations of allies that want to help you regain your castle and lands. A few persons chose not to be included on the list. Someday we'll meet and make plans, but for now I must prepare to battle the Vikings. Take this time to build allies.

I've learned Geoffrey of Hesse is spying on you. He is attempting to learn the location of your family. Break ties with him at once.

Your Servant,

King Henry

The ink again turned to smoke, and then transformed itself back into the original letter.

"Devastating," Zeld whispered, as he placed the letter back into his treasure chest and locked it. In his mind he also locked away his friendship with Matt. Regrettable, Zeld thought, Geoffrey and I worked well together. Then Zeld thought of a brilliantly scathing idea, he whispered, "I know who Geoffrey is - but he doesn't know I know - er - which means - I have the upper hand - and I know how to use it."

Section Two

To "unlock" this mystery you must
find what was hidden
and left behind.

CHAPTER Eleven

Off to the Races

When tournament day finally arrived, Zeld was delighted to learn all of the school's classes had been cancelled. Zeld and the other boys who qualified for the tournament prepared to leave by grooming their horses. The other boys at the school prepared for a journey to the school's lodge. Once Zeld finished grooming Tiger he sat in the Great Hall with the other team members. He wore everything he planned to take. He wondered what took so long. When twenty knights rode through the main gate, his question was answered, but then he had another one.

"Are they coming to escort us to the races?" Zeld asked Brian Boru. Brian shrugged his shoulders.

Sir Tavish had come out of the knights' barracks called 'Bull Hollow' and greeted the soldiers. Evidently they came to guard the school. He spent a few minutes showing them the progress on the castle, and then rang the bell.

"Two minutes!" Sir Tavish called. "Two minutes!"

Zeld scrambled quickly for Tiger. Once they gathered at the front gate, Sir Tavish called out, "Two queues, two queues." The students queued up on their horses in proper formation. Zeld rode near the front directly behind Oars.

"Company – forward – advance!" ordered Sir Tavish with a wave of his hand.

Everyone came running, the head cook, Father Michael, Sir Drain from his area, only the cook's two helpers missed out.

The team followed Sir Tavish while the remaining students and school staff cheered. They paraded through the main gate. Zeld felt a true sense of pride at representing his school. The company turned sharply south and headed for, for, for...... That's when Zeld realized he didn't know where he was going. He swallowed his fear and watched the horses in front of him closely.

After they had travelled for a while, Sir Tavish led the boys off the main road and into a wooded area where he blew his horn. They rode a short distance, coming to the edge of a tall cliff. As Zeld looked over the edge, his mouth fell open in disbelief. He saw a full grown fifteen-foot tall giant with muscular arms and chest rising on a huge cloud from a deep crevasse in the rocks.

The cloud continued to rise until it levelled off with the edge, leaving a small but dangerous space between the cloud and the cliff. Sir Tavish called to the boys, "Follow me and mind the gap."

84

Tiger reached his nose over the edge and touched the cloud before he took his first step onto it. Zeld closed his eyes and nervously urged the horse forward. When he opened them again, he could see everyone had made it safely onto the cloud. He saw Sir Tavish talking to the giant. Stepping closer, Sir Tavish handed the giant a purse and a parchment.

The cloud rose and Zeld felt the wind blowing all around him. The older boys dismounted and sat on the fluffy cloud. When Zeld dismounted, he felt surprised to find the cloud was actually white, silky sand. He asked the older boys about it and a couple of them laughed.

One of them said, "We always ride the giant's cloud to the far away competitions."

The cloud continued south for some time. After awhile it descended until it rested in a large meadow. The students disembarked on their horses and called farewell to the giant.

After the cloud rose into the air again, Zeld spied a wagon at the side of the road. In the wagon sat John and Bract. Zeld pointed to them and said, "There's our kitchen staff." They'd left earlier to set up the midday meal. The white silt around the tires of the wagon told Zeld they had come by cloud as well. They reported seeing no Vikings and had no worries.

The team dismounted and queued for a midday meal of bread and cheese in the meadow. Crispyn of Orange and Tyre Stevens sat pointing out the nearby trees.

"Oak, walnut, I can't remember that one, and sugar pine," said Crispyn.

"I think it's a maple," suggested Tyre.

Sir Tavish interrupted. "That's a mulberry bush. I'll have to report this to Sir Roger."

"Well, Sir, we only missed the one. You don't need to report that," declared Tyre somewhat bewildered.

Sir Tavish laughed, "I'm going to report the mulberry bush, not the pages that couldn't identify it."

"Oh, that's right, fletchers make bows outta mulberry wood," Tyre reminded Crispyn.

"I'll have to remember that," said Crispyn.

Following the midday repast the company mobilized and headed south again. Zeld felt cold and noticed dark rain clouds gathering in the sky. This bothered Sir Tavish who shouted, "COMPANY INCREASE TO A TROT!" The horses went faster.

As the company rode over a hill, they looked down into the valley and could see a castle close by. Zeld was impressed with what he saw; the area resembled a picture rather than a real place. Beautiful farms stretched out looking like a patchwork quilt and the valley was surrounded by a lush green forest. Then a heavy downpour started with hard-hitting drops the size of buckets. The horses fidgeted. Lightning's heavier coat equipped him better for tumultuous weather. Tiger, on the other hand, pitched a fit. He kicked up rocks repeatedly with both hind legs, while randomly moving in a circle to his right.

Sir Tavish commanded the company to take shelter under the trees. He then told them to dismount and move slowly from tree to tree until they reached the bottom of the hill.

When Zeld reached the bottom, he pulled his leather armour over the top of his head to keep the rain from soaking through to his underclothes.

"Everyone choose a mate. I want the entire company in pairs," commanded Sir Tavish. Zeld and Oars found each other immediately.

Dark clouds completely covered the sky and Zeld heard tumultuous thunder and saw bright flashes of lightning. The small creek at the bottom of the hill stopped flowing. He thought this rather odd as it should have swelled with the run off.

Sir Tavish noticed the change and reversed his order. "Everyone back up the hill. Mates stay together."

Some of the horses wouldn't go and their riders faced a dilemma. Should they leave their horse to stay with their mate or should they leave their mate to stay with their horse? Before the problem could be resolved, a deafening sloshing and breaking sound came from up the creek as a wall of water surged down the gully.

A few squires had brought ropes and they threw them to the boys in trouble. Other squires gathered rocks and rolled them into the gully to slow the rushing water.

Zeld and Oars found a fallen log and threw it in. The water changed course slightly, flowing around the log. Presently everyone threw whatever they could find into the gully trying to hold back the flood. The water pushed the logs and rocks together, forming a dam, as if the stream tried to help.

After awhile, the rainstorm grew gentler. The company had inadvertently built a dam that held a considerable amount of water, but in the commotion something, or someone, turned up missing. Zeld called out worriedly for Sir Tavish but he had disappeared. Sullivan de Bruce had vanished without trace as well. In the chaos, the flood had swept them away.

Geoffrey of Hesse organized a search party of squires and Zeld organized a lookout party of pages on the hilltop. Tyre spied two horses with riders in the valley. The pages relayed the message to the squires. They sent out a group to check on the riders; meanwhile, Geoffrey kept searching in the riverbed. In half an hour the riders made their way back with Sir Tavish and Sullivan. The company gave three cheers and reorganized.

Zeld noticed Sir Tavish and Sullivan hadn't been harmed mainly because they rode large war horses. These powerful horses withstood the force of the water where other smaller horses would have certainly drowned. As it turned out, the only loss came when the raging water stripped Sullivan's shoes straight off his feet.

What appeared to be a short ride across a storm-swept valley took much longer than expected. The road to the castle was riddled with a number of undetectable twists and turns. Zeld noticed several check points with towers and archers at the ready.

Once the boys crossed the drawbridge and entered the castle, the schoolmaster, Vancealot du Lake, shook Sir Tavish's hand.

"Welcome to Waltham Forest and Prince Valiant's School of Knighthood," Vancealot said politely. "Your tent has been pitched in the far right corner. It appears you've survived quite an ordeal. I'll send our castle healer to take a look at your company." By this time, several of the students, including Oars, felt ill with chills. Sir Tavish thanked the schoolmaster and led the sickly lot to their temporary abode.

Several pigs roasted at a pavilion and the smell of the cooking pork made Zeld's stomach rumble. The cooks busily prepared the pavilion for a grand banquet.

The ill students toddled off to their tent while everyone else cared for the horses. The healer gave the ill boys pills to take, blue at night and yellow in the morning.

Zeld made it back from the stables and interrupted the healer, "Can you teach me about your medicines?" he asked.

"Yes, they're expensive," said the healer. "I'm too busy to talk medicine right now. Maybe I'll have time tomorrow." The healer trudged his way to the Welch Naval Academy tent. They came in looking much like the C&C team.

After tending the horses Zeld entered the tent with the rest of the team. He found Sir Tavish explaining to the students that it was the Giant Academy's fault everyone felt ill. This unusually odd comment caught Zeld's attention.

"You see, they have clouds for transportation and clouds carry rain. The giants are cunning. Not only do they drench us as we arrive, but also they use the rain to slow us down in the races. We approached King Henry about it and the giants said when they leave home the cloud is dry. They claim English air is wet and this is the cause of the rain. Can you believe that? Our air is wet?" Sir Tavish said laughing. "Have you ever heard anything more ridiculous in your life? I suppose, next they'll tell us Goliath let King David win," he said, rolling his eyes. Sir Tavish played the jester, which put the encampment back into jolly spirits once again.

A black cloud sat on a nearby hill, pouring rain. The villagers had built a ditch to drain away as much water as possible. The Prince Valiant School asked the giants to move the cloud around during the day to water the fields. The giants indicated they would gladly do so.

Three hundred people attended the outdoor banquet, including twenty-four giant youth and one teacher. Zeld had never seen young giants before. Most of the students stood equivalent in height to the knights. The teacher, who wasn't much older than the students, stood taller than Sir Tavish.

After the banquet everyone went back to their camps and sat around the bonfires talking. No one used any more energy than necessary. Zeld and Oars went to bed early; after all, the races started in the morning and Zeld wanted to be rested.

CHAPTER TWELVE

Run

"SIX RAIL RACE, SENIOR DIVISION, SIX RAIL RACE, SENIOR DIVISION!" shouted out the Prince Valiant School's herald, calling the first race precisely at 9:00 a.m. "This is the first qualifying heat with runners from MacNar's and Scotland Naval."

Zeld secretly tested the ground. It felt a wee bit moist but not slippery, although a spot or two on the road appeared a little worse than where he stood. He hoped the moisture would dry off before the horse rescue event started. He watched as the four runners from each school stepped toward the starting line. The course, a wide country road, had railed fences on both sides. A ribbon stretched across the road marking the finishing line.

"Gentlemen, toe the line," the herald called.

The four giants stood to the left while the four naval cadets occupied the right. Zeld could see the tension on the contestants' faces. The herald yelled, "Sprint!" and they ran as swiftly as they could.

The cadets had a faster start and the giants a longer stride. However, before the giants could overtake them, the race ended. All four giants were swept out of the competition.

No one acted surprised. The coach of the cadets yelled, "Way-to-go, sea dogs!"

After the first race much of the tension from the pre-race jitters melted away.

Zeld sat on a wooden bench enjoying the races. Up next came the Dwarven Mining and Welch Naval Academies. The dwarves' shorter legs gave them a disadvantage. One of the dwarves won fourth place and qualified to go on to the next round. The dwarves cheered their hero as if he'd slain a dragon.

The third round consisted of runners from King Arthur's Goblin School and Castle and Caverns. The goblins stood shorter than the dwarves and although Zeld wasn't very good at determining strength yet, he could tell they had less strength than the other competitors. The Castles and Caverns team swept the goblins out of the competition.

The fourth race pitted the Robin Hood and Prince Valiant schools against each other. Seven boys and a human type, which Zeld had never seen before, toed the line. This new boy had long flowing brown hair with a thin build and Zeld could have sworn he had the most pointed ears he had ever seen. The goblins booed and threw things at the strange boy. The strange boy sprinted so fast he left streaks of colour behind. He easily finished first and the goblins booed even louder. Robin Hood qualified three runners and Prince Valiant one.

The strange boy disappeared into the crowd. Shortly afterwards the goblins had a streak of terrible luck. Suddenly, their bench tipped over and a few seconds later, the boy who had booed the loudest howled out in pain. Somehow he'd bloodied his nose.

The final round consisted of two boys from Scotland Naval, two boys from Welch Naval, three from Castles and Caverns and the strange boy from Robin Hood. First place went to the boy from Robin Hood, followed by the three boys from Castles and Caverns.

The schools followed the same process for the 12 rail, 35 rail, 100 rail, 400 rail, 800 rail and 1600 rail races. The long stride of the giants paid off in the 100 rail and longer races because no one could keep up. The giant coach jested about giving prizes to the boys who won the "stretching exercises". He referred to the short races of course.

Zeld cheered enthusiastically when the junior division races started. He knew Brian Boru ran so fast he left streaks of colour too. Brian became the star of the junior division taking first place in the 6 rail, 12 rail, and 35 rail races. A majority of the coaches agreed he was the fastest runner they'd seen in years. Brian slipped and fell in the final race but jumped up and still won by a sizeable margin. At the finish line Brian waited with a smile to shake hands with the other runners.

After eating, Zeld shuffled slowly with the milling crowd over to a new location to watch the wagon races, which started at 1:00

p.m. The course contained several turns and wound through the rolling hills forming a circle, which ended at the starting line. The Naval and Dwarven Academies were swept out in the first rounds because loading ponies aren't built for speed. The giant's weight put them out of this event. The goblins on the other hand did well with their small wagons, winning half the medals.

Zeld felt relieved when his event, horse rescue, finally took place that evening. The horse rescue field lay near several small hills which gave room for spectators to watch. Since this was the last event of the day, everyone came. The crowd buzzed with excitement.

The Dwarven Academy of Mining went first. They had two times of 22 1/2 and 24 seconds. Robin Hood came next, with one respectable time of 22 seconds.

The Giant Academy had two entries. In the first entry, the horse collapsed under the weight of two giant riders and on the second entry, the coach ran out and collected two ponies; then, sprinted to the finish line to the applause of the crowd. "That's how we manage it at MacNar's," he yelled in his gravelly voice.

King Arthur's School took their turn followed by the Scottish Naval Academy, but neither team had a good enough time for a prize. Then Castles and Caverns' took to the field.

The senior division's best time came from Geoffrey of Hesse and Wilhelm of Prussia at 19 Seconds, which tied the all-time record in the event. Then the junior division took to the field. Odin and Oles McMarr went first, finishing with a time of 21 seconds. James O'Day and Crispyn of Orange finished with a time of 24 seconds.

Zeld and Oars took their positions on the field. Zeld stood in readiness and looked over to Oars who nodded his head. Zeld whistled for Lightning and the timer started the ball clock.

Lightning sped to Zeld with precision. His hands reached up and took hold of Lightning's mane as he galloped past. The momentum catapulted his legs over Lightning's back. Faster than ever, they reached Oars who clasped Zeld's right wrist. Oars flew to his position behind Zeld and only an instant later they crossed the finish line. The herald reported the time of 16 seconds, smashing the old record.

Prince Valiant, the hosting school, competed last. They scored times of twenty to twenty-two seconds consistently. They didn't have the fastest time but Zeld felt impressed as they did have the overall best team.

That night after dinner, the Prince Valiant School presented medals at the pavilion. First, second, third, and fourth place medals were awarded, and the coaches received the cash prizes for safe keeping. The giants won the grand prize for the best team. The coach accepted the award but gave the 500 silver pieces to the coach of the King Arthur School to help them rebuild.

92

Zeld wondered what had happened. He leaned over and asked Oars who sat close by. "Did their school burn down?"

"No, the elves destroyed it," Oars answered. "D'you remember the elf the goblins booed at today?"

"That was an elf?" Zeld asked.

"Honestly, d'you always answer a question with another question?" asked Oars.

"I dunno, do I?" asked Zeld.

Just then, the healer from the day before came and sat between the two boys.

"So, what did you want to know about medicines?" he asked.

"Why are they so expensive?"

"Because the plants the medicines come from are extremely hard to find," answered the healer.

"What plants?"

"Well, the Tyfus Mez plant is only found on the plains of North Africa and Huddy Joor comes from the mountains of Denmark. If an herbalist brought, say two dozen plants, of Huddy Joor or Tyfus Mez to England and properly cultivated them, they could make a fortune in about three years," the healer explained.

Geoffrey of Hesse came by to congratulate Zeld.

The healer asked, "So, Geoffrey, are you planning to come learn medicine with me this summer or is your family going to Germany again?"

"Dad is making arrangements to go somewhere but he hasn't told us where yet," replied Geoffrey.

"What was your name again lad?" the healer asked, turning back to Zeld.

"Zeld."

"Well, Zeld, if you're ever in trouble I'm the one to call, my name is Zachary Fillpot. Can you remember that name, Fillpot? It's exceptionally rare but may save your life someday, much like my medicines," the healer said.

"Fillpot. I'll remember," repeated Zeld.

"Excellent, because I'm giving a test on it later," the healer teased.

"That mate should be renamed crackpot," said Geoffrey after the healer left.

"Yeah he's a crackpot all right! But a nice one," said Zeld.

"Have you ever met a mean crackpot?"

Suddenly, Zeld had a revelation of sorts. He had waited for only just this moment since he opened King Henry's letter. He could throw the Hessens off his mother's trail forever. "Sure have, there's this crackpot in Hootsie Land named Dota, that's in North Africa, and he's continually asking me mum to marry him. Now there's a crackpot with a mean streak. Every time me mum says no he starts throwing things around the palace. What a simple minded nimble head," Zeld said with a confident smirk.

Geoffrey's jolly expression showed he took the bait, hook, line and sinker. The McMarr triplets heard everything. They waited until Geoffrey strutted proudly away, and then surrounded Zeld.

"D'you realize you told Geoffrey of Hesse exactly where your mum lives?" asked Odin in disbelief.

"D'you realize there is no such place as Hootsie Land?" Zeld asked back.

"I daresay, you'll probably burn in hell for that one," suggested Oars.

The three boys asked at the same time, "Can we go too?"

"I've never visited down below before," remarked Oars.

"I heard the dragons were dying to get in," said Odin smugly.

"Hottest place 'round," Oles jested.

"I've been there and I'm not going back. However, I wouldn't mind sending that git, Godfrey of Hesse, there – permanently!" Zeld said honestly.

"So, how much will Hesse spend on an assassin to kill Zeld's mother?" asked Oars.

"I thought he might go personally," suggested Oles.

"I don't imagine he'll go personally. I think he'll send a ship of his most trusted scallywags," commented Odin.

Oars blurted out, "Truthfully, I hope he spends a grand fortune. I hope he stays up nights worrying about the whole affair. I also hope when Hesse finally ferrets out it's all a big lie that Zeld survives the aftermath!"

CHAPTER Thirteen

Searching for Jens Jr.

On their return journey from the racing tournament the party of riders reached the C&C supply station near the farms and to Oles' amazement he found a rune carved into one of the posts. He pointed at it. "Look at this - Jens Jr. is alive and in the area!" Oles declared.

The trey born looked at the carving and Odin translated it. "Cottage in meadow - JJ."

"Is that the cottage with the new roof beams?" asked Zeld, who also felt the triplet's growing eagerness.

"Yes," replied Odin excitedly. "I'll go after Father."

"We'll do this properly. Zeld and I'll go after Father while Odin and Oles ride for the cottage. When you arrive, wait for us and if anyone else shows up, spy on them," ordered Oars.

"Why should you go after Father? Maybe we should go after Father and you should wait at the cottage," said Oles unhappily.

"Good question. The answer is - ZELD AND I HAVE THE FASTEST HORSES!" Oars bellowed loudly.

"Smashing answer," said Oles.

With the matter settled, the boys leaned forward and spurred the horses into action.

"HOLD!" yelled Sir Tavish as they whizzed past. "Where are you going? You haven't been released!" The boys ignored Sir Tavish and rode for their destinations all the same. Zeld heard Sir Tavish shout out, "I'm reporting this insolence to Father Michael!"

Wasting no time, Oars and Zeld rode through the front gate of the castle, around the buildings and through the stonemasons' yard. They jumped the stream and headed for the McMarr Manor.

Odin and Oles rode north for the cottage. The horses' hooves rattled the north bridge, and then they passed the dwarven mine on their right and the pool of water being fed by a waterfall on their left. The horse's hooves beat hard on the ground echoing the riders' intense purpose.

Zeld and Oars took all the short cuts Oars knew. This included galloping straight down a mountainside instead of keeping to the weaving road. It also meant jumping over fallen trees and riding through thickets.

By the time Oars and Zeld reached the manor they'd received a considerable number of scratches on their faces and arms. They rode through the main gate and Oars rang the alarm. The manor sprang into action. The armoury door burst open and everyone on the estate took to their battle stations. No one wondered who rang the alarm or where they should go. The defences at the manor were better organized than most castles. Jens Sr. shouted down from his position in a tower, "WHAT IS IT LAD?"

"Jens Jr. has carved a rune," replied Oars excitedly. Jens Sr. slid down a pole to the ground.

"Do we know where he is?" asked Jens Sr., looking intently into his son's face.

"We think so," answered Oars looking up. "The rune said, 'search the cottage in the meadow'."

Jens Sr. turned sharply to his men at the walls and yelled, "Cavalry five minutes, cavalry five minutes."

Zeld's stomach lurched as he knew Jens Sr. expected to find his son and he felt a considerable amount of pressure to make it happen.

Several men came down from the walls and prepared the horses. Jens Sr. called for Dando to join the search party. Dando was 11 years old, a bit small for his age, with dark blonde hair and brown eyes. Zeld recognized him as the quiet boy from the manor, but now he had seen him a few times he felt certain he had known him from before his family went into exile.

"Dando, you watched the cottage in the meadow for a full week after Jens Jr.'s disappearance. Lad, we need to know, did you see anyone or anything - shall we say - magical?" Jens Sr. asked in a somewhat uncomfortable tone.

"One night I had a dream. In me dream the cottage glowed a light blue colour; then, it lifted up in the air and stayed there for a time, and then it slowly came down. In the morning I carefully looked the cottage over, but nothing had changed. So, I knew with certainty I dreamt it," explained Dando.

"Come with us," Jens Sr. ordered calmly.

Jens Sr. marched quickly into the house and spoke with Marta for a moment; and then returned with a bag hanging from one shoulder. "I see you lads raced through the thickets," Jens Sr. mumbled. He reached into the bag and pulled out a cream and rubbed it on the boys' faces and arms. Zeld felt a familiar tickling sensation.

From the doorway behind him Marta spoke. "You lads be careful, we don't want to go looking for any more lost boys."

No one had to tell Zeld twice, he realized this could turn into a dangerous mission in two shakes of a lamb's tail.

She looked directly at Oars, winked at him and said, "You watch your father's back, he tends to jump first and think second when it comes to his sons."

Jens Sr. slowly turned toward her and said, "I'm as healthy as a twenty-five-year-old and ten-times as clever."

Marta retreated shaking her head, as if to say she didn't want to hear such nonsense.

Jens Sr. shook his head, "We're going to the cottage in the meadow."

He mounted his horse and they rode out. The company of horsemen followed Jens Sr. When they reached the cottage, they found Odin and Oles waiting for them.

Oles reported, "Nothing happened on our watch."

Jens Sr. drew his sword, walked right up to the door and kicked it in. Inside he found nothing. The triplets searched the floor for a map or another secret rune. They didn't find anything either.

Undaunted, Jens Sr. cut down a tall sapling; then, used his sword to shape the end of it flat resembling a spade. With the help of two others, he pried the front of the house up in the air, much like a treasure chest lid. The boys looked underneath the cottage and found a large pit. Jens Sr. moved the cottage to one side leaving an opening big enough to climb down. He dropped one end of the sapling down the hole.

Odin and Oles slid down. When their eyes adjusted to the scarce light, they found ropes and rags. One look at the placement of the knots revealed their previous use of hog tying someone. They turned over rocks looking for clues. This seemed mad to

Zeld, a clue hidden under a rock.

Then Oles yelled, "I've got it."

The two boys climbed out of the hole and Oles showed the rock to his father. It appeared to be meaningless scribbling to Zeld, but Jens Sr. could read it.

It says, "Find me, huge boulder, above Baden - JJ," Jens Sr. said quickly, interpreting the rune. The look on his face showed he felt uncertain about which boulder the rune meant.

It didn't take long to reposition the cottage, and the company started on their way to Baden, by way of the school. The shortest route was the same way Oles and Odin came. They rode, determined to bring Jens Jr. home.

By the time they reached the pool by the waterfall, Tiger, Lightning, Meadow and Midnight looked exhausted. Jens Sr. couldn't help but look pleased with his three sons, Zeld and Dando too. They'd shown the leadership and common sense necessary to become wise noblemen.

Jens Sr. turned to his sons and Zeld. "Your horses are played out," he said. "You stay here and when they're rested, take the horses to the school. We'll continue the search. Oh, and please ask Father Michael if we may stay the night and sup with him."

The four boys reluctantly agreed because they couldn't do anything else. The rest of the company went on to Baden.

While the four horses drank and ate, Zeld and the triplets swam in the water and splashed the horses to cool them down. The cool water felt good as the boys had ridden all day. Zeld felt better imagining Jens Jr. being set free in an hour or two.

A few dwarfolk slowly marched out of the mine and asked Zeld, "Have you checked on the mining equipment?"

"I tried but was sent away. These last few days I've been away on a rescue mission and to the Prince Valiant School. I'll give it another go soon."

Hiding in the bushes nearby, two pirates listened to every word.

The four boys headed back to the school. When they started down the last hill, they spied Geoffrey and his father Godfrey of Hesse speaking to each other on the side of the road.

The boys darted out of sight. Oars and Oles held the horses while Odin and Zeld crept within earshot. Zeld couldn't hear everything, but he heard Geoffrey say, "Gold" and he handed his father three gold nuggets. Zeld also overheard the words "flash flood" and "bunch of morons." Godfrey gave the nuggets back to Geoffrey.

The boys inched closer, and Zeld had to smother his laughter when he heard Geoffrey tell his father about Zeld's family. Geoffrey told his father Zeld's mother lived in the palace of Hootsie Land in North Africa.

Zeld caught some of what Godfrey answered.

"I'll have to send my knights...but it'll be well worth it. The palace of Hootsie Land will soon change ownership," said Godfrey. "Secretly obtaining the location of our enemies is as good a deed as I've ever heard." He patted Geoffrey on the back. They turned and walked slowly back to the school together.

Zeld and the triplets huddled.

"We thought Geoffrey tracked the horses after the flash flood but instead he hunted gold nuggets in the gully," Odin informed his brothers in a sad tone. "We should've known the horses and riders would've only gone downstream and found a good place to climb out."

"Didja hear him tell his father about Hootsie Land? He'd believe anything. I should've told him me mum lives on the moon," laughed Zeld, who was in a much better mood than Odin. Zeld couldn't help but feel overjoyed he had sent the Hesses to the wrong part of the world and kept his mother and brother safe.

"Next time, someone else is staying with the horses. I miss all the fun," said Oars.

After a good chuckle Zeld said, "You're not gonna miss out this time Oars. I have a plan."

CHAPTER Fourteen

THE PLAN

Sixty percent of the profits?" asked Grumpes in disbelief as he and the other dwarves who sat around the fire pit in the mine looked up while listening to Zeld's plan.

"Yes, and ten percent for each of us four boys. Now mind the Hessens will also send miners after the gold, so this will be a snatch and go operation," Zeld said stressing his last point.

"How will we reach the mine quickly enough?" asked Grumpes.

"Two of me mates will be here in the next few minutes with a large group of boys to help you on your way," Zeld informed them with a smile and a twinkle in his eye.

The dwarves seemed thrilled with the chance to mine gold and they'd never received an offer of sixty percent of the profits before.

"Where is the gold again?" asked Bushhard.

"In the hills north of the Prince Valiant School. You can't miss it," Zeld said certain the plan would work flawlessly.

"We'll ask Marvin to float us south on his cloud," declared Bushhard. Turning to Zeld he added, "He's helped us on occasion."

"Perfect, Marvin knows exactly where to drop you off. Then you simply follow the road toward the school until you find a small dam blocking the road. The gold is located in the gully below the dam," Zeld told the dwarves.

Odin and Oles rode to the school with the four tired horses, and Oles rang the alarm with the hammer. As everyone came running, Odin called, "We've been on a rescue mission searching for Jens Jr. and could use a couple of fresh horses." The hostler took the reigns of the tired horses and towed them toward the stalls. Odin continued. "Apparently, a band of thieves attacked Jens Jr. on his return journey. Our men need room and board. Oh, and there is a secret mission."

Hands flew up in the air as every boy volunteered.

Father Michael gave permission, somewhat reluctantly, for a few of the squires to assist with the secret mission. He alerted the cooks about their guests, who would arrive soon. The pages accepted the assignment to pitch two large tents for the rescue party to sleep in that night. Friar Jonathan brought out extra blankets from storage. The squires mounted their horses and rode for the dwarven mine. They also took two fresh horses with them for Zeld and Oars.

Once there, they dismounted, helped the dwarves pack and moved the mining equipment from the dwarven mine to the supply station by the farms.

Zeld and Oars rode back to the school with the squires. The plan worked well until Jens Sr. and the other rescuers arrived without Jens Jr.

"You didn't find him?" asked Odin once the rescuers had gathered inside the tent. "We told everyone Jens Jr. had trouble on the road and we could help bring him home."

"Did you tell anyone about the kidnapping?" Jens Sr. asked, placing his left hand on Odin's shoulder.

"No."

"It's me fault," said Zeld in a miserable tone while hanging his head. "I told Odin this would make everyone want to help us."

"Mind he's safe only as long as the thieves believe he's someone else's son," Jens Sr. reminded them.

"Didja find the boulder?" asked Oles.

"Yes, we think so, but Jens Jr. couldn't hear us shouting, because of the boulder's size," Jens Sr. explained.

"You moved the cottage without any trouble, so why not a boulder?" asked Oars as he sat down and removed his shoes while getting ready for bed.

"Because the boulder comprises one third of the hill," explained Jens Sr.

The cook brought dinner for the grateful rescuers. The rescue party, including Zeld and the triplets, ate, and then slept that night in the two tents.

Zeld didn't wake up until he heard music coming from the chapel in the morning. The rescuers left their tents and went over to listen. They sat on the grass outside the chapel and enjoyed

Father Michael's sermon. "I refer to doing good deeds for the sake of doing good. I believe men, no matter their age, should do a good deed each day and good deeds should be done with no thought of repayment. Good deeds are their own reward. Mind the many times Jesus healed the lame in the New Testament, clearly Jesus lived this way. I believe we, at Castles and Caverns, also live this way and last night is my proof.

"Presently you'll go on an excursion to help the local farmers. Learn all you can and toil hard. Farming is an honourable profession. Farmers are close to nature and nature is close to God. Service is close to God. The two together, toiling with nature and service, will most assuredly bring you closer to God."

Zeld's opinion about Sunday had changed. Church really wasn't terrible and Sunday gave a nice change of pace from the rest of the week, but the long afternoons of people spying on each other hardly seemed proper conduct for the Sabbath day.

After the rescue party left, Zeld took Oars with him over to the stonemasons' yard and looked around for the dwarves' unicorn mark.

Oars yelled, "Watch it!" and pointed to something spinning toward Zeld in the sky.

Zeld dodged a silver flash; then, he collected the piece of shiny metal that nearly hit him and ran in the direction it came from. He and Oars couldn't find any sign of his attacker. Zeld examined the object; it was a metal wedge with the unicorn mark.

After searching the area thoroughly, Zeld carried the wedge back to his treasure chest in Eagle Loft. While putting it away he noticed something else rather alarming. A couple of days earlier his treasure chest had appeared new and shiny, but now it had smudges all over it and someone had clearly tried to break in.

Zeld felt uncertain about who would try this, perhaps someone else knew about the secret compartments or possibly they tried to steal his armour? Me life has become more difficult since I moved to England, he thought.

The second-year pages came in and Crispyn said, "We really like your treasure chest."

"D'you know who fiddled with it?" Zeld asked.

"The entire school came by to admire it and Geoffrey of Hesse even attempted to pick the lock but it didn't work. In fact, the lock somehow tossed him across the room," one of the boys explained in a cheerful tone. The others smiled as well.

"Yeah, I wondered who left smudges all over it," Zeld said, relieved to hear what happened from them.

"Anyway, it's time for the midday meal and I'm starved," one of the boys mumbled.

"After we eat, who wants to beat me in a grand game of chess?" Zeld asked.

They laughed and headed for the Great Hall.

"Me first," insisted Crispyn of Orange.

"I know, we can play pass chess. It takes four people and two game sets. When you capture a piece, you pass it to your partner and he can place it on the board for his turn. Its colossal fun," said Brian Boru on the way.

While playing chess in the Great Hall, Zeld learned the next tournament would be held at the King Arthur School of Goblin Training. The events included a treasure maze, house building, two-man boat carving, and fortifications.

That night Zeld had a truly terrible thought as he lay awake in bed. If Godfrey of Hesse sent troops with his miners to the new gold mine, the dwarves could be killed. He slipped out of bed, knelt down and prayed for the safety of the dwarves. Zeld realized his little grandiose schemes could go terribly wrong and there could be the devil to pay for it. People could die and it would be his fault.

He didn't sleep very well that night because he dreamed of the attack on his family's castle again. This time he hid in a wagon and the horses ran as hastily as they could go. One of the horses came up lame and the driver stopped the wagon. Catherine, Wolf and Zeld slipped away and hid under a bridge. The driver pulled a caltrop out of the horse's foot and attempted to back the wagon up when Hessen troops surrounded it. Two of them held the driver's arms while another beat him. The entire time the interrogator demanded to know the whereabouts of the woman and two boys. The driver remained loyal and said nothing. Even while being beaten he said nothing. Then a friendly face appeared in the darkness. Friendly, he thought, yes, but also ugly.

Zeld awoke with a jolt. He sat up in bed with everyone around him still asleep. He slipped out of bed and crept over to his treasure chest, unlocking it with his key. He found the metal wedge and his letter from the king. He lifted up on the armour and saw his coat of arms professionally painted on the left side of the chest. He thought it looked superb, resembling a coat of arms that belonged to someone special. He wondered how King Henry knew his charge; after all, it didn't appear in the Heraldry book of England. Zeld planned to ask him sometime.

He tried to find the secret compartment King Henry wrote about. He pressed every corner, checked on every flat surface, pushed down on every nail, but nothing opened. He wished he understood how secret compartments worked. He couldn't think of anything else to try.

"What are you doing, Zeld?" asked James O'Day.

Zeld jumped, and his heart leapt into his throat. He thought he was the only one awake.

"Looking for secret compartments, but I can't find any," he whispered frantically.

"Maybe there aren't any," James whispered back.

"King Henry said there's one, but I can't find it anywhere," Zeld breathed softly.

"Maybe it's magically sealed," whispered James as he walked over to Zeld. "My father owned a treasure chest he claimed was magically sealed. Supposedly, it required a piece of sea elf gold to open it. My mum always thought it a bunch of O'Day Irish blarney, but maybe not."

"Hang on, what in heaven's name is a sea elf anyway?" asked Zeld.

"We Welch call them water dwellers and the English call them sea elves, because they live underwater," explained James.

"So, a sea elf is someone who lives underwater. Thank you, James. Now I don't have to go to classes in the morning. I've already learned something new," teased Zeld.

"That's not all. The sea elf resembles a land elf except for the webbed fingers and toes and the fact they ride 'round on giant sea horses." James paused, a smile cross his face. "If you taught me something, I wouldn't have to go to class either."

"Dwarves aren't ticklish," Zeld told James.

James gave Zeld a questioning look. Then James bellowed so grand a guffaw he woke half the boys in Eagle Loft.

"It's true," said Zeld with a nod. He lowered the lid on his treasure chest and locked it.

"MIDNIGHT PILLOW FIGHT!" yelled Oles and before Zeld knew what happened, all the boys jumped out of bed and the pillow fight commenced in earnest. Zeld and James didn't make it back to their beds as a flying barrage of pillows knocked them to the ground. A few moments later Friar Timothy entered the room. The boys pelted him with pillows.

He called out, "How dare you have a pillow fight!" He pretended to choke up with emotion. "...without inviting me."

Then Friar Timothy joined in. Pillows flew everywhere for a half an hour. Then Friar Timothy said he'd schedule the next pillow fight on his calendar; that way he wouldn't miss a single moment.

The next morning it became quite apparent to Zeld some of the boys operated on too little sleep. He waited within earshot while Friar Timothy explained himself to Father Michael in the Great Hall without mentioning they had a pillow fight.

"It seems something woke the boys during the night. Whatever it was, it flew all over Eagle Loft and I had a most difficult time stopping it. Fortunately, everyone escaped injury, although at the time it appeared some of the boys were in unmistakable danger."

CHAPTER Fifteen

Take that, Crispyn

I heard about all the excitement in Eagle Loft last night," said Sir Drain, to his class held at the south wall. "If you thought you were in danger last night, I daresay, that's nothing. Today you'll learn the proper techniques used with the battleaxe and how to defend the blows with a kite shield. Zeld, come take the shield." In a matter of minutes Zeld was proud to say he could successfully block everyone except Brian Boru, who possessed super speed.

On Zeld's turn with the axe, he hit Crispyn of Orange's shield so hard the bottom of it whipped around his arm and smacked him in the face. Crispyn fell to the ground stunned. The shield had been split in half from top to bottom.

No one said "fantastic," "crushing," "devastating" or any of the usual words when someone did something brilliant. They merely stood there uncertain what to do.

Sir Drain checked on Crispyn. Then Sir Drain stopped the lesson and called for the pages to come and sit in a semicircle.

"What you see here is called a double one hit. Let me explain. Here at Castles and Caverns, we teach combat through a numbered damage system. You pages already know about the strength of men and animals and you should be learning to assess an enemy's strength. This damage system is part of the whole system you'll learn here. It's based on a game and the game is based on real combat."

Sir Drain shifted his feet and continued. "For example, when we strike with a weapon we're attempting to land the best hit possible. This best hit will cause your opponent's armour to ring and vibrate. A best possible hit doesn't mean you always hurt your opponent. Sometimes even fantastic hits merely glance off.

"In the game, if you roll a one with a die, that's the best hit and the most possible damage is also symbolized by rolling a one with your second throw. When you land a fantastic shot like Zeld and make the best possible hit along with the best possible damage, your opponent's shield will slice in two pieces – er – see it here," said Sir Drain holding up the broken shield.

"This is the result of a one hit with a one damage." Sir Drain's teaching aid proved most effective as the boys wouldn't stop staring at it. "Tomorrow each of you should strive for this result. As soon as the equipment is packed away, you're dismissed. Zeld, may I have a word with you?" Sir Drain asked flatly.

Zeld worried he'd have to pay for the shield. He hoped the dwarves would come back with enough money or he'd be in big trouble.

"Zeld, your father achieved warlord status with a battleaxe. Did you know that?"

"No," said Zeld, with doubt in his voice.

"Do you know what a warlord is?"

"No."

"A warlord is a man who has become so highly-developed with the use of his weapon, in your father's case a battleaxe; he always struck with double ones, much like you did. He'd be very proud of your efforts."

Here it comes, I have to pay for the broken shield, Zeld thought as his muscles grew tease waiting for the bad new.

"Don't worry about the shield. We have items repaired all the time. To us a broken shield means the boys are learning to fight properly." Sir Drain patted him on the back and walked away.

Besides the broken shield, another unusual thing happened that day. In Sir Jaydan's class, held in the library, the pages learned about the fortifications built on the seashore of the Holy Land when the first crusaders arrived. Sir Jaydan looked tall and thin with long legs which resembled a dancer. His hair and eyes were light brown and he had rosy checks.

"Mind this, as it may save your life: the easiest and best defence at the seashore is to roll rocks into a line moving directly inland. In case of an attack the rocks will serve as a barrier between you and your attackers," he said.

"What kind of attackers?" asked Odin.

"What say you to - giant chickens?"

Zeld hooted at Sir Jaydan's jest.

"No...really...er...haven't any of you heard about the giant chickens of Barnstaple?" Sir Jaydan asked seriously. The pages returned blank stares.

"I'll take that as a negative," Sir Jaydan said looking a bit shocked. "Well then, once upon a time, in a cheerful little village called Barnstaple, where every year the crops grew, the cows gave milk and in general, the citizenry lived a good life, a sinister plot arose. A jealous witch and a band of pirates teamed together to overthrow the Duke of Barnstaple and seize the valley for themselves. They made a batch of quick-grow formula and smuggled it to a farm and fed it to a flock of chickens. Presently the giant chickens ran amok. They raced around the town pecking the heads of the peasants and destroyed the fields and shops as they scratched for food.

"After several days of doing battle, the Duke of Barnstaple requested help from the giants in Scotland. The giants came and removed the chickens from the area and marched the duke off in chains as well. They placed in his stead his brother who had married into one of the giant clans.

"The deposed duke escaped and went into exile. The giants posted a thousand gold piece reward for his capture, but no one took it seriously as everyone knows the giants are always empty pursed when it comes to money."

The bell tolled and the boys scampered off to their next class. Zeld felt disappointed he didn't have time to ask any questions.

That night before bed, a pie cart came to the castle. The baker, a newcomer to the area, asked for Eagle Loft barracks. Friar Timothy showed the baker the way to Eagle Loft. The baker looked thin for a cook, but strong with dark hair and eyes. The pie cart attracted the attention of the whole school.

Once inside Eagle Loft the Brotherhood of Air gathered and Friar Timothy asked, "Are these pies for us?"

"Yes," said the baker happily, "I have an announcement. Today, albeit a miracle, we had the first double one or perfect hit from our new class of pages. Since the page came from the Brotherhood of Air, I thought your brotherhood would enjoy giving these pies a few double one hits with your teeth. Signed Sir Drain, knight."

The baker brought apple pies, cherry pies, peach pies, several berry pies, and fresh cream to go on top. It was the jolliest surprise party Zeld ever attended. The baker stayed the entire time serving the pies personally and making friends with the boys and staff. Zeld's mates made a considerable fuss over him and told the baker all about his brilliant hit with the battleaxe.

After the dessert, three friars walked the baker home for safety reasons and to learn the location of the bakery, in case they felt hungry for pie sometime. That night the moon shone only a thin crescent shape and in a few more nights there would be no moon showing at all. Somehow, the moon reminded Zeld of an hour glass with the sand about to run out.

For the next couple of days, classes were held inside due to rainy weather. The boys' barracks and the Great Hall became classrooms. The archery class changed to a demonstration on how to pack for battle.

By Thursday, Zeld couldn't eat from worry, because he hadn't heard from the dwarves. The brothers McMarr worried about Jens Jr. as well.

Late that night, a group of dwarven men came to the castle asking for Zeld. Zeld didn't recognize them straightaway. They came nicely dressed and the men had shaved their beards.

"We brought your share of the money," Bushhard said gleefully.

"Please come into the Great Hall," Zeld said.

"We had the most extraordinary mining experience ever. We found the dam precisely where you said it was and we detached it. Then we rebuilt it on another road that crossed a different stream. A group of Hessen miners arrived but were completely stupefied by our trick for two days. We discovered plenty of gold nuggets," Bushhard said with a broad smile, "while the other miners found nothing."

"We controlled the water with a dam of our own and did rather well until the Hessen miners caught onto our little tricks. They moved below us on the stream, so we opened the dam full bore and flooded them out." Bushhard swung his arms near this chest and stomped his right foot. "They ran like mice and their equipment lay strewn everywhere. Then we scrambled to scoop up every bit of gold. That's when we found a gigantic gold nugget, bigger than any of us had ever seen. We snatched it up and away we went,"

110

Bushhard said, beaming delightfully.

"I found something of yours," Zeld said, not understanding Bushhard's meaning. After all, he had no idea how gigantic the gold nugget would be. He went after the metal wedge. When he returned, he found Friar Timothy talking to the dwarves.

Zeld interrupted. "I looked in the stonemasons' yard like you asked me to and this flung through the air nearly hitting me. It has the unicorn mark on it but the stonemasons' yard didn't have anything else with the mark."

"This disappeared two moons ago. Did you find the person who threw it?" asked Bushhard.

111

"No. I ran in the direction it came from but I couldn't find any trace of the assailant."

"Elves," concluded Bushhard.

"I don't think so," commented Friar Timothy thoughtfully. "It could've been someone with an elfin cloak or amulet of invisibility. Do you remember, Zeld, what happened down at the farms the other day? We found one of our food baskets high in a tree. We would've had no chance of getting it down, if not for James O'Day's mast climbing skills."

"The money, which was stolen from the school, could've also been taken by someone invisible," Zeld added.

Bushhard agreed with Friar Timothy this type of mischief didn't match the elfish style. "I've never heard of an elf stealing money," he said.

The dwarf handed Zeld a purse with gold coins in it. "This is the amount we agreed upon. God be with you my English friends," Bushhard said, with a courteous bow. He rose to leave the castle.

"God be with you, too," repeated the friar.

Zeld went to Eagle Loft where he found the triplets. He opened the purse and counted the money, 400 gold pieces. He gave 100 to each of the brothers. The triplets didn't feel right about their share and returned half their coins to Zeld. Zeld appreciated their kind act and their friendship. He locked his coins in his treasure chest and that night slept like a king.

CHAPTER SIXTEEN

Easy Come Easy Go

A throng of students formed a knot around Friar Martin at the main gate on the morning of the first farm help day.

"Give me room," he called. Then he pounded a nail into the right side door of the main gate to hang the duty roster. He barely stepped free before the knot of people gathered a second time.

The list started -

Johannes farm	*Squire - Marcus Thompson*	*Page - James O'Day*
Hoover farm	*Squire - Wilhelm of Prussia*	*Page - Brian Boru*
Lyman farm	*Squire - Gunter Sims*	*Page - Angus ap Forrest*

Zeld scanned down the page until he found the place that read,

Houston farm	*Squire - Geoffrey of Hesse*	*Page - Zeld de Exile*

Zeld felt betrayed. His thoughts played tricks on him. How could they do this? Don't they know we're secretly bitter enemies? Don't they know as soon as I set one toe over the line of safe haven I'll probably be shanghaied off to China or worse yet, I could have a prearranged fatal accident? This is the end of me.

Looking at the ground he could envision his tombstone: "Here lies Zeld the Idiot, dead at age twelve attempting to recover his family's lands and castle. The same thing will happen to you, so don't try it!" Zeld fumed with anger. He had such a grand life; too bad it only just ended.

Friar Timothy called Zeld over. Zeld ignored him and stormed angrily into Eagle Loft his chest swelling with intense anger and his face blazing red. Friar Timothy followed him.

"Zeld, what's bothering you? Is it your assignment?" the friar asked.

"YES!" Zeld erupted on the verge of a yell.

"I requested you and Geoffrey go together. I saw you helped him with the horse rescue event. I thought you were mates," said Friar Timothy.

"No, we're not mates! The Hesse family killed me father and threw us into exile. That pond scum is spying on me. He's trying to learn the whereabouts of me mum, so his father can murder the lot of us!" Zeld shouted.

"Calm yourself. I'm sure this is all a serious misunderstanding," suggested the friar.

"No, it isn't," said an aggravated voice from the doorway. "The boy is totally correct. Geoffrey has been spying on him and reporting back to his father," stated Sir Drain as he stepped into the room. "However, I've also noticed you've done a fair amount of espionage on Geoffrey," Sir Drain said astutely to Zeld. "And what have you and the dwarves conjured up? I'm sure, whatever it is, the Hesses wouldn't approve in the slightest."

Zeld laughed nervously as he felt his anger ebb away. "It's a money-making adventure."

"You're supposed to file papers with the sheriff making all mining claims legal," said Sir Drain bluntly.

"I didn't know."

"How much did you make?"

"Me share was one hundred gold pieces."

"Not bad for less than a week."

"Oles, Odin and Oars received one hundred gold - each!"

"Four hundred gold pieces - in less than a week?"

"The dwarves kept their share of sixty percent," Zeld added.

Sir Drain rubbed his eyes, as if he had a headache; then, he asked, "So, you found gold. Did anyone else find anything valuable?"

"Er, yeah, Sir Tavish found a mulberry bush."

"Where?"

"At the place we stopped to eat our midday meal while journeying to the racing tournament. I suppose someone chose the place ahead of time because the cooks waited for us there."

"Well, you continue spying on Geoffrey. It's paying interest in information. I must leave but I'll come by to visit with you tomorrow," Sir Drain said as he turned sharply on his heel and left in a hurry.

"You heard Sir Drain's orders - go spy on him!" teased Friar Timothy. Then in a serious tone he said, "You've done well, Zeld.

Don't forget to pay a tenth to God as he has a way of making finances work out right when you pay your tithing."

When the time to leave came, Zeld felt much better. He saddled Tiger and joined Geoffrey at the main gate.

Geoffrey smiled broadly. Zeld could only imagine what type of news would make him that jolly. Perhaps the death of Zeld's mother and brother would manage it, or perhaps Geoffrey had some other sinister plan.

Zeld felt assured his scheme had worked and his family remained quite well. He hoped the foolish Hessens did nothing more than gallivanting around in the wrong part of the world.

The other students packed their belongings and waited for the cavalry to arrive. They waited for an hour with no sign of them. Finally Father Michael told the boys to go to the farms as he felt sure something minor had delayed them. The students rushed to their assignments in order to arrive before darkness fell; after all, no moon shone that night.

Zeld went down the south road to the farms, side by side with Geoffrey, feeling confident he had the upper hand.

When they reached the Houston farm, Mark Houston, his wife Beullah, and their three daughters Rebecca, Elizabeth, and Mary greeted them. Mary, the six-year-old, took Zeld's hand while the two older girls stared longingly at Geoffrey.

After milking the cows, Zeld went down the fence line and found Geoffrey along with farmer Houston repairing several broken rails. Farmer Houston told Zeld a stampede of cows had charged through the rails. The farmer pointed and said, "They charged down the hill on the other side of the road and collided headlong, ruining me fence."

Zeld looked for the path of destruction but couldn't see it well in the darkness; however, he did see a light, so he pointed and asked, "What's that light in the distance?"

The farmer gazed in the direction Zeld pointed and said emotionlessly, "The castle is on alert."

The three of them looked at each other for a moment before the severity of the situation became real.

Farmer Houston suggested, "You boys better return and see what's happening."

Zeld and Geoffrey hurried back to the barn. As they walked, Zeld imagined the school had caught fire; then, another thought crossed his mind, perhaps the black plague had broken out. They walked faster, then jogged, then ran. They saddled the horses in the barn, and raced to the school.

Geoffrey led with Zeld following behind him as they stormed through the gate. To their surprise they found nothing seriously wrong. Father Michael had lit one of the towers, so the missing soldiers, who still hadn't come, could find their way to the school in the darkness.

"I don't understand it. They've never been late before. How could the soldiers have abandoned us?" asked Father Michael, shaking his head in obvious disbelief.

"Perhaps we should send out a search party," suggested Geoffrey who forced a smile from his face every time Zeld looked at him.

"We're already vulnerable due to a lack of manpower," said Father Michael wearing a worried expression on his face.

"Zeld and I could do a short distance road search," suggested Geoffrey.

"We could climb up to a high place and watch for them," suggested Zeld.

"We'll do this by the book," said Father Michael. "Ride into town and muster the militia; then, bring me word."

Geoffrey and Zeld raced for Baden. They passed the place where the squires caught up with the wagon the night of the theft. They continued in the darkness for another five minutes before they saw the town. When they arrived, Zeld looked for an alarm to ring but couldn't find one. Geoffrey banged on a door. A peasant in a nightshirt and cap answered.

"Ralph, call out the militia."

"Geoffrey?" Ralph asked with a slight German accent, "Is dat you?"

"Yes, assemble the militia, several soldiers are missing," ordered Geoffrey.

Ralph did as Geoffrey instructed. He disappeared for a moment; then, reappeared with a horn and blew it over and over again. Presently villagers peeped out their doors for a better look.

"Get dressed for batt'l!" Ralph bellowed.

A feeling of near panic filled the town. After fifteen minutes the wobbly-kneed militia reported for duty. With half the men wearing their helmets backward, they didn't much resemble a fighting force.

Geoffrey took command. This upset Zeld as Geoffrey did not command him nor could he be trusted. Zeld rode Tiger between Geoffrey and the militia asking, "Ralph, what's the militia's duty in such circumstances?"

"To counterattack and regains da castle," Ralph answered.

"The castle hasn't fallen. You only need to guard it," replied Zeld, which comforted the on-lookers. "Geoffrey and I'll meet you there."

"We'll light the other tower, so you'll know all's well," Geoffrey told Ralph.

117

Zeld nodded his head approvingly. The two of them rode back to the castle. When they arrived, they heard clanging, resembling battle practice. Zeld and Geoffrey looked at each other. This could only mean one thing. Zeld's mouth went dry as he reached for his sword. Geoffrey drew his sword as well and together they charged through the main gate.

CHAPTER SEVENTEEN

The Viking Raid

Intense fear gripped Zeld as he and Geoffrey burst through the castle gate. Aided by the darkness of night, Vikings had crossed the back stream and raided the castle grounds. Sir Tavish, Sir Jaydan, Sir Roger, the hostler and the friars formed a battle-line between the chapel and the Great Hall, attempting to hold the Vikings off. Geoffrey dismounted and joined the defenders at once. Zeld rode to the stables and freed the horses. He chased them through the main gate and sent them running toward the farms. This way, the Vikings couldn't steal the horses.

The kitchen staff joined the defenders, throwing pots, pans, bowls and anything else they could find. A group of Viking archers took up positions on the castle walls and fired arrows at the defenders.

Sir Drain rode in, drew his sword and let out a war cry. He endeavoured to outflank the Vikings alone. Zeld drew his sword and followed Sir Drain's lead, hitting one of the Vikings on the back of the head. He fell hard; then, staggered to his feet, ran to a storage shed, broke the lock with his sword and took an armful of axes.

Other Vikings did the same thing, breaking through doors and stealing booty. Zeld saw a Viking carrying his treasure chest and another had the silver crucifix from the chapel. Yet another carried the page's new bows and arrows.

The Viking archers found their marks and shot down everyone except the knights, Geoffrey and Zeld. Had the knights not worn their armour they would have been shot down as well. Zeld's jumbled emotions of panic and fear surfaced from time to time as he reacted to what he saw. He found himself riding deep behind the Viking line, chasing a Viking carrying a load of pole arms. Zeld struck him in the back and the Viking fell, unable to move.

A second wave of one hundred Vikings charged across the stream into the castle yard. Terrified, Zeld turned around to retreat, but Tiger collided face first with a Viking carrying a load of weapons. Both Tiger and the Viking fell to the ground. Zeld raised his right leg to keep Tiger from landing on it and landed on his head instead. He hastily jumped to his feet and swung his sword at the Viking on the ground.

"Zeldain Halfgod," the Viking called breathlessly from his knees.

Zeld froze. He had nearly killed Guulmate the cook from the Viking ship. Zeld couldn't believe his eyes.

Guulmate asked as he rose to his feet, "Vat vould yuu have us du, giver of guud tings."

"Take this war somewhere else," Zeld shrieked.

Guulmate stumbled backward a few steps revealing his new officer's cloak and let out a yell to retreat. The Vikings looked at each other confused. The archers were about to finish the last two knights; then, everything in the castle would fall into their hands. The yell to retreat didn't seem to make sense.

At just that very moment the militia charged through the main gate. The darkness hid the number of men counterattacking and their motley appearance. The Vikings collected what they could and ran. The archers fired a final volley of arrows on the way out. To keep Tiger from running, Zeld held onto his reigns as tightly as he could while the Vikings ran past.

Zeld could hear wagons rolling in the distance. The Vikings must have hidden them on the other side of the stream. They left as quickly as they had come. Once they retreated, Zeld rode Tiger to the main gate.

Ralph, the militiaman, nervously asked, "Vat do ve do?" A couple of militia dully ran into the buildings looking for any remaining Vikings.

"Why are you asking me?"

"Becausen' everyone else is det or unconscious."

Zeld looked around, realizing he was the only original defender, he reluctantly took charge.

"Take me horse to the farms and have the pages and squires assemble at the supply station. When they're all together, have them report to the castle. Leave no one behind and watch for caltrops. After you've delivered the message, go after the healer," Zeld ordered. He handed Ralph the list of boys' names and their farm families that hung on the main gate.

"I can't read."

"Then take someone with you that can."

"Not von of us can."

"Then take this list to the farms, find one of the students, have them use the list to find everyone, and then bring back a healer," Zeld said angrily.

Zeld ordered the militia to set up an infirmary in the Great Hall. He had the wounded laid out on the tables and a few of the militiamen used what blankets and pillows they could find to comfort the victims. Zeld ordered a couple of militiamen to stack the remaining weapons and armour at the front gate. He spied his sword in the pile. He took it up and slipped it into his belt.

Zeld inspected the castle yard. Clearly, the Vikings had achieved a great victory, as they had carried off a fortune in booty. Zeld surmised their wagons raced for the coast where Viking ships waited to load the treasure.

The students arrived before long bringing with them the horses Zeld freed. Zeld's thoughts became fuzzy and his head ached from the tumble he and Tiger took. He felt relieved when the older boys arrived and he was no longer in command. The squires decided to pursue the Vikings while the pages stayed to guard the castle with the militia.

The healer arrived and began his work. Two unconscious Vikings lay on the battleground. Zeld asked how much it would cost to heal them. The healer answered, "Seventy-five gold, each."

Zeld remarked, "I have that much." Then he said, "No, I don't. The Vikings stole me treasure chest."

After awhile, the healer asked to speak with Father Michael. No one had seen him. The pages searched the grounds and found his body in the library. A group of squires carried him atop the knight's shields into the Great Hall. As his body passed through the crowd of silent onlookers, heads dropped and tears flowed freely. Several boys crossed themselves in prayer. The healer prepared Father Michael and two others for burial. Zeld felt stunned when he saw Father Michael's body. He felt betrayed much like he did once he realized his father, Peter, would never come back.

Zeld felt emotionally and physically drained.

Presently some of the squires came back carrying a few items that fell out of the Viking wagons. They claimed they couldn't see well in the dark and the wagon tracks led everywhere.

Despite feeling dazed from the blow to the head and his deep remorse for Father Michael, Zeld thought of an idea.

"I think I know where they're going. Hey mates, I think I know where they're going!" The idea filled him with energy. "Who wants to come with me?"

Thomas Bandit asked in a disbelieving tone, "Honestly, d'you have a death wish? There are Vikings out there and you want to go ambush them?"

"Well, not exactly, I want our possessions back," muttered Zeld as he mounted Tiger. The McMarr triplets went after their horses and so did James and Robert O'Day.

James asked Robert, "What're you coming for?"

"To see you get murdered."

"Robert and James, will you take a wagon instead of riding your horses?" asked Zeld. "If I'm right, we'll need it to haul our property back." Brian Boru and Sullivan de Bruce volunteered to drive a wagon, too.

After travelling a while, Zeld's headache returned. He explained to the boys they were going to a whirlpool the Viking used as a landmark. The McMarrs knew the location well and could lead the expedition. This gave Zeld a chance to curl up in the back of a wagon and fall asleep.

The company reached the whirlpool early in the morning. The triplets rode for the McMarr Manor for help. The others turned the wagons around, so they could return the way they came quickly in case any Vikings showed up.

When Zeld awoke, he looked out to sea. It surprised him the whirlpool remained so close to the shore. It hadn't appeared that close when he and Lightning swam all night. Zeld walked over to it and saw a brown bottle swirling. Sometimes it swung out near the shore and other times it stayed close to the centre.

Zeld retrieved a pole arm from a wagon and tried several times to catch the bottle. He managed to take a few steps into the swirling water and hooked it. Back on shore, he pulled out the cork and found the bottle contained a large clear stone. Something inside the bottle had hardened to form it. Zeld placed the familiar looking bottle on the beach.

He spied something else swirling. It resembled one of his mother's baskets. Then Zeld minded letting go of a basket the night he and Lightning swam in the sea. He tried to remember what he had left behind and hoped to rescue the basket and its contents. Zeld couldn't reach it with the pole arm, so he rolled two rocks into the water, building a break in the whirlpool. He snagged the basket and managed to pull it to the shore.

Although the basket lay thrashed in his hands, he could still see some of the knots his mother had tied to hold it together. He minded his mother's long fingers and watching her work out the details of building baskets. A tear ran down his cheek as he realized how much he missed his family.

He found the dragon meat had remained inside, but hardened and shrunk. It felt heavy; however, it had maintained its original shape, including two holes near the top, like a stone for a necklace. The moment Zeld touched it he felt power surge into his body. When Zeld placed the meat on a rock he felt the power diminish. He lifted the stone again and the feeling came back.

Zeld kept the bottle and the stone-like piece of meat and wandered back to the wagons. The other pages ran around the rocky shoreline. They screamed and laughed but Zeld couldn't understand a single word they said. He situated the bottle on the seat of the closest wagon and held onto the meat.

"We did it, Zeld," said Robert O'Day in a truly jolly voice as he came back from the beach.

Zeld had no idea what Robert meant.

"Loads of bits and snippets are hidden in the rocks," Robert explained pointing to the rocks along the shoreline. Zeld couldn't see a thing, so he climbed onto the seat of the wagon for a better view. The bottle rolled off the seat and shattered on the rocky ground below. Zeld still couldn't see anything, so he climbed down from the wagon and collected the stone from the bottle fragments. The hardened white liquid had taken the shape of the bottom of the bottle, giving one side a rounded edge. It felt smooth and cool. He swept the dangerous looking broken glass away from the road with his foot.

Zeld walked down to the beach with Robert and saw for himself the large amount of treasure scattered among the rocks. The farther he walked, the more he found. By the time he reached the water's edge he could see hundreds of items. Zeld looked for things belonging to the school and found several bows and arrows. He found the alarm bell and finally his treasure chest. The lock was still fastened in its place, which told Zeld everything remained inside.

Sullivan said, "This is the area where the Vikings'll return to next as it has the most valuable items." Brian and Sullivan loaded those items into the wagons first.

Zeld and his mates rolled rocks into a defensive position as Sir Jaydan had taught them to do, in case of trouble. James moved the wagons closer to the work site. Robert moved the bows and arrows to Zeld's rocks along with a couple of axes. The boys carried the items past the line of rocks to the wagons. Zeld placed all of his belongings, including the hard meat and smooth stone, into his treasure chest and took out his purse of gold, tying it to his belt.

Zeld and Brian Boru carried Zeld's treasure chest to the nearest wagon. It landed with a thud. As the thud rang out, the McMarr triplets rode hard and fast over a hill in the distance. At first Zeld saw no need for this, but after they rode fifty yards, four Vikings rode over the hill chasing them. Three more Vikings attacked from a nearby cave. The boys had truly landed themselves in grave danger.

CHAPTER Eighteen

What Are Mates For?

The thunderous sound of horse's hoofs beating on the ground grew louder as Zeld watched the Vikings charging down the beach on horseback. Then he turned sharply and watched as more Vikings came running toward them from a cave. For a long moment the situation didn't seem real. He instinctively wanted to run, but he minded what he had done to the Vikings at the school and knew he wouldn't make it far. The tension grew as the Vikings drew nearer. Just as Zeld realized he would have to fight, Robert broke the silence and ordered, "Everyone take a bow and aim at a different Viking!"

Zeld, Brian, Robert, Sullivan and James dashed for the protection of the stone wall.

"We should aim at the same Viking. I saw it at the castle and it works better," Zeld told the other boys.

"All right, which one do we shoot?" Robert conceded.

"With these bows we had better try for the closest one, and everyone aim here," ordered Zeld, pointing to the V shape on his leather armour.

The McMarrs galloped between the end of the rock wall and the wagons and kept going. The first Viking following them received five arrows in the chest. The blow hit so hard he fell from his horse and landed with a thud on a large stone. The other Viking riders rode around the far side of the wagons, so the boys couldn't have a good shot at them. Then, the Vikings circled around behind the wagons to attack the boys from the rear. The Vikings from the cave joined them.

They decided not to charge their horses through the rocks to avoid injuring them. Instead they dismounted and attacked on foot. The McMarrs saw the strategy and circled around to help.

Zeld and the other pages nervously fired at the closest Viking but every arrow ricocheted off the rocks the Vikings used for cover. The Vikings crept closer giving the boys only just time for one more volley before toe to toe combat. Fear seized Zeld's heart. The group fired on an attacker only 10 yards away and one of the arrows went through his foot, pegging him to the ground. The pages drew their swords and axes.

Meanwhile, the McMarr's clobbered the Viking guarding the horses. Odin and Oles ran to retrieve the pole arms in the wagons while Oars stampeded the Vikings' horses through the rough rocks and into the Vikings themselves. Clearly, he didn't care if their horses were injured. The Vikings dove out of the way to avoid being trampled, except for the unlucky one with his foot pegged to the ground. The pages at the wall watched the horses approach and ducked a split second before the horses jumped to clear the wall.

Zeld ordered the pages to take up the bows and arrows again. They saw the Vikings regrouping and the pages fired a couple of volleys at them. In turn, the Vikings rapidly rolled a few rocks together building their own makeshift wall and causing a stalemate.

Suddenly, the wagons moved. The McMarrs were leading a retreat much to Zeld surprise and relief. Oars rounded up all the horses while Oles and Odin drove the wagons. The pages at the wall made a desperate dash for the wagons. The Vikings hurled Scandinavian throwing axes at them and one hit Sullivan de Bruce in the leg. He fell with a nasty cut. Oles stopped his wagon and somersaulted from the front seat to the back, landing on his feet with his pole arm still in readiness.

The Vikings chased the pages who ran for the wagons. Brian Boru assisted Sullivan into the wagon, and then in a burst of speed ran behind the Vikings. He hit one of them from behind with his sword. The Viking turned unharmed and Brian used another burst of speed to retreat.

Two of the Vikings reached a wagon and Oles struck one of them in the throat with a pole arm. A throwing axe from the other hit Oles hard and he dropped unconscious next to Sullivan. Sullivan reached back clutching the axe that hit Oles. He threw it hard at a Viking standing no more than three feet away. The axe bounced off his skull and the Viking dropped, unconscious, to the ground.

James O'Day climbed into the driver's seat and started one of the wagons moving again. Zeld, Robert and Brian fought toe to toe with the Vikings. The momentum of the battle shifted due to the Viking's larger size.

As he fought, Zeld's mouth went dry and his heart beat faster than he could ever remember. The Viking he fought, sliced him deep enough to draw blood on his right shoulder and instinctively Zeld switched his sword to his left hand.

Sullivan took up a pole arm in the back of the wagon and endeavoured to help. Robert O'Day chanced a lucky blow and stabbed a Viking so hard he fell to the ground, but his sword remained protruding from the Viking's shoulder and he couldn't free it. One of the attackers kicked Robert's hands free of the sword, leaving him without a weapon. Robert received a hard blow from a war hammer that knocked him breathless to the ground.

Lightning charged into the battle pawing his front hooves. He beat down one of the Vikings and chased the last one away. Robert crawled gingerly into the back of the nearest wagon.

Zeld looked around for bandages but didn't find any. He looked in his treasure chest to see if he had anything that could help and Odin darted into the rocks looking for anything that might be useful. He found four crossbows with bolts but nothing that could stop Zeld and Sullivan's bleeding. Zeld looked in his treasure chest and pulled out the smooth stone. Thinking it might feel cool, he placed it against his wound. As soon as the stone touched him, the cut started tickling. He looked down with amazement as he saw the stone healing him. When the tickling stopped, he rubbed the stone on Sullivan's wound. It healed his cut as well.

He rubbed it on Oles' broken ribs. Oles laughed in his sleep, so Zeld knew it had worked. When Zeld removed the stone from Oles ribs, the stone's colour had changed, from a glowing bright white into a pale flat white. Zeld attempted to use it on Brian and Robert, but it had no effect.

A few minutes later, Oles awoke in the back of the wagon. He said, "I had a nightmare." Then he looked at his brothers and teased, "Oh, no – er – it's unbelievable, there really are three of me!"

The boys gathered around to make sure he merely jested and did not suffer from delirium. Of the eight boys, six remained healthy, while Brian and Robert needed medical attention. Staying in the open meant remaining vulnerable, so the boys discussed their situation, hoping to find a way out of danger.

Odin explained what went awry earlier. "We found the road to our manor blocked by Vikings, so we made a run for it. At first, we thought we'd outrun them but everywhere we went, we found more Vikings. Finally, we came here outta desperation."

"Speaking of Vikings everywhere," said Zeld. "Didja see the three who attacked outta that cave?" He pointed in the direction they had come from. "I'm wondering if there's more hiding inside."

"Let's find out, or we could be very sorry," Robert said gravely.

Brian and Zeld drove the wagons near the cave and each of the eight pages held a weapon prepared to strike as they nervously waited to rush inside. Zeld took a deep breath, and then yelled, "NOW!" and the boys burst into the cave. They found it full of English prisoners headed for the slave trade. They'd been tied up with heavy rope and judging by the scratches around the wrists Zeld knew they were desperately trying to free themselves before the Vikings returned.

The boys cut their ropes and told them they had defeated the Vikings. After freeing the prisoners, the pages huddled for a minute to discuss their options. The prisoners gathered around them hoping the boys knew what to do.

"We can stay here or we can attempt an escape. Those are our options," explained Odin.

"If we stay, it'll mean fighting without food or water for an indefinite period of time. If we leave, we must find food and water soon," added Oles.

"You three live 'round here. Where can we go?" asked Robert.

The McMarrs looked at each other and said in unison, "Home."

"The manor is less than five miles from here," said Oars.

The pages stripped the dead and dressed themselves as Vikings. They told the prisoners to climb into the wagons and pretend they were still captured. The boys held on to the weapons they found on the beach or hid them behind the prisoner's backs.

Oars pulled Zeld aside and told him the brothers McMarrs had kept a secret. They spoke their parent's native language of

Norwegian. This was considered an enormous disgrace among the upper class, but in the present circumstances it could prove an advantage. With this in mind, the triplets drove the wagons. If stopped, the McMarrs would speak to the Vikings and attempt to bluff their way through. Zeld felt a little better knowing the boys had a good chance of surviving this sticky situation. After all, the adventure had gone rather badly.

They made their way up the beach a mile and passed a group of archers headed down the beach. The boys tried to manoeuvre past without saying anything.

The commander called, "Are the pests still held up in the rocks?"

Oles face showed relief they hadn't been recognized, he replied in Norwegian, "Yes, and they threw axes at us. We're moving these prisoners closer to the ships and we'll leave the rascals at the beach to you. When we left, they laid down pretending to be dead."

"We'll finish them," replied the commander, motioning for the rest of the men to follow him.

Once out of sight, Sullivan asked, "Does your mum know you're such a convincing liar?"

Oles answered, "No, and she'd better not find out either or I'll set the Vikings after you. I can manage it, too."

Very few Vikings gave them a second look, as they were busy loading and shipping treasure to the coast. Other Vikings stood guard in key locations. The boys urged the horses to go a wee bit faster whenever they came upon a clear stretch. Zeld felt uneasy about the situation and expected the Vikings they sent to the beach to come after them any second.

While pushing forward, the greenery closed around the boys, making it impossible to see what lay ahead. Zeld worried about a possible ambush.

They ran into a check point with several large Vikings. The Vikings told them where to take the prisoners as if they didn't know. The directions they gave took them within a quarter mile of the manor.

"The plan is obvious," said Zeld. "We'll take the wagons as close as we can, and then walk the remainder of the way."

When they reached their turnoff at the crossroads, they didn't take it. Oles led the group straight instead, trying to approach the manor's main gate. Several Viking archers appeared from their hiding places and corrected the wagons. One archer bellowed something and Oles interpreted it. "Turn around! We're not raiding that place!" Then Oles added, "He means the manor." One Viking stepped up to the wagon giving instructions and pointing another direction.

Oles turned the wagon as directed.

"Rats, we were almost there," whispered Oles once out of earshot of the Vikings.

"We'll make it there soon enough," said Odin. "Brilliant try, Oles. We almost drove the wagons through the front gate."

"Where are we going?" asked one of the passengers.

"To the McMarr Manor," Zeld answered.

"McMarr is one of the Vikings, you idiot," the passenger yelled.

"If he's one of the Vikings; then, why did three of his sons jeopardize their lives to save *you*? They could've deserted you or fought for the other side, but instead they rescued you," Zeld said reassuring the prisoners.

"I think it's a trick," the man sputtered fearfully.

"Anytime you want to leave, you're free to go," Zeld said hoping the man had enough sense to stay with the group. Otherwise, Zeld would have to knock him unconscious and bring him along all the same.

The man sat quietly. The look on his face told Zeld he didn't enjoy his dilemma.

"The manor is just there. Each of us McMarrs will lead a group to it," said Oars.

As they travelled Zeld caught glimpses of the manor in the distance. He felt much better knowing they were almost there.

Oles led the weakest group first, including Sullivan and Robert. Odin pulled the wagon to the right side of the road at the bottom of a ravine and hid it with some brush. He then led a second group toward the manor.

Oars drove the other wagon over the next hill hiding it behind a mound of dirt. He brushed away their tracks. Oars led the last group toward the manor and Zeld brought the horses.

Odin's group reached the manor. He yelled something in Norwegian to the men on the walls and the guards yelled back. Odin repeated the message in English informing the guards that three groups and eight horses were approaching the manor. It took considerable time for all three groups to make it in safely but they did.

Marta McMarr ran down from her battle station and kissed her sons' faces once they entered the manor. She told them she'd never seen a worse encounter.

"The Vikings made it all the way to the school and stole everything they could carry," Oles reported through his tears.

"We freed some prisoners and brought them here," reported Odin.

Jens Sr. made it down from his station and looked at the prisoners. "Have you been followed?" He asked.

"No," called the triplets in unison.

"There are archers at the Millington Crossroads," Odin said wearily.

"We saved these people at the southward giant cave near the whirlpool," said Oles.

"What happened to your teachers? Was anyone hurt?" asked Jens Sr.

"Our teachers lay either injured or dead and we've been wounded as well," answered Oars.

"These people are famished, they've been through quite an ordeal," Zeld reported.

Zeld, the other boys and the newly freed prisoners stood watch at the walls, so the kitchen staff could return to their duties. Marta took command of the kitchen crew and served vegetable stew. The delicious stew made everyone feel a bit better.

As he ate, a look of deep contemplation came over Jens Sr.'s face. "Perhaps we shouldn't hide here like frightened mice. Perhaps we should raid the Vikings!" Jens Sr. told Marta.

CHAPTER Nineteen

Frightened Mice

"Y OU'LL NOT TAKE ME BOYS OUT INTO THAT NIGHTMARE AGAIN, THEY'VE SEEN ENOUGH FIGHTING!" Marta shouted out in a fully emotional outburst of panic. "They're too emotionally drained to take more of this savagery!"

"In three hours it will be dusk. I'll take a few of me soldiers and slip out of the manor. I'm certain sure we can save Christians from the slavers," said Jens Sr. in a comforting tone. Marta's countenance changed and she indicated her approval by nodding her head.

When the time came the triplets took Zeld with them to the armoury, where he issued twenty bows. The other boys issued quivers with arrows, swords and shields. The men left the castle in two groups and returned an hour after dusk. Jens Sr. and his men drove the school's wagons into the manor with fourteen unconscious Vikings laying in the back.

Jens Sr. claimed to have set up an ambush at the crossroads even a brown hare couldn't hope to make it through. That night Zeld awoke three times as loads of English prisoners that had been fated for the slave ships were miraculously saved and sent to the manor.

The next morning, Zeld could have sworn he saw King Henry's clerk mysteriously appear out of thin air. Zeld, decided to stay within earshot so he could overhear the clerk's conversation in the yard with Jens Sr., "King Henry has agreed to the following peace terms: One and a half million silver pieces, plus the right for Scandinavians to purchase English land and full citizenship status in the courts and schools. We lost five castles during the attack and five hundred English citizens were enslaved."

Jens Sr. said with a smile, "Make that four hundred." He took the clerk to the former prisoners and showed him the people they'd saved. The clerk made a list of their one hundred and one names while shaking his head repeatedly with a grand smile.

The king's clerk looked most impressed and told Jens Sr., "You've certainly earned a smashing reward from the king and if he hadn't just lost every silver piece in the kingdom, he'd buy you something befitting your outstanding deed. Instead, King Henry is asking a favour. The Vikings can purchase land, they've the money to afford it and there is plenty of damaged property that could sell at a most affordable rate."

"Inform King Henry I'll buy as much land as I can and I'll try to regulate who comes and goes," said Jens Sr., guessing at what he'd be asked.

"Thank you," said the clerk.

Zeld felt extremely nervous, even after the Vikings left. He flinched at loud noises. He felt better when Dando asked him and the other boys to help stockpile a few loads of stone for a couple of towers on his family's lands. At least I'll have something to take me mind off the raid, he thought gratefully. Zeld borrowed a dwarven axe from the manor's stores and showed the other boys how to chip the round rocks into stone bricks. The other boys attempted it but didn't do nearly as well as Zeld.

On Sunday the freed prisoners attended church at the manor. In the afternoon the McMarrs held a feast celebrating the mercies of God in saving the one hundred and one prisoners. They ate roasted pork, sourdough bread, fresh apples and platters of farm-fresh creamed vegetables in the Great Hall. Zeld felt much better after eating well. Somehow, the feast helped bring the entire Viking raid episode to a close.

Zeld and the other pages returned to school accompanied by the host of saved prisoners in organized travelling groups. He noticed members of their lot had sustained several small nagging injuries. He pulled out his healing stone, which glowed brightly again, and went from person to person using it. He saw the astonishment on the people's faces as he healed them. He also heard the words, "Thank you" many times.

As they travelled to the school, a few people turned off here and there in smaller groups on side roads, until only the pages

134

remained.

Quiet anticipation filled the last few miles. Zeld hoped with all sincerity the school hadn't fallen to the Vikings. After all, the Vikings could have regrouped and counterattacked after he and the others left. They passed the farms and the supply station. Oars looked for a new carved message but found nothing. None of the farms showed any type of damage.

As they climbed to the top of the last hill and saw the castle standing ahead of them, they stopped the wagons and looked around. Oles called out, "Come here, mates."

They left their wagons and gathered together in a circle. Oles said, "We don't know what we're gonna discover down the hill. We didn't know what we'd discover when we went after the school's treasure. If we'd panicked and not fought together, some of us would certainly be dead right now. Let's make an everlasting oath to always fight together on the side of righteousness and to keep watch over each other. Everyone hold out your right fist."

The boys put their fists together in the middle of the circle.

Oles said, "Repeat after me. I'll be true to this oath of brotherhood. To fight one another's battles and to always be true mates." Zeld and his mates repeated the oath; then, they looked at each other, Oles, Oars, Odin, James, Robert, Sullivan, Brian and Zeld. They climbed back into the wagons and rode to find whatever awaited them at the school.

As the wagons reached the castle, a funeral procession left the main gate. The body of Father Michael lay in the first wagon and John and Bract, the two kitchen helpers, rested in the second. The pages stood in the wagons and placed their right fist over their hearts, saluting the procession. They joined it and loaded as many mourners in the back of their two wagons as could fit. The procession went to the cemetery at Baden. The friars sang a Gregorian chant all the way to the graves.

At the cemetery the open graves awaited them. Zeld estimated the entire town of Baden attended the services. Sir Tavish, Sir Jaydan, Sir Roger and Sir Drain took turns speaking in reverent tones, of the many things Father Michael had done to shape the school into a highly successful institution. Mrs. Palfreeman cried her way through a tearful farewell to John and Bract.

Zeld felt very uneasy about the battle. The Viking raid felt very wrong. After all, what right did the Vikings have to come and plunder their shores? While at the same time he had raided them back and this didn't feel wrong at all. The deaths of the three men at the hand of the Vikings left Zeld in shock. He thought it odd he knew the three men who had died, but it took attending the funeral before he realized Father Michael wouldn't return. Zeld wanted to cry but somehow his tears failed to come. He listened to the speeches feeling remorse and mournfulness.

136

After the funeral, the townsfolk journeyed home and most of the remaining crowd went to the school. Zeld and his mates watched as the coffin lids were nailed into place, followed by the lowering of the coffins into the graves by ropes. The Baden town militia waited for nearly everyone to leave before using their spades to fill the graves.

That day the school held no classes. The school staff completed an inventory of the remaining supplies. Sullivan retrieved the school's bows from the wagon and turned them over to Sir Roger.

"We found a few items taken from the school. They were hidden on a rocky beach only just south of the Scottish border," Sullivan told Sir Roger. The pages produced an assorted lot of weapons and treasure including Zeld's treasure chest.

"We battled with the Vikings at the beach and Lord McMarr set an ambush near his manor," continued Sullivan.

"The McMarr Manor is across the border in Scotland," said Sir Tavish, looking a bit bewildered as he joined Sir Roger.

"That's correct, and so were we."

"I want to hear all about this adventure," said Sir Tavish showing great interest, "and I want the rest of the knights to hear it as well."

After the knights sat down on benches in front of the chapel, Sullivan told his story. He told them about the whirlpool and the beach, the attack and the cave with the prisoners. He followed that up with their journey to the McMarr Manor. He finished by telling them about the ambushes at the crossroads.

Zeld added that the king's clerk arrived at the manor and told Jens Sr. about the peace terms the king agreed to. "One and a half million silver pieces and rights as citizens," Zeld repeated.

"Blimey, more problems," said Sir Tavish in a disturbed tone. "Part of that money will certainly come out of our school funds, you can tot up on it. We don't have the materials to run a school and we're understaffed. That reminds me, Zeld, the healer couldn't remember what you asked him to do with the two Vikings you struck down, so he healed them and he is waiting for you to pay him."

"I can do that," said Zeld, smiling.

"I believe the next schoolmaster will have a trying time keeping the school open. We're about to lose a king's ransom to pay for the treaty and we'll be unable to replace the equipment we lost. This means we'll have more lessons about living off the land and making homemade weapons instead of learning how to wield the best ones," explained Sir Jaydan.

"Yes, our curriculum has changed," Sir Roger said wearily.

"Most schoolmasters have their own ideas of what should be taught as well. This may bring a bigger change than anything else," said Sir Tavish still showing his concern.

When the pages returned from bathing, Zeld went to the kitchen and nicked an apple. He carried it over to Lightning and fed it to him as a reward. Zeld put his arms around the horse's neck and whispered, "Thank you me friend, that's the second time you saved me life."

The boys spent the remainder of the day playing chess and telling family stories in the Great Hall. Zeld noticed the chess set with Gunter Sims' name on it remained on the shelf. He glanced around and when he couldn't see Gunter, he asked Friar Timothy about him.

"He's one of the squires that went missing during the Viking raid. No one has seen nor heard from him since."

CHAPTER TWENTY

Stolen Goods

Zeld sat reverently in the chapel the next morning and listened as Friar Martin prayed from the pulpit for the safe return of Squires Norton Duval, Gunter Sims and Donald Doolittle. The situation appeared bleak for the missing squires.

To continue classes the knights gathered supplies from several different sources, including the weapons the pages brought back and kite shields from the Baden town militia. This piecemeal approach foreshadowed other future changes the school would go through.

Zeld went with Sir Drain Monday evening in a wagon to the healer's shop. Zeld paid the medical bills for the two Vikings from the raid. The Vikings had spent the last few days assisting the healer with trying to catch up with his work.

Upon the exchange of money, Zeld became the master of the Vikings. According to English law any enemy soldier captured during a battle must pay a ransom for his release. If no money could be raised, the Lord could execute the prisoners or show mercy and let them join his kingdom. The English considered it honourable to save Vikings from death and to keep them as soldiers. So that's exactly what Zeld did.

Zeld pointed to the back of the wagon and the soldiers climbed in. He hadn't thought ahead and was very concerned as to what he should have the Vikings do now he was their Lord. He considered sending them home to his mum but realized they'd simply vanish along the way.

Sir Drain drove the wagon to the sheriff's office. He noticed Zeld's concerned expression and said, "Zeld, you should have the two of them work in your mine."

Zeld found it rather odd Sir Drain would play the adviser to him. Only a family member or trusted ally should do that, Zeld thought. Not wishing to be rude, but wondering what Sir Drain referred to, Zeld asked, "What mine?"

"Come with me into the sheriff's office."

Zeld took a good look at the sheriff for the first time. He had slightly wavy auburn-hair, with a part on the right side, blue eyes and a fair complexion. As the sheriff stood to welcome them, Zeld noticed his height and powerful arms. The sheriff's coat of arms consisted of six spurs arranged in a circular pattern.

Sir Drain, Zeld and the two soldiers walked into the sheriff's office. To Zeld's surprise Sir Drain produced a parchment with a mining claim prepared for signing. Zeld leaned over and signed it atop the sheriff's desk and paid a filing fee of ten silver. With the deed issued, Zeld became the proud new owner of the gold mine in Waltham Forest near the Prince Valiant School. Then Zeld asked about the Hessens miners on his property.

"If they're mining illegally, I'll send men to stop them and confiscate their equipment," said the sheriff in a serious tone.

"Then do it!" demanded Zeld. "I want me mine cleared of thieves."

The sheriff smiled at Zeld's grit. He said, "Let me write the directions on parchment and we'll have your mine free of thieves in a few days."

When finished, Zeld left the sheriff's office but didn't leave town. He took the wagon, with everyone in it, to a shop and bought a few items he needed: a rope, a file and a shoulder bag. At the bakery he bought tarts for his mates. Respectfully, the baker wrapped the tarts in muslin to keep them clean and placed them carefully into Zeld's new shoulder bag.

When they arrived at the school, the cook still didn't have dinner ready. With the cook's assistants gone, the problem of preparing meals on time had grown worse than ever. While they waited in the Great Hall, Friar Timothy asked Zeld if his two Viking soldiers could help in the kitchen. Zeld agreed.

When Friar Timothy spoke to the cook in the kitchen, his suggestion met with stiff opposition. Mrs. Palfreeman was in a right state and yelled so loudly Zeld heard her words in the next room, "YOU WANT ME TO LET THE MURDEROUS SCOUN-

DRELS WORK IN THE SELF SAME KITCHEN JOHN AND BRACT TRIED TO DEFEND!"

Zeld couldn't hear Friar Timothy response but a moment later his two men were busy in the kitchen. As it worked out the soldiers really made a difference, serving dinner in fifteen minutes.

Surprised and pleased, Friar Timothy asked, "Zeld, do you think we could make it a permanent arrangement?"

Zeld agreed. "If they can work for their room and board; then, it's all right." He felt relieved to have a place for his men.

The cook seemed pleased with their work but continued to keep a sharp eye on the two. Zeld wished all of his decisions were made so easily.

141

The king's clerk came a few days later, and in a private meeting with the staff in the library, he gave the school a letter soliciting 100,000 silver pieces from their funds. It also informed them the other schools under King Henry had to contribute as well. It named the five castles that fell, due to explosive dragon bones smashing through the walls: Zebloft, Craton, Meloth, Zorn and Bitzen. Fortunately, the Vikings had abandoned the castles instead of settling a new colony as they sometimes did.

The letter also claimed King Henry placed what soldiers he could spare on guard duty at the castles until all the stonemasons in England could answer his summons to repair the walls, before winter, if possible.

"I daresay, there it is," commented Sir Tavish in an aggravated tone, "Our money and our stonemasons."

"There may be guard duty assignments as well," added the clerk abruptly.

"We'll be glad to send our battle-hardened pages into combat," said Sir Tavish with a forced chuckle.

That night after everyone fell asleep, someone pounded frantically on the gate. Zeld awoke wondering what had happened. He watched outside his barracks door with his mates and watched as the farm families poured through the front gate demanding protection.

"THE VIKINGS ARE BACK!" they cried.

In what had become an all too familiar pattern, the alarm rang, the towers were lit, the squires mounted for action and the pages guarded the castle. The squires rode in the direction of the farms. Some pages appeared terrified, while Zeld and his mates remained calm. Zeld had learned he shouldn't panic until he actually saw the Vikings.

That night a light rain fell making the ground slippery. The cloud cover made the hunt for the Vikings difficult, as not even the sparse moonlight could shine through.

The squires returned and reported to Sir Tavish in front of everyone that they saw several farm animals scattered throughout the woods. They saw a few shadowy figures, too, but avoided fighting with them. Nothing more could be done until morning. The farmers refused to go home. They slept in the Great Hall for the night and the squires took turns keeping watch.

The next morning, the squires found that several farm wagons had gone missing. Zeld overheard one of the squires reporting to Sir Tavish, "Strangely enough no wagon tracks led from the barns, but somehow the farm wagons have vanished all the same."

Sir Tavish set up patrols to look for additional clues. They found that several wagon tracks appeared on the road heading south, and then turned west. The school mobilized to help.

With the combination of 100,000 silver coming from the funds, poor supplies, and now with the possibility of a food shortage, the school was in jeopardy of closing.

Sir Tavish used the school as headquarters for the search parties. He established groups of four by pairing two new boys and two squires. Zeld and Edward of Peele were paired with Richard du Lake and John Dudley. They drew the assignment to search the road west of the castle across the stream.

Zeld knelt down in front of his open treasure chest wondering what he should take. He finally decided on taking his money and his healing and strength stones. He dressed in his chainmail armour for the first time and carried his sword. He locked his treasure chest and left. The armour felt heavy and Tiger attempted to dismount him, showing he didn't appreciate the extra weight either.

The party chanced upon a fork in the road. They chose to explore the right fork, travelling the road until they heard something in the bushes. They found a lost pig. John Dudley sent Zeld and Edward to catch the pig, but wearing armour made the job much more difficult than usual. Finally, Edward caught hold of one of the pig's hind legs and Zeld moved in and lifted it off the ground. The pig squealed and thrashed about but Zeld didn't let go because if he did they'd have to catch it all over again. Edward mounted his horse and Zeld lifted the pig up to him.

"Hold a moment. Use this staff and rope to tie the pig's legs, and then carry the pig on the staff," ordered Richard du Lake.

"Won't the pig hang upside down?" asked Edward.

"Yes, it will, but an upside down pig on a staff is much less trouble than a kicking and squealing pig sharing your saddle," Richard said cleverly.

Zeld and Edward wasted no time. Zeld held the pig while Edward tied the knots. Zeld watched Edward but had no idea what type of knot he tied. Zeld asked, "If you have time will you teach me some knots?"

"Sure," replied Edward politely. "How about on Sunday?"

"Excellent," said Zeld.

Richard and John held the staff while Zeld and Edward mounted; then, the older boys handed the pig to the younger ones. They carried the pig to the castle. Zeld wondered why they didn't tie the pig to a tree and leave it there. It would've saved a considerable amount of time.

Zeld found it interesting that time didn't concern anyone. No one hurried. His whole life he had hurried. He rushed to escape from his family's castle the night his father died. Again they rushed when they first settled in Denmark to find food and build a shelter.

It took forty-five minutes for the pages to reach the castle, deliver the pig and return. They continued the search but only ran into a couple of wild birds and a small herd of deer grazing in a meadow. After awhile, the search party came to a stream where they stopped to water the horses.

While looking down in the water, Richard du Lake saw a Viking gauntlet. He dismounted and collected it. One of the fingers pointed upstream, so he walked in that direction and found a second Viking gauntlet. It too had a finger pointing upstream, so he continued in that direction. Richard excitedly called to the others. John, Richard and Zeld continued cautiously and found more items. The markings led to a small crack in the side of a cliff. The other three boys appeared confused. Zeld understood perfectly what he looked at and used the pig staff to pry open the crack into a doorway.

John Dudley asked, "How'd you do that?"

"It's an old dwarven trick," Zeld answered with a hint of smugness in his voice.

Zeld slipped in and sidestepped to the right. The others followed him tiptoeing. When their eyes adjusted, they could see a mine shaft. They followed it cautiously for two hundred paces, the light growing dimmer with each step. When they spied a crack of light ahead, John said, "I think it's the Viking's headquarters." Zeld stepped forward and silently placed his pig staff into the opening while the others slowly drew their swords. Zeld stepped anxiously around to one side and prepared to pry the secret passage open with one good shove.

He pulled hard and quick, opening the secret passage. The boys charged through the opening only to find they'd stepped straight through the mountain to come out on the other side by means of a dwarven tunnel.

"Braggadocios," said Zeld as the other boys sheathed their swords.

Another road lay only 10 yards away. They looked for wagon tracks but couldn't find any. Zeld had a brilliant idea. He walked down to the new road and scratched a Z in a rock with his sword. The boys watched the road for awhile, and then went back to the other side of the tunnel. Zeld marked a dead tree on this side with a Z as well. The party closed both entrances.

While the other boys could hardly wait to tell their mates about the cave, Zeld thought of ways he could use the tunnel when it came time to attack Hesse. Zeld also thought it would make an excellent place for a camp out. The trail turned cold after that, at least for Zeld's group, and they rode back to the school.

Crispyn directed Zeld up the chapel stairs to Father Michael's office where Sir Roger waited for news from the search. Zeld opened the door quietly and slipped silently into the office. Sir Roger sat in a chair, with his back to the door looking inside a black linen bag when Zeld approached.

Zeld wondered what Sir Roger stared at so intently and leaned over to peek into the bag. He spied a large stone and in the stone appeared riders on horses. Squinting for a better view Zeld could see Odin, Oars, Quincy O'Mally and Jarell Goldenstaff. Zeld watched for a moment and saw the boys riding on the road. A sign read, "Zorn Castle - 3 miles."

Suddenly, Sir Roger sprang to his feet. He manhandled Zeld by tossing him as if he were an intruder against the far wall. He drew his sword and held the tip at Zeld's throat.

"It's me! Zeld!"

"What are you doing in here?" asked Sir Roger as he sheathed his sword.

"I came to report the road we were assigned to search is clear," muttered Zeld.

145

I suppose you saw the amulet of visions?" asked Sir Roger pointing to the black bag.

"Yeah," answered Zeld, rather pleased with his detective work.

"Honestly, try to keep it a secret, will you?" Sir Roger asked.

"All right," answered Zeld.

"Come, sit here, and look in properly," Sir Roger ordered, pulling a chair around for him.

Zeld quickly obeyed and Sir Roger watched the stone from over the top of Zeld's head. They watched as the same group from earlier found wagon tracks on the road. Interestingly the tracks started in the middle of the road as if the wagons had magically appeared there.

Jarell and his companions followed the wagon tracks into Zorn Valley where they ran into a farmer's market day. Through the stone, Zeld could hear the men calling out the prices. The farmers sold the animals at extremely high prices from the back of their wagons, forcing the local people to pay much more than normal or go without food. The four riders rode up and down the street trying to tell the thieves from the farmers. At the end of the market, they huddled while still mounted.

"No one looked familiar to me," said Odin.

"Nor me," added Oars.

"I spied a familiar wagon from the Castles and Caverns farms," said Quincy pointing. "Just there." Jarell led the others over and they surrounded the wagon. He forbade the suspected thieves to sell any of the animals. The boys waited for a reaction and received a doozey. The thieves and farmers alike turned on them, throwing things and calling them names.

Jarell ordered the entire market closed. The people weren't fond of his decision, but they couldn't do anything to stop him; after all, knights and squires had a duty to right wrongs and maintain order. Zeld folded his arms and nodded his head in agreement with Jarell's actions. Jarell further ordered all the wagons and animals remain behind.

Zeld thought it fortunate the thieves hadn't sold many of the animals. The people left together in one ill-tempered knot, mumbling something about finding weapons.

146   The stone changed scenes, and Zeld watch Oles, Brian Boru, Wilhelm of Prussia and Steven Saint James searching on an old mining road. They also followed a set of wagon tracks that merely appeared out of nowhere. They came to an area with a stream on their left and a cliff wall on the right. A large pile of rocks presently fell from the cliff, and with them, a young man. The rockslide missed the party by only inches and the boy fell landing unconscious directly in front of them.

Sir Roger said, "Ah, I see Jens Jr. has returned, with quite a spectacular entrance I daresay."

Zeld looked closely at the boy who had fallen and felt strangely surprised to see he had dark hair and eyes, with a dark complexion. Oddly enough he didn't resemble his brothers.

Oles jumped off his horse and ran to help with Brian close behind. They took care of Jens Jr. while Wilhelm and Steven charged up a slope to the top of the cliff. At the top, a blue light surrounded Steven's horse Blacky. The horse rose in the air and floated toward the cliff. Steven dove off and landed unharmed in the greenery. Blacky floated past the edge of the cliff. Then the blue light disappeared and Blacky fell hard.

Steven ran for an open area and Wilhelm rode to his aid. Steven vaulted onto the horse's back like the boys had practiced in the horse rescue event. The two of them retreated to the safety of the road. Two close calls with death were enough for them.

Steven crept over to Blacky and found she'd died upon impact. Steven stroked Blacky with his hand a few times as if she were still alive, and then with tears streaming down his face, he removed the saddle. When they headed back to the school, they ran into Sir Tavish and reported their adventure. Sir Tavish sent the stonemasons along with several squires to clear the rockslide and remove the horse.

Sir Tavish then rode with a group of six heavily armed squires to investigate the incident. His group also included the original four riders. Once they reached the site they followed the wagon tracks at a quick gallop. The tracks continued for another mile, and then disappeared without trace. The squires split up to search the area, but found nothing.

Zeld heard Sir Tavish's say, "What goes up must come down." After a wider search, in which the riders rode in pairs, they found the tracks restarted on the other side of a steep hill. They also discovered a team of four horses had already followed the new set of tracks.

"That will be one of our groups," said Sir Tavish. The rescue party followed the tracks for nearly half an hour until they stumbled into Jarell's group.

Zeld found it difficult to sit still with so much happening, but somehow he managed to make it through.

Jarell met up with Sir Tavish and reported his decision to close the market. The boys in the rescue party identified all the horses as farm horses from the C&C area, which meant all the wagons came from the farms as well. Sir Tavish ordered everything taken back.

Sir Roger folded the top of the sack over the stone as he could see that the last of the search teams were returning. Zeld and Sir Roger left the office and entered the courtyard where they waited for the others to return. When the four brothers McMarr arrived, Zeld rushed over and met them at the stables. Oars reported, "Sir Tavish told the farmers this couldn't have been done by ordinary thieves. He thinks it's the work of a pirate prince and says every precaution must be taken in future, including a farm community watch."

Then he told them about his brother, "We trey born took Jens Jr. to the town healer in Baden, but the healer wouldn't heal him until we had the money for his treatment in hand. King Henry's clerk came by and he somehow went after Dad. The best part of the story is he had Dad and Mum back in 15 minutes. Oh, and they brought loads of money."

The brothers whisked Jens Jr. away before Zeld had a chance to meet him. Over the next couple of days, Zeld kept waiting for a chance to meet Jens Jr., but it never came. Jens Jr. rested at Eagle

Loft, with his brothers running interference until he looked better. Zeld still didn't have a chance to meet him, because as soon as he looked better he started straightaway on the schoolwork he had missed. Jens Jr. and his brothers didn't try out for the school team as they were obviously too busy. Jens Jr. remained a recluse and he only told his brothers about his grand adventure. He treated Zeld like a total stranger, which of course he was.

Zeld tried out for the team. In one event the boys built a stone wall. Zeld enjoyed watching the event as it reminded him of home. He felt surprised to see how few of the students tried out. It appeared to him most of the students would rather destroy a castle than build one. Zeld easily won a spot on the team, which made sense to him; after all, he had the most building experience. Tyre and Crispyn won places in the plant identification event. No one wanted to cook or do the maze event. A couple of boys decided to try to build a two-man boat.

The stonemasons left in October to rebuild the damaged castles. Zeld's team practiced stonework after classes in the stonemasons' yard. They practiced creating rectangular blocks out of round stones and setting them properly with mud.

Finally, the day to leave came. A small group of twelve students headed south, past the farms three miles, and then east. The hosting school was only three hours away by wagon. When the Castles and Caverns team arrived, at the goblin school, Zeld saw a shabby wooden fort with a Main Hall in the centre, and not a castle at all.

After unpacking inside one of the tournament tents, the teams met in the centre of the fort. Each school queued behind a wooden peg with the initials of their school painted on it. The pegs were pounded into the ground in a semicircular shape and the hosting school staff stood in the opening of the semicircle. The first event had been scheduled for that night. Each team sent two members into the woods to identify trees and bushes.

The contestants wandered around the forest trying to find an elm tree, a yew tree, an ash tree, an oak tree, a sugar pine and a walnut tree. Crispyn of Orange and Tyre Stevens found five of the six and tied for second place behind the goblins. Once the contestants returned, the teams ate supper.

For supper that night the goblins cooked pit roasted geese, baked turnips and fire roasted squash. Zeld queued in the outdoors with the others and ate his meal outside. He thought the food tasted excellent. That night the students slept in the tournament tents. Zeld felt quite a bit less nervous than he had at the last tournament.

In the morning the first event, called, "Cooking in the Field" took place. Each team cooked for their school and for three judges. Each school started with four pounds of bacon, three dozen eggs and a large onion. No one tried out for this activity at Castles and Caverns, so Sir Roger pressed Zeld and Brian Boru into culinary service. The pages made bacon omelettes with chopped onion, and tied for first place.

149

Zeld attended the shed building and two-man boat carving events. He enjoyed watching the elves speed through the shed building process and the giants put on a magnificent show of axe handling skills. The event was held at a nearby stream and the giants also launched the boat into the water as evidence it would float.

When time for the midday meal arrived, they queued again inside the fort and ate something rather odd called a sandwich. The goblin's school staff cut open a small loaf of bread and placed meat and vegetables inside the opening. They washed it down with fresh stream water served in drinking horns. Zeld said, "Braggadocios," when he saw the horns. They resembled the horns of oxen but they had been highly polished and the open ends had been plugged so you could carry them around by their attached leather strap much like a bladder.

During the midday meal break, the students were required to meet two people from another school. Zeld decided to go over to the Welch Naval Academy and asked if anyone knew James O'Day. Some of the students did. They told Zeld about the classes at their school: compass reading, astronomy, map reading, battle preparations for the sea, ballistas and onagers, to name a few.

Zeld watched as Sir Jaydan escorted the schoolmaster from King Arthur's School over to a mulberry bush and explained to him how to make fine longbows from the wood. This bit of knowledge would help the struggling school with their archery classes. Sir Thomas thanked Sir Jaydan for his kind deed.

Zeld felt relieved when it was finally time for his event. He, Brian, Crispyn, and Tyre took their places for Castles and Caverns. The alarm bell tolled and they began work on their enormous pile of stones. Zeld knelt down and waited for Brian to supply him with the stones that needed reshaping. Tyre placed and mudded the best stones immediately into the wall, while Crispyn sorted the stones that would follow.

The giants took the early lead as they went through their pile of stones, snatching the best ones and placing them in the wall. However, they had wagon loads of trouble with the poorer shaped stones. After an hour of frustration the giants tried to reshape their rocks by slamming them into each other. It didn't work. The more they slammed the rocks the more the stones became round instead of square.

The Dwarven Academy did well. The dwarves reshaped the stones independently of each other. When the dwarves started on their third level, C&C was three quarters done with their second.

Brian turned on a burst of speed in an attempt to close the gap on the dwarves and with Crispyn and Tyre both mudding, they managed to move into first place. Zeld's heart pounded with excitement as he moved from stone to stone reshaping them as he went. It was a tight race. However, in the end, the dwarves made a run of their own and the lead slipped away to the dwarves' superior skills.

In the final event for the day, Zeld held the C&C team's receiver stone for the maze event. Each team was handed a receiver glow stone and the first team to find the beeper stone won the event. The school bell tolled and the teams ran from their assigned positions through the trees toward a large hill to the east.

After the C&C team found their first two markers, the stone directed them to go inside a cliff. Zeld wondered if the beeper stone was hidden in the hill. He found a stick and pried it into a crack. Nothing happened, so he tried a different crack. Finally Zeld opened a small entryway only just big enough for the boys to crawl through. Inside they found a stash of weapons, dismantled mining carts and other mining equipment. Zeld became highly suspicious and held up a dwarven axe. He checked one side, and then the other. He indisputably found what he looked for; namely the unicorn mark.

"Mates, we must report this," Zeld said breathlessly.

"Of course, we won the contest!" Tyre exclaimed.

"No, we didn't. We've discovered a stash of stolen goods," Zeld said.

Brian ran back to the school and rang the alarm. Brian led the officials to the cave and the boys unloaded the stolen property. More than half belonged to the old goblin school. Zeld pointed out two sluice boxes and other mining equipment with the unicorn mark of the dwarves.

"Why did the receiver take us here?" asked Tyre.

"Excellent question, and I think the answer is that a second receiver stone crossed signals with the true stone," answered Sir Jaydan. "If I'm right, we should find the imposter stone inside the cave."

The boys went back into the cave to look for a beeper stone. After awhile, they found a secret compartment under a rock on the floor. Inside they found the beeper stone and 20,000 silver pieces.

The goblin school kept the stone and the money. The boys went back for a final look. They found a secret cache of golden necklaces under the money stash. As a reward, the goblin school gave two necklaces each to the boys who found the stash.

At supper in the fort's Main Hall, Castles and Caverns queued first. Officially, the boys ended up disqualified from the event; unofficially, they became the heroes of the day. Everybody came over to their table to shake their hands, which Zeld thought, became a wee bit embarrassing after a while. At the closing ceremony in the yard, Sir Thomas of Malory announced Welch Naval had won the tournament. This brought a small applause but Castles and Caverns received a thunderous ovation when Sir Thomas announced their seventh place finish.

Loyalty is more important than winning, Zeld thought. He and his mates stood proudly as Sir Thomas handed Sir Jaydan a half dozen drinking horns as their prize.

Before Europe became Christian they
believed in a half goat half god who
did as he pleased this is true I
give you no hype. He was known for
playing music on "his pipe".

CHAPTER TWENTY ONE
THE TOWN OF BADEN

Zeld lifted load after load of the dwarves' mining equipment into one of the empty storage sheds on the school grounds, once the team returned from the competition. One of his Viking soldiers came to help and spoke to him in Danish. Zeld couldn't understand him so he waved Oars over to interpret. Oars learned from Peder, that the other soldier, Morten, wanted to bring his wife and children from Denmark. This news shocked Zeld as he didn't know Morten had a family.

"I'll have to think about the journey to Denmark," Zeld told him while Oars translated. "I'm not exactly sure how to get you there and back safely, but I'll think on it."

With a knowledgeable look Oars told the soldier, "Zeld has connections in Denmark."

On Sunday, Zeld received his first knot tying lesson from Edward of Peele in the Great Hall. They worked on the clove hitch and the square knot. After awhile, they played chess. Zeld didn't know how all the pieces moved yet, but he felt eager to learn.

That night at supper, the staff polled the students to see whom they fancied for the schoolmaster position. Sir Tavish MacDonald, Father Ulrich of Kent and Lord Richard Plantagenet finished as the top three. Sir Tavish acted very grateful.

Jens Jr. finally caught up with his schoolwork, which had buried him, and the McMarrs rejoined the living.

After supper Zeld introduced himself to Jens Jr. in the Great Hall. "I'm Zeld de Exile."

"So, you're the famous Zeld who continuously tries to kill me brothers," Jens Jr. said with a stern expression. "I'll have you know murdering me brothers is me own job."

Zeld realized he had another tease on his hands.

"I'm sorry about the time I nearly suffocated them in the cave and for irritating the giant so much he tried to smash us with his club and for the time I nearly drowned them and for that little mishap with the poison and for turning Oars into a pink toad," Zeld said apologetically.

Jens Jr. laughed, "Blimey, you've been busy. Maybe I should take lessons."

"I could write a book, *'101 Ways to Kill Your Younger Brothers'*," Zeld said.

"That sounds splendid, but what friar would copy it a thousand times?"

"Why Friar Timothy, of course. The other day he said he'd do anything to help us boys become successful. Isn't that right, Friar Timothy?"

Friar Timothy had a book in his hands but still managed to overhear them. He answered, "Why, yes I did. What do you need me to do?"

"I need you to make a thousand copies of me new book *'101 Ways to Kill Your Younger Brothers'*."

"I'll do my best to rise to the occasion," said Friar Timothy with a smile.

After a few minutes the friar retrieved a parchment and quill. He wrote continuously for some time only pausing now and then to laugh out loud. Zeld crept over and took a peek at what Friar Timothy had written. Under the title of *"101 Ways to Kill Your Younger Brothers"* was a list of ways you could accomplish the feat. The smile on Friar Timothy's face would've told anyone he felt jolly pleased with his work. Zeld was happy as well. He didn't know what Friar Timothy was doing, but thought it must be something good.

It became evident that night that the students found ways to deal with Sunday's slow pace. Reading increased. Writing letters home did too and several students purchased ink, quills and parchment. A few made lists of personal goals.

Zeld and the triplets went over to the library to acquaint themselves with the collection of books. Oles found a book called, *Bashing About Your Opponent* by Harty Flail and Oars discovered *Jousting for Dummies* by Longfellow Reach. Zeld searched through the library but skipped on *Curing the Black Death* by Oceania

Crossroads and *Remedies for Painful Sores* by Mitus Goldentouch - Alchemist. Odin finally settled on *Severing Limbs Made Easy* by Victor Clever. While Odin queued to sign for his book, Zeld finally found a book for himself. *Proper Armour - Proper Victory* by Stan Strongwill. It demonstrated several types of armour and in which order to use them when dressing a knight. This subject interested him and he studied the book closely.

Zeld looked forward to studying on Sundays instead of sitting around bored. He noticed the friars used part of their Sunday to read the Bible aloud. He and his mates listened in.

In Monday's class, Sir Roger stood in front of the targets at the archery range and told the pages about an archery tournament being held at the Robin Hood School of Knighthood and Elfdom Ways. Zeld felt thrilled when Sir Roger mentioned that he would take charge of the team for this tournament.

Unlike the previous tournament, the entire school tried out. The school had a shortage of bows as Zeld and his mates only recovered a few from the Viking raid and they didn't have the funds to buy more. This problem resolved itself, but by strange means.

One Thursday morning a loud banging sound came from the main gate. When Friar Timothy opened the gate, he found 200 arrows and 15 common bows with a note attached which read:

> *These bows and arrows are the property of Zeld de Exile.*
> *He may use them as he sees fit.*
> *Each bow is labelled with his coat of arms*
> *and each arrow with his cresting.*

The bows were made of mulberry wood; however, they were shorter than the usual longbow length which made them the perfect size for the boys and the arrows had practice tips. Obviously someone, maybe even in the castle, kept an eye on him. Zeld tried to determine who. Sir Roger could have sent the bows and arrows. Sir Tavish wanted to show Sir Roger the mulberry bush when they found one on the way to the Prince Valiant School. Sir Drain seemed harsh to Zeld but he'd assisted in the mining episode and he bought the pies. Sir Jaydan found the mulberry bush at the goblin's school tournament and clearly was the cleverest of the knights.

After thinking it over, Zeld guessed the bows came from the King Arthur School, as a thank you for finding the stolen treasures. After all, the goblins were well known for producing excellent bows and arrows.

Then, one day shortly afterward, Friar Timothy called Zeld and the three triplets out of Sir Drain's class and sent them to the storage sheds. The sheriff waited for them atop his wagon with good news. "Your mine is clear of unwanted guests. We had a spot of trouble removing them peacefully. We found a stash of gold and used a portion of it to pay for the wounded officers' healing costs - that is according to the law, you know. We brought the remaining gold pieces to you, as owner of the mine."

The sheriff handed him a purse with 212 freshly minted gold pieces.

"We also confiscated their mining pans, sluices, pickaxes and other bits and snippets. These are forfeit to you as well. Where d'you want them put?"

Zeld climbed onto the wagon's seat and pointed to the storage shed he used for the other mining equipment. The triplets climbed aboard and the sheriff drove the wagon to the shed. The boys unloaded the wagon and completely filled the shed. Zeld didn't know how everything he unloaded worked. The dwarves didn't always use the same type of equipment as the Hessens.

Zeld said, "Thank you," and the boys hastened back to class.

Mornings grew cold at the school and most of the boys wore new underclothing to keep warm. Brian and James lived a long way from the school and didn't have the money with them to buy such things. This gave Zeld the funny idea of buying the underclothing for them and he laughed several times during his classes, for no apparent reason.

On Saturday Zeld went into town to buy six sets of under-clothes, two each for himself, James and Brian. He entered the clothing shop and found it well organized. Zeld spied scowls, vests, tunics, skirts, dresses, cloaks and aprons. In short a host of different types of clothing in various colours lined the shelves against the walls.

"I'm here for some underclothing for meself and me two mates," Zeld told the clerk that waited behind a counter next to a small stone fireplace.

The shopkeeper asked, "What size do you wear?"

"Er, I dunno," replied Zeld sheepishly, as he had no clue about clothing sizes.

"How much money do you have?" she asked.

"Several gold pieces."

"I remember the time Robin Hood came in with two silver pieces and thought he was rich enough to buy the entire store," she said. "Looking back I wish father would've sold him the merchandise. Imagine the price one could fetch for Robin's first two silver pieces."

Zeld chuckled. This wasn't his first comparison to the legendary hero. He hoped to make the archery team and ask Friar Tuck about the late Robin Hood to see if such stories were actually true.

159

"I'd say you're a size twelve," said the shopkeeper. "Which colours do you prefer?" she asked displaying the colours of purple, blue, green and gray.

"Which is best?"

"The purple and blue are used for nicer occasions and the green and gray for the field," she replied in a knowledgeable sort of way.

"Can I try them on?"

The lady pulled one of the grey undershirts over Zeld's head right then and there. Zeld said in a smothered voice, "I'll take that as a yes." His arms were pinned to his sides by the clothing. She laughed with embarrassment, and then stepped back to have a look at Zeld.

"The grey makes you look like a peasant," she said thoughtfully. "Let's try the green."

Already forgetting her faux pas she pulled the green shirt over the top of the gray one.

"Yes, that looks much better."

While Zeld struggled to take off the undershirts the shopkeeper asked him, "What are your mates' names?"

"James and Brian."

"How tall is James?"

"He and I are the exact same height."

"Well, that's easy," she said brightly, "You're the same size. Now your other mate - er - Ryan?"

"No Brian."

"Is Brian the same height, too?"

"No he's this much shorter." Zeld said holding his fingers three quarters of an inch apart.

"That's fortunate," she said in a cheery voice. "You all wear a size twelve. Select the colours you fancy, and then you'll be ready to pay."

"I'd have them wrapped, with a string and everything."

"For yourself as well?"

"No, only for me mates."

Zeld selected the purple and green for himself, the blue and grey for Brian and the purple and grey for James. He set the clothing on the counter; then, paid the clerk two gold coins and she returned three silver coins from a cracked mug. Zeld held up one of the silver coins and asked, "Would you like to keep the first silver piece of Zeldain de Saxon?"

The woman's face filled with terror as if she would scream; then, it softened. A look of hope surfaced. Then she dropped to one knee and said respectfully, "Me Lord."

That's when Zeld realized he'd used his real name.

"You'd better pretend you're collecting something and don't bow to me in future. You must call me Zeld. Nothing more or less. What is your name good lady?"

"Penelope, but the townsfolk call me Penny," she said. "I was your mother's handmaiden. I helped you escape the night the castle fell under attack."

Zeld looked closely into her face, and then remembered her. "We'll have to pay back our unwelcome guests in kind someday."

"Someday soon?"

"When we're better prepared. Are there other allies nearby?" Zeld asked hopefully.

"Yes, the refugees from the town of Saxon founded the town of Baden. However, there are spies as well," she warned.

"Tell our allies to prepare for our return."

She retrieved a purse from a secret hiding place, handed it to Zeld and said, "This is the money I've saved in hopes that someday the rebel Hesse could be overthrown."

Zeld handed the purse back to the storekeeper and asked, "Is this a safe place to keep money?"

"Yes, it is."

"Then I'll trust you with additional coins and tell no one that the purse is mine."

Zeld handed her 200 gold pieces to hide.

"When I chance upon more money, I'll bring it here," said Zeld, excited to have found an old friend.

They turned as someone opened the door to the shop. Penny dropped down and hid the money in her special place. Zeld looked over and saw Geoffrey and Godfrey of Hesse come into the shop. Zeld stared at Godfrey. He wore a knight's tunic with a large Hessen lion across the front. He also wore a cape and crown. He had a rather large head which Zeld thought wasn't surprising. He wore a stern look on his face at all times and his eyes along with his hair were dark.

"Fined 10,000 gold, can you believe that and if they can prove I sent the miners it'll be much higher. Plus the 50,000 silver for the treaty," Godfrey complained.

Glimpsing Zeld, Geoffrey tapped his dad lightly in the stomach.

"Dad, allow me to introduce you to Zeld de Exile. Zeld, this is my father Godfrey of Hesse," Geoffrey said courteously.

Zeld felt a cold chill run down his spine.

"Zeld, I heard you opened a gold mine and things went well until that sheriff came along. He stole all the money with the exception of a few gold pieces that he turned over to you," said Godfrey in an oily voice.

Zeld knew the mine did well and realized Godfrey of Hesse simply wanted to shake his confidence.

Godfrey added, "I've some men that could work the mine at the usual fifty-fifty split."

"I'm not interested. The mine is played out."

Godfrey said slyly, "It isn't played out. I came from the south yesterday and saw your men working there."

"They're not me men. I'll have to send the sheriff after whoever it is," Zeld said as he brushed his way past them.

Zeld collected his packages, walked out the door and straightaway to the sheriff's office. Godfrey watched him and found that Zeld did exactly what he said he'd do and without hesitation. Godfrey's trick worked. He snarled, "Why would you send the sheriff to chase away miners from a mine that is played out?" Godfrey glanced at his son who lifted his head smiling. Then he added, "The next time I trick that boy, he'll take me where I want him to go: home to his mother."

CHAPTER TWENTY TWO

Mates

BANG! BANG! BANG!

A thunderous knock echoed off the kitchen door. The dwarves had come to the school begging for food. Friar Timothy brought them into the Great Hall. One of the cooks brought food for them while the other went after Zeld. A few minutes later, Zeld joined the dwarves sitting and eating. He felt glad to see them and he learned they'd been raided too. He searched carefully among them but couldn't find one of the dwarves and feared perhaps he may have been killed. He asked, "Where's Grumpes?"

"Right here," answered an astonished voice from behind him.

He turned around and watched as Grumpes materialized out of thin air.

Astonished at what he saw, Zeld's mouth fell open, "Grumpes, how'd you do that?"

"I have an amulet of invisibility." He produced a small purple stone with swirls of white out of his vest pocket and showed it to Zeld. "I made a bet with Bushhard no one would ask about me; after all, most people think we dwarves all look alike."

"I daresay, you lost that wager, me friend. I hope you didn't lose too much," said Zeld hoping to learn the stakes.

Bushhard chuckled, "Only his dignity. He said if anyone asked about him, he'd dance 'round the courtyard in a dress singing 'Seven Peas in a Pot, Look at what I've Got'."

When Zeld took a good look at Grumpes' face he could tell he was truly living up to his nickname. Grumpes struggled to pull a pale green dress over his head, all the while mumbling unpleasant words in dwarfish under his breath. Then, he looked up and his frown slowly turned into a broad grin. He reached into his vest pocket and disappeared. Zeld heard him enter the castle yard singing. Bushhard, red faced, followed the singing around the yard and yelled, "THAT'S NOT FAIR, TURN OFF THE BLASTED AMULET! TURN IT OFF, I SAY!"

Everyone laughed as they watched Bushhard running around the yard yelling to the phantom singer.

Zeld turned back toward the dwarves and held up his healing stone and asked if anyone needed it. One of the women brought a small boy over with a scraped knee and Zeld healed it with the stone.

Friar Timothy watched Zeld use the healing stone, "You have an amulet of healing."

"Is that what it's called?"

Zeld pulled out the dried dragon meat that gave extra strength. He extended it toward the friar and asked, "What do you call this?"

The friar took it and Zeld watched as the energy flowed through the friar's body.

"This is an amulet of dragon heart. It gives the holder greater strength. Where did you find these things?" Friar Timothy asked suspiciously.

"I found them in the sea."

"Did the Vikings have them?"

"Yes, at one time, but they were discarded in the whirlpool."

"The Viking ship must've been very close to you and your horse," said Friar Timothy with a look of disbelief which also carried into his voice.

"The ship came so close it touched us," Zeld explained as honestly as he could.

The healing amulet turned a dull colour, so Zeld put it back in his bag. He watched as Grumpes and Bushhard returned, glaring at each other.

"I have a proposition for you," Zeld said sitting on a bench and leaning toward them. "I'd like you to work for me at the gold mine again. I've filed papers and the mine legally belongs to me."

Grumpes and Bushhard stopped glaring at each other.

"What are the terms?"

"Sixty - forty split, same as last time," Zeld offered.

"The Vikings stole our mining equipment," said Grumpes in a heartbroken tone.

"I found some of your stolen items and the sheriff gave me a bunch more from his raid on the Hessen miners."

This caught their interest, so Zeld and Friar Timothy took the dwarves to the shed where everything waited in storage. The dwarves assembled the carts and filled them with the other items. They left the school and headed south for Marvin.

"That was an exceptionally kind thing you did for them," said Friar Timothy as he watched the dwarves move down the road.

Zeld looked up at the friar wondering what he referred to and asked, "D'you mean the healing or the generous mining terms, or returning their mining tools or the job I gave them?"

"You did all that for a band of outcast dwarves? Well, if it isn't Robin Hood and his elves; then, it's Zeld and his dwarves," said the friar as he released the bar and locked the gate. Zeld felt a pleasantly warm sensation of happiness all through his chest after hearing Friar Timothy's comment.

In the morning Zeld awoke and silently crept through the kitchen. Looking warily around, he tiptoed to the main gate and pounded on it several times with a rock. He dropped two packages with the names James O'Day and Brian Boru on the ground and ran back through the kitchen door. He joined the growing crowd inside the castle yard.

Friar Timothy opened the door, found the two packages and read the note.

These packages are the property of James O'Day and Brian Boru.

They may use them as they see fit.

Each package is labelled with their name and each colour was selected especially for them.

Friar Timothy handed Brian and James their packages. They opened them. When they saw the underclothing, they turned bright red and the boys chanted, "Someone has a girlfriend."

Friar Timothy stopped the chant and instructed them to go and put on the clothing. The boys came back presently, properly dressed for winter.

Zeld acted like the other boys and tried not to smile too much. After all, he knew if he showed the good feeling he felt inside he'd undoubtedly give his little secret away.

On Saturday it fell to the first-year pages, from the Brotherhood of Air, to pick up the food from the local farms again. Exciting things happened at the farms, so Zeld looked forward to it. On the way he saw all the familiar trees. The wagons made their way to the supply station but nothing unexpected happened.

The only excitement came from a new farm family who had recently moved into the area and made plans to build a new farmhouse, barns, railed fences and all the rest. This may've sounded wonderful to the farmers but by the sour look on the page's faces Zeld could tell it didn't sound exciting to them.

Zeld wanted a chance to see the new house and barns go up. He thought it would be lovely to build such things for his mum someday.

The wagons loaded much faster this time as they were not encumbered by a shipment of rocks. This left the rest of the day to explore and have fun. Zeld spoke with the brothers McMarr who rode together on the way back from the farms. "While patrolling we found a secret cave to the west. D'you mates want to go for a romp?"

"Do we look like pansies?" Oles asked sarcastically.

"No, daffodils," Zeld answered and they all laughed.

Word of the romp spread to the other mates. With a sense of pride, Zeld led the others on horseback to his marker and from there up the stream into the cavern entrance. The triplets ran between the scattered rocks inside the cavern, screeching in a multitude of tones and laughing at their echoes. Sullivan de Bruce checked the cavern walls for precious ore.

James O'Day stood on a rock and called out, "I am king of this rock and any who wishes to take it from me must do so one at a time." Zeld answered his call, "I am Zeld the mighty and I say the rock belongs to me." Zeld stepped on the rock next to James and the two interlocked fingers. They pulled and tugged against each other until James fell from the rock. Then it became Zeld's turn to pretend he was king of the rock. Jens Jr. answered his call.

The boys played for hours. When finished they sealed the entrance and rode for the castle. They hadn't gone far when they heard someone call for them to hang on.

166

Zeld turned and looked. To his jaw dropping surprise he saw Norton Duval, Gunter Sims and Donald Doolittle who'd gone missing for three weeks. Norton has to be part giant or something Zeld thought. He remembered him receiving the good deed recognition earlier in the year. Norton weighed 250 pounds with almost as much muscle as Sir Tavish. He had dark hair and eyes with a slightly darker skin tone than most of the other boys.

"What did you mates do, chase the Vikings all the way back to Scandinavia?" asked Jens Jr., jesting.

"Yes, and is my horse tired," replied Gunter.

"The friars prayed every day for your safe return and so did several other mates you might know," Jens Jr. reported.

"So, when didja decide to come back, JJ?" Norton asked.

"Right after the raids, I thought it a wee bit unsafe to skive off anymore with Vikings on the loose and besides, I missed Mrs. Palfreeman's cooking," Jens Jr. teased with a half smile.

"So, where have you mates been all this time?" pried Oars.

"They probably got married," teased Odin in a false voice of suspicion.

"Hey, you quit giving away our secrets," said Norton playing along.

"We stood guard at Zorn Castle and found a few weapons the Vikings dropped," Donald Doolittle said as he pointed to a blanket wrapped around a long bundle.

"Excellent, maybe we can do something besides nature hikes all the time," said Zeld in a voice reflecting his boredom.

"Our group recovered some weapons too," Oars piped up proudly.

"What group?" asked Norton.

"A group of eight pages, Zeld, Sullivan, Brian, James, Robert, Oles, Odin and meself," bragged Oars.

"Eight pages braved the Vikings, who would've guessed?" asked Norton looking impressed. "So, didja chance into any swordplay?"

"Yeah, and we managed to save several people from the slavers," Oars bragged.

"Next time, remind us to ride with you," said Norton laughing.

The lot of boys rode back to the castle together. The whole school seemed glad to see Norton, Donald and Gunter. Everyone shook their hands and patted them on the back, making it a regular homecoming celebration.

Their entrance interrupted a discussion between the friars and a gypsy woman who wandered into the area. She came out of the Great Hall behind the friars, sat on a bench in one of the outdoor classrooms and asked, "Does anyone want their palm read?"

Zeld didn't know what to think of the gypsy. Friar Marcus appeared very offended by her. Friar Timothy acted kind and showed tolerance to her ways.

Sir Roger asked, "Do you have any good luck charms you could sell us? We have an archery contest in a week." He chuckled and the boys laughed.

"The school will do well without a good luck charm," the gypsy predicted.

Friar Marcus spoke in a high pitched angry squeal, "I think - you should leave."

"I have an idea," said Sir Tavish thoughtfully. "We'll pay the gypsy to give five palm readings on a few of the boys. We'll write her predictions down and in a month we'll see if they're true or false."

"Do not tempt the Lord your God by dealing with such pagans," squealed Friar Marcus, still in a huff.

"If the readings prove false, er, we'll have strengthened the boys' belief in God," said Sir Tavish, playing the innocent.

"Do you remember when Elijah the prophet did battle with the unrighteous priests of Baal? This will be a similar type of contest," said Friar Martin to Friar Marcus.

"I don't think so...," began Friar Marcus but before he could finish Sir Tavish jumped to his feet, "I nominate Geoffrey of Hesse."

"I nominate Zeld de Exile," said Sir Roger frowning at Sir Tavish.

Sir Drain pointed into the crowd, "I nominate Brian Boru."

Sir Jaydan said, "I nominate Eric of Markland."

With one boy short and each knight having already chosen a boy it fell to the friars to find the last person. The friars glanced at each other puzzled. Then Friar Timothy stood up, Jens Jr. had only just whispered something in his ear, and the friar said, "I nominate - meself." The other friars smiled and nodded their heads in agreement. Friar Timothy's holy robes were as unmoveable as the sea.

The gypsy woman didn't mind waiting. She sat on a bench and looked about the castle contented. Each of the four boys and the friar queued for a turn.

The gypsy woman took Geoffrey's hand, studied it for a while and then spoke, "You come from a strong family of cunning warriors. They've acquired many riches by strength and cunning. You wonder if you can live up to your family's traditions. You know they depend on you unlike any other. An eminent battle approaches, but you must flee from it or you'll surely die. You'll have the chance to revenge your losses but you must not take part."

The gypsy took Zeld's hand, studied it and then began, "You'll have many companions in your life. Some will be true mates and some will not. You've not found your true purpose in life yet. You make friends with animals. Your family misses you. That is all." Zeld thought it a rather idiotic prediction.

On Brian's turn the gypsy took his hand but didn't analyse it at all. Instead she gasped and said, "I feel your tremendously strong spirit. Your critical purpose in life is to lead men. This school is where you belong and you should develop all your talents." Brian puffed out his chest and swaggered over to the rest of the boys.

Eric stepped up and held his hand out as if he were a soldier doing his duty.

The gypsy took his hand and followed the lines with her fingers, and then she said mournfully, "You've had a hard time expressing your feelings since your tragic loss. Someday a beautiful young girl will come into your life and give you happiness. Your heart will mend, setting everything right again."

Eric's jaw dropped and he gave a startled look at the gypsy before turning away mumbling to himself. As he brushed by Zeld, he overheard him say, "There's no way she could've known."

On Friar Timothy's turn, he sat down and took the gypsy's hand. The friar told the gypsy her fortune, "You're not really a gypsy. You've come here to spy on the school and make plans to steal our valuables. Your name is Edelweiss." The friar held her right hand tightly with his left and used his right hand to pull off her wig.

She attempted to run, but Jens Jr. snatched her tightly from behind and stole away her necklace. The necklace held a shiny blue stone Jens Jr. activated and a blue light shot out and surrounded Edelweiss; then, she floating into the air.

Zeld realized the blue stone had to be another type of amulet. Jens Jr. slowly moved the girl over to the chapel, and then up, up, up, until she sat on the roof. She remained seated there as she couldn't jump without serious injury. Jens Jr. placed the necklace around his own neck and stuffed the stone inside his shirt.

"Call me Merlin the Magician," Jens Jr. said brightly.

170

An awkward silence filled the courtyard. Friar Timothy clapped; then, everyone joined in creating a thunderous applause.

Jens Jr. hugged Friar Timothy and said, "Thank you for believing me."

Friar Timothy called, "Are there any volunteers to go after the sheriff."

Every hand in the school went up, even Zeld's two soldiers.

"Will you go Friar Marcus and Friar Martin?" asked Friar Timothy as if they had received a great honour.

The two friars stood, grinning from ear to ear. They walked out the gate arm in arm singing a marching hymn from the crusades. "Fair is the sunshine, fairer the moonlight..."

That night the sheriff came and took Edelweiss away hog tied in the back of his wagon. Jens Jr. stepped over and spoke to the sheriff privately. Zeld wouldn't have taken notice of what Jens Jr. did, expect the sheriff looked down at Jens Jr. from the seat of the wagon and shouted out, "You want me to take her where?"

CHAPTER TWENTY THREE

Shooting Stars, Shooting Glances

THUD!

"A DEAD CENTRE BULL'S-EYE!" called Sir Roger once he stepped around for a better view of the target.

"YES!" shouted Jens Jr. as he became the first page to make the archery team.

Zeld wondered if he'd make the team at all. Friar Timothy stepped over and said, "So, you and JJ have loads in common."

"We do?" asked Zeld surprised.

"The same mates, the amulets, success, the school, and more," Friar Timothy said tapping his finger on Zeld's bow.

"So, why does everyone fancy him now?"

"Everyone fancies a winner and JJ's in prime form," the friar answered. "It won't last forever. You'll see everyone has a turn playing the hero, as well as the goat."

Zeld said, "Baaaaah."

"Don't worry goat-boy, you're doing fine."

On Zeld's next shot, which was also a dead centre bull's-eye, he became the second page to qualify for the archery team. Zeld felt better. Sometimes it's nice to have a mate remind you you're doing well.

The archery team left early the next morning. Zeld sat on the cloud, waiting to land at the Robin Hood School in Sherwood Forest. The team carried their midday meal and supper with them in the back of a wagon, as it would be an all-day journey due to the unfavourable winds and the horses fidgeted more than usual.

His thoughts turned to his soldier's request of going to Denmark to find his family. "Whom do I know going to Denmark? Whom do I know that knows how to travel to Denmark?" Zeld asked himself and the only answers he came up with were the

Vikings from the ship and Jens Sr. Under the circumstances he thought he'd ask Jens Sr.

Zeld enjoyed riding on the cloud this time. He wandered over to talk to the giant. "Hello, me name is Zeld. How d'you fly a cloud?"

With a mighty roar of laughter the man said, "I learned to fly a cloud before I learned to walk. It's quite easy actually. I simply think up and the cloud obeys my command. Now manoeuvring a cloud is quite a different story altogether. You see it's all a matter of footwork, like swordplay or dancing. If I lean on my right foot the cloud moves to the right."

The giant leaned on his right foot to demonstrate what he meant. Zeld felt the cloud pull hard to the right.

"If I want to steer left I lean on my left foot."

Zeld felt the momentum of the cloud shift to the left.

"To move forward I lean forward."

The cloud increased in speed but at the same time the ride became turbulent, causing small pieces of the cloud to break off. The giant leaned back and the ride became smooth again.

"Too much of that and your cloud will disperse."

The giant smoothly turned a full circle to the right and flew his cloud into a position to catch the cloud fragments that had splintered away a moment before.

Zeld moved closer and could see an opening directly in front of the giant's feet. He looked through and could see the countryside passing below.

"Blimey! You can see everything from here!" Zeld exclaimed excitedly as he turned to look up at the giant.

"You're welcome to stay and watch. I only have to see the ground and I can direct the cloud anywhere I desire. By the way, my name is Marvin, I'm glad to meet you and in case you haven't figured it out I'm on the secret list King Henry hid in the treasure chest he sent you."

"Oh," said Zeld too embarrassed to tell him he wasn't able to find the secret compartment.

The two of them shook hands in what Zeld hoped would become a fast friendship. When the giant let them off, he waved to Zeld and called, "If you ever need an emergency journey, you know where to find me."

That night the team opened their food basket and found Scandinavian scones. Zeld and Jens Jr. reached toward the bottom for the warmer bread. The rest of the boys snatched a flat bread each and spread jam on them. The bread disappeared quickly and several boys looked with hungry eyes for seconds.

After supper the team, led by Sir Roger, found a nearby road and continued their journey. As they approached, a friar stepped out and said, "I'm Friar Tuck, welcome to our school. You'll find the corral prepared on the south hill and your tent pitched on the north hill."

"Many thanks, friar," called out Sir Roger.

"Is that Sir Roger?" asked Friar Tuck sarcastically.

"Yes, it is," said Sir Roger, reaching his hand out to shake Friar Tuck's.

"You boys do know Sir Roger was one of Robin's merry men."

Zeld found it interesting. Not everyone had a chance to be taught archery by one of Robin's men.

While everyone watched Friar Tuck and Sir Roger, a giant crept up on the other side of the wagon. The giant reached out with both arms and lifted Sir Roger; then, turned him upside down. The giant shook Sir Roger until everything fell from his person. Then, the giant held him upside down while Friar Tuck went through his belongings. The schoolboys laughed, including Zeld.

"Six gold and three silver, I see they pay you well at that other school," Friar Tuck teased. "What can this be? Methinks it is a hair brush. Why the Sir Roger I knew never used one. Perhaps you haven't been converted from your thieving ways. Methinks a little humility is in order. Simply lose the archery contest and all prior sins shall be forgiven thee."

The boys watched excitedly as the giant turned Sir Roger around and put his feet on the ground. Friar Tuck handed the spilled items up to Sir Roger and said, "Mind, if you lose, all is forgiven, but if you win, we'll have no other choice, than to get rough."

"How rough is rough?" asked Sir Roger leaning toward Friar Tuck with his hands on his hips in a threatening manner.

The friar placed both hands over his heart and said, "Dear Lord, please take our dearly departed mate into heaven, even though he failed his test of humility. Perhaps dear Lord, you need a gong farmer to clean out the garderobes and I humbly beseech thee to give the job to Sir Roger Fitzwayne."

"So, you have a better team this year, have you? Already making excuses for me loss, are you? Blimey, I may've lost me champion archer to the years of apprenticeship but we didn't come to lose or be intimidated by ruffians. Methinks, we'll do well," said Sir Roger confidently.

The giant put his hands on Sir Roger's shoulders and leaned over the top of the knight's head, "He really did fail the test of humility."

The three of them laughed. Zeld realized why they were called the merry men and relaxed amid the laughter.

After a few more minutes of friendly chat, Sir Roger climbed into the wagon and drove it to the tents and unloaded. He placed the horses in the corral. Zeld heard the rain from the giant's cloud in the distance.

Zeld thought about the upcoming contest. He couldn't imagine any school having an advantage over the others. The giants' size shouldn't hurt them and the goblin's smallness shouldn't hurt their chances either.

That night they ate roasted pigs at a late supper along with all kinds of roasted water fowl. Zeld noticed a couple of kitchen servants, scarred and lame from injuries.

"Everyone listen and mark my words as I will tell you the real story of Robin Hood," Friar Tuck called after the late supper. Friar Tuck stood between two bonfires so he could be seen. The boys sat all around anxiously awaiting every word.

"Robin was a Saxon nobleman. His father placed him into hiding, so the brutal Norman Lord, named Gisbourne, wouldn't find him. Alas, one day Robin's father died, forcing the lad out of hiding at a very young age, in fact, too young to take over the duties of Earl. Guy of Gisbourne, with the help of a German family and the Sheriff of Nottingham, stole Robin's castle and lands.

"Robin fled the area and attended the Castles and Caverns School of Knighthood where he was properly instructed in the ways of war, living in the field, and trusting in God. This was not all; he learned each and every way a knight must live in order to be a man of virtue and knowledge.

"At the end of his school days Robin achieved knighthood. Robin had many friends, including elves, although most people considered this wrong at the time. He learned from the elves and the elves learned from him. Robin took refuge here in Sherwood Forest. Slowly he gained in strength and power, for the sinister Lord Gisbourne brutally oppressed his subjects and they turned to Robin for help.

"When Robin had enough men, he stormed the castle belonging to Gisbourne's German ally. They set fire to the castle using a barrel of pitch, which oozed through the cracks of the stone floors. The stones burst with heat and the castle crumbled into ruins. Robin had defeated one villain and two remained.

"Guy of Gisbourne realized he had a fight on his hands. He patrolled Sherwood Forest with his men. This gave Robin the opportunity to collect weapons and armour, which he did. Robin understood he couldn't hide his large army from his enemies forever, so he reduced his army to his best men, namely, those able to fight three enemy soldiers at once and win. Gisbourne's patrols fell victim to Robin's hand-picked troops.

"Gisbourne himself came up with an idea to rid the world of the Robin Hood menace. They had a duel, Robin Hood vs Guy of Gisbourne. I'm sure Robin would've charged admission if he'd thought of it."

The crowd laughed, and then Friar Tuck continued, "The duel occurred here in this very meadow and at first neither party established the upper edge. That's a little battle humour you know - upper edge."

The crowd groaned.

"During the duel Gisbourne tired and swung his sword much like an axe to save energy, chopping heavy blows at Robin. In return Robin dodged the blows instead of parrying them. Finally, Gisbourne swung a blow for Robin's knee that would've left him crippled and an easy target to finish, but Robin saw it coming. He jumped over the blow and at the same time swung as wide as he could with his elfin blade. The sword slit Gisbourne's throat and he died moments later.

"As for the sheriff, he lessened his cruel hold on the people. After all, no nobles remained who would pay for his wicked favours.

"Robin started this castle before his death and we've continued to build it. We named this school in his honour and you are welcome here anytime." The friar finished and the boys applauded.

The giant who jested with Sir Roger stood up and bellowed loudly, "It's time for bed. We all want to do our best tomorrow and a good night's sleep will help."

Zeld didn't return to the tent straightaway. He helped clear the dishes, waiting for a chance to talk to one of the crippled kitchen helpers. He wanted to see if his amulet would heal him. Finally, the opportunity presented itself.

"Hi, me name is Zeld," he said introducing himself to a boy with a hunchback and a scar down the right side of his face.

"My name is Dowly," a frail voice whimpered.

"Er, I was wondering - " Zeld started.

"I know - how I got this hunchback and scar?" the boy said in his frail voice.

The boy wasn't rude: he had merely answered the same question all his life.

"No, I wondered if this healing stone might help you recover?" Zeld said, holding out the amulet to show him.

They both stared silently at the stone.

Zeld held the stone up and placed it on the scar. The helper laughed as the stone tickled. Then Zeld moved the stone to another position. The boy laughed again. Zeld examined the boy's face closely to make sure he'd healed the entire scar. He leaned back in shock when he discovered the kitchen helper was a girl. He placed the stone on her hunchback but it didn't have enough power left to continue healing.

"Maybe by morning the stone'll have recharged enough to heal your back too," Zeld said hopefully.

The girl held up a silver tray to see her reflection. Then she reached up with one hand and felt the smooth skin. Her tears of joy flowed freely as she saw for the first time in years her face without the brutal deformity. The girl took hold of Zeld's vest; then, pulled him close, and kissed him on the lips. Then she ran toward the kitchen shouting, "MUM, MUM, YOU HAVE TO SEE THIS!"

Zeld raised a platter and looked at himself. He stared at the half embarrassed, half jolly look on his own face. Besides his mother, Zeld had never been kissed by a girl before. He thought, I hope me mates didn't see that.

CHAPTER TWENTY FOUR

Head Splitting Headaches and Other Splitting Shots

"H EY, ZELD, WAKE UP YOU BRAT!" Jens Jr. yelled in his ear as he lay sleeping in the C&C's tournament tent.

It worked. Zeld snapped to a sitting position, and then hit Jens Jr. with his pillow.

"It's time to go split some arrows, Robin Hood the second," Jens Jr. said rolling his r's with a note of confidence.

"All right then. It shall be our finest hour!" said Zeld, reflecting Jens Jr.'s confidence by rolling the r in right as well.

They queued for breakfast at the Robin Hood School's pavilion, where Zeld was served by the hunchback girl with a beautiful face. Zeld received larger portions than the other boys and his service came with a big beautiful smile the other boys couldn't help noticing.

Zeld sat across the table from Wilhelm of Prussia and Norton Duval.

"So, Zeld, d'you fancy girls with hunched backs?" Wilhelm of Prussia asked snobbishly.

"Hunched back or no, she has better manners than you, Wilhelm," Norton Duval snapped.

"So, you do like girls with hunched backs," Wilhelm said to Zeld, paying no attention to Norton.

"Yes, I daresay I do," said Zeld, knowing full well it meant trouble.

Wilhelm started to chant, "Zeld likes hunched back girls." No one had a chance to join in as Norton Duval elbowed Wilhelm in the face giving him a split lip and knocking him backward off his bench onto the ground.

Norton, while still sitting on his bench, leaned toward Wilhelm and angrily scolded, "A little more respect for women might gain a little more respect for your mouth."

Wilhelm shot a look of anger up at Norton; then, reached past him, dipping a cloth into his finger bowl and tended to his injured lip. The hunched back girl walked over to Wilhelm with a dish towel to clean his bloody chin.

"Stay away from me you little toad!" Wilhelm ordered rudely.

Norton turned Wilhelm's direction again and said, "Maybe you need a little more encouragement."

Wilhelm turned to the girl and because of his swollen lip he spoke with a slight German accent, "I apologise for mine rudeness, mine lip will be fine. I do not need any help, tank you."

Norton said nonchalantly, "I always believed he had good manners hidden somewhere deep inside."

Dowly had a look of confusion on her face, but went about her duties.

The teams shot scores of bull's-eyes. It came to this: the first school to miss a bull's-eye lost the round. In the first event of the day, the senior division three rail shoot, all four of the C&C archers hit the bull's-eye but so had all the other archers. A second round hit the targets. Three teams were eliminated as one of their arrows touched outside the bull's-eye area. The next round eliminated two more schools. This meant C&C would take at least third place.

The competition narrowed down to two schools when the Welch Academy had a string break and the arrow spun into the ground. The winner would be either C&C or Robin Hood. Sir Roger looked over at Friar Tuck and Friar Tuck looked over at Sir Roger. They both wore impish grins on their faces.

Zeld wasn't sure how these two knew the contest would end up this way. Zeld wondered if they cheated. Perhaps there really is such a thing as a bull's-eye amulet, Zeld thought.

For the next two rounds all the archers hit bull's-eyes. Finally the contest ended when one of the Robin Hood School's arrows hit the end of an arrow already in the bull's-eye and bounced off. The first arrow didn't split, so they couldn't claim the bull's-eye. Castles and Caverns won.

The herald called, "Junior division step to the mark!" The junior division took to the range. Zeld's first shot was a dead centre bull's-eye. Jens Jr.'s arrow hit so close to Zeld's the tips touched. The junior division didn't have the same skills as the senior division. In the first round, four schools were eliminated, including Robin Hood. The second round removed two more schools from the round. Only C&C and the Giant Academy remained.

The crowd chanted, "Go David go."

The giants appeared irritated and a stymied looking Friar Tuck silenced the crowd with an angry, "That will do!" Zeld noticed the giants did well with archery.

While waiting for his turn, Zeld spied the hunched back girl in the crowd. He waved and she blew him a kiss. He felt so embarrassed he thought he would die. Then he turned pink, followed by red, and then by a shade of scarlet. Sir Roger, who had missed the interaction, saw the colour of Zeld's face and held up the match to see if he suffered from heat stroke.

"Zeld, you don't look well. How many fingers am I holding up?" Sir Roger asked.

"Three," said Zeld faintly as his colour slowly returned to normal.

"Alright, Zeld but if you start to feel ill, let me know."

Zeld nodded his head. He didn't dare look over at Dowly again. When his turn came around, he had his concentration back and shot another bull's-eye. The giants couldn't keep the bull's-eyes coming and fell into second place.

The teams spent the rest of the day shooting and waiting. The targets kept moving farther and farther away until finally no one shot bull's-eyes anymore.

Zeld sat on a grassy knoll eating fried chicken and chips with melted cheese for his midday meal. After serving, the hunched back girl came out and sat by him with her meal. It appeared to be as good a time as any, so he took out his stone and placed it on her upper back. She guffawed so loudly people nearby turned to watch them. Zeld tried to ignore them but his red face showed his embarrassment again. Friar Tuck heard the laughter and came over to check on the problem.

Zeld told him, "I'm attending to her back with this amulet of healing."

Friar Tuck examined the girl and asked, "Dowly, is that you?"

She managed to say, "Yes," through her laughter and held her head up straight for the first time in years. She laughed so hard Friar Tuck started laughing. Then, a few more people nearby joined in and soon it seemed everyone at the whole school joined in. Finally the stone went dark, so the tickling stopped and the laughter died down; which left a beautiful smiling girl with a straight back and a much stronger voice.

"I asked about you. Your name is Zeld, you go to the Castles and Caverns School, your horse's name is Tiger, you are a first-year page, your family lives in exile somewhere and your favourite food is whatever you're having for supper," Dowly said starting a conversation.

180

"That's remarkably close. Me favourite food is scones and me second favourite food is sandwiches," Zeld told Dowly.

"One of my favourite foods is scones too. Especially those with raspberry filling," explained Dowly.

Zeld realized they were talking about two entirely different types of scones.

"I ..." Zeld began to say, I meant the Scandinavian type of scone, but stopped himself as he realized it could give away his mother's location. "I...fancy that kind too," he said hoping he remembered it correctly.

"I've never heard of sandwiches before," Dowly said with a puzzled look on her face.

Zeld took a good look at her for the first time. She had light-blonde straight hair, dark-brown eyes and pale skin. She stood tall and thin and had long fingers which reminded Zeld of his mother's hands. He thought she looked two to three years older than him. Her clothes appeared old and worn but that didn't bother him.

"Why d'you live here?" Zeld asked.

"My name is Dowly A'Dale. My father was Allan A'Dale. His father was the king's forester for Sherwood Forest," Dowly explained.

"So, now you're well, what'll you do?" Zeld asked hoping she had a fantastic answer.

"I'll live here in the forest and wait for both of us to grow up, so you can marry me someday." She spoke as if it would really happen. Then she said, "I suppose you're like the other boys and have mapped out an adventurous life full of dangerous missions on the crusades."

Zeld felt embarrassed by her answer and comment, so he hastily revealed his plans, "I'll become wealthy and build up a kingdom, but unlike the kingdoms we have now. My kingdom will have elves, dwarves, good trolls and anyone else who wants to live in peace."

"Where will you build the castle?"

"Me family already has a castle, but the Hessens have captured it. Someday, I'll reclaim it and force Hesse to retreat to Germany," Zeld said firmly.

"D'you mean, Godfrey of Hesse, who owns vast parts of Germany and two English estates?" Dowly asked with great apprehension.

"He does?" Zeld asked honestly surprised.

"Yes, and I heard he invaded North Africa and is bringing back a fortune in treasure."

"I heard he was fined for misdeeds by King Henry."

"He's so powerful," said Dowly with a shudder.

"I had no idea."

The bell tolled and everyone headed for the afternoon events. Zeld helped Dowly who had trouble standing up straight and walking. To make matters worse everyone stared at her, calling her the-girl-who-laughed-herself-well.

Zeld found his team at the pavilion. Jens Jr. was handed a parchment with a list of animals to hunt and a device which always pointed at the chapel's steeple, so they could find their way to the school from any place in the forest. The alarm bell sounded again and the hunt began. The elves were the first group out of sight. They went into the bushes five feet away and disappeared. The C&C team headed for the closest hill to gain a height advantage. On the way Jens Jr. read the parchment out loud, so everyone could hear.

We have King Henry's permission for each school to hunt one deer.
After you have dressed the deer and delivered it to the school,
then shoot as many brown hares from the farms as
you're able. The school with a deer and the most brown hares
wins the event.

"Deer live by smell and hearing. To shoot one, we must remain quiet and stay downwind," Norton instructed.

Once they went far enough away from the other teams Zeld, Norton and Jens Jr. searched for places to hide. Zeld found an excellent place behind a gnarly giant oak tree. He took up his position and prepared his bow. He readied four additional arrows by leaning them against the tree with the tips down so he could load again quickly. Jens Jr. hid between two large rocks.

Norton climbed the tree Zeld hid behind and made a strange sound resembling a sick animal with his flute. Most of the other team members went further into the woods to keep away from his terrible flute playing. Only Zeld and Jens Jr. stayed behind. Within a few minutes a deer came looking for the music. Norton pulled his bow and fired. He hit the deer low in its right front leg. Zeld shot and hit the deer in the ribs. Then Norton shot again, this time hitting the deer in the neck. The deer toppled over. Zeld went straightaway to claim it.

Norton called, "Don't touch it."

Zeld froze for a moment, and then looked up into the tree at Norton who climbed down, "When killing a deer, you wait five minutes for it to die. They're dangerous animals, especially when wounded. Well JJ, since you didn't put an arrow in the deer, you can dress her out."

Jens Jr. didn't look pleased about it, but what could he say. After five minutes they walked over and Jens Jr. drew his hunting knife and properly dressed the deer. Norton pulled down a sapling and cut away the branches. Zeld swung his rope over his right shoulder, waiting to tie the deer's legs.

Zeld asked, "How didja know the deer would come to that horrible music?"

Norton looked over at Zeld with a sly grin and said, "I grew up in Germany and I would watch the deer play in the meadow not far from my home. One day, when I was eight, I found a fawn tangled in some vines, making a horrible sound. When I went over to help it, I was nearly killed when its mother charged into the greenery. Later, I practiced until I figured out how to make the same noise on my flute and it brings deer every time."

"That's braggadocios," said Zeld, "No other team will know how to call the deer to them. We'll make it back first for sure."

Zeld yelled to the other team members to gather but no one answered. Jens Jr. and Norton called too.

"Which of the boys had the pointer?" asked Norton stiffening with worry.

"Wilhelm," answered Jens Jr.

"I doubt they're capable of getting a deer but they'll at least make it back all right," said Norton as he slipped the sapling between the deer's legs. Zeld spent a moment tying the knots.

With Norton in the lead and Jens Jr. with Zeld on the other end, they followed their own foot tracks back to the school. When they arrived, cheers went up.

"The first deer has been brought into camp," yelled the giant who had turned Sir Roger upside down.

Friar Tuck turned to the giant and asked, "Which school is it, Little John?"

"So, that's Little John," said Zeld somewhat surprised.

"Who didja think he was?" asked Norton somewhat rudely.

"Nobody important."

"Everybody at this school is somebody important."

They handed the deer over to the cooks. The elves showed up with their deer less than two minutes later. Norton didn't waste a moment. "Let's go," he said hastily.

Zeld, Jens Jr. and Norton ran towards the farms. When they arrived, they could clearly see why they needed to hunt the brown hares. They'd torn the land up by digging holes everywhere and they had obviously devoured the crops. Norton pulled out his flute and played a low note that lingered for 20 seconds. A group of several young hares stood tall on their back haunches staring back at the boys. The boys fired their arrows at the same time. Norton stopped Zeld and Jens Jr. from entering the field. While raising his flute again he said, "We'll shoot all our arrows before we retrieve them, so we won't scare away the hares."

Norton turned a new direction and played the note again. They kept this up until the school bell tolled, and then they reported with 67 dead hares. The elves had 43.

The farmers carried most of the dead hares home and said something about cooking them into pies.

The rest of the Castles and Caverns team came in discouraged. They hadn't gotten a deer and had managed to lose three team members. To their jaw dropping surprise they learned their three lost team members had successfully hunted a deer and the most hares. Zeld, Jens Jr. and Norton wouldn't tell them how they'd managed it, so it remained a school mystery.

That night for supper, they ate venison steaks. Dowly sat on the ground near Zeld. He moved over and motioned for Dowly to sit on his bench with him near a big bonfire. They ate Zeld's meal together.

When they finished, Dowly asked bashfully, "Zeld could you use your stone to heal my mum?"

"I didn't know your mum was ill. We can try," suggested Zeld, as he stood to follow Dowly away from the fire. They went a short way and entered a dark hut with a single candle for light.

Inside he found Mrs. A'Dale lying on a bed. He recognized her as the other injured kitchen servant from the other day. He took the amulet from his bag and said, "We want to see if this'll mend you. Where are your injuries?" She lowered her eyes a wee bit embarrassed and explained the cause of the injuries to Zeld. "Both Dowly and me were severely injured by a wild boar years ago."

Mrs. A'Dale mustered her courage, sat up and continued speaking in an exhausted voice, "I've a twisted leg and a shoulder that never healed properly. Even if you can't cure me, I'll always be thankful for what you've done for us already." She looked over at Dowly with a smile on her face. She lifted her hand and Dowly reach over and held it.

Dowly slipped closer to her mother at the side of the bed while Zeld stayed at the foot.

"Which injury should we start with tonight?" Zeld asked chivalrously.

"Me leg," Mrs. A'Dale said, pointing to a spot high on her leg.

Zeld handed the stone to Dowly. "Put the stone where your mother is hurting."

Dowly moved the covers down part way, and then held the stone in place. Mrs. A'Dale giggled; then, she became silent and her face cringed with pain. Then the leg made an enormous popping sound. Mrs. A'Dale moaned for a while, and then she stopped. She lay quietly for a moment. When Mrs. A'Dale pulled back the covers the rest of the way Zeld could see her leg had straightened. She clapped her hands for joy. Her muscles ached but the stone had run out of power, so Zeld could do nothing about the aching.

"Thank you, my dear boy," she said gleefully cupping her hands together and he could tell by her tears of joy she meant it.

Dowly handed Zeld back the amulet.

She hugged her mum excitedly and said, "His name is Zeld."

Mrs. A'Dale turned sharply toward the boy and demanded to know, "Was your father Peter de Saxon?"

"Yes."

"Then your name is Zeldain and your brother's name is Wolfgang."

"Yes – how d'you know?"

185

"It's all written in the Anglo-Saxon Chronicles. You come from an important family and as far as anyone knows you're the last of the de Saxony family, which makes you destined for greatness. Your enemies are the Hesses. You'll have to recapture your lands and castles one estate at a time or you'll have to kill the entire Hesse family in one attack," she insisted, waving her finger at Zeld.

"Castles?" asked Zeld, "You mean there is more than one?"

"Of course, didn't you know?"

"I didn't. I'm not strong enough to take them back or to destroy the Hessens."

"Then become strong," Mrs. A'Dale said unsympathetically.

"I will."

Dowly, seeing her mother's excitement, spoke up, "I think you should rest mum," she said, while rubbing her arm soothingly.

"Yes, Mrs. A'Dale, rest will help the healing process and I need strong allies," said Zeld still confused as to how she knew his family.

"You remind me of Robin Hood in his younger days," Mrs. A'Dale said as she pulled up the covers and slid down beneath them.

"I'll be back after awhile," Dowly told her mother.

She and Zeld went back to the bonfire for the closing ceremony. Zeld felt great happiness in healing Dowly and her mother. By the look on Dowly's face he knew she felt the same way. Little John announced the winners of the events. Castles and Caverns won first place in most of the events and bagged the tournament as well. Dowly stayed with Zeld throughout the presentations. When finished, she walked home blowing him a kiss and waving. He waved sheepishly back.

In the morning Zeld packed his gear and trudged over to Mrs. A'Dale's hut, but she had already left. He searched for her and found her scrubbing pots in the kitchen.

Zeld inquired, "D'you have a minute for a boy in search of an ally?"

"I'll always have a minute for you Zeld," she said, sounding thrilled to see him again.

Zeld pulled out the stone and gently asked, "Where does it go this time?"

She touched her collar bone. "Here," she said wincing in pain.

Zeld sat on the table and placed the amulet atop the injury. Mrs. A'Dale leaned forward to his right side placing her hands on the kitchen table and waited. Presently the tickling started and her mouth twitched as she tried not to laugh. After a few more seconds, the urge overcame her and one outburst of laughter escaped followed closely by another. Her laugh resembled Dowly's and Friar Tuck entered the kitchen to check on Zeld and Dowly. The friar found Zeld with Mrs. A'Dale having another laughing festival.

"Well, young man, you certainly have a way with women," Friar Tuck teased. He shrugged his shoulders. Friar Tuck laughed and laughed. Several new faces peeked into the kitchen to check on the laughter as well.

When he'd finished, Mrs. A'Dale's shoulder had straightened out perfectly and she no longer leaned sideways, but stood up straight.

"Thank you, me boy," she said tearfully as she kissed him on the cheek.

Zeld wondered why women always try to kiss you. His mother did that too. He turned a shade of pink but not the red shades Dowly made him turn the day before. When he walked through the door, he found the Robin Hood School staff waiting for him. They all clapped as he left the kitchen. He hurried to escape his embarrassing moment and made his way over to his team.

Sir Roger asked with a tone of false politeness, "And where have you been - laughter boy."

"Er - in the kitchen."

"In case you've forgotten, we're hosting the next tournament and plan to take the large tents back with us," Sir Roger said while restraining his anger.

Zeld understood this meant loads of trouble, "What d'you want me to do?"

"Scurry over there and help Norton," Sir Roger answered.

He went straightaway. Norton called, "Hold the pole steady - lover boy," and pointed to an unattended tent pole.

Zeld snatched it up. Presently the centre pole came down and the big tent lay on its side. Norton adjusted the flaps, and then the team rolled up the tent. Sir Roger brought a wagon around and the boys lifted the tent into the back of it. They followed the same procedure for all eight tents.

The other schools were in no hurry to leave, so Castle and Caverns made it out the gate first. Dowly ran to catch them up, carrying their midday meal in two baskets. The wagon stopped. Zeld bent over reaching down to take the baskets but Dowly had a plan of her own. She tossed the baskets into the wagon on both sides of him, and then wrapped both arms his neck and planted a long kiss, right on his lips. His mates pried them apart before Sir Roger saw them.

Zeld sat in the back of the wagon, his face an unmistakable shade of scarlet, waving goodbye until Dowly faded from sight.

Sir Roger turned around and asked, "Did they send someone with a midday meal?"

"Yes, a girl only just made a special delivery," said Norton warily as he hit Zeld on the shoulder.

"Excellent, then we're away," said Sir Roger in a happier tone.

The journey home went well. They met the cloud on time and Zeld curled up in a ball and slept until noon. The team had pepper and venison steak sandwiches for their midday meal. Zeld laughed; for a girl who didn't know how to make sandwiches, she certainly learned quickly, he thought. The hot and spicy sandwiches made a grand meal.

"At least she can cook," Norton said teasing Zeld.

He knew he'd receive loads of teasing. He wondered, why do girls always have to embarrass you?

At Eagle Loft that night Odin asked, "Did anything exciting happen on your journey?"

"Didja see Robin Hood's ghost?" teased Oles.

"Friar Tuck told us about Robin Hood's adventures," Zeld said with a gigantic yawn.

"Zeld got married," Jens Jr. said with a smirk.

Zeld sprang up out of bed when he heard it, "I what?"

"I saw the whole thing with me own eyes. Zeld and this hunched back girl went out on a picnic together. While there, he proposed. The hunched back girl laughed and laughed. Presently, Friar Tuck went up the hill as Zeld prearranged and he married them on the spot. The hunched back girl laughed and laughed for two hours; then, she magically turned into a beautiful girl who wouldn't stop kissing Zeld. It was so lovely," Jens Jr. said pretending to wipe away a tear.

"So, what's your wife's name?" asked Oars while trying to join in on this new line of teasing.

"Rumpelstiltskin," Zeld said coldly. Then, he turned to Jens Jr., "So, are you gonna tell them the story of you and that half-gopher girl? She had quite the front teeth you know and the way her mum kept chattering at you. I don't think she fancied you at all. What was the furry girl's name again? Rotting log?"

The triplets laughed. They'd no idea teasing boys about girls with hunched backs and the big teeth could be so much fun.

"Tell us some more," they cried in unison.

"We're exhausted," said Zeld as he climbed back into bed.

"Oh, I've loads more," said Jens Jr. perking up. He told a story about a lengthy duel between Wilhelm and Norton. It ended with Jens Jr. saying, "Wilhelm tired, so he swung for Norton's knee. Norton saw it coming, jumped the blow and in the same move swung his sword cutting the tip of Wilhelm's nose off."

"Is that true or are you stringing us along?" Zeld heard someone ask just before he dozed.

CHAPTER Twenty Five

Norton Dudal

Odin raised his hand at the beginning of Sir Jaydan's class. Sir Jaydan called on him and asked, "Bee in your bonnet?"

"Yes, I noticed a change in the animals. Some spend less time outta their lairs while others scurry about most of the time. Which dangerous animals become more active this time of year?"

"Tree sprites, pythons, non-fire breathing land dragons, bears, snakes, giant-sized rodents, such as rabbits and weasels, and packs of wild poof hounds," answered Sir Jaydan, who always managed to slip something even more interesting into his lesson, or at least Zeld thought so.

"Speaking of dangerous animals, dragons have a certain innate ability to cast an overwhelming sense of fear on humans and other animals. We call it dragon fear and it is a truly devastating, even paralysing condition which makes dragons an especially difficult foe. The more helpful news is humans become immune to it after only two experiences. The regrettable news is hardly anyone lives long enough to experience the trauma twice."

In Battle Preparations class the students learned the proper use of the knife, the saw and the axe. In a roped off area near the targets Sir Roger set up a learning centre. Each boy practiced until they did well. Zeld did better with the axe than any of the other boys. He felt pleased to think he had inherited something special from his father.

On Wednesday the school didn't hold classes. The students went on a woodcutting expedition to the school lodge. They used all the school's wagons and borrowed two more from the townsfolk. The lodge was a two-story building, almost the size of the Great Hall, with a large room on the top floor and a kitchen on one side similar to the Great Hall.

The students were divided into groups and issued wagons and axes. Zeld remembered how the giants used big swings to cut down the trees at the two-man boat carving event. He used their technique with his axe. It looked impressive but Zeld didn't have the proper leverage or the strength to chop down the tree as quickly as the giants, but he felled one all the same.

The students removed the limbs and loaded the wagons. The boys took turns using the axes so no one would tire too quickly. Zeld enjoyed working up a sweat and he found the mountain air had a wholesome smell, quite different from the smoky fires burned at the castle.

At noon they stopped for their midday meal. Zeld and his mates ate sitting on crude benches around two large fire pits near the lodge. None of the students had chopped off their fingers or toes but they did discover loads of slivers. Zeld realized he needed working gloves. He planned to buy himself, James and Brian each a pair.

After their midday meal the boys filled the wagons with the firewood. Once loaded, the staff drove the wagons down the mountain. The boys picked the slivers out of their hands and everyone groaned from sore muscles.

When they returned, Zeld could see the tournament tents pitched in the background. They stood out, making the castle look splendid, reminiscent of a carnival. Zeld helped unload his wagon at the kitchen's woodpile, which rose to seven-feet high and three rows thick. Other wagons were emptied by the south wall with the old firewood. The school prepared for the transition from fall to winter. The day wasn't too hot or too cold and the large number of boys made the work light and fun.

On Friday they didn't hold classes either. Instead the boys were organized to go to the farms early in the morning right after breakfast. Zeld carried his bag with his usual items and this time found himself partnered with Norton Duval.

Just before their departure, the McMarr bothers had a surprise visit from Jens Sr., who told them he planned to take a secret journey for a fortnight.

Despite the rush, Oars called Zeld into the Great Hall and said alertly, "Zeld, tell me dad about your soldier who wants his family brought over from Denmark."

"Oh, yes, one of me soldiers wants to bring his wife and children from Denmark. I dunno if it's possible but I thought I should talk to you about it."

"Where is the soldier?" Jens Sr. asked.

Zeld took Jens Sr. to the kitchen to speak with Morten.

When finished Jens Sr. turned to Zeld and asked, "Is there anything I should tell your mother?"

Zeld realized where Jens Sr. planned to go.

"Please take her this money and tell her I'm doing well," said Zeld handing Jens Sr. his purse.

"I'll tell her about your many adventures."

"Leave out the bad parts."

Norton called from the door, "Hey, lover boy it's time to go."

Jens Sr. looked at Zeld, both of his eyebrows lifted in surprise.

"You don't have to say anything about Dowly either."

"Who's Dowly?"

To avoid answering the question Zeld hurried out the door, mounted Tiger, and rode quickly out the main gate. He stopped and waited for Norton who had been stopped by Sir Tavish. Zeld watched as Jens Sr. stepped outside the Great Hall and rattled the small purse of coins. Jens Sr. opened the purse and looked inside. He found the five pottery shards Zeld had found on his way to England. Jens Sr. poured them out into his hand, jiggled them back and forth for a couple of seconds and threw them on the ground. Norton joined Zeld but not before Zeld saw Sir Tavish reach down and collect something laying the ground. Zeld and Norton rode south for the farms.

Jens Sr. rode out of the castle with his two escorts, and then turned north.

Sir Tavish examined the pottery shards closely; he closed his fist on them; then, turned sharply and walked away.

Norton rode side by side with Zeld to the south to find their assigned farm. They found it in terrible condition due to neglect. Rusty farm equipment lay strewn everywhere. The fences needed new posts, the house and barn hadn't seen repair in years and the fields sat overgrown with brambles and tall weeds. In short, the farm lay in shambles.

Zeld found no one at home, so he carried rusty metal farm tools into the barn while Norton rode the fence line. After Zeld straightened the yard, he joined Norton at the fence. It took awhile but the two of them repaired the fence by reattaching several fallen rails and replacing three posts.

Zeld realized they'd yet to see anyone at the farm and had merely guessed at what to do. Zeld wondered if anyone lived there at all. Norton and Zeld worked straight through and had no mid-day meal. They examined an old weather-beaten wagon. They hitched up their horses and pulled it into the barn.

"This way it'll be outta the rain," remarked Norton.

"Look up," suggested Zeld.

When Norton looked up, he saw several large holes in the roof. He marched straight into the house and found its roof in an unacceptable condition as well. Norton acted disturbed. "Stupid farm," he muttered. "When I get my hands on Fielding ..."

"What are you talking about?" asked Zeld.

"My sister is coming to live at this farm. I thought it best to move her out here - er - she tells me she's no longer safe living at my father's manor. His soldiers are nothing more than pirates hiding behind our family's coat of arms." Norton added worriedly, "We'll have to patch the roofs today."

"The neighbours might have what we need to repair them," suggested Zeld.

They mounted their horses and rode to the nearest neighbour and Norton asked, "Do you have roofing materials?"

The farmer stepped out of his farmhouse. "Yes." then he said cleverly. "Do you have money or merchandise to trade?"

"What d'you need?" asked Zeld realizing he and Norton might end up on the short side of the trade.

"I can't think of anything straightaway."

"How about a wagon load of stone fragments from the castle?" suggested Zeld.

"Yes, I'd gladly trade all me roofing material for a wagon load of stone."

"In exchange would you make sure the roofs on the house and barn at the next farm are repaired by the time the big winter storms hit?" asked Norton pressing for an agreement.

"It's a substantial amount of work and in a short time," the farmer parried.

"Zeld and I'll start the project tomorrow morning. We need you to finish the roofs and provide the materials."

"Agreed," the farmer said abruptly as he reached out to shake hands. "Me name is Michael Woodsman and I'm glad to be of assistance."

He shook Norton's hand, and then Zeld's.

"So, who is moving in?" asked the farmer.

"My sister," said Norton standing to his full height, clearly trying to intimidate the farmer.

The farmer backed away, "Isn't that nice," he said choking on his words.

"We'll be back," said Norton reassuringly. The boys rode to the castle and checked out a wagon from the hostler, who recorded the boys' names in a log book. It took nearly two hours of hard work to fill the wagon. As they left the castle, Zeld jumped down from the wagon and went into the kitchen while Norton waited.

"D'you have anything we can take for supper?" Zeld asked his soldiers in the kitchen.

Morten hurriedly put together some food in a basket, while Peder continued working on an upcoming feast scheduled for the following day. Zeld headed out the door and placed the basket of food into Norton's lap.

"Thank you," he called back to his soldiers.

Then, Zeld drove the wagon through the gate and turned south. Norton opened the basket and ate some cold fried chicken.

"Save a bite for me."

"You wish."

Zeld stopped the wagon next to the Woodsman's farmhouse where the farmer directed him. While Norton started unloading the rock, Zeld ate the two pieces of chicken and a slice of berry pie Norton saved him. When Zeld finished his meal, he joined Norton in the back of the wagon.

When finished, Norton spied a wagon sitting out front of his sister's farmhouse. "Let's go, Zeld. My sister has arrived."

Norton waited impatiently in the wagon seat for the farmer to carry the last of the roofing materials to the wagon, and then he started the horses. The tired horses moved slowly.

Norton parked his wagon next to the one that had brought his sister. He marched into his sister's farmhouse and called, "Sis, are you here?"

"I'm here," said a frail feminine voice.

Norton walked into the bedroom and found two of his father's soldiers building a bedframe in the corner. A teenage girl sat on the floor watching them. Norton knelt down and held her close.

Zeld introduced himself to Norton's sister, "Hello, me name is Zeld de Exile."

The girl looked up at Zeld, and then over to Norton. "Is this the boy everyone's talking about?" she asked.

"Yes, this is the infamous Zeld who strikes fear in the hearts of grown men with castles and armies," said Norton, shaking his head.

Norton stood up and the girl introduced herself, "I'm Norta Duval."

Zeld took a good look at her and smiled because, besides her colouring, she didn't look a bit like Norton and a good thing too. She had a thin build with long brown hair nearly reaching her waist. Her eyes were a beautiful shade of light brown.

Without missing a beat Zeld asked Norta, "I noticed several crates in the back of your wagon. Shall I fetch them in?"

"Yes, please," Norta replied.

Zeld carried several loads of wooden crates into the house. While he worked, another young woman came around the corner of the house and watched him. As soon as the soldiers finished building the bedframe, they went outside and tossed the remaining crates off the wagon. The crates broke into pieces scattering Norta's belongings. The soldiers left, laughing, along with the young woman, who laughed the loudest.

Zeld turned toward Norton who stood in the doorway, watching with a livid expression on his face, as the men left. Zeld said, "If I had a sister living among scoundrels, I'd run them off at the tip of me sword."

Norta, who had stayed in the house the entire time, looked surprised to hear someone speak as if she mattered; only Norton had ever spoken on her behalf before.

Norton carried Norta to her bed, "So, now what are we gonna do? They took your maid with them. I can't leave you here alone."

"Fetch me something to drink please and I'll think it through."

Norton opened one of the crates and found a flask of water.

He handed it to Norta and said, "We're gonna start repairs on the roof."

Zeld walked in with a puzzled expression and asked, "Are you injured Norta?"

"Of course, she is, you numbskull. She can't walk more than a few steps at a time," Norton said, further revealing his anger.

Zeld pulled out this healing amulet, "Perhaps, you should heal her."

Norton shouted, "I WISH I COULD - BUT THE HEALERS SAY IT'S NOT POSSIBLE."

"This healing amulet might manage it."

Norton turned to Zeld, "What makes you think some stone can heal her when the healers can't."

"I used this amulet to heal the hunched back girl at the Robin Hood School," Zeld replied in a hopeful tone.

"You healed the hunched back girl?" asked Norton astonished.

"Well, you saw her kiss me on the way outta the gate."

"That was the hunched back girl?"

"Yes – honestly – why else d'you think she kissed me?" asked Zeld, amazed Norton might've answered him differently.

"I thought she was the gitty village flirt," Norton said astonished at Zeld's good deed.

Zeld stood up straight and said in a serious voice, "This healing comes with a price."

"What price?"

"An alliance between us forever."

"Only if the healing works," barked Norton unyieldingly and pointing his finger at Zeld.

"Agreed," said Zeld with a handshake.

"Norta, where does it hurt?" asked Zeld in a comforting tone.

She indicated her ankles, her knees and her hips.

"Which place hurts the most?"

"My hips ache constantly," said Norta pointing to her pain centres.

"Norton, place the amulet on her right hip," Zeld said handing him the stone. "You simply hold it there." Then, Zeld turned and walked to the front of the house and continued to carry the contents from the broken crates inside.

Norton moved the stone to his sister's left hip.

"It tickles," Norta said through a small laugh.

"Go ahead and laugh, all you want. The tickling means it's working," Zeld called from the doorway.

Norta straightened out on the bed. She laughed a bit but nothing like Dowly. Presently the tickling stopped and Norton tried the knees. He watched as Norta's legs slowly straightened. When he moved the stone to her ankles, it went dark and stopped working. When he called Zeld in to look at it, he told Norton they'd have to let the stone gather power again before they could finish. Norta looked thankfully up at Zeld.

Soon darkness filled the house, so Norton went outside to find some firewood. He found the broken crates and used them. The firelight allowed the two boys to work inside and set up house for Norta. Zeld and Norton slept in front of the fireplace.

The next morning Norton went straightaway in to Norta's bedroom and used Zeld's stone on one of her ankles. This time Norta laughed hysterically. He had never heard his sister laugh so much in her life. When she stopped, he moved the stone to the other ankle. This time Norta laughed so hard she turned blue. When Norton finished, she stopped laughing and stood up. Her legs wobbled a bit, but her face showed how grateful she felt. She hugged them both and cried tears of joy. "It doesn't hurt, it doesn't hurt to walk," she said.

Zeld felt happy for Norta, but he felt even happier when he realized she didn't kiss him. She didn't even try.

Norton returned the stone to Zeld. The two of them worked for a couple of hours repairing the roof of the house. When finished they passed up the barn project as farmer Woodsman would take care of it. Instead they went after firewood. They filled the wagon, and unloaded it by the side of the house.

When the time to return to the school came, Norton insisted on bringing Norta along. This made Zeld a bit nervous until the wagon reached the castle. One look at the school told Zeld exactly why Norton wanted to bring his sister.

CHAPTER TWENTY SIX
THE FESTIVAL

Zeld read aloud from a banner hanging on the castle wall, "Welcome to the Apple Days Festival." As Zeld, Norton and Norta arrived at the castle in the late morning, Zeld saw a vast crowd of shopkeepers and farmers, along with their families gathering for a celebration. The red and white tournament tents stood high in the background. The school's staff served free food to everyone.

"I didn't know we were hosting a festival," Zeld said honestly surprised.

"Sir Roger told us on the way back from the archery tournament," replied Norton.

"I fell asleep."

"What didja think we worked on all this week?"

"Preparing for the next school competition," Zeld answered sheepishly.

Norton smiled and said, "I'd forgotten you're a first-year page. Have you ever attended a festival?"

"Yeah, years ago when me family still had our lands and castle or castles, as I recently found out."

"So, what happened to your family?"

"The Hesse's happened to me family."

Norton looked up at him in surprise. Norta climbed down from the wagon and the squires swiftly seized the opportunity to meet the new beautiful girl who came through the gate.

"My name is Jill," she told them.

"Jill is her middle name," Norton told Zeld quietly, "we thought it best if she used her middle name for safety reasons. If you ever tell a soul..."

Zeld said in a reassuring tone, "Your secret is safe with me, ally."

Norton sat in the wagon with a shocked look on his face as if he finally understood he had become ally to both Zeld's family and the Hesse family.

"What on earth will my father say?" Norton said to himself in a whisper which Zeld overheard as he climbed down from the wagon. "I don't even want to know. I mean - he healed my sister - and - er - I can't - but if I don't - then - they'll come after me."

With all the boys hovering around her, Jill became the main attraction of the carnival. Norton didn't check the wagon back in. He drove it over to the south field with all the other wagons, turned the horses loose in the makeshift corral, and then returned to the castle.

Zeld feasted on hush puppies, glazed gammon and a baked potato. The party went on for hours. Jugglers and tumblers came. A jester entertained, performing every hour on the hour. They had a puppet show inside a food cart with curtains. Zeld found plenty of time to see everything and talk to everyone. The baker from Baden served his famous pies at the end. Then everyone drifted away, some returned home and some packed their wares.

Norton escorted Jill to the wagon and hitched it up. Norton's wagon left first and it didn't come back until dusk.

A few days later, Sir Tavish laid out eight fist-sized highly polished white stones which stood out brightly against the dark grain of the wooden table in the library. He placed a sizeable stone on the end. Eight boys sat at the table, one behind each small stone.

Sir Tavish asked a question and any page sitting at the table could touch the stone in front of him and attempt to answer it. If anyone touched their stone, it would light up and so would the big stone in front of Sir Tavish. None of the other stones would light until the large stone in front of the official was touched, resetting the game. Zeld found the stones fascinating.

The other boys kept poking the stone in front on them with their fingers, but once Sir Tavish regained their attention, he explained the rest of the rules, "The object is to capture 20 questions. Each time a question is correctly answered, it is placed in the team's stack. If an incorrect answer is given, the other team may steal the question by answering it."

It took a little while getting used to the rules, but the boys enjoyed the game immensely. Sir Tavish asked 10 questions, and then rotated eight new boys into the game.

On Zeld's turn, Sir Tavish asked, "What is the capital of Ireland?"

Zeld touched his stone but since he hadn't touched in first, he couldn't answer the question.

Brian Boru touched in first and said, "Dublin."

"Correct," Sir Tavish said abruptly. Then he asked the next question, "What are dragons' teeth used for?"

Zeld touched the stone faster this time. Sir Tavish looked at Zeld and waited for an answer. "Lightning arrows."

Sir Tavish replied thoughtfully, "We'll award you that one. The answer on the scroll says explosive arrows but lightning arrows is also an excellent description."

Sir Tavish continued, "What is the name of the plant which grows in Denmark and is used to heal horse's broken legs?"

No one touched their stone. After three seconds Zeld touched his. "Huddy Joor," he said a bit uncertain of himself.

"That is correct," declared Sir Tavish.

"What is King Henry's surname?"

Zeld touched in. This time everyone stared at him.

"Plantagenet."

Robert O'Day said, "Sorry old champ, but you can't get 'em...."

Sir Tavish interrupted with, "That is absolutely correct."

Robert's jaw dropped leaving his mouth wide open. Crispyn of Orange reached over and closed Robert's jaw with his left hand. Robert stood in place, his eyebrows raised, still stunned.

The game continued, "What is the capital of England?"

Oars touched in and answered, "London."

Zeld felt a wee bit embarrassed not knowing that one.

Sir Tavish said, "Correct." Then asked, "What do Vikings use on their ships to frighten away sea monsters?"

Zeld touched in, "A carved sea monster head."

Everyone laughed.

"That's totally – accurate!" said Sir Tavish and the class laughed even louder. "What is the name of the part of a boat the lookout sits in?"

Zeld attempted to touch in, but he was too late.

James O'Day said, "The crow's nest."

The class waited to hear Sir Tavish's answer.

"Correct," he bellowed.

"Name the magical creature who can unlock a lock with one touch?"

All the students tried to touch in but Brian Boru touched first, "The Unicorn."

"Is that what Sir Jaydan taught you?" asked Sir Tavish apologetically while shaking his head.

The room fell silent.

Sir Tavish answered his own question, "Well then, he's taught you correctly." Several of the pages let out sighs of relief.

"What's the name of the King of France?" asked Sir Tavish. The room fell silent again. Sir Tavish waited patiently. No late response came.

Sir Tavish went on to the next question, "What colour do you create when you mix red paint with blue paint?"

James touched in, "Purple."

"Correct," Sir Tavish said. Then he called for another group of eight boys to participate.

Later that day Zeld stepped into Penny's clothing shop to avoid the heavy snowfall. The shops remained open but they hadn't had many customers due to the storm. Zeld asked pleasantly, "Is your business doing well?"

Penny beamed with excitement when she saw him. "My Lord, I'm expanding the store this spring. I'll have a half basement for storage."

Then she leaned over and whispered, "My Lord, I need you to remove the piles of dirt, so I can make a full basement. This will give us a place to hide an armoury."

"Brilliant," he whispered back.

"I'm looking for some work gloves and a hunting knife," Zeld said out loud. Then he whispered, "I don't have any money today."

Penny whispered, "Pretend to pay."

Penny took Zeld to the work gloves and he took three pairs. Then he looked at the hunting knives and selected one with a six-inch blade and leather sheath.

Penny said, "This is our most popular hunting knife." Then she whispered, "The man who makes them also makes swords."

"Excellent, he does good work," Zeld said out loud.

Penny noticed Zeld wasn't wearing a cloak, "It's bitter cold, do you need a cloak?"

He said a little embarrassed, "I need three of them."

Penny's eyes widened.

Zeld whispered, "Don't worry, they're not all for me and I have money coming."

He removed three cloaks from the display and walked over to the cupboard. He pretended to hand her money and she thanked him for his business. Zeld smiled and walked out.

Zeld had a pleasant surprise waiting for him when he came through the school's gate, "Bushhard!" he called loudly, greeting his friend.

"Zeld, my friend," Bushhard called back. "We've brought you some money from the mine."

Bushhard had a saddlebag resting over his shoulders. "We dwarfolk are living at the silver mine north of here again," Bushhard informed Zeld as they both slipped into the Great Hall.

"You're not mining? What happened?"

"Winter happened, we can't work in the bitter cold," Bushhard explained.

"Someone'll steal me mine."

"Not with the troll living under the bridge."

"What bridge?"

"The people from the Prince Valiant castle insisted we build a bridge because we ruined their road," Bushhard said with his hands on his hips. "We took our money to the lumbermill and there we met a troll who had heard a rumour about the new bridge. He asked if he could build it and live under it. So, I agreed," Bushhard nodded. "He built a stout wooden bridge and added plenty of hidden living space underneath. Tohonnie is a good mate."

"After a while his wife and two children moved in. They grow mushrooms under the bridge to eat," Bushhard said shaking his head. "I thought we dwarves had it unbearable. Living under a bridge and eating a solitary diet of mushrooms is a terrible life, far worse than mine," Bushhard concluded.

"So, how much money did you bring me?"

Bushhard smiled, looked warily around, and then leaned forward and whispered, "12,214 gold pieces."

Zeld tried not to look ecstatic.

"You keep the saddlebag as well," Bushhard said as he held it out for Zeld to take. "I purchased it with your money anyway."

Zeld took Bushhard into the kitchen to find him something to eat, as was customary. He found three rolls which he stuffed with meat and cheese. Zeld's two soldiers came over to help. He showed them his saddlebag with the gold in it, so they would know they guarded more than him alone.

"You are a rich boy?" asked Morten respectfully.

"Only the wealthiest boys go to school here," answered Peder.

Zeld told them, "I haven't heard back from our mates in Denmark yet. This is Bushhard. He's our friend and ally."

The soldiers laughed.

Zeld informed them, "This man isn't taken seriously. That's why he's such a threat to our enemies."

They stopped laughing. Their English had improved and they appeared to have understood him perfectly.

The cooks showed their hospitality by finding Bushhard a slice of pie to go with his rolls. When finished Bushhard rose to leave. He said, "Thank you, my friends, and God be with you."

Zeld called, "Bushhard, d'you need anything?"

Bushhard stopped at the door. "The lady who sells clothing in the town of Baden will not sell to us."

Zeld took out two hundred and fourteen gold pieces and handed them to Bushhard in small stacks, "Give her two hundred gold pieces and say, 'These are from our ally at the school'. She'll let you purchase anything you need after that. Give her the fourteen gold pieces to pay for the clothes I purchased today - she'll understand," Zeld told Bushhard.

"We'll go tomorrow."

"No, tomorrow is Sunday. She'll not let anyone buy on Sunday. It's a holy day," Zeld explained.

"We'll go shopping in two days then."

Zeld nodded approvingly, "Yes, that's all right."

While everyone queued for supper, Zeld went to Eagle Loft and opened his treasure chest. He struggled to fit everything inside.

He poked and prodded around for a while, looking for the secret compartment but couldn't find it. He rearranged the contents and placed the new saddlebag full of gold on the bottom. He locked the treasure chest, and then ran to the Great Hall.

He queued last for supper but first to try a new red coloured custard dessert with fruit chunks inside, called rodgrod. On top sat beaten cream which stood up similar to a hat on a priest. The dessert tasted wonderful. Zeld loved the cook's new recipe.

Mrs. Palfreeman stepped out of the kitchen and announced to everyone, "This is the recipe of my assistant cooks." Everyone applauded and the two cooks bowed.

Zeld lay awake that night thinking. His life had entered one of those quick cycles again and he did his best to keep up with it all. After everyone fell asleep, he arose and took the cloaks and gloves out of his treasure chest. He placed the gloves next to James's and Brian's beds; then, blanketed them with the cloaks. Then he did the same thing with his bed, hoping no one would suspect they came from him. In the morning Zeld acted as surprised as the other boys.

Later that week in Sir Tavish's class Brian Boru, Zeld de Exile, James O'Day and Jens McMarr Jr. were formally named as members of the quiz game competing team.

The other boys took it upon themselves to help them practice, so during meals, between classes, and before bed the boys kept asking them questions. The triplets didn't wait for the answers either. They kept asking the questions faster and faster, which made it nerve racking to be around them for any length of time.

Norton took a group of boys riding horses down to Jill's farm the following Saturday. Zeld noticed the patched roofs were replaced with brand new ones and plenty of firewood lay stacked alongside two rather large mounds of dirt hidden up against the barn. Someone had been digging and tried to hide it.

Zeld became suspicious. When no one looked, Zeld crept into the barn and searched the floor carefully. He found a trapdoor in the floor of the pigsty. He lifted it open and crept down a small wooden stairway closing the door above him. After a minute his eyes adjusted to the sparse light.

He found loads of food stored on shelves. He pushed with both hands to check on the sturdiness of the shelving and one of them swung open resembling a door. Zeld saw a large hidden room with thousands of arrows and several contraptions which would hurl arrows five at a time. He also saw kite shields with the Hessen lion painted on them.

"Where is everyone?" Norton called.

Zeld's heart pounded. If caught in the secret armoury, Norton would surely kill him. It was illogical to think otherwise. Zeld heard footsteps coming his way. He looked up and saw a boot directly above him through the gaps in the floorboards. In absolute silence he slipped into the armoury and hid behind a barrel. He heard the trapdoor to the pigsty open and someone heavy stepping down the wooden stairs toward him.

Zeld held perfectly still. He realized he had started panting so he changed his breathing to slow deep breaths through his nose. He kept as quiet as the grave. He could hear the scraping sound of Norton drawing his sword. The shelf swung open, and then Zeld heard a girl's voice call, "Norton, are you down there."

It was Jill. "Come here this instant," she said urgently. "I have a problem with these nasty green bugs."

Norton climbed back up the stairs and dropped the cover back on top. "The bugs might be coming from down there," Norton suggested.

"No, they're in the house," Jill said. Zeld heard Norton walk away.

Zeld wiped his sweaty face with his shirt sleeve. Then he crept back to the pantry and listened momentarily. He lifted his hand through the trap door taking hold of some straw. He erased his footprints in the pantry; then, he climbed up the stairway and into the pig stall. He brushed the straw back over the trapdoor and left through the back door of the barn.

He saw more than he bargained for in the secret armoury.

Norton yelled, "It's time to go."

The lot stayed less than an hour, but they could do nothing more for Jill until spring.

They rode their horses to Baden. Zeld walked around the shops and visited with the townsfolk. He tried to remember the location of the shops but the town of Baden confused him. It had narrow streets and the shops had been built right next to each other. He was unable to see more than a few feet ahead and every time he went down Main Street the shops appeared to change places. The blacksmith seemed familiar to him but he couldn't remember where they'd met. He went into the clothing store and saw Penny.

"I had a visitor the other day," she said. "A very generous man."

"Did he buy anything?"

"Winter clothing and lots of it."

"Did he pay you for things?"

"Yes, he was a distinguished sort of a man and made sure he paid in full."

"I'd take excellent care of that customer."

They heard a commotion outside and looked out the window.

Zeld heard Mr. Duval yelling violently at Norton, "I DON'T CARE IF YOU THINK HE'S YOUR MATE - HE'S YOUR ENEMY!" Mr. Duval's voice decreased in volume, "and I want him dead. If he doesn't talk by spring, you kill him. Make sure it looks accidental."

Norton remained silent and simply shook his head while obviously waiting for his father to leave. Zeld understood perfectly what this meant.

"Whom does he want murdered?" whispered Penny.

"Me. The Duvals are part of the Hessen alliance." Zeld turned and found Penny's frightened expression. "Don't worry, I already knew they wanted me dead. They're trying to learn the location of me mum, so they can kill the whole family. This has been Hesse's plan ever since I arrived. By the way, your expansion idea, I found the exact same idea already put into place at a local farm. All the dirt piled outside the barn clued me in that something mischievous was afoot."

"Is someone hiding weapons nearby?"

"Yes, and they're doing a proper job of it."

Penny leaned forward grabbing onto Zeld's arm with both hands, "Then it's happening all over again."

"Not if we empty the barn first," said Zeld.

Penny volunteered to help. The alternative would surely be another disaster.

Zeld thought for a moment, and then said logically, "Let me tell you how you can help. It might be a spur of the moment thing - have some money in readiness - er - and see if you can borrow a couple of wagons or sleighs at short notice for a week or so. I think we'll need to take some items far away."

Just then the door to the shop opened and a customer came in.

"I can do that but I can't guarantee the colour you want will arrive," Penny said as if they spoke about something else entirely.

Penny made a magnificent spy, Zeld thought, and it's fun talking to her about things when she makes it appear you're talking about something else altogether.

She said, "Oh, and I have your change from the last transaction."

She went over to the cupboard and took out some coins and handed them to him.

"Thank you, me lady," Zeld said as he waved and slipped out the door.

Zeld searched for Jens Jr. After all, Jens Jr., being the eldest McMarr son, would take the lead for the McMarr family in what Zeld had in mind. He chanced upon Odin who told him Jens Jr. had gone to the bakery. Zeld rode in the direction Odin pointed.

The bakery smelled wonderful and Zeld took a moment to take in the sights and smells. The baker displayed a multitude of baked goods. Large round loaves of wheat, rye and barley bread cooled near the windows. A tray of rolls and cheese rolls rested at the front counter. Treats of sticky buns, honey twists, fruit tarts and éclairs also awaited costumers. The front of the shop held two booths for sitting in while two large bake-ovens were in the back. High stacks of firewood lay heaped on one side of the shop. Zeld stared at everything for a moment, and then he watched as the baker removed eight fresh pies from the oven. His mouth watered as he knew how good they would taste. With a sigh he turned to Jens Jr. to take care of his business.

Jens Jr. had only just bitten into one of the baker's tempting treats.

"What's that?" Zeld asked politely.

Jens Jr. broke a piece of it off and handed it to Zeld. "It's an éclair," Jens Jr. mumbled with his mouth full. Zeld popped the morsel into his mouth. It consisted of a custard cream and icing with a doughnut taste.

"We need a war council," Zeld said in almost a whisper.

"Me Dad is away. Why don't you ask Norton to help you?"

"Norton's a Hessen spy. His father plans to have Norton kill me this spring."

"Sounds as if you could use a few allies," said Jens Jr.

"That's why I'm talking to you," said Zeld, clearly frustrated.

Jens Jr. sat quietly for a few moments. He appeared to be solving a riddle.

"You did know the McMarr's and de Saxons are allies, didn't you?" asked Zeld with a tone of urgency.

"No, I didn't, but it makes sense. After all both you and .... "

"Your brothers never told you?" Zeld interrupted.

"Whom do we invite to the council?" asked Jens Jr.

"First and foremost the McMarrs, then the O'Day's, Brian Boru, and Sullivan de Bruce," Zeld said.

"I'll invite a special someone to join us," said Jens Jr.

"Only invite those you know we can trust. Can we manage it tonight?" asked Zeld with the sense of urgency returning.

"Yes, tonight is good. We'll meet in the library at midnight."

Zeld bit his lower lip pretending he felt nervous, "Wake me up if I fall asleep."

Jens Jr. laughed. "Go away," he said and pushed Zeld aside. Then he added in a serious tone, "I'll see you tonight."

CHAPTER Twenty Seven

Dreamers Dream, Plotters Plot, Schemers Scheme and Pages Do All Three

Zeld asked himself silently, "Where can I hide all the weapons from the armoury?" He thought things through while riding Tiger back to the school. The thieves from earlier in the year tried to make their getaway in a wagon and that didn't work. Under my bed won't work either, he thought. "Awe, yes, the dwarven mine," he said out loud.

Zeld rode the short distance to find the dwarves. He pried open the entrance, stepped inside and yelled, "HELLO." His call echoed down the caverns. A child walked up and closed the entrance behind him.

After a couple of minutes Bushhard came up from a mine shaft.

"Hello, Zeld," he said graciously.

"I came to ask a favour - er - it's dangerous," Zeld explained.

"What is it?"

"I need a place to hide weapons and armour for a few days."

"Do you want to hide them in the mine?"

"Yes."

"We hide things for customers all the time," Bushhard said in a matter of fact tone.

"You do?"

"Of course and for you, we will not charge."

"You charge people?" asked Zeld, who felt a wee bit thick minded. "I had no idea."

"A dwarf has to live you know."

"Sometime soon and probably in the middle of the night, we'll send wagons or sleighs loaded with weapons," Zeld informed him.

"It's always done at night," Bushhard said as if it were obvious to everyone.

Zeld thought Penny had come up with an original plan of hiding things under the store, but she hadn't. He also thought hiding his stash in the mine was original. Zeld realized he needed smuggling lessons.

"Bushhard, don't let me make a mess of this. If I'm doing something amiss, please set it right," Zeld said with a tinge on concern.

"Zeld, my friend, you are about to do something – well – ill-fated. The problem is you're leaving a trail for others to follow. If you have ordered weapons from a shop, the shopkeeper might be persuaded, by whatever means, to betray your trust. Weapons are speedily traced to the owner and are generally easy to find. I will teach you a few clever tricks," Bushhard began.

"Hang on, are you busy at midnight?"

"Are you meeting with others?"

"Yes, we're holding a war council. You see I'm not buying weapons; actually, we're planning the best way to raid a stash of Hessen weapons I discovered at the farms."

"Then, your mates are assisting you?" asked Bushhard.

"Yes and we're meeting at midnight to discuss our plans. Can you be at the kitchen door of the castle five minutes before midnight?" Zeld asked hopefully.

"Yes, I can."

"Thank you and I'll let you in. I must go before I'm missed. D'you need anything?"

"Food."

"I'll work on it." said Zeld, "God be with you."

He rode to the school's bathhouse and bathed early. Despite the cold water Zeld washed his hair and his clothes. Zeld worried about taking the weapons. He asked himself, what if we are discovered? He wanted to forget the whole adventure, until he remembered the attack on the castle. How many more castles would Godfrey of Hesse take? How many more people will die or have to live under his cruel boot. The consequences of not taking the weapons were inconceivable, yet truly sinister.

At supper Zeld had regained his full courage and he told his soldiers in the kitchen a secret guest would arrive at midnight.

"Vat about de odder guest dat is coming tonight?" one soldier asked confused.

Zeld's heart skipped a beat, "What other guests?"

"De visidoors for Geoffrey of Hesse."

"Does he have visitors often?"

"Yeah, his fadder sends somevone every couple of veeks."

"Peder and Morten, I want you to spy on them," Zeld said, "Report back to me what they talk about. This is a test to see how your English is coming."

"Yeah, ve vill du it guud," said Morten with excitement.

The wind blew that evening and the temperature became dangerously cold. Zeld wondered if it would keep people from coming to the school. It felt as if a century passed before bedtime arrived, and then he couldn't sleep. He arose at ten o'clock and tried again to open the secret compartment on his treasure chest. He toyed with it unsuccessfully for a half an hour before he gave up.

He felt cold, so he climbed back into bed and fell asleep. He dreamed of the day when he and Oars won the horse rescue event. As they crossed the finish line, he awoke with a jolt. He looked around to see if someone had come to wake him but found no one.

Zeld dressed and crept over to the McMarr's beds to wake them but found they had already left for the meeting. He crept outside only to find snow coming down in the castle yard. He made his way toward the Great Hall when he heard a voice say, "This way." The voice sounded familiar, but he couldn't recognize it straightaway. He didn't obey the voice. Instead he dashed for Eagle Loft, but looking over his shoulder he saw two people stepping out of the Great Hall. He hastily dove under a bench in one of the open classrooms. He lay on his stomach unable to see anything. What a terrible place to hide, he thought; after all, I'm laying in full view but I've no place else to go. He listened to the sound of footsteps as they walked toward him.

"Why are you limping?" he heard the familiar voice ask. This time he recognized Geoffrey's voice. He felt someone sit down on the bench he hid under.

"It's an old battle injury," the second person replied. Then he added, "Blimey that's strange."

"What?"

"There's an intense tickling feeling in my foot."

Geoffrey changed the subject, "Do you think the giants will agree to it?"

"Your dad is sending them a thousand gold pieces in advance, with another thousand when the job is done," the other person answered.

A door opened and beams of light filled the courtyard. Zeld turned his face away from the light just as Sir Tavish asked, "Whose there?"

Zeld tried to think of an excuse for the late hour and hiding under a bench in the middle of the night, but couldn't think of a proper one. Perhaps if he pretended to sleepwalk, he might have a chance to play the innocent.

"Rat blossom," said Geoffrey giving the password and the two walked toward Sir Tavish's voice. "Your limp in gone," commented Geoffrey.

"That's strange, maybe it's a good omen," said Geoffrey's companion.

Zeld lay still for a few more seconds, and then the light in the courtyard disappeared. He rolled over realizing he had made it through the ordeal without being caught. He tried to stand but managed to hit his head on the bench instead. He reached into his vest pocket for his amulet but found it empty.

Zeld panicked. He fretted to himself, it could be anywhere. He tried to remember where he saw it last. Then he minded the tickling feeling the man who sat on the bench mentioned. He searched in the mud and found his stone in the bottom of the heel print. He almost shouted for joy. Instead he wiped off the mud and put the amulet back in his vest pocket.

With a sigh of relief he crept silently to the kitchen. He opened the door and looked for Bushhard. He watched as a pair of footprints made their way through the snow and into the kitchen. Once inside, Bushhard appeared, standing in the last set of footprints.

Zeld and Bushhard made it to the library two minutes late. The boys and their guests could speak normally, as the library had thick walls.

"Come in," said Jens Jr. brightly to Zeld when he opened the door.

"This is Bushhard," Zeld said, introducing the dwarf as the two of them stepped into the room.

"D'you know Garth Wheelwright, the blacksmith from Baden?"

"I've seen him 'round."

Garth stood up and shook Zeld's hand.

212

"I held the post of Fletcher in your father's army," Garth said respectfully.

"Excellent, I'm building an army again soon," Zeld told everyone.

"You can begin with what is left of your father's army," suggested Garth.

"How many soldiers is that?" Zeld asked hoping to hear a goodly number.

"Eleven soldiers and one commander," said Garth.

"We'll need their help, if this goes the way I imagine it," said Zeld.

213

"I'm in contact with the other eleven and they live close by."

"Does that count my two soldiers in the kitchen?" Zeld asked, trying to determine whether or not everybody knew who belonged in the growing alliance.

"The assistant cooks are your soldiers?" asked Jens Jr. revealing he was still behind on current events.

"Yes, I knocked them out in the Viking raid at the castle, or so they tell me."

Sullivan came in followed by Brian, James, and Robert. They closed the door behind them.

"Is this everyone?" asked Jens Jr.

"Everyone attending this meeting. The Hesses meet regularly and I saw them gathering into Bull Hollow. I only just escaped capture as they arrived. My soldiers are spying on them," Zeld said.

"Shouldn't we ambush them?" asked Jens Jr. urgently.

"No and for two reasons; firstly, it would violate the rule of safe haven, and secondly, I want to know who I'm up against," Zeld said.

"That makes sense," said Jens Jr., nodding with approval.

"Let me explain why I asked for this meeting. I found a secret stash of weapons with the Hesse family markings under the barn at the farm where Jill lives. I spied thousands of arrows, kite shields and those things which fire arrows in groups of five," Zeld started.

"Mongonels," interrupted Jens Jr.

"I didn't have a chance to see everything but this much I know - they're planning to attack someone. I believe the most likely place is the five damaged castles, because they're weak and out of food and money. Norton Duval stayed in the area for three weeks on guard duty after the Viking raid and he would know exactly how to attack them.

"I propose that we," Zeld paused, "secretly appropriate the weapons and send them to the McMarr Manor. Bushhard is an expert smuggler and I've asked him to teach us the best way of doing this without getting caught," Zeld said with an air of mystery to the group.

Everyone looked with surprise at Bushhard who spoke, "I am Bushhard. In the past I have helped conceal many secret stashes in the mines I have worked. The mine we're in is underground and has many excellent hiding places. The mine is not a problem but smuggling the weapons in and out of the mine is. This is where most jobs go awry and if you are caught, there'll be the devil to pay.

"I believe we should take special precautions, so the goods aren't discovered missing. Firstly, we must replace the weapons and armour with something which resembles the goods," Bushhard said setting one finger on the edge of the table. "For example, we could have the arrows replaced with broken arrows or merely the feather parts of the arrows, so the enemy thinks he still has his weapons."

"Secondly, the exchanges must look like ordinary events, in case someone is watching," Bushhard said setting a second finger on the table top. "Another example, if you schoolboys took loads of goods into the mine, it would look suspicious, but if another family of dwarves moved into the mine; then, no one would suspect a thing," explained Bushhard.

"Er - you want to replace the weapons with - phoney - look-a-likes - and then store the weapons in the mine until we - smuggle them over to the manor?" asked Jens Jr. with a painful expression on his face.

"Yes, or something similar," Zeld responded.

"When Edelweiss captured me, I pretended to join the gang until a chance to escape came along. I learned the mine you live in is watched by pirates. They've stolen equipment from you several times."

"We've had many items stolen. We blamed the elves until Zeld and Friar Timothy proved to us we were mistaken. We never knew about the pirates," said Bushhard in a concerned voice.

"I know they watch you day and night," said Jens Jr.

"Then we can't use the mine," concluded Bushhard.

"There are several places we could hide the goods temporarily. Perhaps behind the big rock overlooking Baden or the double-sided cave, and there is the McMarr Manor itself," explained Zeld.

"Garth, can you work on the replacement goods?" asked Jens Jr. directly.

"I'll need to know roughly the numbers of mongonels, shields and arrows," Garth answered.

"I'll help with the numbers. I recruited Penny at the clothing store to find some wagons which couldn't be traced back to us," Zeld said, revealing another portion of his plan.

"Penny asked if she could borrow me wagon on short notice for a week or so. I told her yes, but that all happened before this meeting," Garth commented, sounding discouraged because a part of the plan had already failed.

"Did she tell you why?" asked Zeld, hoping Penny hadn't said too much.

"No, she's done a lot of peculiar things lately. She's planning on remodelling her store with a basement storeroom. I told her the mice would eat anything down there, but she won't listen to me."

"She's making room for an armoury," Zeld said.

"I've already built a storeroom in me attic and have made several dozen arrows. Do you remember the 15 mulberry bows someone delivered to the castle in Zeld's name? Those came from me," Garth said proudly.

"Thank you, they're the best part of our training," Zeld said surprised.

The other boys nodded in agreement.

Zeld continued, "Let's take what we've learned and formulate a master plan with so many intricate details it is impossible for any would be spies to ferret out what we're doing. In order to identify our side, we'll need a sign. Put both of your fists together and bring them down in a motion resembling the snapping of an arrow in half. This will be very fitting, as you'll see when you hear me plans."

It took an hour to finish planning, but when they did Zeld felt very satisfied. Everyone had work to do and the switch would take place during the next school competition. Any complications which arose during the week would be discussed on Thursday evening.

Zeld sneaked Bushhard quickly back through the kitchen door. He then made his way to Eagle Loft. As far as Zeld knew, Jens Jr.

sneaked Garth in and out another way. Zeld slept well that night even though he felt excited about the plan.

In the morning Zeld's soldiers appeared very tired while serving breakfast in the Great Hall. Although Zeld felt great anticipation to hear their report he decided to wait all day and heard it that night after supper.

That evening they reported. "Day said dat day vere going to put more tings wid friends. Yah, de mill and de lodge," said Peders.

"Yah and dat it vill be a big prize for sir," said Morten trying to explain something was a big surprise.

Zeld completely misunderstood his men's report. He had never heard of anyone named De Mille or De Lodge. He supposed they were Hessen allies who had won a big prize. In truth, Hesse planned to hide more weapons with his spies at the mill and the lodge.

"I've other soldiers, didja know?" Zeld asked his cooks.

"No," answered Peders who spoke better English than Morten.

"You and they will help me with a secret smuggling mission," Zeld informed them.

Their eyes grew rather large as the two of them looked at each other.

CHAPTER Twenty Eight

Button, Button, Who's got the Button

Zeld's heart pounded as he watched Friar Timothy enter Eagle Loft Monday evening. Zeld looked over at Oars who quickly took his position. They made eye contact. Zeld gave the signal by nodding his head and the game was afoot.

"I need a storage shed," said Oars to Friar Timothy.

"Why."

"To hide some Christmas presents."

Zeld interrupted right on cue, "You could use the storage shed the school keeps the archery equipment in. There's plenty of room and I'll cart away any of the old broken arrows."

"I wanted to buy you a present too and if you need something in the shed, then you'll see it. Friar Timothy, may I please use an empty shed?" Oars pleaded.

"Yes, you may use a shed, but mind it's freezing and you shouldn't put anything out the cold will damage," said Friar Timothy.

"I want a shed too," whimpered Oles.

"And me, too," whined Odin in a deliberately obnoxious tone. Zeld rolled his eyes as he thought Odin overplayed his part.

"You may use whatever space you need," said Friar Timothy waving his arms and stepping through the small crowd as if he were glad to be rid of the problem.

Zeld and the McMarr triplets wandered nonchalantly to the storage shed which held the bows and arrows. On their way Zeld held up two fingers to James and Robert O'Day. The two fingers meant it was time for Act II. Once at the shed the boys took out all the arrows, good or not, and broke them in half; then, they broke each half in half. This gave them eight hundred seven-inch arrow shafts to work with. They placed the shafts in Zeld's bag.

The snow in the castle yard had melted and mud puddles lay everywhere. Five minutes after Zeld gave the two finger sign, James and Robert began a row, both of them ending up in the mud right outside the Great Hall. This allowed Zeld and the McMarr triplets to return to Eagle Loft unnoticed.

Friar Jonathan scolded the brothers, "I've had it with you two constantly rowing. Now go to the bathhouse and wash up. Don't forget to use soap."

"I'll collect it for you - er - I don't want all that mud in Eagle Loft. I - I - I'm on clean up duty," Jens Jr. said, playing the innocent with a stutter.

A broad smiled crept across Zeld's face when he heard Jens Jr. as he thought he played his part perfectly.

Jens Jr. returned with a bag full of towels, soap and the broken arrows. James and Robert went to the bathhouse shooting pretend angry looks at each other. They washed their clothes, faces, and the cresting marks from the broken arrows, so they couldn't be traced back to Zeld. When they finished washing, they returned to Eagle Loft and gave Jens Jr. the bag. Jens Jr. took out the towels and soap and dumped the rest of the contents into a wooden rubbish bin.

Jens Jr. then carried the rubbish bin out the main gate to the kitchen stoop and switched it for an identical bin. He stepped back a couple of paces and wiped his forehead with a cloth. Then he walked back to Eagle Loft with the empty bin.

Sullivan de Bruce peered down from the north tower, waiting anxiously for his signal. When he saw Jens Jr. wipe his brow, he pulled out a red scarf from his vest pocket and waved it in the breeze.

Garth Wheelwright sat waiting in his wagon on the north road. When he saw the scarf, he drove down the road. He stopped at the kitchen stoop and unloaded several empty crates.

He collected the box which Jens Jr. had abandoned and asked, "Did you need me to repair this?"

"Yah," Morten replied as if he had done something grand.

Garth put the wooden bin into the back of his wagon, covered it with a cloth and then drove away. Zeld sat on the battlements above the main gate. As Garth turned for Baden, Zeld could see the bin bouncing around in the back of the wagon. He felt very satisfied with how things had gone so far.

Once at his blacksmith shop Garth carried the wooden bin in and buried it under his work for the day, with a half smile on his face. His shop, the largest in town, held room enough for two large wagons to park inside and that didn't include the work space. Garth had a large hearth with a bellows at its side. Nearby stood an anvil with a large hammer for pounding the hot metal into horseshoes or whatever else might be needed and next to that awaited a water barrel for cooling the red-hot metal.

An assortment of tools rested on a table: casting moulds, smelter bowls, large tongs and various sizes of hammers to name a few. Racks on the sides of the shop held finished projects waiting for customers and long metal rods waited to be shaped into something useful.

When his workday ended, Garth carried the rubbish bin up to his attic room and removed the broken arrows. He diligently glued three feathers on every plain piece, giving them the appearance of arrow tops. When he finished, he had 800 fake arrows. The sunrise extended the first light of the new day as he went to bed.

Two hours later he sleepily arose after hearing a banging at his door. Six men made a delivery. The men had cut barrels to the exact shape of kite shields. Each wooden shield lay face up while the men painted them silver. In relatively little time they prepared 50 shields.

A few minutes later another shipment of tin and flimsy boards arrived. This second work crew cut, glued and tacked together what resembled a box with a bow attached to the front. When they finished, everything was hidden in the attic room. The men vanished by early afternoon leaving only one more job to do; namely, building the last of the crates.

Penny dropped by. "It's another quiet Tuesday afternoon," she said while taking up the hammer on Garth's work table.

"Yes, a regular day," Garth agreed as he pointed out the place for the next nail to go.

"Do you have any tacks or glue you could donate for an excellent cause?" Penny asked teasing him. He smiled and leaned against the crate to hold it steady. Penny tapped the nail into place. The work went much faster with Penny's help. After awhile, Garth grew too exhausted to continue. Penny guided him to a seat where he promptly fell asleep. She finished the last three crates on her own; then, slipped out the door only to return a few moments later with a steak supper for Garth. Zeld paid for the meal, along with everything else, out of the money he had given Penny.

Wednesday was an even busier day for Zeld. The pages from the Brotherhood of Air volunteered to collect the food that morning. The cooks sent extra crates to the farmers. They waited as the cooks loaded the empty crates, which Garth had secretly provided.

"Why are we delivering crates to the farmers?" asked Friar Stephen, a bit confused about the arrangements.

Peders answered, "De farmers are needink some more boxes for de extra fuuds."

"Your English is doing very well," Friar Stephen said.

"Tank you."

On the way to the supply station, the pages quizzed the team. Zeld was bombarded with questions. "What is the capital of Germany?" "What is the capital of Scotland?" "What is the name of the King of France?" "What species of tree makes the best bows?" "What type of arrow gives a bleeding wound?" "What dagger gives a bleeding wound?" The questions seemed endless; however, the journey went much quicker since they had loads to go over.

At the supply station, Zeld and the boys switched the empty crates for the waiting food. They rode back to the school quickly. Zeld felt anxious about the next phase which had to be completed by the few survivors of the de Saxon army. He had no choice but to place blind faith in his father's old soldiers.

On Wednesday evening Zeld's plan went into effect. Two wagons arrived at the supply station and the men driving loaded the page's allegedly empty crates. From there they drove directly to Jill's farm.

"Hide the wagons behind the barn," the man in charge told the others.

The work crew opened the secret passage in the pig's stall, removed the stash of weapons, replaced them with the phoney weapons hidden in the crates, then hid the real weapons inside the crates. They found a few extra hidden surprises on the far side of the room; namely, bottles of healing pills, vials of poison and two catapults. The soldiers fit the extra items into the wagons without any trouble. They dropped off the crates at the pick up station and raced for the blacksmith shop.

"We found a few more items than Zeld told us about," said Kanock.

"Bring the wagons into the shop," Garth told them as he looked warily around to see if anyone spied on them.

The wagons pulled in. Garth took one look and said, "It's nearly impossible to hide the catapults. Unless someone has a better idea we'll cover them with dirt and sneak them to the Robin Hood School. Friar Tuck will undoubtedly know what to do with them. As for the bottles of pills and poison, I know exactly where to hide them."

221

"I wonder why Zeld didn't mention the catapults and the pills?" Kanock asked.

"We discovered them hidden in the back," said Hans. "Maybe Zeld didn't see them."

"I'm sure you're right Hans," Garth agreed.

"Either that or the Hessens are still making deliveries," suggested Kanock.

On Thursday morning Garth went down to the clothing store and asked Penny, "Are you expecting a shipment of glue and beads?" Garth nodded his head slightly.

"Yes, I'm entirely out of glue," she said, playing along.

"I think the delivery wagon must have sent your shipment to me blacksmith shop by mistake. Could you drop by at noon and see if this shipment is yours?"

"I surely will."

At noon Penny walked into the blacksmith's shop and saw Garth painting in red the word glue on a few bottles.

"Penny, this is poison for dipping arrows into. It came as a bonus last night and these are healing pills. We need you to hide them in your store as if they were merchandise, but don't sell them," Garth said while lifting up a small crate the perfect size to put everything in.

Penny took the crate from Garth, set it on his work table, and then quickly loaded it full of the bottles. She carried them to her store where she put them down behind the counter and left them to collect dust.

That same morning a number of crates went to the pick up station in wagons from the school again. The allegedly empty crates from the day before, which were now filled with the stolen arms, sat next to the filled farmer's crates waiting to go back to the school. The empty crates were switched for the full ones. Once the filled crates reached the school the cooks sorted them. Some crates went to the kitchen, other crates went to the outdoor roasting pits, and still other crates went to storage sheds for later use. It all appeared perfectly natural.

Also, on Thursday morning, the school prepared to host the Quiz Games Tournament. Zeld and Brian Boru sat on the battlements above the main gate and excitedly watched the other schools' teams make their entrances. The Giant Academy arrived at the school first. Their cloud drifted to the west side of the castle and presently snow fell in that direction. Their cloud landed and several giants emerged from the fog to check in. The Castles and Caverns School didn't have a schoolmaster and no one knew who should take charge.

Friar Timothy suggested, "Sir Tavish, you should take charge for the next few days."

Sir Tavish said, "I can't do it without interfering with me tournament duties. Let's have you take charge, Friar Timothy, er, I mean, for a couple of days."

Friar Timothy accepted, "All right, but only for a couple of days."

Friar Timothy welcomed the giants. "I am Friar Timothy, your welcoming committee."

"I thought it took more than one person to make a committee," argued the giant humorously.

"That being the case, I'm your welcoming person, place or thing."

"I liked you better as a committee," the giant teased.

"Your wish is my command."

"We plan to leave our cloud to the west. If that's all right?"

"Yes, it is, unless an additional storm comes along. They usually come from the west which would blow you over the top of the castle and from there to who knows where," jested the friar.

"That's true; we'll watch for incoming storms."

"What's your name?" asked the friar reaching to shake the giant's hand.

"Anthony," said the giant extending his oversized hand as well.

"Do you have a full team this year?"

"Yes, but we have one ling who is suffering from travelling sickness."

"What is a ling?"

"Some people say lad and others say boy, we giants say ling. You know - as in giantling or elfling."

Friar Timothy said while turning to find someone, "Zeld and Brian, would you two collect the healer and take him to the giant's cloud to attend to an ill student?"

Zeld and Brian looked around and saw the healer speaking with the hostler. Brian put on a burst of speed and approached the healer well before Zeld. He asked, "Will you attend to a giant boy who is ill?"

"Yes, well, duty calls," the healer said to the hostler.

Zeld came scampering up.

"Do you need me to see someone, too?" asked the healer.

"No, I'm with Brian," said Zeld pointing to his mate.

"Have you two ever seen the inside of a giant's castle?" asked the healer.

They both shook their heads.

"Shall we go and face the giants in their lair?" the healer asked dramatically while handing each boy a wooden medicine kit to carry.

"Indubitably," said Brian.

Zeld was excited to go along but didn't know what to say, so he shrugged his shoulders. The different reactions from the boys made the healer laugh as he led the way to the cloud.

It grew colder under the cloud with the shade and the snow. Zeld felt glad he wore his cloak and he watched as Brian wrapped his cloak around his shoulders to keep warm. When they reached the highest point on the hill, the healer looked up into the cloud and hollered, "I've come to examine the boy who is ill."

The cloud lowered and the three of them stepped onto an unusual stone path. The stones floated in the air, each one a little higher than the one before.

"Devastating," whispered Zeld.

"Onward and upward," said the healer.

The three of them strolled up the stone path to the front gate of a castle. They clapped with a knocker at the gate and heard footsteps approach. The gate opened and they stepped into a magnificent, radiantly white-stone castle. It resembled Zeld's healing stone, when fully charged.

The giant who opened the gate didn't speak at first, but through gesturing led them to a barracks where several of the students studied for the tournament.

"The ling is over there," directed the guide.

While Zeld and Brian tagged along, the healer examined the ling and found he suffered from a stomach ache.

"Is this your first tournament?" the healer asked.

"Yes, it is."

The healer rubbed some peppermint oil on the ling's stomach, and then gave him two peppermint sticks to eat before bedtime. The healer tousled his hair. "You'll feel better soon. Remember to have fun on your journey. Fun is a good medicine for stomach aches."

As the three of them walked toward the gate, Zeld glimpsed the Great Hall and kitchen. He could see the stables in a far corner. While examining his surroundings, he heard something above him and turned in time to recognize a giant chicken roosting on the top of a building. At first he thought it was an odd sort of decoration. Then he heard the smothered sound of a chick. The chicken moved to one side and the chick lifted its head out of the nest. He recognized the bright red colour and face of a baby dragon. He froze while an all-encompassing fear took control.

Brian called over his shoulder, "Zeld we're leaving."

Zeld didn't move. Brian ran back and stepped right in front of Zeld's face.

"What's wrong?" he asked.

Zeld couldn't speak. He merely pointed toward the chicken. Brian turned around and looked where Zeld pointed.

"It's one of the giant chickens we learned about," commented Brian.

"N-n-no, the ooother b-b-bird," Zeld stuttered.

"You mean the red thing?"

Brian saw the creature move its oversized head and he froze in place.

"It's a d-d-dragggon," Zeld managed to say through his intense fear.

"How d'you know?" asked Brian.

224

"Bbbecccause I fffought ooone once."

The healer called to the boys, "I know it must be wagon loads of fun seeing the courtyard of a giant castle but honestly we must leave now."

Zeld and Brian turned, no longer petrified as the dragon's curse had worn off. They ran full speed side by side, leaving streaks of colour behind them. The healer called, "Wait for me!" However, Zeld couldn't make out the words as they raced too quickly trying to reach the safety of the school. He wished he hadn't worn his cloak, so he could run faster.

CHAPTER TWENTY NINE

THE QUIZ GAMES TOURNAMENT

Zeld and Brian returned to their lofty perch on the battlements atop the main gate trying to warm up in the afternoon sun. Zeld wondered if he should tell anyone about the dragon. They watched as Scotland Naval entered the school below them. The cadets acted very confident. Friar Martin who happened to be nearby told Zeld and Brian, "Scotland Naval has won this competition for seven out of the last eight years. This is their school's moment to shine. Much like the archery competition belongs to our school year after year, Scotland Naval dominates the thinking games."

The two boys didn't wait around for the other schools to arrive. They'd seen enough to know their real competitors. They walked over to the hostler who assisted the arriving schools by placing their horses into stalls. Brian asked, "D'you have any advice for us? We're competing in the quiz game event."

The hostler thought for a moment, and then said, "I seem to mind they save questions about rare and unusual animals until the end of the match. This means, in a close match the game goes to the school which knows the most about unicorns, dragons, griffons and other unusual or rare animals."

Zeld said, "Thank you."

Zeld and Brian rushed immediately to the library and each found a book on rare animals. Zeld found the book, *Finding Unicorns Across Our Flat World* by Antonio Columbus. He read from the introduction, "Unicorns have long since lived in the region of the world known as the Holy Land. The first influx of unicorns brought to Europe in great numbers occurred during the first crusade."

"Blimey!" exclaimed Brian after reading something interesting in his book. Brian said nothing further.

Zeld read out loud to Brian, "Most unicorns are white in colour but occasionally an orangish-brown colour has appeared. Unicorns are fond of things which flow gently like a stream or banners in the wind. One unicorn was timed for over five hours watching a woman's robe drying in the breeze. OOOH! Quite an ugly scene occurred when the wash lady retrieved the gown."

"What does your book say about griffons?" Zeld asked after glancing at the cover of Brian's book.

228 Brian lifted his book and read, "There are male, or land griffons, and female or flying griffons. The males keep watch over the females by guarding the lair in a circular shaped perimeter defense. The males, once they are grown, are removed from the lair and never return."

"Fascinating!" said Zeld who secretly hoped this information would come in handy during the match. "Who wrote that book?"

"It's called, *Flying and Non-flying Griffons* by Cumulus Heights and Lowly Foote."

"Heights and Foote, now there are a couple of blokes who know about griffons," said Zeld.

The bell tolled and everyone gathered for the feast. Friar Timothy welcomed one and all to the Castles and Caverns School again. He introduced Sir Tavish, who read the list of games and times to the contestants. While reading, he also pointed out the various buildings the events would be held in.

Their spiritual thought for the evening came from Friar Jonathan who told the story of Samson from the Bible. After reading from the bible he likened the strength of Samson to the gifts of God in the boy's lives. "It's true some people are physically strong and we must all keep ourselves physically fit no matter our age but some people have other gifts from God.

"Some men are great readers while others are superb writers. Women generally have a great love and conviction to care for their families and neighbours. God certainly takes notice of such talents and rewards those who share their gifts not only with blessings here, but also blessings waiting for us in heaven above. It is important that you find your talents and serve God with moral conviction."

Zeld hoped he and his friends were doing just that, but he felt entirely uncertain about how moral war and secret operation were viewed by God.

Sir Tavish wished everyone good luck and sent the boys to bed.

Darkness fell and most of the boys appeared exhausted from travelling. Zeld headed for Eagle Loft when he came across Norton Duval who sat on the same outdoor classroom bench which Edelweiss had sat upon. Zeld overheard him mumbling to himself, 'honour thy mother and thy father' and 'thou shalt not kill.' Norton bent over looking as though he suffering from stomach pains. Sir Tavish took a seat next to Norton and spoke quietly with him. After a while the two of them walked to Bull Hollow together.

Zeld turned toward his barracks when someone crept up behind him and put their hands over his eyes. An artificially deep voice asked, "Guess who?"

Zeld played along, "The man on the moon."

The strange hands moved away and Zeld turned around to find Dowly. He stepped back getting a better look at her. She stood there bundled up in several sets of clothing to keep warm.

"Is your back still all right?" Zeld asked.

"It aches only a little, I'm doing much better than I used to." Then she added, "Come and see my mum."

Dowly led Zeld through the Great Hall and into the kitchen. Mrs. A'Dale gave Zeld a big hug and asked, "How's our favourite schoolboy?"

"I'm doing well, but there is something I need you to do for me."

"Is it sneaky, conniving and going to give the Hesses their comeuppance?" Mrs. A'Dale asked hopefully while leaning toward Zeld.

"Like a bloody nose," Zeld responded.

Mrs. A'Dale leaned down and he whispered in her ear what he needed her to do.

"Is that all?"

Zeld leaned forward and whispered again.

"Now you're talking!" she said while placing her fists together and giving the broken arrow sign. He returned the sign and they both leaned forward and giggled nose to nose.

Zeld and Dowly left Mrs. A'Dale and went for a little walk around the castle grounds. He made a quick tour out of it because of the freezing temperature. They said goodnight at the door of the Great Hall. Dowly puckered for a kiss but nothing happened.

He saw what she was doing and slipped away as fast as he could.

Zeld found his mates in bed. They'd stayed up visiting.

"Where have you been?" Jens Jr. asked suspiciously.

"Out for a romp with Dowly," Zeld said, still shivering from the cold.

"Ooohhh, lover boy," said Jens Jr. and the other boys howled with laughter. When it quieted down, Jens Jr. asked with a note of irony, "Isn't Dowly the hunched back girl from the Robin Hood School?"

230

"At one time she had a hunched back," said Zeld realizing Jens Jr. had set him up for more teasing. "Her mum is here too. She asked for a couple of additional crates - er - you know - to put in the back of the wagons - so the boys can sit on them and have a better view as they travel."

"My mates requested the same thing for their wagon," said James, acting surprised.

"I thought the additional crates the kitchen staff used might be the right size," suggested Zeld.

"They should be done with all those bits and snippets by the end of the tournament," said James.

Oars said, "I talked to the boys from Scotland Naval to see which road they would return on, I'd hoped by way of our manor, but apparently not. They said they planned to return by way of the north road past the dwarven mine. I planned to send several of my Christmas presents home with them, but I'll have to find some other way."

"I'll talk to the man on the moon and see if he can change the weather," said Zeld.

"While you're talking to the man on the moon could you ask him to make Danish sweet rolls for breakfast?" asked Jens Jr.

"Whatever you say JJ," Zeld said through a yawn. He had turned the tide on Jens Jr. and knew who would receive the teasing now.

"Don't call me JJ!" Jens Jr. said angrily.

The other boys in Eagle Loft teased him unmercifully by calling him JJ. The more Jens Jr. told them to knock it off, the more they kept it up. Finally, Jens Jr. gave up and went to bed with a pillow over his head.

The Great Hall filled with chess players early the next morning carrying their chess sets for the first round of the tournament. Unfortunately, the boys' minds kept sleeping due to the early hour. Stringham, the chess champion from Scotland Naval, drew the white pieces and opened the game by moving the pawn in front of his king's bishop two spaces (P-KB4). His opponent, Quimby from the goblin school, countered by moving the pawn in front of his king two spaces (P-K4). The champion moved the pawn in front of his king's knight two spaces, next to the pawn he moved first, trying to take control of the centre of the board (P-KN4). Stringham let go of the piece.

Quimby celebrated by dancing and singing in goblin, more commonly called gobbledy gook. Stringham moved the piece back. The judges of the tournament ruled if you touch a piece you must move it and if you let go of the piece you can't take it back. Stringham repositioned the piece. Quimby moved his queen diagonally to the right as far as it would go (Q-R5) check mate. The champion had lost in two moves.

Quimby reported his win to the scorer's table. Stringham went over and sat by his coach with his head in his hands.

"It's not over yet. One surprise loss won't make a difference in the end," the coach said in a knowledgeable tone.

The quiz events started on time as well. The Castles and Caverns School played against Welch Naval. Zeld, James, Brian and Jens Jr. sat in their seats at the library's biggest table.

James looked across and saw his mate Scott. James turned to the other team members and said, "This is my mate Scott from Penarth." The two teams shook hands with each other. Then James said, "I hate to have to do this to you Scott, but you're on the other side of the table."

"Do what?"

"Embarrass you with this terrible loss."

"Do your worst."

"You asked for it."

"Yes, I did," said Scott confidently.

The official called for quiet, and then he asked the first question, "What is the name of the warm celestial object which moves 'round the earth?"

Scott touched in first, "The sun."

"Correct," the official responded, placing the question to his left in what became the first card of the score stacks.

"What is the name of the sea near Arabia?"

"The Persian Gulf," Scott answered.

"What direction does a compass always..." The official stopped when Scott touched in.

"North," Scott said with a confident smirk.

"What is King Henry's surname?"

Scott beat them to the touch again, "Pendragon."

"Incorrect," said the official, "C&C, you may steal the question."

Zeld touched in, "Plantagenet."

"Correct," said the official.

Scott looked over to his coach with a devastated expression on his face. His coach threw out his hands in a questioning manner. When Scott turned he missed the next question but James answered it, "A pulley."

"Correct," said the official, showing no preference to either team.

"What building is the most awe-inspiring in the world?" No one touched in for that one.

"Snakes belong to what animal family?"

Jens Jr. touched in, "The dragon family."

"That is correct," said the official.

The score was tied three answers per school, and both schools were trying to capture twenty questions for the victory. Questions and answers filled the room as the game heated up.

"Spain, Mongolia, Italy."

The Castles and Caverns team went on a run, shooting far past the other team, 12 to 3. Scott hadn't touched in since his incorrect answer.

"Name the bush which makes excellent bows?" the official asked.

Zeld touched in, "Mulberry."

"Correct. Name the arrow which has goose feathers on it."

Scott touched in, "Gray goose shaft."

"Correct," said the official.

Castles and Caverns went on another roll and the game ended C&C 20 Welch Naval 4.

The next two teams filled the seats while the C&C and Welch Naval teams shook hands as they walked toward the door.

"Let's go to breakfast," suggested Scott. Zeld guessed Scott wanted to avoid the rub.

As the boys wandered into the kitchen they were put to work immediately. They prepared a breakfast buffet with four queues setting out what Jens Jr. ordered the night before: Danish sweet rolls with milk and fruit.

"How didja get the cooks to make Danish sweet rolls?" asked Jens Jr., a bit bewildered.

"That's me little secret," said Zeld. Truthfully he didn't do anything. The cooks merely happened to make them.

"Don't forget to change the weather while you're at it," commented Jens Jr. in a doubtful voice. "He thinks he can change the weather," said Jens Jr. quietly to his brothers with a small mocking laugh.

"Oh, I'm glad you reminded me," called Zeld as he approached the giant's coach and whispered something in his ear.

"We'll take care of it," assured the coach.

"I'll bet he asks the giants to move their cloud," said Odin.

"You should be nicer to Zeld," Oles told Jens Jr.

While walking to the next round of the quiz game Zeld's right side was plastered with heavy snow fall. Zeld looked up and saw the cloud moving north of the school. Zeld hoped no one else would notice straightaway, at least not until the road became impassable.

Jens Jr. stepped alongside Zeld. He watched the cloud as well, then said, "That will do Zeld, that will do nicely."

The Castles and Caverns School took their places against the goblin school for the second round. Zeld felt a sense of superiority, sitting across from the shorter goblins. This feeling quickly died away when the goblins captured the first 10 questions.

The next five questions pertained to sea animals, and James correctly answered all of them. Questions about foreign languages came up. Jens Jr. captured a question about Swedish, and Zeld knew one about Dwarfish. The other three went unanswered.

"What is the name for the type of armour which can't be broken?" asked the official.

Zeld touched in. "Proof Armour."

"Correct," said the official.

The next four questions were easy pickings for the C&C team. The score favoured C&C 12 to 10. Then the categories switched and favoured the goblins again. The goblins captured four out of five questions about rare shrubs. They also captured the first two questions about insects and the score tipped in favour of the goblins 16 to 13.

"What is the type of insect which eats wood?" asked the official.

234 James touched in, "The tree beetle."

"Correct. What is the name of the insect which sits on water?"

James touched in, "The water skeeter."

"Correct. What colour of insects do fish fancy the most?"

James touched in again, "Red."

"Correct," said the official.

The score was tied at 16 apiece. Everything depended on the last category of questions. Would they favour the goblins or C&C?

"What is dragon bone powder used for?" asked the official.

Zeld touched in, "Explosives."

"Correct," responded the official. "What is the name of the lake in Scotland where sea monsters live?"

Jens Jr. touched in, "Loch ness."

"Correct. What is the name of the tree monster with the half-crazed laugh?" asked the official.

A goblin touched in, "Tree sprite."

"Correct," said the official.

"What's the name of the poisonous plant from Scotland?" the official asked.

Jens Jr. touched in, "Hemlock."

"What are the lungs of a dead dragon used for?"

Zeld touched in, "To filter sea water into fresh water."

The official looked at the card, and then at Zeld. He looked at the card again.

"I need a ruling, would someone please retrieve the judges from the Great Hall?"

Brian touched his stone, "Yes," he said as if answering a question.

The entire room broke into laughter. After all, he'd answered the official's question. It didn't take long for the two judges to come to the library. The official read the question from the card, then repeated Zeld's answer and showed the answer on the card to the judges.

A judge asked politely, "Have you ever seen it done?"

Zeld touched in accidentally and answered yes with a red face.

The crowd sniggered again. Zeld hadn't meant to touch the stone.

The other judge's face held a bewildered expression as he asked, "Where?"

"Me family lives in exile. I can't tell you where without exposing their location," Zeld explained.

235

"It is scientifically sound, and I rule that he's captured the question," the first judge said. The other judge nodded in agreement.

Zeld looked at the official minding the fact this was question 20 for his team.

"The game goes to Castles and Caverns," announced the official.

Zeld felt a slight sense of relief and sighed as he slid back into his chair. He felt a little better, but knew he would only feel truly better once the mongonels left the castle.

Brian stood up and bragged about their score, "17 to 22, I guess you could say we won."

They shook hands with the goblins. Zeld reassured them it all came down to the last category of questions. Zeld respected the goblins for their preparation.

With less than an hour until noon, Zeld went to the kitchen to help. He didn't mind working alongside Dowly as long as she didn't kiss him.

The kitchen staff busily baked. They used racks to expand the amount of useable oven space. This improvement allowed them to bake more food, which made the Danish sweet rolls possible. The staff used the racks to bake bread rolls.

Zeld asked carefully, "If these rolls are for supper, where's the midday meal"

Mrs. A'Dale and Mrs. Palfreeman pointed to several picnic baskets sitting in the corner of the kitchen. Zeld noticed for the first time the two ladies looked alike.

Dowly said with an enormous smile on her face, "We're having sandwiches. It was my idea."

Jens Jr. popped his head in and said, "Ingenious and beautiful. You better watch yourself Zeld, that's the best kind."

Zeld flushed a cherry-red. "When did you become an expert on young ladies?"

"The same day Edelweiss kidnapped me."

"That must've been some adventure."

Jens Jr. had an abnormally funny look on his face. He didn't say another word. He simply went back to work, helping prepare the Great Hall for the midday meal.

With the boys' help the staff had the midday meal ready ahead of schedule. After grace, the boys queued and chose between jam, meat, and vegetable sandwiches, along with fruit and milk. The queues flowed smoothly. A spontaneous debate sprang up about which sandwich tasted best and each sandwich had a following of boys. The debate concluded as a three-way draw, because they ran out of time.

The last round of the day started at 2:00 p.m. with Castle and Caverns going against the Dwarven Academy. Zeld felt thrilled to spend some time with the dwarves. The dwarves didn't seem very jolly, as they entered the library.

The teams took their seats and the official read the first question.

"What is the name of the fire-worm which lives in Scotland?" the official asked.

Jens Jr. touched in, "Dragoneus."

"Correct," called the official. "What is the name of the worm which eats poisonous plants in England?"

James touched in, "The tomato worm,"

"Correct," said the official.

The match was a complete blow out 20 to 0 for Castles and Caverns. After the match Zeld spoke with the dwarves.

"Didn't you know the answers to any of the questions?" Zeld asked surprised.

"All we know is mining," one of the boys answered.

"We dunno anything about plants or animals," another one pitched in.

"We have an hour before team time, what d'you want to know?" Zeld asked.

"Money, we don't understand money," one of them said with great interest.

"Coins are minted outta gold and silver," Zeld said confused.

"We understand that. What we don't understand is why most people refuse to sell basic items to us and how to prosper when half of what we mine is payment to the landlord," The dwarf asked.

"You won't prosper," said Zeld, then he paused. "Let's go sit in the Great Hall and I'll explain everything I know about it."

They found a quiet place in a corner of the hall and Zeld began, "Gold is worth ten-times more than silver."

"What does ten-times mean?" a dwarf asked.

"It means if you have enough silver coins to buy a dwarven axe, that's good. However, the same number of gold coins will buy 10 dwarven axes," explained Zeld.

"So gold is better?" asked another dwarf.

"Yes, always mine gold if you can. The best way to make money is to own the mine yourself. This way you're the landlord and you keep all the gold or silver. If that's not possible, you'll have to do your mining in secret," Zeld explained looking furtively from side to side.

The dwarves asked several questions about the best places to mine and for directions. Zeld didn't know all the answers, but he told them about the dwarves who mined north of the school and explained they had great expertise in these matters.

Before long team time had arrived. The dwarven coach found himself bombarded with requests to go see the silver mine north of the school. He told them they could go in the morning; they had other things to do right then.

Zeld went to his team meeting in the library and learned his team would compete in the championship round. The senior quiz game's team made it to the conciliation round and would compete for third place in their division. The chess team had two players going into the championship round.

Zeld went to the kitchen to tell Dowly but found her sleeping on a long bench in the Great Hall. He doffed his cloak and laid it over her. She didn't wake up. Mrs. Palfreeman came from the kitchen drying a pot with a dish rag.

Zeld looked up and asked, "Are you related to Mrs. A'Dale?"

"Why, I'm Ellen's sister."

"I noticed that you look alike," Zeld said with a drowsy smile. "Well, goodnight." Then he scurried over to Eagle Loft.

Everyone appeared exhausted or perhaps worried. Qualifying for the finals made Zeld wonder if his team really was the cleverest pages in all England or perhaps the luckiest? He wondered, can we win? Then his thoughts deepened, can we beat Hesse at his own game?

CHAPTER Thirty

Merely Jesting

Sleepy boys, full of yawns and sporting various styles of hairdos which could all be classified under the 'stick up hair' category filled the Great Hall in the morning. They moved slowly through the breakfast queues, delaying the matches by twenty minutes. This gave the boys more time to worry, which adversely affected their abilities. Zeld didn't worry about the tournament very much. To him it made a splendid alibi in case someone discovered their smuggling scheme. He worried much more about the reaction from Hesse. If caught I'll have to flee for my life, he thought with a cold shudder.

The two leading teams of the junior division sat in their prearranged seats in the library and soon afterwards the questions began. With all the rushing here and there, Zeld didn't notice the players on the other team until the first question. When he looked over, he saw the giants.

A new official, dressed in a deep brown friar's frock, sat at the head of the table. He wore a small round cap on his head and spoke with a Kentish accent. His hair shone a silver-grey colour with alert watery-blue round eyes.

"What rodent lives by the thousands in caves?" asked the official.

Zeld touched in. "G - Bats," he answered.

"Correct," said the official.

Zeld almost said giants by mistake. I need to concentrate on the game more, Zeld thought. A botch like that could cost us the match, not to mention a black eye.

"What is the German name for the famous magical forest in Germany?" the official asked.

A giant touched in. "The Black Forest," he answered in an exaggerated dark voice as a jest.

"Sorry," the official said, "We asked for the German name. C&C, you may steal the question, if you know the answer."

James touched in. "Schwarzwald?" he guessed.

"Correct, but I'm honestly surprised Zeld didn't touch in on that question, seeing how his ancestors come from there as well as Saxony," said the official.

"I'm English," said Zeld confused.

"Only on your mother's side," the official informed him.

"Can you tell me more about it after the tournament?" Zeld asked a bit surprised at the officials comment.

The official nodded, and then read the next question.

"What is the first day in May called?"

A giant touched in, "May first."

"No," said the official apologetically.

Brian touched in, "May Day."

"Correct," said the official. "Name the pillars which guard the waterway in and out of the Mediterranean Sea."

James touched in, "The Pillars of Hercules."

"Correct," said the official in a pleased voice.

The C&C team took the early lead, capturing the first seven questions.

"Name the village in England where a flock of chickens drank a magical growing formula."

A giant touched in, "Barnstaple."

"Correct," said the official nodding his head.

This started a five question run by the giants.

"Name the capital of Ireland."

Zeld touched in, but Brian Boru touched in faster.

"Dublin," Brain answered.

"Correct," said the official. "What is the name of the plant used to soothe swollen gums?"

A giant touched in, "Yarrow."

"That is precisely - accurate. Name the river which runs through Egypt?" the official read.

James touched in, "The Nile."

"Correct," the official called. "In what country does the plant Huddy Joor come from?"

Zeld touched in, "Denmark."

"Correct," the official said.

The C&C team pushed ahead until the questions turned to Scottish history.

"The Stone of Scone is used for what purpose?" asked the official.

A giant touched in, "To stand on while crowning the Kings of Scotland."

"Correct," called the official. "In which country was the largest sword made?"

A giant touched in, "Scotland."

"Correct," said the official.

The crowd murmured something about the largest sword being the German Zwiehander. The official quieted them down. Then, he reminded them the largest sword on record was a claymore cast exclusively for Lonnie Lorne, head of the Giants of Lorne in Scotland.

The score stood at 10 questions for C&C to 8 for the Giant Academy. The giants had clearly made headway.

"I'd hate to do battle with him," said Jens Jr.

"Me too," said Brian.

"By what means did Samson burn a village of the Philistines?" the official asked.

Jens Jr. touched in, "Flaming fox tales."

"Correct. What animals had David killed with his sling before his battle with Goliath?" the official asked.

Brian touched in first, but the whole C&C team tried.

"A lion and a - bear," Brian said in a hopeful tone.

"Correct," said the official.

C&C captured all five of the Bible questions and the score leaned heavily in their favour at fifteen to eight. The team could tell they'd most likely win. The rumour of C&C's eminent victory reached the Great Hall. This inspired the C&C chess players who sat up properly and somehow appeared more confident, which in turn helped them play better.

"Vikings believe Olga, the Goddess of the Moon, comes each year to take what?" the official asked.

Zeld touched in, "Ten horses."

"That is correct," said the official. "What mountain region in Denmark is known for its magnificent horses?"

Zeld touched in again, "Paladorian."

"Correct again," said the official. "What is a horse's worst enemy?"

Brian Boru touched in first, "Caltrops."

If the team could capture the next two questions about horses, they'd win.

"What is the most famous horse in history?" asked the official.

No one touched in. The official repeated the question. Finally Jens Jr. touched in.

"The Trojan Horse," he said with borrowed confidence.

"Correct," said the official.

The crowd grew tense and the mood desperate for the giants.

"What is the name of King Henry's horse?" asked the official.

James touched in, "Mercury."

"Correct," called the official.

The C&C boys cheered thinking they had won, but the official cut them off by telling them to sit down. He read another question. "What is the name of the flammable rock used in onagers?" he asked. The room stared silently at the official.

"Merely jesting," he said humorously.

A huge sigh of relief came from the crowd. The C&C team really had won. They shook the giants' big hands and went outside for some air. The giants went with them.

"I'm glad it's over," commented James.

"Us too," agreed a giant. "Most people think giants are big and stupid." Our coach said, "We must do well, in order to gain respect."

Zeld said, "I imagine the dragon in your castle will bring you all the respect you need."

"You saw the dragon?" the tallest giant asked.

"Yeah, and it frightened me nearly to death."

"I saw it too," bragged Brian Boru.

"The English have trouble with Vikings every fall and we have a dragon invasion early every summer. When the hatchlings grow big enough to leave the nest, they spread destruction wherever they go. It usually doesn't stop until we've killed a couple hundred of the beasts. The dragons eat our cattle, burn down our houses, and if we don't hunt them down soon enough, they start eating people. We're trying to raise some friendly dragons so when the hatchlings see them, they'll go somewhere else."

"Why is your leather armour blue instead of red?" Zeld asked.

"Because it's made from the blood of a blue dragon instead of a red one," the ling answered.

Zeld felt confused.

"Er - you know - blue dragons - they shoot lightning outta their mouths - they're more dangerous than the red ones."

Zeld shook his head cluelessly. He had never heard of blue dragons.

"A dragon's scales are so hard you can't hurt them with a sword. So what's the best way to kill a dragon?" Zeld asked.

"We use ballistas and hunt them down in their caves where they can't attack us repeatedly from the air," answered the tallest giant. "I almost forgot we're supposed to attend the consolation round. Follow me," he said to his mates.

"Honestly, good luck with your dragons," called Jens Jr.

"See you later," called the tallest giant as they hastened to the match.

Zeld and the other three boys headed for the kitchen. When they walked into the Great Hall, it caused a major distraction. Several chess players called out, "Did you win?"

"Yes, we did," James told everybody proudly.

A knot of people gathered around, congratulating them.

After a few minutes they made their way to the kitchen, where the cooks busily baked bread and prepared stew. Dowly wasn't present so they made their way through and found her outside loading kitchen pots and pans into a wagon. The boys took over the work.

"The food has been excellent, Dowly," said Jens Jr.

Dowly looked impatiently at Zeld. With her hands on her hips she said, "Zeld, I need to talk to you, over there." She motioned to the far side of the woodpile. "Are you really only twelve years old?" she asked, grimacing.

"Yes, didn't I tell you?"

"I'm nearly fifteen. Zeld, it's the thirteenth century. A girl should be married at age sixteen. By the time an unmarried girl reaches nineteen, she's considered a spinster." Dowly's tone made Zeld feel as if he was the accused at trial. He had no clue what made her so upset.

"Zeld, I'm too old to marry you," she said nervously.

"That's all right. You can marry someone else," Zeld said without hesitation.

Dowly hung her head, covered her face with her hands and briskly stepped into the kitchen, trying to hide her tears. He threw his hands out; then, walked over and helped his mates. The boys finished loading in an embarrassing silence.

When finished, they re-entered the castle through the main gate. The time had come to load the crates on the other school's wagons. The Scottish Academy's coach insisted he couldn't take the two large crates to the McMarr Manor until Zeld pointed out that the road he planned to take had been snowed in. He no longer had a choice as to which direction to go, so he reluctantly agreed to drop off the crates as they passed the manor.

At the storage huts Zeld and his mates loaded two crates for the McMarr Manor, one for James' grandfather, and two more for the Robin Hood School. At the same time the giants loaded the tournament tents as they would host the fencing competition next month.

The bell tolled and the award ceremony started at the outdoor classrooms. It seemed as if it would go on forever. Zeld, James, Brian, and Jens Jr. stood up front to receive their first place prize in the junior division quiz game. Castles and Caverns School won the tournament overall.

As Zeld left the stand one of the Scottish cadets collided into him intentionally, and then said in a very unsportsmanlike manner, "Just you wait until next year - we'll show you whose master of this tournament."

Zeld smiled, "Right then, I'll see you next year."

Zeld and his mates watched from the battlements above the main gate as the visiting schools left carrying the crates. The last wagon in queue belonged to the Robin Hood School. Only fifty feet outside the gate Zeld saw Godfrey of Hesse, Mr. Duval and Wilhelm's father riding toward the wagons. Godfrey lifted his hand and patted the crate as the wagon passed. A wave of panic flowed through Zeld's body and his breathing nearly stopped. He felt certain sure they'd been caught in the act. He wondered if he should run for his sword or his horse. The three men rode past the wagon and straight into the castle. They dismounted and calmly asked the hostler where they could find their sons.

Then it dawned on Zeld they'd done it. Right under everyone's noses, they had shipped the weapons in and out of the school and no one was the wiser. Zeld and company had hoodwinked the Hessens. He breathed normally again. Hopefully, it would take weeks or months before Hesse discovered the missing weapons. Zeld felt a tremendous burden lift from his shoulders. He wanted to shout out a victory cry. By the looks in his mates' eyes he saw they felt the same way. He thought it best if they slipped away from the castle. While holding up three gold coins, he cried, "I feel like celebrating. Let's go into town, buy some pies and have a party."

Jens Jr. agreed and Oles said, to no one's surprise, "We should have a party every day."

Zeld checked out a wagon and the boys went to Baden town. Every time Zeld went to Baden, he became a wee bit confused while trying to find his way around. It seemed as if the streets played tricks on him. Jens Jr. suggested the boys go up and down the streets, shouting out to everyone they had won the tournament.

The boys entered town, passed a few shops and then reached the main junction. Jens Jr. told Zeld to turn right on the other side of the pub. He did so and found more shops. At the end of the town he found the blacksmith shop. He turned the wagon around and travelled back to the main junction where he turned right again. He discovered Baden had two main streets and not just one. These two streets formed the junction in the centre of town, causing his confusion. Driving the wagon in all four quarters of town one after the other solved his problem. The best part was Zeld didn't have to tell a soul about getting confused now and then.

He parked the wagon in front of the bakery. The boys jumped down and barged through the bakery door. The baker didn't seem to mind the intrusion. "Come in mates," he said with a smile. Zeld bought eight pies and the boys sat in the booths and held a pie eating contest. When finished their faces were a mess and they had all lost the contest, because no one could finish a whole pie.

They all agreed they'd never had a better time losing. The baker said he had never enjoyed watching so many boys lose a contest. He thanked them for their business and told them how honoured he felt to be among them. The boys bought two more pies for the chess champions and they climbed back into the wagon. The baker waved as he cleaned up the mess they left behind.

When they arrived at the school, they couldn't see any of the teachers. When they asked, the other boys told them about a series of meetings in the library. Zeld wondered if something had gone amiss with the tournament.

"D'you suppose someone cheated?" asked Sullivan.

"No, it's either something really important or nothing at all. Me guess is it's nothing," said Jens Jr.

When the staff entered the Great Hall for supper, Zeld recognized the official from his final round who had stayed and met with them. A man of some importance, or so it appeared, by the way the staff treated him. Zeld had plenty of time to watch him as he couldn't eat much supper due to all the pie.

246

That night the boys bathed together at the bathhouse and complained about the water.

"It's freezing," said Odin.

"It's positively the coldest liquid of all God's creations," Oles concluded.

Zeld piped in, "It's glacial."

"It's wickedly cold," added Oars.

"And it's ours," said Jens Jr. as if he'd made a fabulous discovery.

That comment brought a laugh.

"It's barbaric," sneered Sullivan.

"You're barbaric," called Robert rudely.

"DID YOU HEAR THAT, MEAN CRUEL WORLD? FOR ONCE I AM NOT THE BARBARIAN!" shouted out James.

"Oh, sorry, Sullivan, I thought you were James," apologized Robert.

"THAT'S MORE LIKE IT!" called out James. "I'M JAMES O'DAY, THE WELCH BARBARIAN!"

Brian pushed James into the stream.

"Now you're the wet Welch barbarian," Brian laughed.

Robert pushed Brian into the stream.

"Now you're the wet Irish barbarian," Robert said, not realizing what he had started.

Presently wet barbarians from all around the world hit the water as boy after boy tumbled in. The fun didn't last long, due to the freezing water. The boys ran shivering for the hearthrug in front of Eagle Loft's fireplace. Their noise echoed all over the castle grounds.

Late that evening the entire school met in the Great Hall. Friar Stephen called for everyone's attention.

Then, he announced, "King Henry has selected a new schoolmaster for Castles and Caverns."

Friar Stephen then motioned for the new friar to stand. "This is Father Ulrich. He is a well-known scholar from the great library in London."

Sir Tavish stood up and clapped while nodding his head. The boys stood and clapped as well. Father Ulrich bowed. After a few seconds he raised his hand with his two forefingers extended like a priest doing his duty in church. This quieted the applause.

"I really didn't want this job and I hate violence, sooo - I'm closing the school," said Father Ulrich in a desolate tone.

The shocked students looked at each other in disbelief. A couple of pages looked like they were going to cry.

Then Father Ulrich said, "Merely jesting. I pulled little jests twice today. I'm not sure which time I enjoyed most."

The boys breathed a sigh of relief and everyone listened to their new schoolmaster.

"Let me tell you boys about my life. At the age of seven, my parents died in a Viking raid. My brother and I went to a monastery to be raised. Well, first we went to an orphanage, but we didn't fancy it, so we burned it down. Then we went, well were forced is more accurate, to the monastery to pray for our sins. My brother escaped by successfully impersonating a squirrel and I've been in hiding ever since, pretending to be a friar."

The schoolboys gave an uncertain sounding laugh, but Sir Jaydan found this comment more humorous than the boys for some unknown reason and gave a hearty laugh.

The Father continued, "One day while dusting the banister, well, actually I slid down the banister while trying to slip away from the cook, as he kept throwing bricks at me. Well, they weren't really bricks, but they hurt like them and tasted like them too. The cook always called these bricks - soft rolls."

More laughter filled the room.

Father Ulrich continued, "If you think that's atrocious, you should've tried the hard rolls. I lost many a good tooth on those. Anyway, there I sat at the bottom of the stairs having dusted the banister when I overheard one of the friars asking another, 'Who can we assign to work in the great library?' Well, I figured anyplace was better than the monastery, so I volunteered for the job. The friar eyed me up and down and said wagging his finger at me, 'Absolutely not.'" Father Ulrich pointed his finger at the proper moment for effect.

More laughs filled the room.

"I refused to become discouraged in the slightest," the Father continued throwing his hand out waist high with his palms up. "I found out who they selected to work in the library and I accidentally stole some transfer papers. Well, it might not have been a pure accident. Anyway, the king's guard, stationed up the road, filled the transfer forms out for me. The guard hated that friar because he always whistled. Rain, snow, sleet, hail, it didn't matter, he whistled all the time. Come to think of it, I don't mind if I ever heard him speak," Father Ulrich said while rubbing his chin thoughtfully.

"Oh well, that's not important anyway. The important deed or perhaps I should say misdeed, occurred when the poor unsuspecting friar read he'd been transferred to Switzerland, with the papers signed by the pope himself. That's exactly how the guard signed it, 'the pope himself'.

"Well, the guard found himself in plenty of trouble after botching that little forgery and they transferred him to the Castles and Caverns School up north somewhere. I hope I never meet him again." Father Ulrich looked over at Sir Tavish and jumped back as if one of his worst fears had only just come true. "He left very angry with me, I'll tell you." Then leaning toward Sir Tavish he added, "But I think he's the forgiving sort." Sir Tavish played along by folding his arms and shaking his head.

"Anyway, the friar landed in trouble as well, especially when I explained the whole idea behind the forged papers was so the friar could manage an all-expense paid tour of Europe." Father Ulrich stretched his arms open widely as if rejoicing when he said the word Europe. "The archbishop became so angry he sacked him. That's right, he up and sacked the friar. No need to feel concerned about it. I heard he's working at that same school up north." Father Ulrich cupped his hand to the side of his mouth and whispered loudly, "That's where they send all the rattle brains."

"Well, to make a short story long, that's how I landed the job in the library. The only problem came afterwards when I found out the library resided in the basement of the monastery." Father Ulrich placed his hands on his hips and leaned forward. "So, for the last 900 years, I've been cooped up in the dungeon of a monastery with 2000 books for company and I can't read."

Pacing three steps to his left, while keeping his left hand on his hip and extending his right into the air he continued in a nervous voice. "The other day King Henry came by and accidentally took a wrong turn. In case anyone mentions the story of the crazed librarian and the knife, it's totally false. I don't know who makes up those kinds of stories but they ought to be flogged. Anyway, I merely suggested to the king 'Let's slip out the back door,' and he said 'Right then. You grab a knife on the way, in case anyone tries to stop us,' so I did.

"The next thing I knew the king's guards wrestled me to the ground and plotted my demise. My good friend, the king, personally intervened on my behalf and saved my life when he said, 'Don't kill him I have a better plan. Let's send him to the school up north to deal with all those spoiled brats instead.' So, here I am, the luckiest man in the world."

The school sat for a moment, waiting to see if the father had indeed finished. When they concluded he had, they clapped and cheered.

"The truth is I was born to a wealthy family and joined the holy order to benefit mankind. I worked at an orphanage, then in a monastery, then the great library in London and today I'm the new schoolmaster at Castles and Caverns. The only problem is the true story isn't very exciting, so I improved it," said Father Ulrich grinning triumphantly as he sat down.

Sir Tavish stood and announced bed time. "Tomorrow is Sunday and some of us need to practice repentance, so catch a good night's rest and be prepared to repent in the morning." He said the last bit while throwing a look over his shoulder at Father Ulrich.

"The father is fun or perhaps senile," one of the boys mused as they filed out.

"Either way he fits in nicely," Zeld observed out loud. However, this isn't what he truly thought. Deep down Zeld wondered how Father Ulrich knew so much about his family and more importantly he needed to know which side of the de Saxon and Hessen war he supported.

CHAPTER Thirty One

Voyages

Jens Sr. watched as the first heavenly rays of light shone through the cloudy morning sky. It had been only two days since he visited with Morten. With a torch for light, Jens Sr. led his crew into the secret cave, where he stored his Viking ship. The ship hung upside down, its dead weight supported by four heavy chains. The crew lowered the chains on one side of the ship and raised them on the other until the bottom rested directly above the surface of the water. The ship's dark timbers reflected in the water below. Then the crew slowly lowered the ship as if it were a casket until its full weight pressed against the surface of the water.

The crew busily set the boarding planks and filled the ship with cargo. When ready Jens Sr. boarded and gave the order, "Oarsmen to your posts."

The oarsmen promptly found their seats and slid their oars into position.

"Forward. Quarter time," called Jens Sr.

The drummer pounded a slow beat and the oarsmen matched the rhythm with their rowing. The ship pushed its way through the canal from the cave and was reborn into the ocean. Three days later Jens Sr. arrived at Blackdane. His ship docked and he disembarked. Jens Sr. breathed in the invigorating smells: the aroma of fresh baked bread, candles being dipped and wet cheeses going into the press.

He spoke in a cheerful tone to the workers at the dockyard. "I am Jens Marrsen of Norway," said Jens Sr. giving the Scandinavian version of his name. "My crew is Danish and they want to use their booty to start a new village."

The other Danes informed them of the best farming ground in the area.

"We'll look there and perhaps a bit further," Jens Sr. said in a polite voice.

Jens Sr. and a landing party walked into town. In the middle of the lot stood a smaller passenger wearing a brown cloak with the hood pulled up as if the wearer tried to hide inside.

Jens Sr. was no stranger to Blackdane. He led his party directly to the blacksmith who was an old mate as well as the man who could re-mint his English coins into Danish currency. Jens Sr. did this to convince people he had participated in the last Viking raid. When they finished visiting the blacksmith shop, he rented two wagons with horses and his friend gave him the exact location of Zeld's mother. He loaded the wagons with supplies and started to climb the Paladorian Mountain Range. Part of the crew stayed behind to guard the ship and to perform a secret mission.

The wagons rolled soberly up the mountains that evening and into the night. The party continued their journey until well after darkness fell. In the morning Jens Sr. removed a jar from the back of the wagon. He rubbed some cream on the horse's legs which readied them for several more hours of travelling. Jens Sr. kept up a quick pace and often looked over his shoulder as if checking to see if anyone followed.

On the second day they made eight miles and passed a group of soldiers on a march up the mountain. Jens Sr. simply nodded as they passed. He didn't stop to speak with them as it could prove unwise.

On the morning of the third day they reached Catherine's farm. Zeld had described a small struggling farm, but Jens Sr. found it doing rather well. He found a comfortable stone house with four extra rooms. Two pigsties held a dozen pigs and the barn housed a milk cow and several chickens ran in the yard.

Catherine came out and greeted them in Danish.

Jens Sr. replied in English, "I'm a friend of your son, Zeldain. Me name is Jens McMarr Sr. and I've brought you winter provisions."

A look of terror crept across Catherine's face.

"Zeldain has not betrayed your trust. His horse and other clues gave away your location," Jens Sr. said honestly. "I've concealed the clues, so no one else will be able to determine your location."

"What have you brought us?" she asked, the sound in her voice giving away her uncertainty of the situation.

Jens Sr. showed her the first crate. It held flour, salt, yeast, bread pans, cutting boards and new kitchen pots. The second crate held heavy winter clothes, including fur coats and snowshoes. He handed her a small purse with gold coins in it and informed her, "These coins came from your son. I had them re-minted in Blackdane."

Catherine took the purse, looked inside and gasped, "Where'd my son chance upon this much gold?"

"From his new gold mine, I suppose," answered Jens Sr. "I can see I've a lot to tell you. However, first things first, I have brought a difficult task for you."

"What sort of task?" asked Catherine, still looking worried.

Jens Sr. stepped into the small crowd of soldiers and escorted out from among them the person wearing the brown cloak with the hood still up.

"This maiden," he said, gently pulling the hood of the cloak back. "She stands in need of proper instruction in the art of womanhood. She has lived among thieves and learned their ways. In England her life is endangered from both a band of pirates and the law."

Edelweiss stepped cautiously out of the robes. Catherine's face softened. She hugged the girl as if she were a long lost relative and told Jens Sr. she would gladly have her stay. Edelweiss cried and looked overwhelmed with joy by Catherine's kindness. Catherine welcomed the soldiers to her home.

Jens Sr. put his soldiers to work straightaway unloading the wagons. They carried several items into the kitchen. They assembled some shelves, making a place for the food they brought. Catherine thanked Jens Sr. for his kindness.

Wolf walked into the house and saw the men working. He held the dwarven axe in one hand and the bow with two arrows in the other. On his shoulder sat Hammer, the mountain sprite.

Hammer stood three inches tall and was covered in a soft, tan fur. He walked upright and resembled a little hairy man. His little pointed ears barely poked out of the fur on the top of his head. He moved hastily to Wolf's other shoulder and his long tail wrapped around Wolf's neck.

Edelweiss gave a soft squeal of delight and reached out for the little creature who cracked his tail like a whip and disappeared.

Wolf gave her an exasperated look and shook his head. "You scared him. He isn't used to strangers. He'll most likely hide until dark."

Edelweiss gave a muttered apology and they both turned to look at Jens Sr.

"Who's this Viking lad?" asked Jens Sr., sounding befuddled.

"This is my son Wolfgang," Catherine stated proudly.

Jens Sr. reached out to shake his hand. Wolf looked at his mother who nodded. Wolf dropped the axe and shook Jens Sr.'s hand.

"How's Zeldain doing?" she asked.

"We call him Zeld as we don't want people to connect dain and Denmark. Anyway, Zeld is doing well. He found his way over to Scotland on a Viking ship. He escaped the ship when the Vikings attempted to kill him. We McMarr's took him in for a couple of days, and then he joined me sons on their way to Castles and Caverns."

"How many of your sons attend the school?" Catherine asked.

"Four."

"That must cost a king's ransom."

"Yes, it does," said Jens Sr., grimacing.

Jens Sr. and Catherine sat down. He could see through the open doorway his soldiers working on a wooden lookout tower in the trees. Catherine leaned over and took a glimpse at what they were building.

"Zeld has done many courageous deeds since he arrived. The Vikings raided the school and he fought them. He and several other boys, including three of me sons, led a raid against the Vikings and freed more than thirty prisoners. King Henry sent Zeld a treasure chest and suit of chainmail armour for his distinguished bravery. Zeld also has a suit of dragon's blood leather armour. I don't know where he chanced upon it."

The news caught Catherine's attention. She looked up from her seat at Jens Sr. and asked, "Does my son fight Vikings and dragons regularly?"

"Mum, I want to attend that school," Wolf interrupted.

Catherine turned abruptly and said with a stern expression, "I'm not raising you to become a barbarian."

Jens Sr. looked over at Wolf. He'd outgrown his clothes during the summer and wore furs similar to the Viking men.

Jens Sr. laughed and he kept laughing until Catherine asked, "What's so funny?"

"Have you looked at your 'non-barbarian' son lately?"

Catherine looked Wolf over from top to bottom then back again.

"Tell me truthfully, how often do they fight monsters and invaders?" she asked sounding weary.

Placing a comforting hand on her shoulder, Jens Sr. said, "The only time the schoolboys fight is if they're attacked first."

"We'll have to purchase a horse for you sometime next summer," said Catherine looking over at Wolf.

"Do we have the money for it?" asked Wolf.

"The Viking women came and picked the yellow flowers again," she said with a pleasant smile. Then turning to Jens Sr. she added, "I don't know what they use them for, but payment is in gold."

"Let me take a few flowers with me and see if I can discover what they are." Changing the subject Jens Sr. commented, "Perhaps the lad should come to school as a Viking and not as a de Saxon. Vikings may attend school in England now. King Henry signed an agreement. He'll need the horse you mentioned, a suit of Viking armour, and his tuition money. From the looks of him he'd pass as a Viking."

"Will you stay the night?" Catherine asked, gesturing toward the extra rooms she rented out on occasion.

"Your home is bigger than I expected but I'm afraid we can't stay long. We must hurry back to Scotland before the winter storms catch us, and every minute counts," Jens Sr. said, clearly concerned.

"How does Zeldain get along with the other boys?" Catherine asked.

"He gets along well with the good boys and is a true mate to me four sons. We've trey born sons. The youngest is Oles, he is the emotional one, he is the first to cry and the last to stop. He wants to play games all day and have parties every night. The middle

255

son's name is Odin. He states things as facts. The moon is round and the trees are green. He likes simple statements. Oars likes fast horses. He also likes to make plans and work hard.

"Then there is our oldest lad, Jens Jr. He sees plots in everything around him. He's a schemer and has many secrets. Zeld is something akin to Oars with his fast horse and Jens Jr. with his many secrets," Jens Sr. explained.

One of Jens Sr.'s men ran into the house, "The soldiers we passed yesterday are coming."

"How often do soldiers come to the mountains?" Jens Sr. asked Catherine with a suspicious look.

"Never."

"Hide the wagons. Edelweiss, cover the wagon's tracks, so they can't tell we stopped here. Everything and everyone must be hidden by the time they arrive," Jens Sr. ordered.

"I'll greet them as if they are customers," Catherine told Jens Sr.

"NO! That's how Maid Marian was murdered."

Catherine and Wolf hid behind a rather large rock where they could watch the farm. Ten minutes later the soldiers arrived. They didn't march up the road as most travellers did. Instead they spread out in order to raid the farm. Two - Four - Six - Eight, Jens Sr. counted silently while his lips mouthed the words. One of the approaching soldiers stopped and pulled his cloak back. On his chest the image of the Hessen lion stood out.

Section Four

"Ten" sailors you'll need to
solve this not find the hidden
"Roman numeral" on this boat.

CHAPTER Thirty Two

Early Christmas Presents

The pigs at Catherine's farm squealed as three of the Hessen raiders chased them. One of the raiders slipped into the barn looking for eggs, but Jens Sr. introduced him to his oversized double bladed axe instead. The axe hit the raider on the side of his face, throwing him out of the barn and back into the yard. He used his left hand to try to stop the bleeding.

Three arrows shot out of the trees, striking one enemy soldier's shield. He tumbled to the ground, but barely injured. The six standing soldiers attacked Jens Sr. Edelweiss ran to find Wolf and Catherine. The element of surprise hadn't worked and they needed Wolf's bow and axe.

Wolf, Catherine and Edelweiss ran hastily toward the metallic clanging sound that rang through the air. By the time Wolf arrived, Jens Sr. had already struck two excellent blows with his axe and the raiders had only hurt him slightly. Another volley of arrows hit a soldier in the back. This time the arrows penetrated his body and he fell over dead.

Wolf took aim and shot at one of the men who had trapped Jens Sr. against the barn. Wolf's arrow didn't hit the intended target, because the raider Jens Sr. had hit in the face stood up directly in the line of fire and the arrow hit him instead. He collapsed a second time.

Wolf aimed his second arrow at the same soldier he'd aimed at the first time but the battle shifted and Jens Sr.'s position made the shot too dangerous. Wolf looked for a better shot. The raider who fell from the first round of arrows managed to stand. He drew his sword, let out a war cry and advanced upon Wolf. Wolf froze with fear for an instant; then, fired at the charging soldier, hitting him in the stomach.

Edelweiss and Catherine arrived in time to see the arrow hit the soldier. With a determined look Edelweiss ran headlong at the man and swung the family's dwarven axe with her left hand hitting him in the chest. He keeled over backward and lay motionless.

Jens Sr. hit one of the Hessen raiders in the left thigh with the blade of his axe. The man stumbled back out of the toe-to-toe combat right into Edelweiss's 'tender loving care'. Edelweiss used her right hand this time to swing the dwarven axe into the soldier's neck. He fell dead.

260 Jens Sr.'s two men, who left to hide the wagons, returned. They lifted their axes, and without making a sound hit an unsuspecting raider from behind. He dropped to his knees and threw his head back in pain. Jens Sr. saw the raider on his knees and knew exactly what to do. He took a giant step, and with one mighty swing decapitated the raider.

The other raiders saw the blow and ran in a horrified panic. Catherine ran and dove in front of the fleeing soldiers tripping them. One rose to his knees and raised his sword's hilt high in the air to stab Catherine. Wolf rushed in and seized his head from behind and twisted it hard.

The soldier swung his elbow down into Wolf's belly and they both fell onto their right sides. Edelweiss planted her axe in the raider's exposed left side and he went limp.

Catherine clung on to the remaining raiders to keep them from leaving while Jens Sr.'s two axe men caught up with them. The axe men unmercifully finished them off. By the time it ended, all the raiders lay dead and Jens Sr. rested on his axe while suffering a great deal from numerous small wounds. His men assisted him into Catherine's house.

None of Jens Sr.'s cuts or bruises appeared serious. However, they still needed treatment so Catherine followed Jens Sr. into the house and washed them. His men dabbed a healing ointment on the cuts. As he lay injured in bed one of his men gave him a blue pill.

"He'll sleep for a while," said Halver, one of Jens Sr.'s trusted soldiers.

"I thought you were in a hurry to leave?" questioned Catherine.

"Yes we are, but this postponement can't be helped," Halver explained.

Jens Sr.'s men searched the bodies. They took all the raiders possessions into the house and placed them on the kitchen table, including the clothing. They buried the bodies a good distance from the farm.

A man in the lookout tower spied dwarves armed with axes coming down the road. Jens Sr.'s men took defensive positions again. With a warm smile Catherine told the soldiers her dwarven friends were coming to defend her.

She ran out into the yard. "I'm still here," she called to them in Dwarfish while waving.

They ran to Catherine, forming a protective circle with their backs toward her. They hunched over with their axes raised behind them and their shields in front, prepared for battle. They continuously circled to their right in what looked like a war dance. Still looking for the enemy, they drove Catherine back, forcing her toward the mountain.

She pushed her way out of the circle and said in a disappointed tone, "Stand properly. You look ridiculous. These men aren't our enemies."

They stood upright, looking embarrassed. Catherine led them to the house and introduced the dwarves to Jens Sr.'s soldiers.

"They defended me in the battle. They're our allies," Catherine told the dwarves.

"Did your enemies run away?" Dort asked, looking confused.

"No, we killed them all," Catherine said, with a frown, which showed she took no pleasure in what they did.

"Someone will search for them when they do not return," warned Dort.

Interrupting his comment, three goats ran down the mountain and straightaway into the stall next to the cow.

Catherine laughed, and then warned the others, "I guess I ought to tell all of you, a grand storm is on the way. An old man gave me those goats. He had grown tired of their peculiar behaviours. They were once caught in a lightning storm and scared nearly to death, so they run for cover whenever they sense an approaching storm. They're the best weather predictors I've ever seen."

The men and dwarves laughed, but only for a moment. Both groups needed to rush down the mountain quickly. Jens Sr.'s soldiers hitched the horses to the wagons and the dwarves went after their families.

Edelweiss brought out sliced bread and goat cheese for the soldiers. Afterward she packed the leftovers for the soldiers to take. Wolf loaded a stack of firewood into a wagon.

Meanwhile, Jens Sr. awoke and wandered into the kitchen. He found some bread and cheese left out for him. As he ate, he searched through the clues on the table. "German swords - Danish coins - English shoes - and five pottery shards," he said aloud. Jens Sr. examined the shards closely; then, collected them and rattled them in his hand. They made a familiar jingling sound. He realized they were the exact pottery shards he'd thrown to the ground at the Castles and Caverns School.

Groaning, he slipped the shards into his purse and said to himself, "How foolish I am. We were extremely lucky. Since they weren't looking for Catherine herself, they obviously didn't know this farm belonged to her. This must've been a search party, which means - Hesse is unsure where Catherine is hiding - and - there must be a German ship at the docks in Blackdane - which also means - I must take the ship - then do something - something to keep Hesse from ever sending soldiers here again."

Jens Sr. paced in deep contemplation for a moment, then he looked up as if he had an idea, drew a deep breath and let out a sigh of relief. He walked outside and found his men prepared to leave.

"Catherine has predicted an eminent storm," Halver reported through laughter. He then told Jens Sr. about the goats.

"We must leave immediately," Jens Sr. said. He turned to Catherine, "God be with you, me Lady, and thank you for the care you've given us. I've a feeling we'll meet again. Perhaps someday I can welcome you and yours into my home and return the favour of your hospitality."

Jens Sr. noticed the bed waiting for him in the back of one of the wagons. The other wagon held the supplies for travel. Jens Sr. went into the house, gathered the enemy's belongings; then, climbed into the back of the wagon with the bed and lay down while his soldiers waved farewell.

Shortly after they left, the dwarves hastily passed the farm, also on their way. As the dwarven children passed, they waved to

Wolf and said, "Bye, Beo." Beo being the dwarven word for Wolf. They'd played many adventurous games with Beo during the last few months and by the heart-rending looks on their faces they'd truly miss him.

The journey down the mountain went quicker than the one going up. Jens Sr.'s men drove the wagons for less than two days. When they arrived at Blackdane they went directly to the ship and found several additional people had boarded for their voyage home, including Morten's wife and three children.

Sterner, the soldier in charge, reported on his secret mission to Jens Sr. "We delivered the four Gospels as planned, the problem is 50 people want to come with us and we unfortunately don't have enough room to accommodate everyone."

Jens Sr. reported, "You think that's a problem - try this one, Sterner. We killed eight of Godfrey of Hesse's soldiers on the mountain. We must commandeer their ship and slay the crew before Hesse figures out what we've done."

"In broad daylight? With the other ships nearby? That's nearly impossible. Besides we don't know where the other ship is located," Sterner said.

"True, but the Hessens are from Germany so we know the ship is of German design and build," said Jens Sr.

"I'll conjure up an attack plan," Sterner promised.

"Wonderful. I've other things to do."

Pressed for time Jens Sr. used the wagons to go to market and purchase a large amount of food for the coming voyage. While in town Jens Sr. asked the butcher about the yellow flowers on top of the mountain. Jens Sr. learned they were a key ingredient in making the yellow healing pills that restored vim to tired and achy muscles. He also learned the location of the German ship.

Once the wagon held enough food for the return journey, Jens Sr. and his soldiers delivered the food to the Hessen ship as if they had purchased it. Hesse's men smiled mischievously and accepted the food. The crew naturally divided into two groups, one below bossed around Jens Sr.'s men and the other on top which made sure everything was loaded onto the ship. Straightaway Jens Sr. counted five men guarding the ship and two mongonels fully loaded with five arrows each. The mongonels rested in strategical locations on the main deck with extra arrows kept in readiness.

As Jens Sr. came up from the galley, he walked over to a mongonel and fired it into the back of one of the enemy sailors who stood by the stairwell to the lower deck. Jens Sr. reloaded the mongonel and set it back where he found it. Halver snatched up the dead sailor and stashed him into a storage closet below.

The other topside sailor heard the mechanical sound of the mongonel and ran to investigate.

"They broke a crate," Jens Sr. said as he walked past the crew member, pretending to be on his way to the wagon after another load. The last topside sailor went down to see.

On his return journey Jens Sr. switched the food crate he carried for a mongonel. The sailor hurried on his way back on top when he ran into Jens Sr.

"They didn't break a crate," he scolded, as Jens Sr. fired the mongonel.

If the five arrows, fired at top speed didn't kill him, the fall down the stairs would have as he landed extremely hard. Jens Sr. handed the mongonel to Halver, who reloaded it and started down the stairs looking for the next victim. Jens Sr. took up the second mongonel on deck and followed Halver. It didn't take long for the two of them to eliminate the remaining three Hessens.

Two of Jens Sr.'s soldiers impersonated the dead men on the deck. They acted bossy, so none of the neighbouring ships noticed any difference. They hid the corpses in the captain's closet. With the food properly stowed, the time to board the remaining 50 people had arrived.

Jens Sr. took the wagons to his Viking ship and turned them over to Sterner. "Since this ship is full, I need you to take the wagons and bring the rest of the passengers to the Hessen ship which is docked on the far side of Blackdane. Have them sing aloud as if they're at a party. Then sail to the entrance of the fjord. We'll wait for you there," Jens Sr. ordered.

"What about the enemy sailors?" Sterner asked looking worried.

"They're dead," Jens Sr. answered.

Sterner looked surprised for a moment, and then asked, "Why did you assign me to think of a plan if you already had the situation under control?"

"You never know when you'll need a secondary plan," Jens Sr. answered.

The passengers obeyed their instructions. They sang songs and crowded onto the German boat for a little cruise down the fjord. Jens Sr.'s ship waited for them and the two ships sailed for the McMarr Manor. Once they reached the sea, they respectfully wrapped the corpses in some old sails and sent them to the bottom of the ocean with a Christian prayer.

The voyage to Scotland lasted five days. When they arrived, Marta ran down from the manor to the docks and kissed Jens Sr.; then, tickled him under his beard. The McMarrs led the new group of refugees to the manor and learned their previous occupations. Jens Sr. matched their skills with what the dukedom needed. The men also became soldiers in Jens Sr.'s army. This secret activity of converting the Danes to Christianity and then having them sail for Scotland is how he steadily built his kingdom.

As soon as the new converts had disembarked, the soldiers prepared the ships for another voyage. Marta spied the preparations as she led a couple of families to their new homes. When she returned she reminded her husband with a doleful appearance, "The winter sea is very dangerous."

Jens Sr. saw the concerned look on her face and explained, "I've commandeered the ship of an enemy and have to return it secretly before he ferrets out what I've done. I'll simply return the ship and sail home. It's a short journey if the weather conditions hold."

"I'll do what I can to help the new ones adjust while you're away."

"That's grand, and I'll return as soon as I'm able."

Marta searched from high atop a nearby cliff every evening for over a week before she finally saw Jens Sr.'s approaching ship. When they at long last reached the shore Marta sent new oarsmen to row the ship into the cave. The McMarr dukedom prepared for a celebration. When Jens Sr. and his crew staggered off the ship, the joyous mood nearly vanished. It was the hardest voyage Jens Sr. had ever taken and he could no longer take them well. Jens Sr. told his wife, "After a hard voyage, I'm grateful to spend another Christmas here with you." Marta merely smiled as she assisted her husband up the walkway to the manor. Her smile told the others, we will celebrate even though the crew is exhausted.

Two days after Jens Sr. started his second voyage, students from the Scottish Naval Academy arrived at the gates of the manor and asked for food and lodging. Snow had blocked their usual travelling route. Marta beamed with delight when she saw them. She learned Castles and Caverns won the quiz games tournament and Jens Jr. had participated.

The boys slept in the guest hall and the cooks offered them so much food they couldn't possibly eat it all. The cooks even warmed stones in the fireplace for their feet that night.

266

In the morning the Scottish Academy's team left, having enjoyed the hospitality they'd received. They jested that if they needed any other deliveries at the manor, they'd help, anytime.

They gave Marta the crates from her sons. They told her not to open them as they were Christmas presents. She had them placed into a storeroom, having no idea they held dangerous weapons nor did she know what Hesse would do if he discovered where they were hidden.

CHAPTER Thirty Three

Christmas Holiday

Zeld enjoyed the handmade Christmas decorations that filled the walls of the Great Hall at supper time. Pictures of Figgie pudding, snow flakes, angels, shepherds and a stable complete with a manger scene were on display. "Christmas is coming, are you gonna spend the holidays with us?" Oles asked Zeld while examining the pictures from their dinner seats.

After a short pause, Zeld replied, "After thinking it through, I've decided to spend Christmas at the manor; besides, no one else asked me."

"That's because I already told everyone you planned to stay with us," said Oles with an impish grin.

"Thanks a lot, you squirrel," said Zeld, punching him on the arm.

Oles did an impression of a squirrel by showing his front teeth and taking small bites from a slice of bread he held in front of his face with both hands, much like a squirrel eats a nut.

"You must be Father Ulrich's brother," Zeld teased.

Odin and Oars laughed, but Oles didn't.

Just then Jens Sr. appeared with Morten's wife and children. Zeld watched as the woman and her three children entered the Great Hall. They surprised Morten while he wiped the tables. He dropped his bucket with the cleaning rag and tripped over several benches trying to reach his family. The boys chuckled a bit at his momentary clumsiness. When Morten reached his wife, he kissed her and held her as if she were his most treasured possession. Then he lifted his three small children into his arms all at once and sang a Danish lullaby.

Later that day, wagons left the school's main gate every few minutes as the boys returned to join their families for the Christmas holiday. The brothers McMarr and Zeld loaded their belongings into the wagon Jens Sr. brought. Jens Sr. helped them until he tried to lift Zeld's extremely heavy treasure chest.

"What do you have in this?"

"A suit of armour and loads of gold," Zeld confided quietly.

"How much is loads?"

"More than 10,000 pieces."

The look on Jens Sr.'s face showed he didn't believe Zeld, as it seemed quite impossible.

268 Zeld, the triplets and Jens Jr. rode their horses accompanying the wagon to the manor. The cold air and the sunshine battled to determine what sort of day it would be. The morning started out cold, but the sun took command and warmed the countryside for a few hours. Before dusk the cold air regained the upper hand, and the temperature dropped below freezing again.

It took four hours for the wagon to reach the manor. Once inside the boys cared for the horses. That night the boys sat in front of the fireplace in the den and anxiously listened to the stories of Jens Sr.'s exploits in Denmark.

Zeld's face turned crimson with embarrassment when Jens Sr. handed him the pottery shards; after all, they did lead to a lost treasure, only for the wrong side. He would have to puzzle out how they had gone from Sir Tavish's hand to Denmark. Zeld felt very pleased when he heard about the improvements at the farm, more chickens, a dozen pigs, a milk cow, weather-predicting goats, rooms for travellers to rent and Edelweiss. He hoped Edelweiss wouldn't ruin everything.

Over the next few days, Zeld went with the brothers McMarr who showed him around the countryside. The boys explored plenty of small caves and a couple of larger ones. Zeld saw the small port and the farms. One day Jens Sr. went with the boys and showed them his new land purchases in England. He owned all the stone and woodland needed to build a port town, which Jens Sr. had dreamed about for ages. With a port the size he planned, a major city could be built.

When Christmas day arrived, the entire kingdom celebrated by holding a special church service in the manor's chapel where the local people play-acted the Christmas story. A narrator read the story in both English and Danish. The new converts played as many of the roles as possible. They performed the play twice, so everyone could attend. On Christmas night the McMarrs held an exceptionally grand feast with roasted pork and a host of creamed vegetables. Zeld tried several new foods.

Jens Jr. whispered in Zeld's ear, "All these marvellous cooks and not one of them can make brown hare pie."

Zeld whispered back, "Thank goodness."

Christmas was a jolly occasion filled with family and friends. The converts celebrated Christmas for the first time and they glowed with the joy of their new faith.

269

Jens Sr. spent the next few days in his den preparing diagrams of the land surrounding his manor. He marked the locations for new farms, roads, towers and his port town. While looking for supplies, he stumbled across a couple of large unlabelled crates sitting in storage. He opened them and found they contained mongonels and arrows.

He asked Marta about his discovery, "I don't recognize the crates in the storeroom. Did they come from the ship we captured?"

Marta went into the storeroom and examined them before she remembered where they came from. "Oh, the boys sent them home with a group of cadets from Scotland Naval."

Jens Sr. called the boys in and asked them, "Where the blazes did these mongonels come from?"

Zeld answered proudly, "After you left for Denmark, we discovered a Hessen store of weapons at a farm near the school. We think Hesse is planning to capture the damaged castles from the last Viking raid. So, I ordered me father's soldiers to take the weapons and replace them with phony items. Then we smuggled the crates out of the area and they've been hidden here nearly a month."

"I counted twelve mongonels in the storeroom. It must've been a profitable raid."

"We sent six to James's grandfather in Wales and twelve more to Friar Tuck," Zeld explained.

Jens Sr. pulled out one of the mongonels. He discovered the Hessen lion painted on the front. He also pulled out a few arrows and found the Hesse family cresting.

"Lads, you better wash this paint off before I'm caught with stolen goods in me manor," said Jens Sr. in a serious tone.

Jens Sr. left the boys to their task and wrote a letter to King Henry updating him on the situation.

The boys spent quite awhile in the storeroom washing the paint off the arrows with wet rags, and then they repainted them with the gold and black rings that made up Zeld's cresting. They had to scrub with a horse brush to remove the lions on the mongonels. Zeld didn't mind the work. To him this kept the Christmas holiday from getting too boring.

The next day they had a surprise visit from James and his grandfather.

"I am Sir Rosser ap Phillip," James' grandfather said once through the manor gate.

"I am Jens McMarr Sr. Please come in and tell me why you came all the way from Wales."

Sir Rosser dismounted slowly and went into the manorhouse. James and all the other boys, including Dando, followed. They went into the den where Jens Sr. had maps and drawings strewn all around. Jens Sr. gathered them into a stack. Presently the den filled with men, young and old.

"My grandson, James, informs me you are at war with Godfrey of Hesse. Is this true?"

"Yes, I killed thirteen of his soldiers this month," stated Jens Sr. soberly.

"My grandson further states he desires to participate in this war."

Zeld stepped boldly forward. "He already is part of the war. You see the war is between the Hesses and the de Saxons. Godfrey of Hesse stole me family's castles and lands. In the process he killed me father. Me mother escaped with me brother Wolf and meself. I've returned from exile to reclaim me lands and castles. James has helped me raid a Hessen store of weapons."

"How will you finance a war? You're merely a boy," said Sir Rosser, looking him up and down.

"Me gold mine has done very well, so far," Zeld said gratefully.

"How much gold do you have? Twenty or thirty pieces? That is woefully inadequate," snapped Sir Rosser.

"I've more than 10,000 gold pieces."

"Show me," insisted Sir Rosser sceptically.

270

Zeld led his mates to his treasure chest and they carried it back into the den. Zeld opened the treasure chest and took out his possessions until he reached his saddlebags on the bottom. He untied one of the bags and showed the freshly minted gold coins to James's grandfather.

Sir Rosser raised a gold coin to his mouth and bit it. His teeth left a mark in the soft metal.

"It's real gold," said Sir Rosser looking astonished.

Jens Sr. could hardly believe his eyes.

"You really do have thousands of gold pieces," Jens Sr. said sounding happily surprised.

"Enough to buy a battleship..." Sir Rosser began.

"...but not enough to win a war," Jens Sr. finished.

"True, but this is a fine start," remarked Sir Rosser. "I see you're making maps."

"Yes, now the Vikings may purchase land in England, I've bought all I can. I plan to build a port city here," Jens Sr. said while pointing to a location on the map for Sir Rosser to see.

"The Vikings will destroy it," said Sir Rosser.

"Other Vikings are purchasing land in England as well. They'll not destroy themselves. They'll raid other lands instead," explained Jens Sr.

"I hope it isn't Wales," said Sir Rosser in a somewhat desperate tone.

"If the Welch opened trade with the Vikings this spring, it would almost guarantee their safety," explained Jens Sr.

"What sort of merchandise will they need?" asked Sir Rosser.

"They'll need building supplies, nails, tools and lumber," answered Jens Sr. "They would also need additional household supplies, perhaps food and blankets."

"I believe it's worth a try. If allowed to open a store on your land, I can fill it with goods by spring."

"Agreed," said Jens Sr. reaching for a handshake.

"Now, about those six mongonels sitting in my boat shop. Why do I have them? And who do I surrender them to?" Sir Rosser asked.

"They belong to me," stated Zeld. "Someday I'll need them to recapture me family's castle but for now I want them hidden."

"May I have permission to use them occasionally?" Sir Rosser requested.

"That's sounds fair enough," Zeld said.

Sir Rosser put his hands together and gave the same broken arrow sign the boys had used earlier as a salute to Zeld. Zeld gave the sign back.

James asked his grandfather, "May I stay here and return to school with the others?"

"That's all right by me," said Sir Rosser. "It reduces my busy schedule by one journey."

"It's good with us, too, and Sir Rosser you must spend the night. It's cold and it appears a storm is brewing," added Jens Sr.

"Thank you. My amulet of wind should only be used during daylight hours. One mistake could cost me a ship and crew."

"You boys sleep in front of the fireplace in the guest hall and Sir Rosser will stay in the guestroom," called Jens Sr.

Zeld and the others cheerfully moved their things. James told them how his grandfather made him scrub the coats of arms from the mongonels and cresting from the arrows and they'd come to the manor to make certain sure James hadn't made up the story. The boys told James they had to do the same thing.

That night they stayed up late in front of the fireplace. They really didn't have much to say other than they missed Robert, Brian and Sullivan.

"I think Brian and Robert went with Sullivan for Christmas holiday, at least I overheard them talking about it," said Odin.

Zeld looked at Dando. "So, Dando, tell us about yourself? Are you English?" asked Zeld sarcastically. It felt good to ask somebody else that question.

The triplets joined in, "Are you purple with pink polka dots? Are you as mellow as apple juice? Does the hair on the back of your neck stand out when you whistle? Can you blow fire from your nostrils when you get angry? Is there anyone more annoying than we three? Would you like us to torture them?"

Dando ignored everything after "tell us about yourself?"

"I came to live at the McMarr Manor when me family fell under attack by Godfrey of Hesse. Me father is in hiding. When the time is right, we'll retake our lands. Then we'll build a castle bigger and better than any castle before," Dando said.

"I know how you feel, and I'm glad to know you're one of us," Zeld said as if an old mate. Dando gave Zeld a strange look, but he didn't see it.

In the morning the triplets practiced their parts for the school play and they wouldn't let the other boys watch. "THIS IS A CLOSED REHEARSAL!" shouted out Oles as he slammed the door of the chapel in the other boys' faces.

Boredom finally set in, so the boys invaded the kitchen and took cooking lessons from Marta McMarr. They learned how to knead and bake bread, rolls, sweet rolls, cornbread and short 273 bread. They also learned how to make a one pot supper with meat, vegetables and dumplings on top. Cooking was jolly fun. They started cookbooks with recipes which they copied from Marta McMarr's file box.

To Zeld, the time passed quickly when suddenly the day came to return to school. The boys packed their belongings into a wagon which waited for them in the yard. Zeld and James thanked Lady McMarr with a hug for letting them stay the holiday; then, they shook Jens Sr.'s hand. The triplets followed and they hugged their mum and shook their father's hand too. The triplets thanked their parents for letting them stay the holiday as well. Jens Jr. stood back shaking his head and covering his eyes with his hand in obvious embarrassment.

Two soldiers drove the wagon to the school for safety. After all, the law of safe haven did not apply until they entered the school's property. The journey took longer than usual because of inclement weather; namely, it snowed, lightly at first, but then the storm turned fierce. The wagon bogged down in the deep snow forcing the party to find shelter and wait it out.

Zeld searched up and down the road looking for his marker. When he found it, they abandoned the wagon and the boys carried their belongings up the frozen stream and into the cave. The soldiers gathered firewood for the night on the way.

The cavern held plenty of room, so the boys brought the horses inside and planned to spend the night. A strange sound came from far behind them in the darkness. Zeld guessed the sound came from bats at first, but then realized its deep and flowing pitch sounded similar to the ocean. The darkness of the cave made it hard to see. They started a fire, and then crept to the back of the cave with a flaming stick. They found a hibernating black bear snoring in the far shadows.

"What do we do now?" asked James.

"We build a barrier," answered Zeld.

Zeld laid his shoulder bag on top of his treasure chest and joined the other boys in rolling large rocks to form a wall. To Zeld the rocks felt heavy and cold and they required three or four boys to move each one. One particularly larger rock rested heavily in the ground. The boys loosened the dirt around it before it rolled.

Once the stone moved, the boys found a large black pit hidden under it. Jens Jr. pulled a flaming stick out of the fire and held it above the pit. All the boys stood around the dark hole. Jens Jr. lowered his flaming stick for more light. Inside the pit lay a secret wooden stairway. Oles and Zeld retrieved a couple more flaming sticks from the fire.

Jens Jr. took a deep breath and said, "Ready or not, here I go." He charged heroically down the stairs. One of the stairs broke and his foot went straightaway to the ground. "OOOUUUCH!" he screamed loudly. He dropped his torch.

Odin and Oars reached down and pulled Jens Jr. out of the pit. They found a caltrop imbedded in the bottom of his foot. Zeld examined the caltrop and saw a big red sore already forming around the wound.

"Throw me bag," Zeld called to James.

James grabbed the bag and hastily tossed it. Zeld reached in and took out the healing stone with his right hand while he pulled the caltrop out with his left. Blood and poison poured out from the wound. Zeld placed the stone to the side of the wound. Jens Sr.'s two soldiers made their way through the small crowd with a flaming stick and watched as Jens Jr. lost consciousness slumping on the ground.

"Death venom," one of them said in a bitter tone.

"What does death venom do?" asked Zeld frantically.

"It spreads rapidly through the body, and then you die. There's no cure," said the soldier with a sad nod of his head.

Zeld reached into his bag and took out the dragon heart. He placed it in Jens Jr.'s hand. The spot where Zeld held the healing amulet formed a big blister that popped. Blood and poison drained out of the open wound. He moved the stone to another place on

Jens Jr.'s foot. Jens Jr. turned red in places as the poison spread through his body.

A second blood blister burst under the healing stone and more mess flowed. Zeld moved the stone directly on top of the original wound. Jens Jr.'s body turned entirely red as the poison hadn't stopped spreading.

Zeld squeezed Jens Jr.'s hand with the dragon heart in it and said, "C'mon – c'mon – fight - never give up – c'mon - JJ."

Jens Jr.'s body changed colour to a lifeless grey.

As the boys stood around traumatized, one of the soldiers said, "Let me carry him to the wagon. It's not right we should have to sleep with a dead boy."

Zeld looked up with a boiling anger at the soldier and screamed, "HE'S NOT DEAD UNTIL I SAY HE'S DEAD!"

"HONESTLY, WHO DO YOU THINK YOU ARE, A GRAND WIZARD THAT CAN DO THE IMPOSSIBLE?" the soldier scolded.

"I am a great healer. You go outside if you don't want to sleep with him. We're not done here!"

Zeld leaned over and listened for breathing. He heard nothing but the snoring bear. Zeld turned to the McMarr boys and said, "Bring me some snow."

With tears streaming down their faces, the triplets went outside. Zeld pulled Jens Jr. clothes off. The brothers returned with big snow balls.

"Wash him with the snow," Zeld ordered.

The boys rubbed the snow all over his body. Zeld held the healing stone over Jens Jr.'s chest. It had very little power left. Just as Zeld lost hope, he thought he felt a heart beat.

Hastily feeling for it again he announced, "His heart is beating! We must get him to breathe."

James pushed down on Jens Jr.'s ribs, and then he released his hold causing the chest to move up and down as if he were breathing.

"This is the way it's done with drowned men," James said with a hopeful expression.

"Good, keep doing it," said Zeld.

After a while they turned Jens Jr. over and pushed on the back of his ribs. Jens Jr. coughed and wheezed. They stepped back. Jens

Jr. sat up weakly with his back against the cavern wall.

After a moment, he opened his eyes and asked, "Where's Edelweiss?"

The lot nervously laughed.

"Gone fishing, she'll be back tomorrow," answered James.

"Oh, I'll wait here then," said Jens Jr. and he leaned back and closed his eyes.

Zeld laughed, this time with great relief. The soldiers' mouths fell open in amazement.

276 One soldier said to Zeld, "I apologize for doubting you - I never would've - but I saw it with me own eyes. I'd fight on your side of any war."

Jens Jr. shook from the cold, so Zeld wrapped him in a blanket and the soldiers stayed to watch him while the rest of the boys headed down the stairwell again. This time they checked on the sturdiness of every step by clubbing it with a stick from the woodpile.

They found more caltrops, expertly hidden. Zeld went back upstairs, unlocked his treasure chest, took out his gloves and emptied the coins from the saddlebag. Using his gloves he carefully collected each caltrop, including the one Jens Jr. stepped on and dropped them into the saddlebag

At the bottom of the stairwell the boys discovered a trail of brittle small animal bones which led to a storage cavern where several blankets hung over three large wooden crates. Zeld could tell by the amount of dust the secret passage had been sealed for years.

The boys checked for traps before they paid attention to the crates. They didn't find anything, so they slowly pulled off the blankets and checked the crates for booby traps. They didn't find any, so they carried one crate away from the others and opened it.

"GERMAN ZWEIHANDERS!" Odin shouted out excitedly as he identified the giant swords in the crate.

"Only a strong man could handle one of these," declared Oles.

They opened another crate.

"Fiddle shields," said James, as he hoisted one out of the crate.

The fiddle shields were the size and shape of two dinner plates sitting side by side. Each shield had nine sharp studs protruding out the front, which made them a vicious weapon as well as a shield.

"Look, the Hessen lion," Zeld observed.

One by one the boys looked up at Zeld with a smile.

"I think the McMarr Manor would make a better home for these swords and shields," said Zeld.

"There's plenty of room under my bed," Oles jested.

"Mine too!" added Odin.

"Well, we'll have to stack a few on top of my bed," said Oles.

The boys took the swords and shields but left the empty crates behind in their original places. They used the blankets to cover the crates and the room appeared as it had before they found it. After the boys double checked to make sure they had taken everything, they rolled the original boulder back on top of the stairwell. Then they packed dirt around the boulder's edges to hide their intrusion.

Zeld washed Jens Jr.'s sore foot with snow again. The party had nearly run out of firewood, so the soldiers gathered more. Zeld stood in the entryway and watched as the full-blown blizzard hampered the soldiers' efforts. Zeld called to them several times and they called back in an attempt to keep everyone located.

Once they returned, Zeld said slyly, "Watch what I can do." Then he reached down, closing the mine entrance. "That should keep the cold out," he said confidently.

"You are clever, aren't you?" asked Oles.

"What type of amulet d'you need to close cavern entrances?" asked Oars.

"This is a dwarven door, no amulet required," said Zeld as he showed them where to pull the door to make it open and close.

That night as the boys huddled around the fire to stay warm Oles asked, "D'you imagine we'll ever be clever enough or strong enough to overthrow the Hessens?"

No one answered. The boys looked back and forth at each other not knowing what to say. A long silence occurred. Their faces grew heavy with shadows as the firelight diminished.

In the morning Odin and Oars rode into the castle and checked out a sleigh. They used their horses plus two school horses to pull the sleigh through the deep snow.

While Zeld waited in the cavern, he used his amulet on Jens Jr.'s foot. The two soldiers loaded the new swords and shields into the McMarr's wagon.

After turning the school's sleigh around they speedily finished their journey. Zeld felt better once he reached the school.

Zeld watched as Robert, Brian and Sullivan arrived shortly after them. Robert reported they had spent the night with the dwarves in the silver mine, having been caught in the storm as well. They learned a lot about mining and tried dwarven cooking, which they claimed was delicious.

Oles showed his happiness to be safely back by hugging the teachers, his brothers and even his horse.

Odin showed his feelings by saying, "I'm glad to be back." That was Odin's logical way, say it and be done.

Oars on the other hand kept asking about going out again. Even though they looked alike, the triplets had their own way of approaching life.

That night in Eagle Loft, Zeld used his stone to finish healing Jens Jr.'s foot. Jens Jr. took off his shoes and rested his foot across the end of the bed. Zeld placed the stone on the wound. This time it really tickled and Jens Jr. kept laughing, even after the stone was packed away. Once his laughter stopped he turned to Zeld and said, "I know I've been overly critical of you in the past and I'm sorry. I want to say thanks and that you're a true mate. Oh, and one more thing I've never had so much fun, secretly dishing it out to the Hessens. I can't wait to see what we're gonna do tomorrow."

CHAPTER Thirty Four

School Play and Swordplay

The schoolboys crowded around Friar Stephen leaning this way and that for a peek at the schedules for the new semester. Friar Stephen set the schedules down on the ends of the tables in the Great Hall as the morning classes restarted. After most of the crowd dispersed, Zeld made his way to the tables, found his schedule and read it intently.

Awake and arise 6:30 a.m.
Chapel at 6:45 a.m. (promptness required)
Breakfast at 7:15 a.m.
1- 8:00 a.m. Friar Martin   Healing without a Healer
2- 9:00 a.m. Sir Jaydan Razor   Characters and Creatures II
3- 10:00 a.m. Sir Roger Fitzwayne   Battle Strategies
4- 11:00 a.m. Friar Timothy   Map Making
Midday meal at 12:00
5- 1:00 p.m. Friar Marcus   Money and Foreign Trade
6- 2:00 p.m. Sir Drain Bracken   Castle Design and Management
7- 3:00 p.m. Friar Jonathan   World Politics
8- 4:00 p.m. Sir Tavish Macdonald   Field Exercises
Supper at 5:30
Time for homework and school sports or teams. Library open.

Zeld noticed the teachers taught in the same order as before, but the subjects had changed or advanced. In a couple of classes the teachers planned to put the boys' knowledge of war to use in the Castles and Caverns Combat Game. Zeld felt anxious to get started. The Christmas holiday seemed too long for him.

The McMarr triplets stayed busy in the evenings with play practice. The long and harsh winter felt terrible. Zeld grew tired of only having five hours of light per day and longed for the summer sun. This dreary boredom lasted three weeks, that is, until the school play came along.

After supper one Wednesday night the tables and benches in the Great Hall were rearranged for the show. A pieced curtain hung over a rope. The performers went behind the curtain and put on their costumes. Several visitors came to see the production, including Jens Sr. and Marta.

Zeld watched impatiently as the play started. Friar Timothy stepped in front of the curtain, his face and hands painted red, dressed in red, with red horns on his head and holding a tall red pitchfork. He stood in front of the curtain and spoke while the acting took place first on one side and then on the other. All the props and actors remained hidden behind the curtain and the actors stepped out on cue.

280

Friar Timothy began: *"Listen here and I shall tell of the worst plague upon mankind.*

This plague steals, lies, plots and schemes. It always leaves you in a bind.

What is this plague above all others?

Why it is that of younger brothers.

So, listen here and listen well, be he blood or be he friar.

When he is through with you, your ox will be in the mire.

If a journey calls you far away and your true love you'll be missing,

Take her with you, don't let her stay, or your brother will do the kissing.

If your true love and younger brother soon are to be wedded

Why sit back all forlorn, when you can have them both beheaded?

Why should you wait until this is true?

Why not kill him now, without further ado?

Teach him of nature and things he should do-

So, that life can be jolly, at least for you.

Up north in the caves they saved you a dragon.

Merely walk right on in; its tail is a waggin'.

The best part of being little is that you can fly.

What, I'm your older brother, I wouldn't lie.

Swimming with the animals is fun for goodness sakes-

Barracudas, eels, alligators and occasional snakes-

You stand right here while I chop down this tree.

There are bees trapped inside but soon I'll have them free.

That brother of yours, does he not pester?

Then send him to school and turn him into a jester.

If he refuses to go and become a clown,
  Then take him out back and teach him to drown."

The actors put on short displays, acting out the verses. The triplets played the victims. First, one was beheaded on one side of the curtain. As he left the stage, another triplet walked out with his big brother and went nervously into a dragon's den. Every death became a comic scene.

All together the boys were beheaded, eaten by a dragon, eaten by water monsters, stung by bees, drowned, poisoned, eaten by dogs, crushed under a wagon, stabbed, tortured on a rack, crushed in a rockslide, used as whale bait, sold to a mad alchemist for body parts, and finally eaten by cannibals.

The last line ended with Friar Timothy saying,
"The moral of the story is quite clear and plain.
  Learn to hate your brother, then go and raise a little Cain."

The boys from the school clapped and cheered, but the guests appeared shocked. They'd never before seen a play where the Devil encouraged the murder of younger brothers.

Father Ulrich stood and congratulated the cast for their outstanding efforts.

Then he said something that eased the visitor's minds, "I believe after seeing this play, Lucifer, the father of lies, will have a much harder time convincing people to commit sin. The Devil is exposed magnificently in this play and I recommend every man, woman and child in England see it."

Father Ulrich's statement guaranteed the copies of the play, on sale at the school, would sell out. Friar Timothy became the hero of the day. The proceeds from the play were used to buy food for the starving people from the Viking raid.

That night after Zeld went to bed, he saw Friar Timothy quietly enter Eagle Loft. The friar still had traces of the red paint here and there. He walked silently over to Robert O'Day's bed and whispered, "Robert, are you awake?"

Robert bolted into a sitting position, "I am now."

"Fantastic. I wanted to make sure you knew exactly where this came from."

Then Friar Timothy pulled a pillow out from behind his back and hit Robert in the face with it. "Midnight pillow fight," yelled Friar Timothy.

The boys hadn't expected this, so Friar Timothy managed several more excellent whacks before the fighting came to equal terms. Everyone jumped out of bed and had a jolly time clobbering each other. The fight ended with everyone breathing hard and sitting in a large group.

Friar Timothy talked for a few minutes about the play and the effort of the triplets to make it funny. He told the boys how grateful he felt to be their adviser. "I feel like I'm helping God shape your destinies. It's indescribably awe-inspiring." Zeld went back to bed wondering what that meant and Friar Timothy left.

He thought momentarily about the things Friar Timothy did for others. He'd exposed Edelweiss, sold copies of his play to feed the poor and discovered the missing gold on the first day of school. He was truly an outstanding man.

Tryouts for the fencing competition started the next day. The boys lighter than 85 pounds comprised the first group and each additional group grew 10 pounds heavier. Each weight class had three divisions as well, full armour, sword with shield and sword only, categories. This meant a team of 24 boys would participate for C&C at the tournament.

The boys used their own armour and wooden practice swords to avoid injury. Zeld didn't fight well wearing his heavy armour. He fancied the sword and shield event but didn't win that place on the team, because of Brian Boru's quickness.

Zeld tried for the sword only competition and successfully won a spot on the team when Angus ap Forrest dropped his sword in the qualifying round. Angus complained to Sir Tavish but to no avail. "Dropping your sword is bad luck - it happens - it happened to you and you lost fair and square. No one cheated. You have no case," explained Sir Tavish.

Zeld noticed Geoffrey stood nearby listening in on what Sir Tavish said. Geoffrey dropped his sword in a mocking way when Angus walked passed. Geoffrey's mates all laughed.

In short, Zeld lucked out. However, luck could be a grand companion. He couldn't complain.

On the scheduled day for the tournament none of the usual preparations took place. No one packed clothing or prepared any food for the journey. The horses and wagons remained undisturbed. Zeld waited in the courtyard prepared but he wondered if the schedule changed. Brian Boru came out of Smoky Glen, also prepared. Presently all 24 boys waited to compete. Then a soft white cloud floated overhead. It gradually descended until it reached the ground. Recognizing the Giant Academy, Zeld hoisted his bag and marched toward the cloud. Brian did the same. The rest of the team cautiously followed. Zeld and Brian called to the team to hurry as the two of them walked through the front gate. The rest of the team followed in a nervous bunch.

They could hear a distant voice say, "Preparing for lift. We're up."

They felt the ground move under their feet as the cloud slowly drifted upward. The team walked over to the Academy's Great Hall where they joined the Scottish Naval team.

The cloud stopped moving after awhile and descended again. Shortly afterwards they saw Scott and the other Welch Naval cadets coming through the gate.

Zeld yelled, "Scott, we're over here."

The Welch boys marched into the Great Hall as the cloud rose again. The cloud stopped next at Prince Valiant followed by all the other schools. The ride ended when the castle touched down on top of a mountain. The main gates opened and the students toured the rest of the school.

Some giant students practiced archery with huge war machines they called ballista. Their targets were heavy two-inch thick oak boards with small red dragons painted on them. The ballistas fired eight foot long spears that hit so hard, they knocked the heavy targets backward. It appeared to be an intimidation tactic, but Zeld certainly knew better. He minded what the lings told him about hunting dragons with ballistas inside their caverns.

The athletes followed until they reached the outer courtyard. In the middle of the court was a square with a sunken floor in the white solid stone. The spectators watched the matches in the centre while sitting on the steps surrounding the square.

The matches started in the afternoon with the full armour division competing first. The eight smallest boys dressed in their armour reported for combat rounds in the bottom of the square and were paired into four matches. All four started at the same time in the open courtyard with an official assigned to each match. No coaches were permitted to attend because of alleged cheating in the past. Zeld was never told who or how they cheated.

Crispyn of Orange competed against a tall, thin giant who used a move C&C hadn't seen before. He swung his sword wide from right to left, bullying Crispyn's sword out of the way. Then, the giant hit Crispyn in the face with his elbow knocking him to the ground. The giant followed by putting his sword at Crispyn's throat for the first score in the best of five match.

In the second combat stance the giant tried the same thing, but this time Crispyn ducked the elbow and made a hasty lunge with his sword into the giant's left armpit. In real combat Crispyn would've killed the giant, as there is a weakness in the links of chainmail in the armpit area.

The third combat stance went much differently than the other two. The giant swung his sword up and down; then, without warning lunged forward. Crispyn parried the giant's sword. The giant swung his sword in the same motion. Crispyn caught on to the rhythm and as the giant lunged he spun a complete circle to his right, swinging his sword wide but low, hitting the giant behind his left knee. The giant lost his balance and fell. Crispyn placed his sword on the giant's throat for his second point.

The fourth combat stance relied more on brute strength than skill. The giant swung chopping blows, driving Crispyn into a corner. Crispyn countered by lowering his shoulder and throwing himself directly into the giant to push him back. The thin giant dodged out of the way and Crispyn tripped over the giant's foot, landing face first. The giant leaned over placing his sword on the back of Crispyn's neck.

On the fifth stance Crispyn swung with hard blows, but the giant matched them. The crowd's attention shifted from the other matches as this one showed grand intensity. After about three minutes of hard hitting, the giant dropped low to the ground and swung his leg around Crispyn, tripping him backward. Crispyn quickly curled up into a ball and rolled onto his back, and then over his head landing on his knees.

The giant, surprised at Crispyn's ability, moved in and found Crispyn couldn't defend himself as well from his knees. The giant kicked Crispyn hard in the chest and he landed on his back. The giant held his sword to Crispyn's throat and the match ended. The giant helped Crispyn up.

The crowd cheered at the brilliantly fought contest. The four winners received no rest as they went back into combat as soon as the last match concluded. The giant easily beat his next two opponents.

Zeld noticed the giants won every match until they reached the upper weight divisions. The 145-pound division came down to the giant Brutus Bragg against Geoffrey of Hesse. Both had easily won their earlier two matches. Geoffrey broke tournament rules by striking Brutus's hand with the flat of his sword early in the match. Brutus couldn't hold his sword properly, due to the injury, so Geoffrey won without much trouble. Neither Brutus nor his school could file a protest because of the financial arrangements the giants had with Geoffrey's father.

Norton Duval fought as the heavy weight from C&C. He won his first match and fought with a giant in his second. The giant weighed 100 pounds heavier than Norton. Norton manoeuvred around the giant with ease. Once behind him he seized the giant around the neck and threw him to the ground. The crowd cheered as Norton used his superior skill to defeat the giant.

In the next event, swords and shields only, Zeld saw plenty of pounding, tripping, lunging, parrying, and even occasional biting. The giants won seven of the first eight matches. The only loss came to Brian Boru, who used his speed to slip around his opponents and take them down the way Norton had done. Zeld enjoyed the astonished looks on the boys' faces when Brian wrestled them to the ground.

On Zeld's turn he stepped down into the square. He felt a wee bit nervous but nothing like the time he fought the Vikings. Zeld's opponent happened to be a goblin who tried various tricks to throw him off. He kept switching hands with his sword and at times bobbed his head up and down. Zeld didn't fall for the tricks and made short work of the goblin.

Zeld watched the others fight. The younger boys didn't appear to be very good fencers. He wondered if he fought better than the others. He remembered fighting with the Vikings and he knew he must be the best in this set of boys.

Next he duelled Scott from the Welch Academy. Scott fought better than the goblin and could parry most of Zeld's thrusts. Zeld used a strategy and tried a false thrust on the right side followed by a real one on the left. Scott attempted to block the fake lunge and Zeld hit him with the real one.

In their second stance Scott tried to disarm Zeld with a circular motion followed by a whipping motion. Zeld held tightly to his sword and the whipping motion took Scott's sword out of proper position. Zeld took advantage and scored with a thrust over the heart.

Zeld defeated Scott with a wild full arm swing over his head and around his back, and then with a quick lunge once the sword rose even with his waist. Scott never saw the sword coming.

Zeld's final match came against a tall, thin giant who had a very long reach. Zeld understood in order for him to win he had to block the giant's first lunge; then, advance and strike promptly.

The giant had a terrible time lunging with accuracy. He kept missing for no apparent reason. Zeld thought the giant was trying to lure him out of proper position with false lunges. After a while he attempted lunging back to see what would happen. He scored with a hit in the giant's belly.

The giant experimented with a brute force tactic. Zeld retreated, taken by surprise and the giant scored with a hit in Zeld's ribs. Zeld decided if the giant came at him with brute force again he would give the Norton Duval move a go.

The giant attempted it on the very next stance. Zeld tried to spin around the giant on his right side but tripped over his own feet and landed sprawled out across the floor. The giant quickly lunged for a score but somehow missed. Zeld rolled toward the giant and switched hands with his sword. While still on the floor he reached up hitting the giant in the stomach. The crowd laughed at the giant's terrible luck, crushing his confidence. Zeld easily scored his final point, winning the match.

At supper that night the boys ate giant pies in the Great Hall. The MacNar School staff sat at the head table. When the staff cut their pie, a dozen blackbirds escaped flying around the room, and then out the windows. The staff sat red faced as all the other schools laughed at their expense. The cooks delivered a second pie and this time they ate it.

The giants gave away shields as prizes during the closing ceremony which they held in the Great Hall following supper. Geoffrey, Norton, Brian and Zeld were called to the head table and each awarded first place kite shields, with a rounded stud centred on the front.

After the ceremony most of the boys marched out of the Great Hall to the cloud. Zeld hurried over to see Brutus Bragg. He found him sitting at the giant's table.

"How's your hand?" he asked earnestly.

The giant held it up, and it appeared mangled.

Zeld asked, "May I heal it with this stone?"

Brutus obviously didn't trust Zeld; after all, he and Geoffrey came from the same school. He asked suspiciously, "You're not toying with me are you?"

Zeld placed his healing stone on top of the giant's hand. The giant could feel the tickle that came with the healing but suppressed the urge to laugh. It didn't take long for the hand to heal. Zeld felt the cloud move and ran to catch his team up. As he left, Brutus called after him, "Thank you, me friend." Zeld waved as he ran to catch the cloud, proudly carrying his new shield.

When the cloud landed, Zeld walked out the main gate with his team onto solid ground. They were back. The entire event took less than a day. Zeld and Brian showed their shields to the other pages. Norton and Geoffrey sat in the Great Hall surrounded by the older boys as they told them how they beat the giants.

Sir Tavish stayed in the Great Hall interested in hearing all about the fencing. The older boys stayed up late telling their exploits. Zeld and his mates simply congratulated each other, and then went to bed. Zeld felt pleased having won his matches, but it didn't seem right to brag about every good move. After all, some of the students who lost, like Crispyn, did some of the best fighting.

As soon as Zeld and his mates left, the conversation in the Great Hall changed.

"Did it take much effort?" Sir Tavish asked Geoffrey.

"Zeld did well in the first two rounds but, I had to work my magnetic amulet very hard in the third. In fact, I broke a sweat before he did," Geoffrey reported. "That little trick I pulled on Angus causing him to drop his sword so Zeld would qualify for the team was nothing compared to what I did in the third round. Zeld tripped and landed face down giving his opponent a wide open view of his back. For a moment I felt tempted to reverse the polarity of the stone and have the giant's sword pierce straight through him."

"I'm glad you didn't. Remember we want the entire family - not merely Zeld. You're sure they awarded him the special shield?" asked Sir Tavish.

"No question about it!" answered Geoffrey.

"Good! The trap is set!"

CHAPTER Thirty Five
Waiting for Spring

Penny lifted the mysterious bottles of multicoloured pills from under the counter at her store and showed them to Zeld and all his mates; namely, Oles, Oars, Odin, Sullivan, James, Brian, Robert and Jens Jr. They had ridden together into Baden town one Saturday morning.

"These came from under a barn," she said, and Zeld caught her meaning. "We're not exactly sure what each colour of pill does," she added.

Zeld stashed one of the bottles in his bag. He trusted Friar Timothy implicitly so he planned to show the pills to him to see if he could unravel the mystery.

"Do you think I should branch out my stock and order in different types of merchandise?" Penny asked, and added in a hushed tone. "Meaning armour?"

"I would continue stocking what you usually sell," Zeld said. "After all, I don't have an army yet."

Penny stared at Jens Jr. with a puzzled look on her face. Zeld realized she probably didn't know him. "This is me true mate Jens McMarr Jr. He plans to remove the dirt when you dig the new basement."

"At one time I felt sceptical about the project, but I can see its merits, now I've thought it through," said Jens Jr.

Zeld bought a few items: waterproof boots, a stand for his armour and shield, a bag for the poisoned caltrops, parchment and three colours of ink. He planned to sketch a few maps that might help him regain his castle.

Zeld and his mates visited the bakery for a treat and to call on their friend, the baker. Afterward they rode north to visit the dwarves.

When Zeld entered the mine, he quickly noticed all the men were gone. One of the women said they went hunting. Meanwhile, the women and children waited impatiently for their return. Zeld looked into the kitchen just inside the mine's entrance and saw the empty cupboards and nothing hanging on the meat hooks. He realized the dwarves didn't have anything to eat. He remembered Bushhard had said they needed food. Zeld felt ashamed for enjoying treats at the bakery while the dwarves went without food.

The boys took immediate action and broke into two groups. The triplets rode to the school and checked out a wagon while Zeld and the rest of his mates rode into town with money.

Oles found Tyre Stevens and Crispyn of Orange sitting around looking bored to tears in Eagle Loft and swore them to secrecy. Then Oles marched into the kitchen with Tyre and Crispyn trailing behind. "The dwarves have run outta food," Oles said. Zeld's soldiers gave them a half a burlap sack of turnips and a couple loaves of bread. "Thank you," said Oles as he left the kitchen.

Oles rode his horse with the turnips draped down from the saddle horn and Tyre and Crispyn rode with a loaf of bread each to the dwarven mine and presented the food. The women thanked them, put the turnips on to boil and fed the bread to the children.

Odin and Oars took the wagon into town. Zeld filled it with two fat geese, flour, sugar, salt, milk and three gigantic burlap sacks of vegetables. After delivering the supplies, they left the dwarven women cooking and headed home.

Tyre and Crispyn beamed with joy from the satisfaction of helping with their first real rescue mission. Zeld understood how they felt when they begged him to include them in any future good deeds.

Tyre and Crispyn joined the others in their Saturday night bath. Tyre became the Holy Land barbarian and Crispyn the Dutch barbarian. As usual the boys ran back to Eagle Loft freezing, dried off standing on the hearthrug in front of the fireplace and then slipped into bed. All except for Brian, who said goodnight and marched for his own barracks.

"These are floor plans," said Sir Drain during map reading class in the library as he unrolled several parchments and placed bookends for paperweights on each corner. The class leaned in and learned the symbols. "This castle map is complete with walls, buildings, defensive gates, drawbridges and secret passages," said Sir Drain. The castle on the map somehow seemed familiar to Zeld. He was convinced he had seen this castle at some point. Sir Drain assigned the class to make a scale model of the castle out of small wooden blocks.

It took a week of class time as well as some evenings and most of the following Saturday to complete the model castle. Once finished, Sir Drain gave the boys dozens of round wooden coins to serve as attacking and defending units of soldiers. The boys took turns attacking and defending the castle in mock battles. They rolled dice and used the charts for major battles found in the Castles and Caverns Combat Game. The pages found the castle impossible to capture.

Then, Sir Drain gave Robert a turn as the invaders. His soldiers attacked with mongonels instead of bows, and zweihanders instead of common swords. Sullivan's soldiers were unable to defend the castle. On Crispyn's turn, Sir Drain gave the local farms a militia to help defend the castle. However, the militia's poor weapons gave them little combat value.

Sir Drain tipped the scales further in favour of the attackers when, on Oars turn, he gave the invaders poison arrows for their mongonels. Oars attacking force shredded Brian's defenders.

Sir Drain assigned the boys to come up with new strategies to fortify the castle in order to beat the invading army. They could choose any weapons and add any new structures. Odin tried mongonels while Oles tried catapults. These weapons hurt the enemy, but they couldn't stop them. James had the idea of building two new towers to serve as crow's nests. This enabled the defenders to see the enemy as they approached and the defenders fired down on them sooner. This added to the overall strength and eliminated several attacking units of men, but the castle still fell once the enemy smashed through the front gate.

Other boys tried different solutions. Tyre had the militia attack the enemy using mongonel fire from the castle to support them. The weak militia simply had no lasting impact. Oles' plan called for traps in the kill zone around the castle. The traps did very little damage to the large invading army.

Zeld puzzled it out and thought of a plan similar to James'. He built a second castle wall inside the castle, higher than the first. He stationed soldiers on both walls with mongonels which fired in predetermined locations based on most likely troop placements due to the lay of the land.

Zeld also added two giant sized catapults, called onagers, to shoot the rear line of attacking soldiers. He had the militia enter the castle by a secret passage to strengthen the defenders' numbers. His plan worked well enough. The invaders failed to take the castle and settled for a siege to starve the defenders.

Sir Drain assigned one more round of attacks. This time the invaders used death venom arrows. The game became completely lopsided again. The only solution Zeld could think of was to give all the defending soldiers dragon's blood armour to neutralize the poison and to shoot dragon bones out of onagers to blow up the enemy.

Zeld felt pleased as his plan worked brilliantly. The invaders fell prey to rapid destruction while the castle lost very few men. He wished in real life he could give every one of his men dragon's blood armour and to have an unlimited supply of dragon bones. Only dragon hunters in Scotland would come close to having such supplies. This gave Zeld a brilliantly scathing idea, which he kept to himself.

Zeld and his mates studied both the combat charts in Sir Roger's class and the battle strategies in Sir Drain's class; so much so, they neglected their other studies and didn't do well when they tried out for the school's tracking team. Zeld tried out for the 'fox on foot' event, but managed to lose his fox when it doubled back on the far side of a tree branch.

James tried out for the blood hound scent competition. The judges dragged a deer hide for a quarter of a mile and the dogs were supposed to track the scent. He chanced upon a live deer in the woods and his blood hound gave chase, dragging poor James behind. Needless to say none of Zeld's mates made the team.

The day for the tournament arrived. The tracking team left for the Naval Academy of Wales and the rest of the Castles and Caverns schoolboys packed for an overnight stay at the school's lodge on Cavern Mountain. The well-supplied lodge had plenty of firewood and the cooks roasted an ox over an enormous outdoor pit.

After supper, the boys attended meetings to help them prepare for the war games held at the end of the school year. Zeld learned of his assignment to the purple team. He had no idea they had teams, let alone, that he'd been on one all school year.

Keeping the war game activities quiet helped the boys learn to keep secrets. To violate the code of secrecy meant banishment from the game. Considering its importance, as the highlight of the school year, it meant you had truly thrown away something valuable, like a gem, if you revealed anything about your team. A second consequence existed but it fell along the lines of a human nature type punishment rather than something imposed by the school. Namely, the boy who revealed anything about the war games became ostracized or friendless.

Brass Stevens, Tyre's cousin and a fifth-year student led the purple team. He held a team meeting in the upstairs classroom. Zeld listened intently to the briefing as Brass explained, "The purple and red teams compete against each other as enemies and so do the orange and blue teams. In order to win, the purple team must capture or outlast the red team in the field. The title of grand champion will go to the team that outlasts all the others. The teams will go into the field with only a one week supply of food, but we must survive for a fortnight."

Zeld leaned forward to see better when Brass showed his team a map of the area and told them, "We'll be dropped off in this valley which has several streams. Our location is vulnerable to attack from a nearby hill. I plan to move the team atop the hill straightaway. This move will not only eliminate that problem, it will also give us a grand view in all directions. Perhaps we'll discover the red team's location."

As the meeting progressed, Zeld reported the best place to find food in the wilderness was near the streams. Brass assigned Zeld and James as members of the food acquisition squad.

"Can we take anything we want?" asked Zeld.

"No, we can only take what the school allows," answered Brass as he handed Zeld a list.

Zeld read it carefully looking for something he could use to help catch fish. Zeld thought feeding his team was a gigantic job. Other boys drew the assignments of caring for the horses and doing the cooking. Assignments for spying and raiding parties hadn't yet been given.

Zeld studied the maps. He found a place where three streams connected less than a mile away from their drop point. This should be a reasonably good place for fishing, he thought. He wondered if the other teams would start out near the water.

That night Zeld dreamed of sneaking through the woods and finding the other camp's food. He nicked their crates and carried the food away to his own camp where they congratulated him and sat down to a splendid feast.

During the night James awoke ill. He went outside and spewed out his dinner. In the morning he still looked ill.

"Remind me not to eat oxen," James said wearily.

Everyone agreed they would. Zeld couldn't help wondering if James had a serious illness. He became ill quite often and always during or directly after supper. Zeld minded that James didn't have this problem at the beginning of the school year.

"The marketplace will not sell food to us dwarves," Bushhard told Zeld as the two of them sat on a crude wooden bench in front of the fire pit in the dwarven mine. Zeld had gone to visit them after the school's journey to the lodge. He took Bushhard with him to the largest farm south of the school and asked the farmer, "May Bushhard be allowed to purchase food here every week?"

Farmer Johnson took one look at the dwarf and demanded, "Let me see the money!"

Both Zeld and Bushhard took out some coins. They showed them to the farmer and he bit into one to make sure his teeth left a mark in the soft gold.

"I've heard rumours the dwarves are using counterfeit coins to pay for things," said farmer Johnson.

"Who told you that?" asked Zeld. He and Bushhard both showed despondent faces.

"A couple of the new farmers. They moved in last fall," Farmer Johnson said pointing toward a farm across the valley. Zeld noticed the fields near the house hadn't been planted.

"Since they didn't plant in the spring, they haven't had any produce to sell. Which means they wouldn't know whether the coins are counterfeit or not," reasoned Zeld.

"You're absolutely right," said farmer Johnson in an apologetic tone. "You may buy food here any day of the week, except Sundays."

"Then I will return tomorrow morning with a wagon," said Bushhard sounding delighted to have his problem solved.

Zeld took Bushhard back to the mine. He waved and left for the school.

When Zeld arrived at the school, Crispyn and Tyre asked Zeld what he and the dwarf had been doing.

"I assisted with the food shortage," Zeld said thinking of the dwarves.

"How didja do that?" asked Jarell Goldenstaff.

"By setting up a wagon run," Zeld answered.

"I thought Friar Timothy helped with the food shortage?" asked Crispyn.

"Oh, he does," answered Zeld now thinking about the starving people from the Viking raid.

The boys quit pestering Zeld as they had found their new target, Friar Timothy.

During the week several of the boys asked Friar Timothy to let them help feed the poor. The friar organized a food drop for the following Saturday and the schoolboys would drive the wagons.

"Well, Zeld, since you started this, I think you should drive a wagon too," said Friar Timothy at Thursday's midday meal.

"Certainly," Zeld said even though he wondered how he started it.

For the next couple of days, everyone talked in the Great Hall about the school's effort to help the poor. Zeld felt a sense of school pride unsurpassed even by the school's competitions. In fact, he felt chivalrous. The other boys beamed as well and Zeld felt pleased knowing they would make a real difference.

The best lessons of the week came from Sir Roger's class in the Great Hall. He taught about the individual combat charts in the Castles and Caverns Combat Game.

"The chances of hitting an opponent with a common sword are about 50-50. In order to make the combat simulations more realistic, we have adopted a chart for common dice. This means the first three numbers of one, two and three represent hits while the later numbers of four and five represent misses. The number six represents a repose or blunder and gives your opponent the chance to injure you on your turn."

Zeld thought the class appeared flustered. After all, he couldn't remember all the rules and numbers.

"If you'll examine this chart, it will help," said Sir Roger as he pulled out the hit and damage chart for the common sword.

3-3 Chart (Common Sword)

Hits/Damage	1	2	3	4	5	6
1	4A	3	2	1	0	0
2	4	3	1	0	0	0
3	4	3	1	0	0	0
4	M	M	M	M	M	M
5	M	M	M	M	M	M
6	R	E	D	O	S	E

The boys gathered around examining the chart.

"What does the 'A' stand for?" asked Oars bewildered.

"The 'A' means you split your opponent's armour, like Zeld did to Crispyn earlier in the year," explained Sir Roger.

Zeld found the chart fascinating. James asked, "Why didn't Sir Drain have us use these charts when we played the castle invasion game?"

"Because on major simulations the charts take too long."

"Do we have a competition with the simulation game?" asked Oles.

"No, Castles and Caverns and Robin Hood are the only two schools using it," said Sir Roger. "But I'll bring it up as a suggestion to Father Ulrich."

The boys played a fencing duel between two swordsmen with dice, ink, and a parchment to keep track of the diminishing strength points. It surprised Zeld how long it took to battle with two swordsmen.

During the week, Sir Roger taught them additional charts for the different weapons. The boys played swordsmen against pole arms men and all sorts of combinations. They played all week learning the various charts as they went.

Zeld and Jens Jr. drove a wagon to the castle of Zorn on Saturday while several other boys made similar journeys to their assigned areas. Zeld entered the castle with the wagon bed heaping with farm fresh vegetables in five pound burlap sacks.

Someone shouted to Zeld, "Hello, aren't you one of the boys from the McMarr castle."

Zeld looked over and saw a familiar face. "Yes," Zeld called back while attempting to turn the wagon around. He was unable to do so due to the large numbers of peasants forming a knot around the wagon. The food disappeared in seconds. Not a soul remained to hear them say farewell and no one said thank you. Zeld and Jens Jr. only heard the slamming of doors. As they drove back to the school, Zeld wondered if he seemed ungrateful at times and decided to thank people more often.

"Blimey!" said Jens Jr. "I expected a warm welcome and instead we received the cold shoulder."

"Too right you are!" said Zeld.

The mid-March days felt warmer to Zeld and the ride back to the school passed quickly. The trees didn't have their leaves yet, but some showed little fuzzy buds. Zeld picked one and gently rubbed it on his face. It tickled, so he kept it in his bag with his other things.

Springtime meant loads of work and that sent the boys to the farms again. Zeld was partnered with Jarell Goldenstaff. They cleaned out the drainage ditches, moved rocks and dug huge brambles with spades. Zeld felt fortunate he owned a pair of work gloves. After clearing the ditches, they replaced some damaged logs on a pigsty.

Zeld watched as farmer Beasley fed his pigs slop from a bucket. It landed in a trough and splashed all around. Some landed on the farmer's leggings. He simply brushed it off with his hand and went about his business. The pigs heard the noise and ran grunting happily toward the trough. They ate the slop and liked it. Zeld's stomach turned and he thought he might be sick. He'd seen food scraps before, but these had been left out in the sun for a couple of days, so they looked terrible and smelled worse. The farmer laughed at Zeld. Zeld decided he didn't fancy pigs or at least he didn't fancy what they ate.

The sleeping arrangements consisted of a bare wooden floor in the hayloft. Zeld awoke with a stiff back, but still did a good amount of work the second day. He opened the turnip cellar and sorted out the spoiled turnips.

Jarell ploughed all morning and looked exhausted by noon. Presently Zeld started planting the good turnips in the furrows Jarell had ploughed. The whole family helped with the planting including their elderly grandfather, two women in their thirties and two young boys ages five and six. As they finished, they saw the rain clouds rolling in. The family cheered as the rain fell on their newly planted fields. Zeld and Jarell simply rode back to the castle. Zeld was so tired he didn't feel like cheering. That is, until he arrived at the school.

CHAPTER Thirty Six

Spies and Assassins

Throughout the castle the smell of roast beef permeated the air. Zeld's mouth watered as he couldn't wait for his first bite of juicy meat. The boys sat at their tables in the Great Hall for supper and Zeld watched James, who had been served first, cut a good sized chunk of beef. He speared it with his knife and placed it in his mouth. He chewed a moment, and then swallowed. Two seconds later he turned a greyish-green colour and ran for the door. Zeld felt badly for James and went to the kitchen and explained to his soldiers that somehow the beef made James ill and asked them to find something else for him to eat.

"Yah," said Morten handing Zeld a bowl of cold leftover chicken and dumplings from a couple of days before.

"Where is your wife?" asked Zeld who realized he didn't know the arrangements.

"Fadder Ulrich said dat ve can live at de farm," Morten said pointing in the direction of the farms.

"Excellent," said Zeld.

Zeld carried the bowl of food to James who ate it without getting sick.

After supper the whole gang, including Crispyn and Tyre, checked out two wagons and went for a romp into town. Zeld kept a watchful eye on James and the fresh air seemed to do him good.

They passed the clothing store and saw heaps of earth behind it. They didn't stop but headed directly for the bakery instead and visited with their mate, the baker. While there, they ate berry pies with cream. James looked loads better. His colour returned and he laughed and jested with the other boys.

On the way back to the school, they stopped behind Penny's store and Jens Jr. lifted piles of dirt into the wagons with his amulet of levitation. The boys enjoyed riding in the back with the dirt. They threw dirt into each others' hair and had a jolly time.

The boys stopped several times on the way home to fill the road ruts made by the spring runoff. Jens Jr. used his amulet to place small mounds of dirt on the ground and the boys compacted the dirt into the ruts with their feet. Jens Jr. used the remaining dirt to repair a ditch. By the time the boys arrived at the school they were filthy from head to toe and gave each other new names including, mud man, creature from swampland and dirt brain. They checked the wagons in and ran for the bathhouse.

The barbarian push turned into the barbarian jump. The boys had gotten good at making big splashes. As they dried off, the boys heard a voice up the stream where the staff bathed.

Father Ulrich yelled, "I'm the holy barbarian." Immediately following the words, landed a big splash; then, the sounds of Father Ulrich climbing out of the water half frozen. The boys laughed and continued drying themselves. Once they finished, they ran for their barracks as usual.

On Monday the schoolboys competed for places on the forestry competition team. Zeld identified plants in the wilderness and took a written herblore test in the wagon on the way back. He felt dim-witted when he learned how badly he did on the written portion of the test. He did poorly because he couldn't remember all the uses for the plants. He knew the plants of Denmark better than plants in England.

As before, the team went to the competition and the other boys went to the lodge while 25 knights guarded the castle.

At the lodge Zeld found some wild onions. He bit into one, and the sharp taste flooded his memories. He minded the onion and potato stews his mum used to cook. Then he remembered how much he missed his family and how long it had been since he had seen them. Tears came to his eyes.

"Zeld, what's wrong?" asked Oles.

"It's the onion."

Zeld figured Oles could tell it wasn't the onion but hoped he wouldn't pry further.

"Oh," Oles said.

Godfrey of Hesse watched the C&C team arrive at the dwarven academy where he secretly waited for them. Godfrey signalled to his son; then, Geoffrey and the other Hessen allies followed, leaving the rest of the team to make camp. Hesse and the boys walked into the huge mouth of the mine, down a passage and then into a comfortable, well lit room, with a wooden floor. Several large tables stood together. A giant map of Great Britain rested on them. Atop the map military figurines marked the current locations of Hesse's troops. All the Hessen allies in Germany had representatives at the war council.

"We've had two of our secret stashes raided, here and here," Godfrey said pointing to the map, which also corresponded to the locations Zeld and company had made their discoveries. "To make up for the losses, I'm having 600 extra men shipped up the Thames on the day of the attack. That'll give us 3000 men north, on Tower Hill, plus 200 cavalrymen and the catapults and onagers. On the ships we'll have 1800 men and the ballistas.

"I see no possible way King Henry and his 700 men will survive. We'll need a retreating and regrouping point. I've selected the Castles and Caverns School. I realize it's a considerable distance from London but I really can't imagine we'll need it for anything more than a regrouping centre to launch the second phase," Godfrey placed both his hands on the table. "I've ordered the Baden town militia to capture the Castles and Caverns School and place my banner on the wall once it's secure."

"Our job today is to coordinate the attacks and set the date. When is the jousting tournament?" Godfrey asked.

"In 15 days, travel begins the day before, for most schools," said Sir Tavish in a clever yet sinister voice.

"Show me where the travellers will come from," ordered Godfrey gesturing toward the map.

Sir Tavish showed him the location of each school and estimated the time of day they'd leave to arrive on time for the tournament. Godfrey seemed most concerned about the roads that led from the de Saxon castle to London by way of the magical shortcuts. It took a considerable effort, but Hesse made a schedule that kept his troops from running into the school teams who would also travel that day.

"Read the orders, son," Godfrey instructed Geoffrey.

Geoffrey read, "All the wagons must be hidden in Sherwood Forest no later than 1:00 p.m. The wagons will move again after they see the boys from the Robin Hood School leave for the tournament, at approximately 2:15 p.m.

"The horses are to proceed up the magical road on Dragon Hill and turn left once they reach the main road. This will take them past the Prince Valiant School in Waltham Forest, and then south through Forest Gate to London. They are to assemble the catapults and onagers at the top of Tower Hill. The attack begins at 5:00 p.m.," Geoffrey read.

"Sir Tavish, I want every Hessen ally out of the school before the militia attacks," ordered Godfrey.

"Easily done. With a little help from Geoffrey's magnetic amulet, they'll all make the jousting team," Sir Tavish said with a confident smirk.

"Wonderful, let's keep the boys out of the first attack. We'll need their help coordinating the regrouping efforts for phase two. I plan to capture the five weak castles two days after the first attack and in the process capture all the master stonemasons in England," said Godfrey.

"When do I kill the de Saxony family?" asked a man who stepped out from the shadows. It was none other than the Baden town baker. Zeld had visited the bakery many times over the school year and would've been horrified if he'd known the baker's true identity was Hesse's personal assassin.

"When Zeld returns home for the summer, follow him. We've planted a little tracking amulet in his kite shield that he thinks he won fair and square at the fencing competition. Actually, Geoffrey rigged the de Saxon boy's matches with his magnetic amulet. We've tracked his shield ever since. You simply follow him home with this tracking amulet at the end of the school year and murder the entire family," said Godfrey.

"I could poison him and his mates now," said the baker, "or I could easily sneak into the castle and kill him in his sleep. I know which bed belongs to him as I watched him carefully one evening when I brought pies for a celebration."

"No, I want the entire family killed," said Godfrey slightly irritated. "We've gone to a lot of trouble to deceive this boy into thinking we would go after him in another way. Stevenson Duval

302

here, ordered his son, Norton, to kill Zeld one day in Baden, and we're sure Zeld heard him give the order. Of course the whole idea was to throw Zeld off."

"Zeld jumps every time I go near him," Norton lied convincingly. The group had a good laugh at Zeld's expense.

Godfrey continued with his meeting. "Are there any other concerns?" Everyone paused.

"I have one. How'll we sneak our allied pages out of the castle when they're not allowed to compete in the jousting tournament?" asked Geoffrey.

"I'll require each of the winning jousters to choose a page to go with them and that will clear the allied pages out of the school," said Sir Tavish. Geoffrey nodded his head approvingly.

"Anything else?" asked Godfrey. An awkward silence filled the room, until Godfrey himself spoke again. "Well, I have a concern. Do you remember the pottery shards? I sent a crew of 13 men in a ship to Denmark with orders to find and kill the de Saxony family, if by chance they lived in the Paladorian region of Denmark, as the writing on the pottery shards suggested. We found my ship two months later on the coast of Germany with the plague flag raised. We found only dried-up bloody clothing and believe they fell victim to some sort of mind plague while at sea. This is a dangerous plague, so I'm ordering the field commanders to execute any soldier who shows abnormal behaviour."

The commanders smiled when they heard the news.

"If there are no further concerns; then, we're at war in 15 days," said Godfrey in a rakish voice.

When the C&C team returned from the tournament, they looked miserable.

"It must've been a disaster," said Jens Jr. watching the faces as the humiliated team paraded through the main gate.

"I think the team forgot to pack their brains. Some of the mates missed even the easy questions. We finished in last place in every event. If I didn't know better, I'd say we lost on purpose," Jarell Goldenstaff said, shaking his head unhappily as he told Zeld what happened.

Zeld went to his favourite place above the main gate and watched the boys who had gone to the competition. Jens Jr. went with him. Zeld spied Norton Duval who looked as if his stomach pains had returned and worse than ever. Sir Tavish, on the other hand, appeared very jolly and Zeld wondered why he would after such a defeat.

As the boys walked to the barracks, Jens Jr. suggested they repair a few ruts in the road that needed tending. The gang of eleven boys climbed into two wagons.

"Why are we suddenly responsible for the roadwork?" murmured Tyre.

When they had moved a considerable distance from the school, Zeld turned to Tyre and said, "We're on a secret mission."

Tyre and Crispyn looked at each other as if to say they didn't believe him.

"We're glad you let us become mates. Most of the boys at school won't have anything to do with us ever since our fathers filed legal papers against Godfrey of Hesse for encroaching on our lands," explained Tyre.

"We do fun things with you, including secret missions. Feeding the poor was fantastic, but I can't see how roadwork counts as a secret mission. Perhaps we should call it a good deed instead?" Crispyn offered.

"We aren't really doing roadwork," said Jens Jr. "We're really hiding from the spies in the town of Baden, the amount of dirt that's being removed to make Penny's basement."

"Spies in the town - are you mental, JJ?" asked Tyre a bit aggravated.

"Penny is the name of the lady who owns the clothing store. She's digging out a place for a secret armoury. She told her neighbours she's digging a partial basement to throw off suspicion. It's our assignment to hide the heaps of dirt, so the spies won't be able to tally the amount and realize she's actually digging a full basement," explained Zeld, while trying not to show his disappointment with Tyre.

Then Tyre laughed, "You mates make up brilliant stories. You're really good. You almost had me believing you."

When they reached the back door of the clothing shop, Zeld swore Tyre and Crispyn to secrecy. Penny stepped out the back door and inquired, "Are all these mates of yours, Zeld?"

"These two didn't believe us when we told them why we're hiding the dirt," answered Zeld.

"Can you mind a more suitable place for a secret armoury than the basement of a clothing store?" she asked them. "Shipments have come and gone from this store since before I was born and no one ever suspected my late father or me of smuggling weapons and armour for the de Saxons, but we have managed to do plenty of it."

Tyre and Crispyn's mouths dropped opened.

"You mean - they told the truth?" asked Crispyn, still in disbelief.

"We also needed a place to hide the things we've taken from Godfrey of Hesse," explained Jens Jr.

"You mates nick stuff, too?" Crispyn blurted out.

"Only from our enemies," Zeld answered quickly.

"Yes, we're not a bunch of common thieves," stated Oles.

"No, we're actually quite excellent thieves," jested Jens Jr. and they all laughed.

"We stole two stashes from Hesse already and he doesn't even know about it yet," bragged Odin.

Jens Jr. used his amulet to lift the dirt into the wagons and they headed east filling the ruts as they went. Crispyn and Tyre became full-fledged members of the alliance. Zeld thought overall things went famously.

The boys continued their roadwork activity for a while, and then dumped the rest of the dirt in two sunken graves in the cemetery. They overheard some men talking in a grove of gnarled yew trees as they left. Zeld thought nothing of it until he heard the word Hesse. He stopped the wagon on the other side of the hill and crept back through the yew trees with Jens Jr. The other boys stayed behind and threw the last handfuls of dirt at each other.

Zeld and Jens Jr. saw the men digging a new grave. Zeld turned to leave when something caught his eye. He stopped and turned back. That's when he discovered, it wasn't a new grave, but an old one.

Zeld and Jens Jr. climbed into the wagon and raced to the blacksmith shop. "We'll be right back," Jens Jr. told the others. As Zeld entered the shop, he held his fists together and gave the broken arrow sign. Garth excused himself and hurried over.

Zeld quietly whispered, "The town militia is at the cemetery digging up an old grave."

"An old grave?" asked Garth, with a puzzled expression.

"Why would the militia dig up a grave?" Zeld asked.

"Maybe they're attempting to frighten someone or perhaps they're trying to spread a disease," said Garth quietly.

"No, they'd acquire the disease themselves and the only people they'd scare are peasants," replied Zeld.

"I'll alert our friends. Maybe they know why someone would dig up a grave," said Garth. He turned and went back to his customer.

While arriving at the school Zeld spied Friar Timothy. Zeld minded he needed to visit with Friar Timothy briefly. The friar used all his spare time to make copies of his play to sell. Every show wagon in the country had ordered a copy. Zeld climbed down from the wagon and approached Friar Timothy.

"Have you finished making copies?" asked Zeld.

"It'll take another week or so," replied the friar.

"Can you tell me what these are?" Zeld asked, taking the pills out of his bag.

"The blue ones are sleeping pills, the yellow ones restore energy, the green ones heal you and I don't know what the orange or grey ones do," Friar Timothy replied.

"Thanks," Zeld said and he scurried off.

Zeld missed the concerned look on Friar Timothy face.

Zeld and his mates brooded that night and the fun at the stream didn't pull them out of it. Zeld noticed the Hessen allies also acted worried. He had no way of knowing the reason they acted the way they did was because of the eminent battle at London Castle.

CHAPTER Thirty Seven

Jousting

CRASH! Zeld watched Norton Duval unhorse Gunter Sims in the first joust on Monday. The next two boys queued for their turns in the jousting lists as if charging their horses toward each other and breaking lances on their opponent's armour were natural occurrences, like the sun rising in the morning. Each squire wore their family's tunic and bore their coat of arms on their shields. The various bright colours greatly added to the pageantry of the event.

The school held the jousting team tryouts on Tuesday and Wednesday afternoons. Zeld thought it looked extremely dangerous and he was unquestionably correct. During one joust Geoffrey used his magnetic amulet to clear away Jarell Goldenstaff's shield only just before impact. As a result, regrettably, Jarell's arm became mangled, and the injury appeared life crippling. Zeld watched as Jarell was carted off to the infirmary. He waited for his chance; then, pulled the heavy green curtain back and ducked inside. Jarell's arm had been splinted. He lay motionless, still in shock from his injury. Zeld reached into his shoulder bag and pulled out his amulet. He put his finger to his lips so Jarell would remain quiet, and then he placed the stone on the injury. "I've come to heal you me friend," said Zeld.

In the silence Zeld could hear a low pitched creaking sound resembling an old door with rusty hinges slowly opening. Jarell winced in pain and hit the side on his bed repeatedly with his good hand. After a minute and a half Zeld removed the amulet, not because it had gone dark, but to give Jarell a chance to breathe. When Jarell was ready, they continued. Zeld gave Jarell two more breaks as the treatment continued. When they finished the shattered bones were completely healed. Jarell thanked Zeld over and over. Then Zeld crept out the way he had come.

Jarell slowly rose to his feet, and then walked outside for some air. His shoulder felt stiff so he swung his arm around in circles to stretch it. The arm worked as if nothing had ever happened. Norton Duval saw him stretching it and asked, "Did Zeld do that?"

"Yes," replied Jarell in a grateful tone.

Norton's stomach pains came back. He bent over and whispered to himself, "I've delayed this decision as long as I can and now I've finally made up my mind." Norton stood up straight and took a deep breath, his painful expression relaxed.

308   On Saturday Zeld went into town and checked with Garth to see if he had learned anything further about the grave mystery.

Garth reported, "I waited until the middle of the night; then, sneaked out to the cemetery and dug the grave again. It was easily done with the loose soil. I brushed away the dirt atop the casket and slowly lifted the lid. I glanced inside only to find it empty. I could hardly believe my eyes. I didn't know what to expect but I daresay an empty casket came as an absolute surprise. I rested the lid against the mound of dirt and looked for clues. The only clue present was curved rust stains on the bottom lining."

Zeld didn't know what to make of it. An empty casket with rust stains seemed odd indeed. He pondered on the mystery while visiting in the town of Baden.

A monstrous rain fell so Zeld took shelter in Penny's clothing shop. She reported her basement had been completely dug and she'd hired the dwarves to build the false walls and a floor. She had a worried expression, "Our plan could be easily discovered but the dwarves don't seem to understand this. They need to complete the job straightaway."

"Tell them to include a secret passage underneath the floor," said Zeld.

"That's the problem - they're not listening to me," Penny said nervously.

"How about I tell them," Zeld suggested. He thought it best to ease Penny's mind on the matter.

The cloud burst cleared, so Zeld rode north and visited the dwarves. Once inside the mine Zeld asked about the basement plans.

"We have already completed most of the construction here in the mine and plan to install the various sections tonight. Zeld, we've discussed it, and when we're done with Penny's basement, we'd fancy going to work for you at the gold mine again. If that's all right with you?" asked Grumpes, who sounded uneasy about something.

"Yeah, that's all right with me. Can you make a secret passage in the floor of Penny's basement? It would be grand to have loads of secret compartments," Zeld reminded them.

"No worries, we planned two floor passages and four in the walls," said Bushhard, a bit calmer than Grumpes but still troubled by something.

"Thank you," said Zeld.

He wondered why everyone seemed stressed. He realized his allies were having a harsh spring but he didn't know why. He minded what a lovely spring he, his mum and brother had in Denmark, and he wondered why England felt so different.

When Zeld returned to the school, he spied Sir Tavish sitting on the porch of the chapel, sharpening his sword, whistling and in a grand mood. In the mist of all the melancholy, Sir Tavish actually enjoyed spring. In fact, Sir Tavish seemed extraordinarily cheerful.

"Why is everyone in such an unpleasant mood but you?" Zeld asked Sir Tavish who sat examining the sharpness of his sword.

"Springtime is a busy time," said Sir Tavish.

Zeld wasn't satisfied with his answer.

Sir Tavish continued, "The farmers are worried about their animals - will they have enough piglets and lambs for the year? They're worried about the amount of rain - will the plants grow? The shopkeepers are worried about little things, should I place the winter underwear on sale and do I have enough money to buy spring items?" Sir Tavish went back to sharpening his sword but continued speaking. "The baker's wondering if his berry patch will produce enough berries. As for me, the only thing I have to worry about is competing with the spring weather for the attention of me students. In other words, I don't have problems with spring like everyone else."

Zeld hadn't trusted Sir Tavish ever since the incident with the pottery shards, so he thought perhaps sharpening his sword had more to do with his good mood than anything else.

Sir Tavish watched Zeld walk away; then, said under his breath, "What an idiot!"

On Wednesday and Thursday large numbers of Holy Pilgrims turned at the junction in front of the Castles and Caverns School. They came from Baden and turned left, marching toward the farms. Friar Martin's class went to watch. Zeld could have sworn he saw a tip of a scabbard dip below one of the pilgrim's robes as he walked. Then, it dawned on him it must have been the tip of a silver crucifix instead. After all, Zeld thought laughing to himself, why would a pilgrim need a sword?

Early on Friday morning the Castles and Caverns jousting team paraded out the main gate for Scotland Naval. A half hour later Zeld saw the Prince Valiant School and Welch Naval Academy pass by the school, travelling together.

At that very moment the Robin Hood School waved goodbye to their team from high atop a hill. As they watched their team journey north, they spied a large convoy of wagons headed south on another road.

One of the students called, "Look, Friar Tuck, a circus is headed south." Friar Tuck could see the wagons but even after squinting couldn't make out the words on the signs.

Friar Tuck said, "Gashua, Field, and Wainbright, I have an assignment for you. I want you to sneak down there and tell me what's written on the sides of those wagons and tell me what they are transporting. Don't show yourselves and bring me word."

The three elflings crowded onto one horse and made their way down the hill. When they reached the bottom, they used bushes to make themselves invisible. They watched as two of the wagons went by. Then one of the bushes rolled half way across the road. Gashua's head appeared above the bush for a moment, and then the bush rolled back again. The elflings rode up the mountain to Friar Tuck.

"It's a circus caravan from Germany, we think. The words weren't written in English. The wagons had tent poles in the back," said Gashua alertly.

"What colour of tents?" asked Friar Tuck.

"I didn't see any tents, merely poles and metal parts," replied Gashua.

"You three come with me," ordered Friar Tuck.

Friar Tuck took them to the Robin Hood School's lodge and opened a large storage compartment.

"Did the tents poles resemble these?" he asked, showing them the catapults that Zeld's men had sent.

"Yes," said Gashua, "I rolled behind one of the wagons and saw everything in the back. These are the exact type of poles and metal parts I saw."

Friar Tuck called all the boys from the school together, and they hurried to the Great Hall. When he arrived, he rang the alarm and within seconds everyone surrounded him.

"HESSE'S ARMY IS ON THE MOVE! THEY'RE HEADED SOUTH FOR LONDON AND KING HENRY! WE MUST ALERT THE OTHER ENGLISH SCHOOLS AND EVERY NOBLEMAN IN THE SOUTH TO SEND AID TO DEFEND THE KING! WE'LL SEND MESSENGERS ON HORSEBACK!" shouted Friar Tuck with as much confidence as he could muster.

Mrs. A'Dale made sandwiches for the messengers, and then for an army. The kitchen staff would find the next couple of days an extreme burden. It didn't take long for the messengers to receive their directions and leave for their assigned castles. The merry men immediately prepared for battle as their duty was to protect the king.

At the Castles and Caverns School the remaining boys packed for a journey to the lodge. Zeld went through his treasure chest selecting what items he would take.

Suddenly, Mrs. Palfreeman screamed as the Baden town militia poured through the main gate swinging weapons and firing arrows. Zeld and Oars ran to the door of Eagle Loft. Zeld realized they were under attack and he ran back to his treasure chest. He scooped up a handful of random items in his shoulder bag, locked his treasure chest and ran for his horse. He instinctively ran for Lightning and Oars for Tiger. Zeld's mates didn't have any weapons with them and the storage sheds were empty, compliments of Sir Tavish. They rode out the eastside of the castle, where the wall hadn't been built yet; then, jumped the stream and into the woods. Three dozen additional boys followed their lead.

They promptly made quarter staves from saplings and searched for logs to use as clubs. Another dozen boys rode out of the school with a hailstorm of arrows whizzing past.

Zeld crept cautiously closer for a better look at the castle yard. He watched as the militiamen carried bodies into the Great Hall, but he couldn't tell if his mates lay wounded or dead. The well-prepared militia had attacked the school with mongonels and poisoned battleaxes.

Brass Stevens was one of the last stragglers to escape. An arrow protruded from his back. His cousin Tyre led Brass to Zeld, who took out his stone from his bag and healed the wound. The arrow slipped out with very little effort.

Once Brass was healed, Zeld and he kept a close eye on the militia. The boys watched as the militia climbed the stairs to the ramparts on the castle wall.

Jens Jr., Oles and Odin joined Zeld as the boys regrouped for a counterattack.

"Now we know what the militia hid in the coffin," Jens Jr. said to Zeld.

"Battleaxes," answered Zeld, "and they're a Hessen militia in case you haven't figured that one out. I should've known it. During the Viking raid, Ralph, the militiaman not only knew Geoffrey but he obeyed Geoffrey's orders."

"You're starting to sound as if you were me," said Jens Jr. warily.

"Oh lovely, now things have really gone from bad to worse," Zeld teased.

"Look at that, they're in defensive positions at the walls and that group is draping the Hessen banner for all to see," Jens Jr. said while pointing out the militia's archers.

Zeld twinged when he heard something sneaking through the bushes to the west. Zeld, Brass and Jens Jr. lifted their quarter staves in readiness for combat. They found Mrs. Palfreeman and Zeld's two soldiers from the kitchen. They had escaped by running out the kitchen door and hiding under the stoop. Zeld's soldiers brought four baskets of food with them.

"They won't find anything to eat, because we emptied the kitchen," blurted out Mrs. Palfreeman in a tone that let everyone know she had already struck the first defensive blow.

"Let's cut off their supplies and send for help," said Jens Jr.

A voice from behind him said, "Brilliant plan."

They turned around to see who had spoken and found Sir Jaydan, Sir Roger, the hostler and Sir Drain. They'd escaped through a secret passage with the friars and Father Ulrich. Father Ulrich had sent the four of them to locate the boys while he and the friars spied on the castle from another location.

"Let's divide into work crews and set this plan into motion," commented Sir Drain as he put his fists together and gave Zeld's secret signal.

The boys grinned. Zeld truthfully believed they could take the upper hand.

Oles and Odin rode on fast horses to the McMarr Manor. Sir Drain instructed them not to trust anyone on the road. Jens Jr. took the assignment of building a small fort of rocks and fallen logs with his amulet, so they could ambush the militia if they came for water at the stream. Sullivan and James went to the silver mine to ask the dwarves for help. Steven Saint James took a large group of boys down to the farms to organize a roadblock. The three knights took another group of boys to set up an ambush between the school and Baden.

Zeld and Brass volunteered to sneak inside the castle through the kitchen door and rescue as many injured boys as possible. The two of them wasted no time and crept around to the kitchen's woodpile. Once there they flattened themselves against the castle wall, sidestepping until they reached the stoop. They hid under the stoop and listened before they entered. Zeld didn't hear anything, so they proceeded as quietly as possible through the kitchen and into the Great Hall, where the militia had neglected to place a guard.

Zeld and Brass sneaked silently over to the wounded. Zeld used his stone on Jarell Goldenstaff's wounded leg, healing it enough so Jarell could walk.

Brass found Thomas Bandit moaning with a severely displaced ankle. Brass pulled on his foot while Thomas bit down on a piece of leather to keep from crying out. The bones snapped back into place and although he limped, Thomas could walk.

Swen and Swan Christensen had both taken blows to the head. Zeld used his stone on them, but it ran out of power part way through. He searched in his shoulder bag and found the pills he'd shown Friar Timothy resting under his bag of poisoned caltrops. He slipped two green pills from his bottle into the twins' mouths. Brass used direct pressure to stop Gilbert Stuart's bleeding.

Once everyone could walk, Zeld led them to the kitchen door and looked outside to his right and left. All was clear so Zeld sent them sidestepping along the castle wall. The escaping boys dripped sweat from pain and fear as they made their way toward freedom.

A voice rang out, "THERE THEY ARE!"

The wounded boys panicked and ran the best they could across the road into the greenery. Zeld felt relieved when no arrows flew their direction. A militiaman had sneaked down to the stream for some water. Once he bent over to fill his bladder Jens Jr. leaped half way across the stream and clubbed him with a quarterstaff. A second militiaman saw the ambush and shouted out, "There they are." Arrows flew but Jens Jr. escaped unharmed.

Zeld quickly realized he could use this distraction. He and Brass seized the opportunity to cross the road with the last of the wounded boys in what should have been full view of the militia. The militia looked back toward Jens Jr.'s scrimmage. The boys escaped unseen and hid in the trees. Once safe they made their way toward the knight's ambush site between the school and Baden.

Meanwhile the militia launched an attack on the small fort Jens Jr. had built by the stream. Dwarves from the silver mine reinforced Jens Jr.'s position.

As the militia charged, sticks and stones rained down upon them from the air. Just when it appeared they had a chance to shoot back, poisoned axes and bolts from crossbows carried by the dwarves hit them as well. The militia attempted to retreat but more stones and bolts struck their ranks. Five of the ten militiamen lay on the ground unconscious. Jens Jr. promptly used his amulet to lift three of the militia's mongonels to his side of the fort.

The dwarves sharpened sticks to fire out of the mongonels. The sticks wouldn't be accurate for long range, but they would do well enough for close combat.

The militia didn't return for water or to retrieve their wounded men. They stayed at their posts and kept looking up the road toward Baden, obviously waiting for reinforcements.

CHAPTER Thirty Eight
Death Venom

Sir Drain spied what the Baden militia waited for from his ambush site; namely, he watched the baker of Baden pushing his bakery cart, which looked fully loaded, down the road toward the school. Sir Drain stopped him.

"Where might you be going on this fine spring day?" he asked.

"I'm headed for the school with this generous order from Father Ulrich," he replied.

"I'll take it from here."

"Father Ulrich hasn't paid me yet," the baker said.

Sir Drain took out his purse and said, "I'll pay you. How much is it?"

The baker looked worried but played along as if ignorant of the attack on the castle. He knelt down beside the cart as if reaching for a bill; then, without warning pulled out a small dagger from a hidden sheath strapped to his calf under his leggings. With one swift stroke he stabbed Sir Drain in the leg right above his ankle. Sir Drain fell to the ground dying.

He called out in a weak voice, "Death venom," then his head fell to the right, his eyes closed and he went limp.

The baker cackled in triumph. "Don't feel too bad," the baker said to the dead knight. After all, I murdered 36 knights in a single evening. Not to mention over 200 red squires at the same banquet. I poisoned their wine you know." The baker cackled again. "There is no other assassin as clever as I."

From behind the baker came a mighty blow from an axe that penetrated deep into his body. The baker fell dead in the middle of the road. Sir Jaydan said to the dead baker, "Your murderous career is over, and your cohorts waiting in the castle will never know what became of you!"

Sir Drain stood up, pulling the dagger out of his leg.

Sir Jaydan said, "You did an amazing job of play acting. You had me convinced you were dying and we planned this together."

"I told you, this dragon's blood leather neutralises all poisons," said Sir Drain.

"Was it death venom then?" asked Sir Jaydan.

Sir Drain smelled the dagger, "No question about it."

Sir Roger stepped out of his hiding place and teased, "Honestly, if you mates will quit babbling we can move this cart into the greenery and eat."

"What do we do with the baker?" asked Sir Jaydan.

"*You* exterminated the traitorous scum, *you* bury him," said Sir Roger as he pushed the cart into the bushes.

Sir Jaydan lifted the dead baker's hand to drag him away when Sir Drain called, "Hang on," and reached for the baker. He took the sheath off of the baker's leg and placed the poisoned knife into the sheath.

"Don't forget, we need his clothes, and now you may bury him," said Sir Drain waving his arm graciously.

Sir Drain sent the various baked goods to every group surrounding the castle. Sir Roger put on the baker's clothes and pushed the baker's cart back to Baden. Inside the cart he placed a black linen sack which Zeld recognized at once as the hiding place for the amulet of visions. After seeing the linen sack, Zeld volunteered to go along. As they journeyed through Baden, they passed several people from the village. He didn't know who he could trust and neither did Sir Roger. Zeld's mouth went dry from worry. He felt suspicious of everyone, and if anyone came too close, he talked to Sir Roger as if he were the baker.

When they arrived at the bakery, Zeld closed the door and built fires in the bake-ovens. Sir Roger took the amulet out of the black sack and set it on the kitchen counter where he could watch for new developments while he worked. Zeld saw Hessen soldiers waiting on ships to disembark. To his horror he watched as the throng of holy pilgrims he had seen earlier in the week gathered on a hilltop and removed their robes revealing they were Hessen soldiers. He also saw elfin riders leaving Sherwood Forest. No matter how hard he tried Zeld simply could not ferret out how the elves were involved.

Five minutes later Mrs. Palfreeman and Zeld's two soldiers arrived. Zeld recruited more help when he went for Penny and Garth. They all gathered at the bakery. Garth brought his wagon with two large crates of arrows and a dozen longbows.

While the bake-ovens heated, Penny made bread dough, Mrs. Palfreeman kneaded the bread, the men split firewood and Zeld stoked the fires. Once 50 loaves of bread were baked and cooled, Garth used them to fill the remaining space in his wagon and left. He dropped off half the longbows and some of the arrows at the ambush site where the baker died, and then hastily whipped past the castle to take bread to the boys at the farm blockade. The archers on the walls fired arrows at Garth when he drove past the school, but no arrows hit the wagon, save one, and none managed to come close to him.

While at the farms, Garth recruited a couple of farmers, and they loaded five wagons from the farms full of the food that would've gone to the school's kitchen. They planned to take the five wagons to the bakery in Baden but were unsure how to manage it safely.

The crew in the bakery kept cooking until they had a three-day supply of bread. They ate and drank as well to sustain their energy.

Meanwhile, Jens Jr. took advantage of his surroundings. He used his amulet to retrieve the sticks and stones they hurled earlier and managed to retrieve two more mongonels as well as several of the dwarves' battleaxes to his side of the stream. He moved wood from the school's main woodpile and made several small stacks around the courtyard. He planned to burn the wood that night to ensure the militia stayed awake and couldn't sneak up on his little fort. This strategy coupled with the fact the militia had no food would weaken them hour by hour.

While Zeld loaded bread into baskets in front of the bakery, he heard a horse galloping at full speed. When he looked up, he saw an elfin boy carrying two bows and a quiver full of arrows on his back. He ran out into the street, hoping to wave down the rider. The elfling recognized Zeld and stopped.

When the elf caught his breath, he explained, "Hesse's catapults are moving south. He's attacking King Henry in London."

Zeld took the elf to Sir Roger inside the bakery where he told the whole story.

"Friar Tuck sent this bow especially for you, Sir Roger," the elf said.

Sir Roger took the bow reluctantly, and then a look of determination little by little settled on his face. He promptly gave orders. Penny took Zeld's two men and ransacked her and Garth's shops. They took everything that resembled a weapon. Zeld and the elfling rode double to the ambush site and explained the new developments to Sir Drain, who called everyone off the siege at the school except the dwarves. Then they moved south and gathered the boys at the farm blockade. Sir Drain sent the boys door to door recruiting as many farmers for battle as they could muster.

While at the farms Sir Roger and the rest of his group from the bakery caught up with the rest of the school. Penny had retrieved the healing pills and poison vials from her store. Mrs. Palfreeman saw them and revealed what the last two colours cured, "The orange pills stop bleeding and the grey ones neutralize poisons. I don't know where you chanced upon all these pills, but I'm surely glad we have them."

Sir Roger begged Penny and Mrs. Palfreeman to set up an infirmary near the battle and they agreed. Zeld slipped Penny his bottle of pills with a sigh of relief.

The friars came out of hiding. They moved stiffly at first from sitting too long but joined the others marching down the south road. The wounded boys queued at the aid wagon. Each received the proper medication.

Zeld noticed Sir Drain limping. He called him over to Penny's wagon. She reached up to put a pill in his mouth when her eyes met his and she stopped. Sir Drain's eyes gave away his true identity! Penny spoke his name, Lord Barrack, but no sound escaped her lips. Zeld saw her lips move; however, he was unable to tell what she had mouthed. Zeld didn't know it, but Sir Drain was his uncle Lord Barrack de Saxony. The same man who led the counterattack the night the Hessens captured the castle and the same man who had been engaged to marry Penny. Everyone believed him dead.

She fed him the pill the same way she used to feed him grapes and looked again into those eyes. He jerked away hastily to catch the other soldiers up. Penny had discovered his secret even though

Zeld had not.

Penny's face showed delight and dejection at the same time. She uttered in a whisper, "He's alive! Why hasn't he said anything? Why hasn't he come for me?" She hung her head and sobbed.

Mrs. Palfreeman came over and put her arm around Penny, "It'll only be hard for a few days, and then things will return to normal." Mrs. Palfreeman spoke as if Penny felt disturbed by the eminent battle and tried to calm her fears. Penny went back to her duties even though the expression on her face clearly revealed her broken heart.

Sir Roger caught up with the crates of arrows, taking two dozen for himself. He carried the bow Friar Tuck sent him, holding it gingerly.

Sir Jaydan gave Father Ulrich his seat in the back of a wagon and stayed close to him as if on guard duty. Zeld wondered if Sir Jaydan felt guilty about losing Father Michael. This would explain his extra protective behaviour with Father Ulrich.

They marched to the great chasm. Sir Roger blew his horn and the cloud rose from the depths.

"Marvin, we must reach London with all haste. The king is under attack," said Sir Roger.

"You know the price," said Marvin holding out his hand.

Sir Roger handed him his purse. The entire attack force loaded onto the cloud while Marvin counted out the money and returned the purse to Sir Roger.

Meanwhile, in Scotland, Jens Sr. spied his two sons riding fast toward the manor. "Here we go again," he muttered as they rode through the gate, then directly to the alarm and rang it.

"WHAT IS IT THIS TIME?" Jens Sr. called from the hay loft as his men scrambled to their positions on the wall.

"THE BADEN MILITIA ATTACKED THE SCHOOL!" Oles reported.

Jens Sr. shouted in a stern voice, "ALL SOLDIERS PREPARE FOR THE FIELD! ALL SOLDIERS PREPARE FOR THE FIELD!"

It took 25 minutes to load the wagons, empty the armoury and bring the farmers in from the fields. Jens Sr. prepared for war with 243 soldiers and 3 mobile kitchens that could cook while travelling. Zeld's 12 mongonels were Jens Sr.'s only pieces of siege equipment and Zeld's zwiehanders, his best toe to toe weapons. He had thousands of Scandinavian throwing axes and hundreds of wooden shields. Jens Sr. kissed Marta farewell and marched with his small army south.

Some of the kitchen staff came as well and kept busy in the wagons, mixing bread dough, while others gathered firewood along the road. "The school will have to wait. We must fight Hesse's men at the five damaged castles," Jens Sr. told his troops.

320

The army moved out with horses and riders flanking both sides of the road in case of an ambush like the C&C School did. The army advanced faster than the kitchen wagons. Jens Sr. ordered a few men to stay with the wagons while the main body of men forged ahead.

They reached the first castle and found no battle had taken place. Relief showed on Jens Sr. face. This meant he wouldn't have to fight at each of the five castles.

The villagers hid when they saw Jens Sr.'s Vikings. He called out to the villagers informing them Hesse's men were on the march, and they'd come to defend them. He also said he would feed anyone wishing to join in defending the king.

This had no impact on the villagers until the food wagons arrived. The smell of food brought out volunteers. Some volunteers owned weapons and some did not.

Jens Sr. led his army toward the five castles and when he arrived at each one he had the same experience. No battle, but food gathered new recruits.

Jens Sr. spoke to himself out loud, "If Hesse didn't march here - then - he has found some other prize - something bigger - bigger than five castles - and that would have to be - the whole kingdom."

He spied a large group of stonemasons repairing the far side of the fifth castle. He approached them and asked, "Have you been paid for your work?"

"No," one of the muscle-bound men replied.

"Did you know King Henry is under attack by Hesse's army?"

"No," the same man replied with more interest.

"Did you know if Hesse wins the battle you'll never be paid?"

The stonemasons had worked for months without pay and learning they may never receive pay aroused their attention.

"I'm counterattacking Hesse as soon as we arrive. Would you care to join me in defending the king?" Jens Sr. asked.

Eighty-seven stonemasons joined his force. He'd also increased his army by 116 men and boys from the ranks of the starving villagers.

The stonemasons brought hammers to fight with, and they had a couple of other surprises as well. The derricks they used to lift stones onto the walls converted into trebuchets. These heavy duty siege weapons could throw rocks exceptional distances with accuracy. The stonemasons loaded the trebuchets into four wagons, and the castle had one working mobile catapult they brought along.

The stonemasons dismantled an old iron gate to use the parts for spears and clubs. For shields they used whole doors with leather straps on them. It took only minutes for these muscular men to prepare for battle.

In Sherwood Forest the Robin Hood School had mobilized as well. They'd sent 22 boys to recruit soldiers for the field and still had 37 soldiers to attack with. They took Zeld's two catapults, twelve mongonels, one wagon full of food, and one wagon that carried a kitchen. They also made the decision their retreating station, should the battle go ill, would be atop Dragon Hill.

An elfling galloped into the King Arthur School and rang the school's bell. The goblin boys took defensive positions at the wooden fort walls while Sir Thomas Malory approached the young elf.

"Hesse is attacking the king in London," the elf said. He followed with, "Friar Tuck sent me."

Sir Thomas rang the bell, and the goblins ran to him.

"We're at war with the Hessens, prepare for battle. I want every weapon brought and stacked here. Meanwhile, I want Glop, Gash, Frulu, and Zim to each pick a lookout tower and see if anyone's on the roads. Report to me in 15 minutes."

They didn't resemble a grand fighting force, but Sir Thomas did his best and brought out the school's two small wagons and four ponies. Three of the boys owned ponies as well. Sir Thomas loaded the weapons evenly into the two wagons. Each goblin carried a bow and 14 arrows with various colours of feathers. Some of the boys wore leather armour.

The four goblins returned from their errand. They'd seen no one on the roads.

"If Hesse wanted this area for a retreating station, we would've seen someone. That means he must've chosen the Castles and Caverns School or the town of Baden. That's where we'll go fight the enemy," said Sir Thomas in a courageous manner, attempting to inspire his young warriors.

They loaded the wagons with food and moved out. The boys took turns riding and walking. They didn't use flanking guards as they didn't have enough ponies to manage it properly. The elfling stayed with the other 27 small and frightened looking warriors from the goblin school. The Battle of London would soon begin, but they had no means to travel there in time.

Another young elfling urgently rode past the Hessen circus wagons, entered the Prince Valiant School and rang the alarm. The school leaders slowly answered the distress call as they hadn't had a real emergency in three decades.

When they finally spoke to the elf, he told them the circus wagons carried Hessen catapults and onagers to attack the king. The schoolmaster, Vancealot du Lake, slowly climbed the tower stairs. Once at the top he looked down and saw the catapults and onagers in the wagons. He stood for a moment astonished, but then ordered a guard to shoot a special arrow that erupted into a red flare.

The guards in the various towers throughout the valley panicked. A red flare meant they had fallen under attack. The next colour would tell them where the enemy could be located. They made mad scrambles for their aged instruction scrolls. The second flare burst into a yellow glow, which meant the enemy, was on the road. They snatched up their bows and looked down on the circus wagons. Some of the guards promptly recognized the disguise, while others remained unsure of what to do.

Presently arrows from the towers fell on the speeding wagons. The castle guards fired their catapults. It took several tries before they hit a wagon, but when they did, it was a spectacular sight. The wagon flipped over and the two drivers somersaulted through the air.

The archers in the towers shot two driving teams leaving two wagons speeding down the road without drivers. The horses ran into ditches upsetting the catapult parts which spilled out onto the ground.

When the last wagon cleared the valley, the guardsmen left their towers and checked on the men they'd fired upon. The castle sent out wagons to retrieve the captured catapults. This impromptu scrimmage meant the Battle of London had commenced.

323

Chapter Thirty Nine

The Battle of London

The Robin Hood School poured into the Prince Valiant Valley riding on horseback in pursuit of the war machines. This jump started the hearts of the tower men and sent them running to their battle stations as what appeared to be a second wave of invaders started through the valley. The first tower gave the all's well signal and the other tower men stood down.

The Prince Valiant Castle mobilized for battle. They brought 2 onagers and the 3 catapults they'd just captured. In addition, they equipped a force of 20 knights, 60 footmen, 28 militia, and they brought 6 portable lookout towers, various tents, blankets, and food wagons with 700 meals. The armoury held 200 sets of swords with shields and 200 crossbows with 2800 bolts.

Friar Tuck sent several boys ahead to shoot down as many drivers as they could. This proved an excellent strategy because the enemy's horses had tired. The boys captured 5 more catapults before they reached the battlefield.

At the castle, Hesse's catapults and onagers were assembled and loaded for battle. The missing catapults left holes in the attack line, but the newly arriving men couldn't report the capture of the war machines as the field commander's location was top secret. The field commander waited for the missing war machines to arrive before he started. The Hessens found themselves at an impasse. Finally, a catapult fired on the castle without permission, breaking the stalemate.

Presently the entire northern army engaged in earnest combat. In the second volley an onager fired an outstanding shot, smashing through the tower gate. The field commander raised the banner to stop firing, and then signalled for the foot soldiers to attack.

The king's men rushed valiantly to the opening as well. They used poisoned arrows and fired stones from catapults. They drove the attackers back or so it appeared. In truth the invaders played cat and mouse with the defenders. Once they located the catapults in the castle, the footmen withdrew and the onagers fired, aiming for the catapults and damaging three of the four.

Then, something strange happened: the onagers stopped firing not by commander's orders nor because they ran out of ammunition. The problem came from Friar Tuck who had opened fire on them and timed the release of his catapults to match the release of the onagers. Because he was on the other side of the battlefield the commander only learned about the counterattack once his onagers stopped firing.

The onager crews were pelted by fist-sized rocks that broke down their machines and caused many casualties. Several of the onager crews turned on Friar Tuck's forces with poisoned battleaxes.

Godfrey of Hesse hadn't positioned rear guards, nor had he given the onager and catapult crews shields. This proved a tremendous mistake. Two hundred crossbows fired on the charging Hessens three times before they reached Friar Tuck's band of merry men, who easily mopped up the rest.

Some onager crews stayed behind, repairing their onagers by salvaging the useable parts from the other damaged machines. The men in the castle repaired their catapults, using the same tactic. The king's troops also tossed stones into the hole in the castle wall to slow the invaders' inevitable advance.

The one functioning castle catapult took aim on a Hessen catapult that appeared to be in range. They missed the catapult but clobbered three of the five crewmen.

The two surviving crewmen began arming the catapult to return fire, but 20 bolts from Friar Tuck's crossbows changed their minds. They retreated down the hill toward their footmen in a panic, leaving the catapult behind.

When the commander of the footmen saw the two soldiers leave their catapult, he ordered his footmen to kill them. After all, Hesse had told them to take every precaution to prevent the spread of the mind plague, and leaving their functioning catapult behind appeared as a sign of madness. When the two men reached the

safety of their fellow soldiers, they watched as those nearest them, reluctantly drew their swords and struck them down.

The onager crews finished their repairs and fired on the merry men. The merry men had moved to a new location and watched the rocks fall harmlessly from the sky onto their old position.

Hesse's field commander ordered his 200 cavalrymen to search out and destroy the enemy, meaning the merry men and their war machines. The cavalry bounded over the hill, swords and axes drawn.

Marvin landed his cloud south of Forest Gate, and Sir Roger's attack force looked for the best way to join Friar Tuck and the merry men. Sir Roger sneaked a peek inside his black sack, and then said aloud, "Ah, yes."

As Marvin left, Sir Roger handed him his black sack, he didn't want the amulet to fall into the hands of the enemy. "Keep this safe," he ordered, "and retrieve Jens Sr.'s army. They are at the five damaged castles up north."

The two onagers from Prince Valiant joined the battle. As the cavalry advanced in the general direction of the merry men, fist-sized rocks fell on them from the sky. After the deadly rainstorm of stones, 20 of the Hessen knights and their horses lay strewn across the battlefield. The boys from Prince Valiant scoured the countryside looking for more stones.

The rest of Hesse's cavalry accelerated their advance, attempting to avoid a second showering of death. They rode into the trees at the top of the hill. The merry men fired Zeld's two catapults into the charging knights. Seven knights and their horses went down, smashed by the stones.

Despite their losses Hesse's cavalry found their targets. A knight blew his horn three times, and the cavalry divided into three groups in order to crush their opposition.

The battle grew fierce. Two volleys of bolts flew into the knights before the man-to-man combat started. One of the three groups of knights rode into the ranks of the merry men. Unable to get out of the way, the knights trampled the merry men or struck them with their long swords.

The second group of cavalry attacked Little John's lot of elf-lings, who had captured the catapults on the road. Little John fired the catapults at the cavalry with large stones; then, he ordered his elflings to draw their weapons and attack man to man. As the elflings ran into the battle, they turned invisible.

This part of the Hessen cavalry experienced terrible problems. The horses became spooked, some of the men sustained injuries from no apparent enemy and several of the horses' reins appeared to break, leaving the riders with no control. This was the worst luck many of the cavalrymen had ever encountered.

The third group of cavalry attacked the two onagers that had only just joined the action. The two onagers fired small stones into the attacking cavalry causing considerable damage, but not enough to stop the advance.

While the onager crews desperately hurried to reload, soldiers from the Prince Valiant School formed a defensive column in front of them. Then, using mongonels they had concealed in a ditch, they fired upon the charging cavalry. Eight knights fell, while the others continued the charge. As the charging knights reached the column, a second volley of mongonel fire hit them, dropping another nine.

The first vicious swings from the cavalrymen hit with such force they split the defenders' armour. Clearly the Robin Hood and Prince Valiant Schools, even though they had bled the enemy, had lost the battle. Their men broke ranks and ran. The Hessen cavalry chased them down, hitting them from behind in an all-out-rout. Hesse's cavalry overpowered the entire battlefield.

The goblins, meanwhile, hadn't yet reached the Castles and Caverns School. They wouldn't have any impact on the battle to the south. Jens Sr.'s army remained in the wrong part of England, literally hundreds of miles away and couldn't reach them in time.

The Hessen cavalry commander gave the field commander the victory sign. The field commander turned his attention back to the assault on the castle. He started with a barrage against the outer wall, as he had done earlier.

When Sir Roger saw the victory signal, he issued the attack order. Zeld heard the pounding of the horses' hoofs on the battle-

field in London and the dreadful screams of the men the Hessen cavalry caught up with.

Sir Roger stepped out in the open and fired an arrow from his bow, hitting a Hessen knight pursuing a Prince Valiant squire. The blow from the arrow knocked the knight off his horse; then, the arrow ricocheted and hit a second knight's sword out of his hand. Again the arrow ricocheted, this time puncturing the horse's skull. The horse dropped immediately. The knights riding closely behind couldn't stop, and three of them took headlong spills onto the field. It was truly an amazing display of archery skills and Zeld couldn't believe any living man could make that shot, but he'd seen it for himself.

Zeld watched as the German knight who had attacked the onagers retreated, but they didn't make it far. More brilliant shots from Sir Roger crushed the retreating knights in the third group. Sir Roger sent his footmen, meaning his students, to recapture the war machines.

As Zeld ran for his new position he choked on the thick dust the horses had kicked up. He spat, rinsing out his mouth. He saw the Prince Valiant knights take up his 12 mongonels and load them with small stones. They advanced on the knights who had smashed their way through Friar Tuck and the merry men. The mongonels made a major impact. The Prince Valiant knights had the German knights on the run in three volleys.

Little John ordered his elflings to abandon the Hessen cavalry they harassed. They turned visible and retreated to the onagers. The mongonels opened fire once the elves had retreated to safety. The remaining German cavalry scattered like mice in a dark dungeon when the torch is first lit. With all three of the cavalry groups defeated, the tables turned and Hesse's knights rode for their lives.

Zeld and his mates collected stones with the elflings, to fire out of the war machines. While the Hessen field commander once again played cat and mouse with the castle, King Henry's men rushed to defend the outer wall. Then the field commander ordered a retreat of the ground troops before they engaged in combat and ordered the onagers to fire flaming stones upon King Henry's unsuspecting men. The contemptible trick worked. More than 100 of King Henry's men died or lay severely injured and many more received lesser wounds.

The field commander signalled for another ground assault when the remainder of the retreating cavalry rode up in a frenzy.

"They've taken the hill," said one of the knights, pointing back the direction he had retreated from. The field commander looked in the direction the knight pointed but, alas, too late.

All of Hesse's onagers lay crushed under a heavy bombardment of rock. The momentum of the battle shifted, but the German commander hadn't finished conjuring unworthy tricks out of the air. He signalled for the ships to attack. Giant arrows flew from the ballistas mounted aboard the ships and ground troops rowed for the shore.

The amphibious assault became the commander's last order as a giant rock landed on top of him, leaving no trace he'd ever existed. Hesse's men fired back with their catapults at the English defenders, but they were no match for the much larger onagers that pounded them in return.

A Prince Valiant knight stopped his horse and ordered the C&C boys to the crest of Tower Hill. Zeld found himself running along with the other schoolboys toward the frontline with onagers and catapults firing back and forth over their heads. He had worked up a sweat from running and his heart pounded with fear and anticipation. Sweat from his forehead stung his eyes and he wiped his face with his shirt sleeve. He hadn't yet seen the other side of Tower Hill, but he felt certain, the Hessen army waiting there would be enormous.

After a lengthy, desperate dash the boys reached the top of Tower Hill. They dove onto their bellies, raised only their heads over the crest, and looked down on the castle. Zeld saw the castle wall giving way to the giant arrows which came from the ships. He also caught glimpses of landing parties rowing to shore. The remnants of the German cavalry regrouped to Zeld's left, and directly in front of him stood the 3000 footmen near the base of the hill. The footmen faced the castle, awaiting orders.

Zeld saw the abandoned catapult which Hesse's two men left earlier. It sat in range to attack Hesse's footmen at the bottom of Tower Hill. The Hessen footmen waited patiently for the attack signal from the dead field commander.

Zeld said, "Let's capture the catapult and fire it at the enemy footmen."

As Jens Jr. opened his mouth to let out a war cry, Zeld put his hand over his mouth. "I'd rather not announce our arrival."

"Excellent point," said Jens Jr., nodding his head.

On a silent signal the boys ran for the catapult. They made it three quarters of the way there before the enemy noticed them. When they reached the catapult three of them cranked the turning handle to lower the firing shaft into position. Four boys loaded the largest rock from the ammunition pile. Jens Jr. yelled, "Stand clear," and gave the boys a half a second before he pulled the firing rope. The rock flew high in the air and then landed, striking several footmen who were facing the other direction.

Hesse's cavalry, or what remained of it, saw the attack and charged the catapult riding hard and fast. Zeld saw them and froze with fear for a moment.

"Turn the catapult," ordered Robert.

The boys grabbed hold of the corners and turned the catapult in the direction of the charging cavalry.

Sir Roger stepped out alone between the charging Hessen cavalry and Zeld's catapult. He raised his bow and fired an arrow. His first shot hit a knight's helmet spinning it around in front of his face. Then the arrow ricocheted and cut the reigns in the hands of a different knight. Finally, the arrow bounced off another charging knight's axe. The axe flew through the air and sent the arrow flying dangerously close to Sir Roger. The arrow landed directly in front of his feet. He collected it and fired it again into the charging knights.

The knight, whose helmet had spun around blocking his vision veered to his right, colliding with a group of seven other knights who all crashed into a crumpled heap of armour and broken bodies. The other knights, riding directly behind, steered around the calamity.

The knight with the severed reigns couldn't control his horse, which caused a second collision. Four more horses landed hard on the ground with their riders sprawled across the battlefield.

A third collision came from the battleaxe that flew from the knight's hand. The axe became a whirling dervish, spinning around in the air until it made contact with its victims. Three crashes from the axe reduced the total cavalry force to a mere six knights.

Jens Jr. fired a load of small rocks from the catapult and four of the six fell. Brian Boru put on a burst of speed and one of the knights followed him round the catapult. Jens Jr. swung the launching shaft at Brian who saw it coming and ducked. The knight didn't fare as well, as his horse ran headlong into the shaft. Zeld and company mobbed the knight and pulled him to the ground as he shouted something at them in German. Sullivan stood on the knight's sword which remained in his hand while Crispyn broke the knight's nose with a rock.

332   The last knight stopped and ordered the men behind him, "Chase da brats into da voods." Then, he turned and saw all of his men lying in heaps. The nine boys chased the knight, who turned his horse around and galloped away.

From behind the boys came 12 tired but determined men carrying Zeld's mongonels. Unable to catch the knight up the boys ran back to the catapult and loaded it. Presently catapults, mongonels and onagers lined the battlefield with crews to work them. Penny and Mrs. Palfreeman had created a makeshift infirmary, hidden in the trees, on the north side of Tower Hill. Over 100 rescuers had been treated with the healing pills and rejoined the battle.

Sir Roger ordered the bombardment of Hesse's footmen. The first volley angered them and they instantly counterattacked straight into Sir Roger's forces. Yellow lights in the western clouds reflected the sunset. As the footmen charged up the hill, Zeld remembered his poisoned caltrops. He trembled at the sight of the three thousand charging men, but managed to pour out his caltrops from their bag, creating a death trap.

Zeld's chest swelled with heavy breathing as he watched the footman making headway toward him. The smell of horses hung in the air and his leather armour creaked with every breath.

The charging footmen received hit after hit of lethal barrages from mongonel and catapult fire. The footmen manoeuvred to concentrate on Zeld's position. Sir Roger countered by ordering a rider to have the pages retreat, but the rider couldn't get there in time to save Zeld and his mates.

Zeld spied an assault on the south side of the castle as well. The Hessen landing parties rowed toward a central location, which meant the ballistas had breached the castle's outer wall.

Mongonel fire shot down several of the footmen attacking Zeld's position. The catapults and onagers joined in. However, it fell woefully short of the firepower needed to stop the throng of footmen who charged undaunted toward Zeld and company.

Out of the first eight men to reach Zeld's catapult, four stepped on caltrops. Each did the same thing: he reached down pulling the caltrop out right before the poison hit his system. Then, they fell over leaving the caltrops exposed to take additional victims.

Sir Roger ordered the crossbow men to fire on the attackers. They did until they ran out of bolts. Sir Roger then ordered everyone to meet the charge at Zeld's position. Sir Roger personally led this force, which included the C&C knights, the merry men and the knights from the Prince Valiant School.

Several elves appeared, delivering more stones to fire from the mongonels. They disappeared as quickly as they came. The two sides became locked in a massive toe-to-toe struggle.

Zeld's mates drew their swords and lifted axes in readiness. As soon as a footman made it through the caltrops, the boys swung their weapons at him. This surprise tactic proved effective at first but later too many men made it through.

The boys fought five footmen and then ten. Once outnumbered the situation became hopeless. A footman struck a solid blow on Tyre's left shoulder. He screamed and dropped.

Sullivan followed as a blow to the head knocked him unconscious. The footmen ran through the battleline toward their next objective, the other war machines.

Zeld felt a sense of morbidity with what he planned to do. He forced it from his mind; then, sprang anxiously forward onto the dead bodies in his poisoned caltrop field of death. He found himself surrounded by enemy footmen. He jumped from the body he stood on to a second and then a third. The men chased him. Three of them stopped, reached for their feet, and after pulling out the caltrops, they collapsed. Zeld's plan worked.

Two of the footmen swung at Zeld, but he escaped their lethal blows by leaping back across the dead bodies. He slipped and fell on top of the last body and in order to stand properly he stretched his left foot toward the ground. Just before he stood he checked for caltrops and spied one directly under his foot. He pulled his foot back, rising to his knees.

Just then he felt a sharp pain from a hard blow on the left side of his head. The images around him blurred and then went black.

Meanwhile, the goblins reached the Castle and Caverns School and the dwarves greeted them at the outskirts of the castle. It didn't take long before the goblins and dwarves conjured up an excellent plan. Phase one consisted of setting an ambush, and phase two meant tricking the enemy into it.

Two goblin boys ran out in full view of the archers on the wall and yelled, "We're telling King Henry on you and we're coming back with a whole army."

The militia sent four men to kill the goblins. The four men chased them up the road and over the hill toward the town of Baden.

Once the men advanced out of sight, Sir Thomas called back as if he belonged to the militia, "Hey, there are more than two of them, send a dozen men to help." His comment was followed by an awkward silence.

Six men went instead of a dozen. They ran over the hill and again more silence.

Sir Thomas called back for more men, but only two men left the castle. The awkward silence returned. The goblins used blue feathered sleeping arrows on their enemies. Once hit the victim slept for hours. The goblins hog tied and gagged the militiamen who had fallen into their trap. The militia's numbers had dwindled severely. They'd lost some men at the stream and a dozen had mysteriously vanished over the hill.

Back in London, Zeld had fallen unconscious to the ground and landed on his bag. His healing stone started working on him immediately. He awoke just minutes after the crushing blow, with his sword still in his hand.

The battle raged up the hill. Zeld struggled to pull himself up and stepped from one body to the next while crossing the field of death. When he reached his mates, he found six of them lying in one group, injured, but still breathing. A great sense of relief filled his soul. The half brothers, Robert and James, were missing. After a brief search, Zeld found Robert up the hill, unconscious from a blow to the back of his head, but alive. He found James under a footman.

Zeld rolled the footman away, revealing that James lay mortally wounded. Shocked at the sight he placed his healing stone inside the deep cut that stretched from his chest to his right hip. The stone began to heal James. Then, Zeld took out his dragon heart and placed it in James' hand, so he wouldn't lose all of his strength.

Zeld spied three abandoned mongonels. He covered James' wound and left the healing stone in place. Though exhausted, Zeld dragged the mongonels to the top of Tower Hill and fired at the footmen who had their backs to him fighting the last of the king's rescuers. The mongonels dropped 10 enemy soldiers. Zeld reloaded with whatever he could find: sticks, rocks and broken arrows. He fired again into the crowd of footmen and watched as more of them fell. Zeld continued firing and the footmen kept falling.

The final few footmen ran away and six men on Zeld's side were left standing. A terrible noise arose from the castle. A group of 400 Vikings standing in battle formation with large rectangular wooden shields held over their heads approached from the west. The shields lowered in unison and suddenly dozens of battleaxes flew from the advancing army. Zeld's heart sank as he realized King Henry wouldn't survive.

CHAPTER FORTY

After All
You Can Do

G O DAD!" cheered Jens Jr. in a weakened voice after raising himself onto his elbows atop Tower Hill and seeing the commotion at London Castle below.

Zeld looked at the battle again. He realized these Vikings weren't the enemy. Jens Sr.'s army had arrived and grown significantly. Zeld's heart suddenly swelled with hope. From the east side of the castle he heard knights blowing their horns. All types of colourful banners preceded a great number of superb horses, along with hundreds of knights and squires who took to the battlefield, attacking the German forces. The battle raged on two sides of the castle and it appeared some of the defenders had survived inside the keep.

The sun went down and darkness descended. The goblins and dwarves at Castles and Caverns switched tactics for a night-time of fun. They went around the castle to the stream and found small stacks of firewood waiting to be burned in the courtyard. The goblins shot flaming arrows into the woodpiles. The fires made it look like the whole castle was ablaze.

The militia couldn't sleep because of the fires and smoke, not to mention the trepidation in their hearts. A few of the men climbed down from the walls and attempted to smother the fires. The goblins shot them down with orange coloured poison arrows. Unquestionably the dwarves and goblins would win this battle as they held all the advantages over the physically and emotionally weakened militia.

Penny and Mrs. Palfreeman drove the aid wagon over Tower Hill near London castle in the quiet of the early morning. They issued the last of the medications. The food wagons filled the air with the scent of freshly baked bread.

Zeld felt a surge of relief when he spied the king's banner still flying over the castle. Hesse's troops had crept away in the night. King Henry had won the day.

Soldiers cleared the battlefield by carting away the wounded and the dead. The mortally wounded were transported to a shady area where a large wooden cross towered above them.

The pills from the infirmary had run out by the time they found James. Mrs. Palfreeman waved for the wagon with the mortally wounded to come. Zeld ran down and waved it off, telling them he'd tend to James' wound. The recovery team didn't argue; they simply left James behind.

The healing stone had regained some power during the night, so Zeld repositioned it and the healing process renewed. He removed several hard black stones that had formed in the wound. He felt most curious about them so he turned the bag that had held the caltrops inside out and kept them.

Sir Roger came by. He examined James and with a tear in his eye said, "Take the boy home to die."

Zeld found a small wagon and Robert carefully lifted his dying brother into the back. Robert laid him down gently, using his tunic as a pillow. He obtained instructions from one of the castle guards to find James' home town of Penarth. They received a couple of day's rations from a cook wagon and began their journey.

Zeld drove the wagon while Robert tended to his brother. It took the better part of three days to reach James' home. They travelled as far as they could each day, tending to James' wound with the healing stone and washing the wound with water regularly. When they arrived, Sir Rosser left his manorhouse to greet them.

Sir Rosser looked into the back of the wagon and saw James' ghastly wound. A look of anger filled his eyes. The anger was slowly replaced by a profound sadness. He appeared to recognize Zeld. Then, he looked over at Robert.

"Are you his mate, too?" asked Sir Rosser uneasily.

"No, I'm his brother," said Robert awkwardly. An uncomfortable silence followed.

"I'm Sir Rosser ap Phillip, James' grandfather," Sir Rosser said. "Thank you for bringing him home."

Sir Rosser carried James into the house. Zeld and Robert followed. Zeld carried his bag over his shoulder. They laid James on his bed in his small room. It was time for another treatment. Zeld used the amulet and more black stones formed in the wound, so he picked them out and added them to the others. Sir Rosser told them to wait for him while he fetched some alcohol. He returned with a dusty brown bottle. Sir Rosser washed the wound thoroughly before Zeld resumed the healing process with his stone.

The black stones came back and Sir Rosser picked them out. This slower pace of healing, which included removing the black stones and washing the wound at the same time, worked better than anything Zeld had tried before.

"His breathing is improving," said Robert who placed his hand over James' heart. He added, "His heart is growing stronger, too." A feeling of relief crept into Robert's voice.

The stone eventually ran out of power. Zeld took out his dragon heart and placed it on James' chest. The three of them left the house to talk privately.

"Tell me about the war. There are rumours Hesse attacked King Henry?" said Sir Rosser stiffening with concern.

"Yes, from Tower Hill and from the Thames," Zeld confided.

"Did they use warships on the Thames?"

"They fired ballistas from the decks of the ships," answered Robert.

Sir Rosser turned sharply on his heel and hastily walked to the stable. He saddled the fastest horse and rode swiftly toward the coast without saying a word. After he disappeared, Zeld and Robert looked at each other with an amount of uncertainty about what they should do or where they should go, so they slipped into the house and waited. They sat on the floor outside James' room so they wouldn't disturb him and fell into an exhausted sleep.

A beautiful slim blonde-haired woman who appeared no older than 20 awoke them.

"You must be James' sister," said Robert reaching to shake her hand.

"No, I'm James' mother, Gwendolyn," she said, reaching with her hand. Then, she asked, "Did they dismiss school early this year?"

"No, Hesse's men attacked the school," said Robert.

A thunderstruck expression crossed Gwendolyn face and it carried through to her voice, "Where is James?"

"He fell wounded in the Battle of London and we brought him home," said Robert pointing to the bedroom.

Gwendolyn hurried in to see her son who lay nearly lifeless on the bed. His wound had healed to only one quarter of its original size, but it still looked terrible. His eyes were sunken with black rings around them and his skin had turned a pasty white.

She fell on her knees and lifted her son's hand to her face; then, she cried the tears of a grieving mother. Zeld came in and removed the stone from his bag. Robert cleaned the wound and Zeld applied the stone. As the black stones appeared, Robert plucked them out. The wound completely healed on the outside. James' colour was nearly normal and he rolled over on his side.

Gwendolyn had never seen a miracle before. An expression of total shock and joy froze unto her face. Her mouth fell open but she could not speak for several minutes.

"I'm Zeld de Saxon."

"I'm Robert O'Day."

Gwendolyn could see a younger version of Robert's and James' father standing in front of her.

"Yes, you are," she said, recognizing Robert. With both hands she reached out and hugged him like her own son. "Thank you, for bringing him home," she said as politely as her tears would allow. She softly kissed Robert atop his head.

Robert cried as Gwendolyn held him.

"I'm sorry," Robert said.

"For what?" asked Gwendolyn.

"I always thought of you as a terrible monster who stole me father away. I called you terrible names and continually hazed James at school," Robert confessed.

"Thomas O'Day deceived both your mother and me. Rumour has it we may not be the only two. One thing I'll say for Thomas, he always wanted to be worth a fortune and from what I learned about his criminal past, he is. That is if you count the bounty money on his head. Someday he'll be caught and most likely beheaded!"

Sir Rosser entered the bedroom with an impish grin on his face and muttered to himself, "When those Germans sail for home, they'll have a very warm welcome waiting for them." He added in a lower tone, "Nobody does this to my family. With the amulet of wind my men will sail circles around the other boats and chase those ships all the way back to Germany. That's if any of them make it that far."

Sir Rosser quietly checked on James, and then went into the kitchen to cook supper. Supper sounded wonderful to Zeld. Neither he nor Robert had eaten all day. Sir Rosser made fish and chips. Zeld loved them and ate his fill, and Robert ate more than Zeld did.

341

The boys gave James a couple more treatments that night. James awoke in the morning fully healed and asked, "Is there anything to eat 'round here? I could eat a whole giant chicken - by myself." His mother appeared overjoyed. She hugged James and cried tears of happiness. The two walked arm in arm to the kitchen. Sir Rosser cooked all the fish and chips James could eat even though he had previously cooked the same meal the day before. The lot sat around the kitchen table while James stuffed himself.

"Fish and chips are sure better than beef or oxen, wouldn't you say?" Robert said, teasing James.

"They surely are," mumbled James as he obviously forgot his manners and used his fingers to shove another fillet in his already full mouth.

"James, are you having trouble eating red meats?" asked Gwendolyn.

James nodded, too busy chewing to answer.

Gwendolyn and Sir Rosser looked at each other.

"Have you gotten any black spots on your stomach?" asked Gwendolyn.

"No," he mumbled.

"We removed a lot of black stones from his wound," Zeld reminded everyone.

"By the stars, that's right," said Sir Rosser, who abruptly pounded on the table with his fist as he and Gwendolyn looked at each other again.

"James, do you remember the stories of your grandmother, the water dweller?" asked Sir Rosser.

James looked thoughtful for a moment, and then a look of astonishment came to his face. He swallowed and asked, "Grandfather, am I turning into a sea elf?"

"Yes, I'm sure of it," answered Sir Rosser. "The first stage is the underwater lungs. As they develop you become allergic to red meat. The second stage is the black spots on the belly. Later stages include webbed feet and hands. The last stage is the pointed ears whenever you get wet."

"Pointed ears?" asked James with an exasperated expression.

Zeld pretended to be a reporter and said, "I'm from the Anglo-Saxon Chronicles. So, Robert, honestly, how d'you fancy the idea of your little brother transforming into a sea elf?"

342

Robert remained silent for a long while; then, he turned to Sir Rosser and asked, "Is it catching?"

"No, Castles and Caverns School of Knighthood will not suddenly become the Castle and Caverns School for Sea Elves," said Sir Rosser reassuringly through his laughter. Turning to James he added with a wink, "Your grandmother had a lot of grand adventures being a water dweller you know."

The next day, Zeld and Robert took their belongings and left James with his family. They didn't go straight back to school. They went to Robert's manor instead. Robert hugged his mother when he arrived. Zeld and Robert spent the evening telling her about the school and the battle they'd gone through.

Bright and early the next day the boys headed back to the school. Mrs. O'Day's servants packed plenty of food and water for the return journey. It so happened they didn't need it, as Marvin the cloud giant found them and gave them a lift north, as requested by Father Ulrich. The journey took three hours instead of several days.

When they approached the castle, Jens Jr. called from the battlements above the main gate, "Zeld, gigantic news! The king has requested an audience - WITH YOU!"

Chapter Forty One

The King's Request

The Castles and Caverns' main gate slowly opened, the heavy wooden doors seemed to take forever in the morning light. Once Robert drove the wagon inside, Zeld asked in a worried tone, "Er - did I do something wrong?"

"No, the truth is I've been working on a brilliant scheme for the last few days and the king really did request an audience. You'll definitely need to bring along your money and your soldiers to guard it," Jens Jr. said trading places with Robert as he obviously planned to go with Zeld.

"You told him then?" asked Father Ulrich who approached the wagon from his office.

Jens Jr. nodded.

"I insist you leave at once," cried Father Ulrich. "When the king requests an audience, then you must not delay a single moment."

"Jens Jr. says I'll need me two soldiers to come along and guard me money," Zeld told Father Ulrich even though he still didn't know what was happening.

"Agreed," said Father Ulrich.

Jens Jr. parked the wagon in front of Eagle Loft; then, Zeld and Jens Jr. carried the treasure chest to the wagon. His two soldiers waited outside the Great Hall prepared to leave. When ready, the small entourage headed south and stopped at the cliff to hire Marvin to float them to the king.

Marvin appeared surprised to see Zeld so soon and out of friendship, waived the fee for the journey. Two hours later, he set the cloud down as softly as he could, right outside King Henry's castle. It caused quite a stir, as the soldiers had remained on full alert.

"Me name is Zeldain de Saxon," he called to the soldiers on duty.

"ALL'S WELL, IT'S MASTER ZELD," one of the guards called over his shoulder.

A group of eight guards accompanied the wagon to the keep's main entrance.

Two soldiers carrying halberds marched Zeld through the doorway. They escorted him through the hallways to see the king. The guards stopped at the entrance of the last hallway, and one told Zeld in a voice only slightly more than a whisper, "Go straight toward the set of double doors. The king is waiting on the other side."

Zeld's steps echoed in the hallway as he approached the large set of double doors, he heard someone call to him, "The injury on my shoulder has become painful again, could you look at it?"

The voice came from a room off to the right of the double doors. Zeld looked in and saw what appeared to be a healer's shop. Various sized cauldrons rested against one wall with rows of glass jars filled with pills and other ingredients for potions resting upon numerous shelves.

The man who called out sat on an examination table. He appeared 19 or 20 years of age. He had dark hair and a muscular build. His back faced the door and his shirt was pulled high on one side, revealing several battle injuries. Zeld stepped in the room and spied the nasty wound on the man's shoulder, so he took out his healing stone and began to heal it. The man laughed because it tickled.

The man questioned, "What is that, Pomfrey?"

"Sir, I'm Zeld de Saxon."

"So, you're the famous Zeld," said the man light-heartedly while turning around.

"Yes - I suppose I am - famous - er - these days."

"We heard you personally dropped 60 men on the battlefield by using poisoned caltrops and firing mongonels," said the man in a bragging tone.

"Yeah, I did that."

"Only Robin Hood, himself, did better."

"Robin Hood is dead, Sir," Zeld said believing the man's injuries were temporarily confusing his mind.

"No, he isn't dead," said the man. "We gave him a new identity after Maid Marian died, and you know him very well. Haven't you guessed?" The man paused. "Sir Roger must be doing an excellent job of hiding, if you didn't recognize him."

"Er – you mean Sir Roger – is really Robin Hood – and to think – he taught me how to shoot!" Zeld said in jaw dropping surprise. Then, he began to wonder with whom he spoke. He must be some sort of magistrate, Zeld thought. After all, only someone with real power could legally change Robin Hood's identity.

The man continued speaking, "We heard he made some spectacular shots with his famous bow. You'll keep his secret of course. He served my uncle, King Richard, well, and kept the people safe from my wicked father. He deserved a better life than that of an outlaw, so we gave him one."

With an even greater expression of surprise, Zeld bowed and said, "Sire!"

"We bid thee rise. Follow me please." The king finished putting on his fancy shirt, walked out of the examining room and through the double doors. He continued, "We have discovered many of Godfrey of Hesse's men are not loyal to their master and have expressed a desire to become turncoats. We understand by means of a letter sent from Jens McMarr Jr. you have enough money to pay for the healing of 100 footmen. If you choose to pay this cost, you will become the new master of the said men, and as you know that will make you, the Duke de Saxon. The total cost comes to 7,500 gold pieces."

Zeld crossed the threshold of the double doors and into the king's royal chamber. The room was filled with extravagant furnishings from across the world. He scanned the room trying to absorb his surroundings. The largest tapestry he had ever seen stretched 40 feet along one wall. A series of pictures, which told the story of the Battle of Hastings, had been woven into it. Royal blue curtains hung around the king's four poster bed. Rich purple drapes, with golden stitching of a forest scene, divided the bedroom from the dressing area. The throne with its peaked top rested against a wall. It housed the stone of scone underneath and somehow the chair stood as if on guard duty. The high backed chairs held cushions both to sit upon and to lean back on as well.

King Henry stepped around his brightly polished mahogany desk and sat behind it while Zeld stood in front.

"Yeah, I have that much money and more," Zeld said, almost forgetting where they were in their conversation.

"You'll need the rest to buy land and build farms. These land deeds now bear your name. The castle, lands and people of Saxon all belong to you," the king said, reaching backward and handing Zeld some scrolls. "Oh, yes, while I'm thinking of it, we deemed Hesse a pirate. He has a price of 25,000 gold pieces on his head. I know it's not much but we must drive Hesse out of the country somehow." Then the king handed him a second scroll and said, "The land deeds for your cousin Dando are in his name as well, and thank you for your diligent service," said the king with a slight nod of the head.

346

"Dando is me cousin?" asked Zeld, whose heart skipped a beat. He didn't wait for the king to answer as he spied another injury. He moved the amulet to a burned placed on King Henry's face. The burn healed instantly.

"Yes, he's your cousin. What is that little thing?" the king asked, pulling Zeld's hand in front of his face to examine the stone.

"A healing amulet, Sire."

"Crushing," replied the king with a look of wonderment on his face as he closely studied the amulet for a few seconds.

Zeld found it comical to think the king used words like 'Crushing'. He worked on other injuries until the stone ran out of power.

"Whom shall I pay the money to?" Zeld asked when he finished.

"Oh, bring it here to me."

He went to the wagon, unlocked his treasure chest and pulled everything out, trying to reach the bottom quickly. He and Jens Jr. counted out 7,500 gold pieces, and Zeld carried the heavy saddlebag into the king's room. The king gave Zeld a letter releasing 100 men and called for one of his knights.

"Sir Walter, please take our new duke down and release his men," the king ordered.

"This way, Master Zeld," said Sir Walter with a sweeping bow.

As Zeld followed Sir Walter, the king called out, "One more thing, Zeld, have you found the hidden compartments in the treasure chest I sent you?"

Zeld turned to look at the king, and then shook his head unhappily. The king laughed and said, "I daresay, I'm sure when you actually need it, you'll figure it out. We'll meet again soon and thank you for healing me."

He watched the king put his hands together and made the broken arrow sign. Zeld returned the sign and bowed. The king waved goodbye and Zeld followed Sir Walter.

Down in the dungeon Zeld found 100 German men waiting anxiously for their release. Only a few of them spoke English. He marched his soldiers outside and found King Henry's men had finished filling his wagon with food for their return journey.

Once finished with his audience, Jens Jr. had a suggestion. "I've been snooping through your belongings and I found these necklaces. I think we should go to a jeweller and put your amulets on these gold chains."

"First things first, we need more wagons and farming equipment," Zeld said thoughtfully.

"The soldiers don't have any weapons either," Jens Jr. reminded him.

"Jens Jr., did you know Dando and I are cousins?"

"I thought everyone knew that."

"I remember playing with me Cousin Danny when I was little, but I never knew the two of them were one and the same person."

"Zeld, your cousin Danny and Dando are the same person. Don't say I never tell you anything," Jens Jr. teased.

"Thanks a lot, you brat."

"You're welcome a lot, you brat," Jens Jr. teased again.

A sapphire, ruby and diamond were painted on the sign hanging outside the jewellery shop in London town. The coo-coo clock showed 1:30 p.m. as they entered the shop. Zeld watched nervously while the jeweller added the healing stone to one of his necklaces by setting the stone inside a solid metal ring, and then fusing a loop to the top of the ring. The necklace was then strung through the loop. The jeweller used another metal ring looped through the heart valves to attach the dragon heart to the second necklace.

Zeld put them both around his neck and paid the jeweller one gold piece for each job. The jeweller seemed grateful for the business. Jens Jr. cut his finger with his knife, and then placed the healing amulet on the cut to make sure the jeweller hadn't switched stones. The cut healed, and Jens Jr. smiled at Zeld, most satisfied.

Zeld sent Morten and Peders to buy two wagons, and he took his 100 soldiers with him to buy ploughs, pitchforks and spades. They bought everything in sets of six as he planned to start six farms. Zeld hoped six was enough.

His men came back with three wagons instead of two.

"We found them on sale," Peders boasted.

"Good. Now go and buy six farm horses," Zeld said while handing Peders more money.

Peders took a dozen men and did as Zeld requested. They returned 20 minutes later. The horses were hitched to the wagons and the company marched to find Marvin. Presently the company found Marvin waiting in a large meadow. The ride home excited and frightened Zeld's new soldiers, as none of them had ever ridden on a cloud before. They mostly sat on the sand with their eyes closed. Zeld minded his first ride and how he sat nervously waiting for it to end.

After they landed, the march continued. While approaching the farms, they ran into Father Ulrich and several members of the staff.

"Jens Jr. hinted you might return with several new soldiers, but I had no idea he meant this many." Father Ulrich looked into the wagons and saw all the farming equipment. "There are three farms for sell close by, er, if you're interested," Father Ulrich informed him.

"How much?" Zeld asked, definitely interested.

Sir Drain interjected, "1200 silver for all three."

"There is one small catch. You'll need to forcibly remove the pirates from this farm," said Father Ulrich pointing to a nearby farmhouse.

"Are they the farmers who started the rumour that the dwarves use fake coins?" asked Zeld suspiciously.

"Yes, I see you are familiar with their sinister plots," said Father Ulrich with his head tilted forward and his eyebrows raised.

"Oh, yes," replied Zeld.

Then he ordered his men to prepare for an attack. They looked around for something to fight with. Twenty of the soldiers hoisted a log to use as a battering ram while others collected sticks and stones. When the two pirates in the farmhouse saw the battering ram coming, they ran out the back door. Zeld agilely jumped on Sir Drain's horse and chased after them. As Zeld caught up with the two pirates, he hit them from behind with the flat side of his sword, one at a time. They tumbled onto the dusty back road unconscious. His soldiers watched and cheered.

348

"Take them to the healer, and then to Garth's blacksmith shop, I think he'll know what to do with them," Zeld ordered his men. Fortunately, a few of Zeld's new men had served under Hesse at the de Saxon castle so they were able to obey Zeld's order.

Jens Jr. counted out Zeld's money for the farms but wouldn't pay it until he had a receipt and that meant going to the school. Before leaving, Zeld directed the majority of his men to their new farms where they began work at once by hitching the ploughs to the horses and taking to the fields.

While waiting for his receipt, Zeld was within earshot of some of the German boys talking about transferring to another school next year. He wondered why they'd do that; then, it dawned on him the boys in the Hessen alliance would no longer feel comfortable at the school. They had lost the war and perhaps they'd return to Germany.

Sir Drain and Jens Jr. stepped into the Great Hall and Sir Drain wrote out the receipt and handed it to Zeld. That's when Zeld realized he had nearly run out of money and didn't have enough to pay for seed, stock animals and the three additional farms he planned to purchase. He immediately talked the matter over with Jens Jr.

"Let's raid the Hessen farms. They belong to you. Let's go reclaim what's yours," insisted Jens Jr.

After Zeld thought about it he said, "We'll take the farmers and everything they can carry. It would help if we found some quick-grow formula for the crops too!"

"What quick-grow formula?" asked Jens Jr.

"You know, you pour it on plants and they grow really fast. Mind the story of the Barnstaple chickens," Zeld explained.

"That works on plants?"

"Yes, it does."

"A map might help us," said Zeld who pulled out his deed maps from the king, so he and Jens Jr. could look them over. They tried to come up with a workable plan to steal Zeld's farms away from Hesse. He and Jens Jr. finally arranged something achievable after three hours. Part of Zeld's land lay in the mountain area near the goblin's school south of the de Saxon castle. Zeld understood he couldn't fight the Hessen army, but if they moved the farms, including the farmers, livestock, ploughs and everything else over the mountains with Jens Jr.'s amulet, they could restart the farms in a new, yet hidden, location. The move would take several days of hard work, Jens Jr.'s amulet, and expert planning, but if they timed it right, they could strategically evacuate the farms without getting caught. The boys planned to start moving the farms on Monday.

The Hessen allies drew up tables and benches in their own area at the Great Hall that night at supper. It became obvious the Hessen allies felt unwelcome.

Grace before the meal included a blessing on the boys going into the field for the next two weeks. That's when Zeld realized he had landed in a sticky wicket. The war games were scheduled to start on Monday. They couldn't do both, evacuate the farms and go to the war games. Zeld couldn't think of any solutions, save one: ruin the war games as quickly as possible, and then return to the real war.

That night Zeld, Jens Jr., the triplets, Robert and James O'Day, Sullivan, Brian, Tyre and Crispyn met secretly in the library. They didn't have time to include anyone else. Zeld revealed the farm relocation plan. "The problem is it's spring, and we have to act now while the farmers can still plant crops. In other words, we can't wait until the war games are over."

"Are we gonna abandon the war games?" asked Oles, with a smile.

Zeld spied a scar on Tyre's forehead. He removed the necklace with the amulet and healed him. His mates had grown accustomed to him attacking them frequently with his healing amulet. Tyre strained not to laugh but the urge became too much. He stuffed his shirt sleeve in his mouth to keep the noise down. When Zeld finished, he asked if anyone else needed it. Most of the boys did, and Zeld gladly took care of them.

Running about healing injuries in the middle of an important meeting might bother some folks, but Zeld didn't mind doing both at the same time.

"Very last chance, does anyone need the stone?" Zeld asked.

Brian raised his hand, "I've an injury in a personal place."

Zeld handed him the necklace, and Brian placed it on his rear end. His mates tried not to laugh and they didn't snicker much. Zeld thought it was because someday they might have an embarrassing injury and they didn't want anyone to laugh at them.

"Let's take inventory of the teams; then, perhaps we can formulate a better plan," suggested Jens Jr.

"Our group, the blue team, is about half Hesse allies and they are fighting with the other members of the team. We can easily manipulate them into making mistakes," said Brian returning the necklace to Zeld.

"I'm on the purple team. We only have two Hessen allies. I imagine I could get them captured by the red team," Zeld suggested as an option.

Oars spoke up, "The orange team has enough de Saxon allies that we could assist anyway you need us to."

Oles said excitedly, "Our team, the red team that is, always hazes us..."

Odin added, "It would be wagon loads of fun to double-cross them." As the two brothers looked at each other with impish grins, Zeld almost felt sorry for the red team.

"I've got it!" blustered Zeld. "Tyre, go find your cousin."

It took several minutes but Tyre returned with Brass. When Brass entered the room, Zeld stood up and congratulated him on winning the war games. Brass looked around and saw the pages from the various teams.

"I must say, this looks a bit dodgy. What are you up to, Zeld?" asked Brass suspiciously.

Zeld explained the plan to take the farms from Hesse. He then submitted a new idea, "Instead of ruining the war games let's make them our alibi."

"I love it, but I want a more active role," requested Brass.

"Not this time," said Zeld. "You're irreplaceable where you're at for this operation.

"Does that mean there will be other times, in future?" asked Brass in a hopeful tone.

"Does this war look finished to you?" asked Zeld.

Brass appeared immensely pleased to help overthrow Hesse, and the guarantee he'd take part in future put a sparkle in his eyes.

"Here's the plan: on the first day Brass will get his two Hessen allies captured by the red team. Brian, as soon as you can, take all the food from your team over and give it to the purple team. The orange team will take their food over on day four. If the red team is still in the field on day eight, the traitors, Oles and Odin, can make sure life becomes unbearable," Zeld said as he looked over at the brothers. They nodded with a sinister chuckle.

"Where are the teams' drop off points?" Brass asked cleverly.

They all reported their drop off points by drawing them on a parchment map.

"Brass, if anything goes amiss, you have to set it right," said Zeld.

Brass nodded his head.

Jens Jr. turned to the boys and said, "Zeld and I'll leave the first day to evacuate the farms. If any of the staff asks about us, you saw us earlier or we're out getting food. You must cover for us."

Everyone nodded and Zeld said, "Class dismissed."

They ducked out of the library with smiles on their faces and went back to their barracks in small groups. The next day Zeld read up on farming again. He wanted to make sure he hadn't forgotten anything.

The following day Father Ulrich asked to see Zeld privately in his office right after supper, "Zeld, while we're out in the field for the next fortnight, we'll need men to guard the school. We'd welcome your men to do the job as we can no longer trust Godfrey of Hesse's troops."

"How many men'll you need?" asked Zeld, uncertain of how many he should take with him and how many he should leave.

"Twenty-five will do; we'll feed and pay them," said Father Ulrich, adding encouragement.

Zeld agreed to have 25 of his men guard the castle. This would also be his retreating station should anything go awry.

"I'll go tell them," Zeld said pleased to have an excuse to fill his soldiers in on the farm evacuation plan.

"Take some of your mates with you for safety," Father Ulrich reminded him.

"Men, we have a dangerous mission ahead of us," Zeld said, standing in the back of a wagon surrounded by his men in front of one of Zeld's new farms. "Starting in the morning, we will split into two groups. Twenty-five men will guard the school while the rest will help me steal away Hesse's farms." Zeld, Jens Jr., Brian, Oars and Robert had to wait for one of Zeld's men to translate what Zeld said into German. The soldiers reported they had nearly run out of food. "After tomorrow food will no longer be a problem," Zeld informed them.

Chapter Forty Two

Sabotage

Friar Stephen, the purple team's assigned staff member, handed out coloured armed bands to the boys who loaded the two wagons with their week's supply of food. The entire school sat in the wagons on Monday morning while waiting in front of the Great Hall for Zeld's men to come and guard the castle before they drove through the main gate.

"Sorry, we're late. We had to procure some weapons," one of the men explained in a loud voice so Geoffrey could hear him. Zeld counted a dozen longbows with arrows and a couple of swords as well. He guessed the bows and arrows came from Garth.

The Hessen allies gave Zeld's men repugnant looks when they saw them enter through the gate. Geoffrey of Hesse made the ultimate of rude gestures by biting his thumb at Zeld's men. This usually led to swordplay but one of Zeld's men diffused the situation by simply looking at Geoffrey cross-eyed and sticking out his tongue.

The wagons started away within a minute of the soldiers' arrival and they hadn't gone far when, with a wink to his mates, Zeld jumped out. He dove into the greenery and hid under the north bridge. Friar Stephen didn't suspect a thing. Zeld waited for the final group to cross the bridge then, crept back into the school through the kitchen door. One of his soldiers led Lightning to the stoop. Zeld mounted his horse and rode south. His soldiers saluted with fists together, but not breaking the arrow, as he rode away.

Zeld made excellent time getting to the rendezvous point, which was on the north slope of the mountain located five miles south of the Hessen farms. His men remained eager but hungry; they hadn't eaten so far that day. He ordered them to approach the farms and start the move. He watched from a vantage point two thirds the way up the mountain from atop a crest as his men loaded the farm wagons. The men didn't leave the farms all at once; they took their time and left in small groups, so they wouldn't attract attention.

Zeld looked carefully down the road to the west for Jens Jr. but couldn't see him approaching.

Several wagons pulled in from the farms and Zeld asked his soldiers to unload them before returning. They didn't seem to understand, so Zeld showed them by removing items, that he wanted the wagons unloaded. His men joined in once they saw him working.

Finally, an English-speaking soldier arrived driving a wagon. Zeld told him to ask the farmers to feed the men. The soldier gestured to the back of his wagon and Zeld realized the farmers had already taken care of the problem as the back of the wagon was already filled with baskets full of various foods.

Wisely, Zeld kept with him the soldier who spoke English. This proved useful on a number of occasions. This particular man stood the tallest of all his soldiers. He had black hair with pale skin and deep set dark brown eyes. His height helped him look the part of a good leader. He claimed he used to be a Hessen commander and gave his name as Einhorn von Kessler.

The evacuation of goods went on into the night. As a precaution Zeld established a roadblock to stop anyone from approaching the farms from the west.

In the morning Zeld still didn't know what had happened to Jens Jr. He kept the wagons moving and explored his surroundings for a way to reach the mountain top. He secretly hoped to chance upon a way over the mountain. He had to settle for the discovery of an old road which led near the top of the slope. Zeld's men properly cleared the old road and the wagons carried the goods further up the mountain.

The horses tired before sundown on the second day so Zeld let them rest on the morning of the third day. With borrowed axes and spades from the farms, his men built animal stalls and corrals that morning. The horses went back to work on the afternoon of the third day. Zeld worked the horses all night. He gave them the fourth day off until after dark, and then the time came to move the livestock. Zeld brought the feed first and the animals were herded away during the night.

On the fifth day, Zeld still found no sign of Jens Jr. Zeld would have to move ahead without him somehow. He sent a group of 10 men to explore the mountain and find the best location to lift the goods over the top. Their plan called for three derricks, an oversized one on the farmer's side of the peak and two smaller ones on the other side. Zeld searched the remainder of the day for cargo nets and hooks in order to make the plan work.

On the sixth day, with the farms nearly empty, Jens Jr. finally arrived. Zeld felt greatly relieved to see him. He had a lengthy story to tell Zeld. They found an appropriate vantage point in the top of a tall tree to lift the goods. Zeld and Jens Jr. climbed the tree and Jens Jr. worked as he told Zeld about his adventures.

"When we left the castle, I waited for a chance to escape. A wild boar ran across the road in front of us. The wagon stopped and I made a desperate dash for it. Norton Duval, who happened to ride in the next wagon, shot and killed the boar so quickly, I didn't have time to slip away into the greenery.

"In one shot? How did he do that?" Zeld asked a bit befuddled.

"No idea. However, Father Ulrich ruled half the meat would go to each team. So instead of getting away, I was trapped skinning a wild boar in front of everyone.

"When we reached our drop off position, I tried to slip away pretending to go hunting. Friar Timothy stopped me because we had plenty of boar meat. About that time one of the boys caught two prisoners from the orange garrison." Jens Jr. shook his head. "I drew the assignment of building a prison and guarding the prisoners.

"I worked as hastily as I could, but Friar Timothy came over determined to show me exactly how to build it. He also told me, in exquisitely painful detail, all of his adventures, since birth. I never knew he was 300 hundred years old and his whole life consisted of one dwarven adventure after another!" Jens Jr. was enjoying himself and Zeld laughed. "That night Brian created a diversion by 'accidentally' lighting a signal arrow and giving away our position. As the team moved camp, I slipped away.

"I inched me way nearly outta the game area, when I chanced upon me two brothers digging a ditch – and – er – well – I only wanted to frighten them – a little – I mean – er – I wouldn't see them for a week – you know – and after all – what are big brothers for? So, I jumped out at them just as the stream changed course. They lost their footing in the loose soil and keeled over backward into the ditch and zoomed away in the flood. I followed the stream trying to catch them up with me amulet but it doesn't hold on to wet things very well. I didn't know it at the time but the ditch carried the water back to their camp. I used this dial on me amulet and finally lifted them outta the water so they wouldn't drown.

"As I turned to leave, Norton Duval congratulated Oles and Odin on capturing me! They attempted twice to help me slip away, but Norton kept too close an eye on me and I ended up locked away in their prison for a few days."

Jens Jr. rested a plow atop the mountain crest and continued speaking. "When I finally escaped, I came as speedily as I could. Didja know almost the entire red team is Hessen? No wonder me brothers wanted to doublecross them.

"Oh, by the way, they're blaming everything, shall we say, unusual, on you," Jens Jr. said laughing almost hysterically for several seconds. "And thanks for helping me escape too. You probably don't remember it; after all, you've been really busy. I mean raiding other teams' food stores and all."

"I have?" asked Zeld.

"That and much more."

As Zeld listened to Jens Jr.'s brilliant story he mostly laughed or shook his head. It took Zeld's men a couple of hours to build a suitable platform with a ladder, so Jens Jr. and he could stand rather than remain cramped in the tree.

Jens Jr. worked his amulet all night. In the morning Zeld took over, relieving Jens Jr. and giving him a chance to rest. After a couple of hours, Zeld needed men on the other side of the mountain to build corrals. He handed the amulet over to Jens Jr.

Zeld's men made ladders, so they could go over the mountain without using the amulet. They also prepared rockslides in key locations as if there would be a battle.

A heavy rainfall poured from the sky with ominous thunder and lightening that hammered the ground. Work on the mountain stalled. Once the rain passed Zeld had the farmers drive their last wagon loads of seed to his other farms near the school. The Hessen farmers had been busy digging up the plants that had been previously planted so they could take them as well. Zeld sent six of his soldiers to accompany the wagons.

Once in a while something went awry. One of the wagons broke down and Zeld didn't have replacement parts, so he abandoned it. Jens Jr. accidentally dropped a wet chicken coop, which fell thirty feet, killing the chickens. To Jens Jr.'s chagrin they ate chicken pie for supper that night.

On the ninth day, the mountain was nearly clear of farm goods, as Jens Jr. had completely made up for his absence. The time had come to free everyone who wanted to leave. Zeld sent as many of the farmers as he dared, to the castle itself and to the town of Saxon located close by. They invited everyone they trusted to join them.

One of the men loyal to Hesse overheard one of the conversations. He left the town of Saxon, marched to the de Saxon castle and reported the news to Hesse, who became enraged. He sent soldiers to stop the exodus and he placed the castle on full alert.

Zeld had anticipated this. When Hesse's soldiers reached the town of Saxon, Zeld ordered the farms burned. The flames caught the attention of the soldiers.

The soldiers were divided as to what to do. Some volunteered to return to the castle while others stood guard at the town of Saxon. Once the soldiers who wanted to defend the castle left, the others became turncoats and helped the shopkeepers escape to freedom. Zeld's men waved to him as they passed with their families. Most of his men gave him a two-fisted salute as they went up the mountain. Day nine best symbolized their success.

Hesse and his closest allies, Duval and Prussia, looked down from the ramparts of the de Saxon castle. Hesse saw he'd lost his town and his farms. "So, this is how King Henry chooses to retaliate," Godfrey of Hesse said. He did three things to regain the upper hand. Firstly, he sent to Germany for food, farmers and shopkeepers. Secondly, he gave his assassin Grunfeld the tracking stone to follow Zeld home. Thirdly, he sent his soldiers up the mountain on a search and destroy mission.

Thirty-five of Hesse's loyal cavalrymen went to search the mountains trying to find and then kill the turncoats before they completely vanished. Zeld hadn't thought to hide the wagon tracks. Hesse's men broke into groups of five and followed the tracks up the various mountain roads. Zeld's men let loose the rockslides forcing Hesse's soldiers to retreat momentarily. Zeld's men used the few minutes the rockslides bought them to climb the ladders to safety, but not all could make it over the mountain's crest in time. Jens Jr. lifted the last seven men in one group over the top with his amulet.

The Hessen cavalrymen arrived too late to catch their former mates up. Zeld felt very pleased with how everything had gone until he realized he and Jens Jr. were out of bounds and still in immense danger. "We must make a run for it," Zeld warned. "We're out of the school's boundaries and the rule of safe haven doesn't apply here."

"The rule of safe haven didn't keep the militia from attacking the school either," Jens Jr. commented quietly. There was a momentary yet intense pause. "They may not have seen us," Jens Jr. whispered.

"The blue beam of light which lifted the soldiers came from that direction," cried one of the Hessen riders to his commander.

"They're on to us! Let's ride!" Zeld breathed.

The cavalrymen rode to search in the area of Zeld and Jens Jr.'s platform. The two boys slid down the ladder and dashed for their horses. Their noisy retreat gave away their position. The cavalrymen rode toward the two boys, who wasted no time in mounting and galloping away. The Hessens pursued them in a dramatic race of life or death.

Lightning stood sixteen hands high, was well kept and ready for the challenge. However, Jens Jr.'s horse, Bluebell, was much smaller and slower due to age. Within the first 300 yards Bluebell had fallen two horse lengths behind. Zeld knew he had to do something or the Hessens would catch Jens Jr. so he veered to his right off the road and into a thicket of trees. Jens Jr. followed.

The Hessens followed with ease. Zeld rode into an even tighter clump of trees and was forced to ride on the side of his horse to keep from being unsaddled by low hanging limbs. Jens Jr. leaned forward and avoided a similar fate. The first three Hessen riders were able to slip through as well; however, the next group didn't do as well. Some slowed to a halt while others made their way slowly through the danger zone. The last group of riders charged headlong into Zeld's trap and were tossed to the ground. Two of the riderless horses made it through, while the others blocked the way.

Zeld raced for the road with Jens Jr. trying to keep up. Zeld looked back and saw his pursuers: three in the front, with a second group of seven behind them, and bringing up the rear were two riderless horses. This gave Zeld an idea. He darted again to his right into a clump of trees. Jens Jr.'s horse tired and he rode to the right of the trees trying to avoid the trouble they might cause.

Zeld continued riding to his right completing a semicircle. The Hessens rode without incident through the trees all the while narrowing the gap. He once again cut to the right and this time held the circular pattern. He rode until he saw in front of him what he was looking for: the riderless horses. He pointed at them and Jens Jr. nodded his head. He watched as Jens Jr. rode up alongside one of the horses and leapt from his horse to it. He also saw the group of Hessen riders still in blistering hot pursuit. Zeld spied the road to his left and quickly manoeuvred toward it. Once they reached the road, the horses hooves beat hard on the ground. Suddenly, from the other side of the road three faster horses emerged from the greenery.

Zeld and Jens Jr. kept to the road and ran the horses as fast as they could. Their pursuers trailed off behind them. After two miles Zeld looked back and saw only the three fastest horses remained in sight and of them only one had gained ground. He felt somewhat relieved. The Hessen horse that did well was a tall magnificent black stallion war horse, which matched Lightning's powerful build and speed.

Only after a right turn and three more miles which took them past the farms, did Zeld look back again. This time the black horse had closed the gap even further. Zeld could see the school ahead. Jens Jr.'s horse faded once they reached the first tower of the castle. Zeld spun around to help but was too late, as the Hessen rider held his black battleaxe aloft and swung at Jens Jr. Jens Jr. desperately dove onto the ground and the battleaxe struck his horse with a bone crushing thud in the back of the head, killing it.

Someone shouted from the wall in a German accent, "Archers to de vall."

Seven men appeared and fired at the Hessen who was still trying to kill Jens Jr. All the arrows missed but not by much. Jens Jr. ran for the gate but was cut off by the dark horse. The rider again swung at him, forcing Jens Jr. away from the gate. Jens Jr. pulled out his amulet and held both the rider and horse frozen. An arrow whizzed down from the wall striking the rider in the back near his right shoulder. The battleaxe fell toward Jens Jr. who bent down and collected it. Once he knelt down the beam of blue light left the horse and rider. When the rider saw Jens Jr. held the axe, he dismounted and ran the best he could in the direction he had come. The horse walked peacefully over to Jens Jr. and bowed. Jens Jr. did not know it but this axe was magical and whoever owned it also owned the horse.

Two other Hessen riders arrived on the scene. They watched as the horse bowed to Jens Jr. They retrieved their wounded companion and rode in the other direction with a volley of arrows landing around them. Zeld and Jens Jr. hastened inside the castle walls where it was safe. The boys took their horses back and locked them into their stalls.

When he removed the saddle Jens Jr. read the horse's name, which was engraved on the underside. He turned to the horse and called to him, "Goliath, is your name Goliath?" The horse nodded and Jens Jr. stroked him on the neck. The two boys fed and watered their horses; then, went over to the kitchen to see if they could find something for themselves.

After a warm meal and plenty to drink, the two boys sneaked through the forest to rejoin the war games. Zeld found his garrison and his team leader, Brass Stevens. Zeld wanted to fill him in on the grand adventure but he realized Brass needed help.

"Our rations are gone and we've more prisoners than men," Brass said updating Zeld quietly.

Zeld took a bow and a quiver of arrows and headed for the best hunting ground. He shot a brown hare and found a gigantic patch of watercress. On the way back to camp he killed three edible snakes with his sword. When he returned to camp, he washed a pot and prepared the snakes for cooking.

Friar Stephen stepped over to see what Zeld was doing.

"I haven't seen you in a couple of days," said Friar Stephen concerned.

"I went hunting – er – I brought some food," Zeld replied alertly, while laughing to himself.

The friar seemed impressed, "I still can't believe the way you took all the blue team's food on the first day. It'll go down in school history as the best tactical manoeuvre ever achieved in the field. The way Brass lifted you up and carried you on his shoulders. Oh, it was grand, me boy."

"I can't remember, how many boys am I feeding tonight?" asked Zeld, as he imagined Brass carrying him on his shoulders and wondered who really received that honour.

"Thirty-eight," said the friar raising his finger in a knowledge-able way.

"I'm gonna need more food," said Zeld, who realized his efforts had fallen short.

363

Zeld walked over to Brass, "Can someone finish cooking this, so I can go after more food?" Brass assigned James to do the cooking.

Zeld spied three good sized fish in a shallow part of the stream, so he slipped off his shoes and rolled up his leggings. He sharpened a stick with his hunting knife and speared at the fish. After spearing two of them, he laid down in the tall grass to rest for a moment. He heard something moving in the thicket, so he sat up slowly hoping to find an animal they could eat, and saw instead a unicorn approaching the stream from the other side.

He watched silently as the unicorn lowered its head toward the water. Zeld heard another noise from upstream. This time he heard boys looking for food. The unicorn's horn glowed and it jumped across the stream directly at Zeld.

Startled, Zeld lifted up his hands to cushion the blow, as he thought the unicorn would land on him. The unicorn and Zeld touched while the unicorn flew through the air. To Zeld's surprise the unicorn's horn fell from its forehead. Zeld turned to see if it was alright and the unicorn turned around as well.

A new horn, bright and glowing formed on the unicorn's head and the old one lay on the ground still glowing. The unicorn reached down with its nose and pushed the old horn over to Zeld, who collected it. The horn stopped glowing as soon as Zeld touched it. Then with a single bound the unicorn vanished into the greenery. Zeld examined the horn for a moment; then, he slipped it into his bag. He couldn't help smiling.

"You simply follow the stream and it takes you directly to the watercress," said Eric of Markland.

Zeld watched Eric, Thomas Bandit, Jarell Goldenstaff and their team adviser Father Ulrich pass by him; then, he loaded his bow and crept up behind them.

"YOU'RE CAPTURED!" roared Zeld using a deep voice that echoed through the forest, and then adding in a higher voice. "We have you surrounded."

The group turned around looking in the undergrowth for the boys who caught them. Zeld bent over and picked up two handfuls of rocks, tossing them into the stream. The splashing sounds resembled people closing in on an ambush.

"On your bellies," demanded Zeld with the same deep voice.

After they lay down, Zeld ran to them and yelled, "I get to tie them up."

Zeld play acted an inexperienced page and it worked. He tied them up and took their belongings. They had three brown hares, their team's hunting bow and the boys' personal hunting knives.

"All personal belongings will be returned at the end of the fortnight," Zeld reminded them.

Zeld marched his prisoners into the purple team's garrison and Brass tossed them into the overly crowded makeshift prison. Zeld gave James the three additional rabbits and two fish.

Father Ulrich asked Zeld, "How did these boys arrive back at camp so quickly?"

"They never left camp."

"I heard them down by the stream."

"Why? Because I threw a few rocks in the water and used two voices?"

"How many boys ambushed us at the stream?"

Zeld held up one finger. The father shook his head in disbelief.

Zeld spent the next couple of days fishing, hunting and gathering watercress. At the end of day 12 the last opposing team was unhappily removed from the field, due to lack of food, and the purple team was declared grand champions. In the morning the boys reclaimed their personal effects, tore down their garrisons, loaded up the wagons and went back to the school.

At noon they held a grand feast. Brass was honoured above all, as the winning team captain. He received a standing ovation for his efforts.

For the rest of the day, Zeld heard about all the brilliant things he did at the war games. While sitting in the outdoor classroom, he was surrounded by the other boys who asked loads of questions. Someone asked how he put sand in the red team's meal on the second day, so they went hungry that evening. Oles and Odin sniggered when Zeld was asked about it. Zeld said, reaching for an explanation, "Er – sometimes the wind blows sand into cooking pots – after the cook has tasted the meal."

The red team also asked about the fire ants in their bedrolls. He answered, "Bread crumbs attract ants."

"How did you change the watercourse to make the stream form a lake in the red team's camp?" asked Friar Martin, who looked totally bewildered by it. Before he could make up an answer, someone else asked how he attracted the snakes that kept the red team from retrieving their belongings.

"That's a family secret," Zeld said and everyone appeared satisfied with the answer except Sir Drain.

By the end of the day the stories stretched a little and Zeld had captured an entire team single handed and robbed the food from another to feed them.

The following week was the last of the school year. The boys took their final tests and packed away the school for the summer holiday. This included the library books and weapons. For the last two days of school, the boys gathered stones from the mountains and left them where the woodpiles usually went. The stonemasons would use the stones once they returned.

Zeld's belongings sat in a neat pile outside Eagle Loft, waiting for Jens Sr. to collect them on the morning of departure day. Jens Sr. parked the wagon in front of the pile and the boys loaded their belongings into the wagon bed.

"I've arranged for you to meet a boat which will take you home for the summer," said Jens Sr. Suddenly, Zeld felt eager to see his family.

Zeld said farewell to his mates. Robert and James travelled south together. Crispyn, Tyre, Brass and Sullivan headed north. Brian Boru planned to sail home for Ireland. The Hesse allies left together in one company heading east.

Some of Zeld's men arrived to guard the castle during the summer. Zeld climbed into the back of the wagon with the triplets and Jens Jr. and they started on their way. The travellers ran into a road blocked by a rockslide, which upset Jens Sr.

"Dash it all, if Zeld's not at the docks before four o'clock, he'll miss his voyage home," Jens Sr. said.

Zeld mounted Lightning and the other boys mounted their horses. They took all the shortcuts and rode as hastily as they could, which meant the assassin, Grunfeld, had a difficult time following. When the boys arrived at the docks, the boat had already left. Zeld had no choice but to spend part of the summer with the McMarr family and catch up a later boat to Denmark, if he could find one.

The McMarrs attempted to cheer him up as they rode toward their manor. "So, what would you have for supper Zeld? D'you like broccoli? How about some snake and watercress? Would you prefer some tree bark on the side? How about a raw onion?" the triplets pestered him.

"How about – er – some fish and chips?" Zeld answered.

Grunfeld, although not successful in his attempt to follow Zeld home, was able to learn his destination was in fact Denmark. This information alone would certainly bring the downfall of the de Saxon family. He watched Zeld go safely inside the manor from his hiding place among the rocks near the manor's main gate. He turned around to report back what he had learned when the mechanical sound of a mongonel firing rang out. The assassin took five poison arrows in the chest and then keeled over backward, sprawled out upon the ground. His assailant rifled through his belongings and took out a glowing amulet stone.

Back at the roadblock Father Ulrich loaded building stone into the back of a school wagon. He said to his companion, "I'm pleased you found this excellent stone Sir Drain, it'll really help in our remodelling project this summer. However, I don't understand why you blocked the road; the McMarr's planned to journey this direction."

"After the goblins took back the castle from the Baden militia, one of their beeper stones located a receiver stone hidden in Zeld's kite shield. Norton Duval told me Hesse hired an assassin and gave him a receiver stone to follow Zeld home. I deliberately sabotaged the road, so Zeld couldn't catch his boat on time. With the help of me son Dando and one of Zeld's soldiers, I set an ambush for the assassin. Hesse isn't the only one with a secret spy network you know," explained Sir Drain.

Father Ulrich's jaw dropped in surprise when he heard Sir Drain's cunning answer.

"I brought the deeds to your lands," Zeld said while holding out the parchments the king had given him in London for his cousin. Dando pushed his dinner plate aside and broke the hard wax seal. Zeld watched as Dando read for a moment, and then clutched them to his chest like a grand treasure. He felt better about missing his boat. He planned to leave the deeds with Jens Sr., but felt delighted to personally see the joy on Dando's face.

Following the late supper, the boys prepared for bed. The McMarr's would share their attic bedroom with Zeld and Dando for the summer.

"So, Zeld, now that you can't go home straightaway, what'll you do?" asked Jens Jr.

Looking thoughtful, Zeld pondered on the question for a moment, and then his eyes sparkled. He thought this was the proper time to reveal the plan he had conjured during the Castles and Caverns Combat Game classes. He said with his usual enthusiasm, "I think, I'll go dragon hunting!"

"Red dragons or blue dragons? D'you like dragon meat? Do dragons have toes? D'you have toes? Do dragons like cheese? Are you a nutter? Can we come?" asked the triplets, as they gathered around.

Jens Jr. dove for his bed and pulled the blanket over his head as he yelled, "OH, NO!"

Acknowledgements

I would like to thank my family, 1 wife, 8 kids, 5 in-laws, and 14 grandkids for their stickitituti. Special thanks to my son Josh who drew two of the pictures and my wife who struggles with my strange "city slicker" ideas.

Another thank you goes to the members of the Kigalia Fine Arts Writers Group for the many hours of editing, teaching and friendship over the years.

I would also like to thank the extended family and friends who lent a hand in the many steps that brought the book together.

A special thanks to Gary B. Shumway from Shumway Publishing who caught the spirit of the book and showed exceptional spiritual inspiration and artistic expression in its creation.

Some books are meant to be. This is one of them.

Zeld and the Pirate Prince

In Zeld's second year at Castles and Caverns he and his mates go toe to toe in a battle of wits with a new rival. Mistaking Zeld's efforts as an act of revenge by King Henry Godfrey of Hesse leaves his castle in the hands of Fielding and his band of pirates. Godfrey journeys to Germany to collect new farmers, storekeepers and soldiers. He also begins the lengthy process of rebuilding his army. Cunning as a fox this one, Fielding uses his magical amulets to stay one step ahead of the game in his attempt to best Zeld and keep the de Saxon castle in the possession of Godfrey of Hesse. Aided by a magical growth formula Fielding takes unfair advantage and creates a disaster so big it makes the story of the giant chickens of Barnstaple pale in significance. Will Zeld and company best him? Will Fielding be able to hold out until Godfrey returns with reinforcements?

With new mates, new spies and a new opponent Zeld is in for the adventure of a lifetime! It's all coming your way in Castles and Caverns II - Zeld and the Pirate prince